D0016867

A KIND OF PARADISE

A KIND OF PARADISE

Helen Cannam

Michael Joseph

London

First published in Great Britain by
Michael Joseph Ltd,
27 Wrights Lane
London W8 5TZ
1987

© Helen Cannam 1987

All rights reserved. No part of this publication
may be reproduced, stored in a retrieval system,
or transmitted in any form or by any means, electronic,
mechanical, photocopying, recording or otherwise,
without the prior permission
of the Copyright owner.

Cannam, Helen
A kind of paradise.
I. Title
823'.914[F]   PR6053.A6/

ISBN 0–7181–2800–1

Printed and bound in Great Britain by
Billing & Sons Limited
London & Worcester

For Vivien, without whom . . .

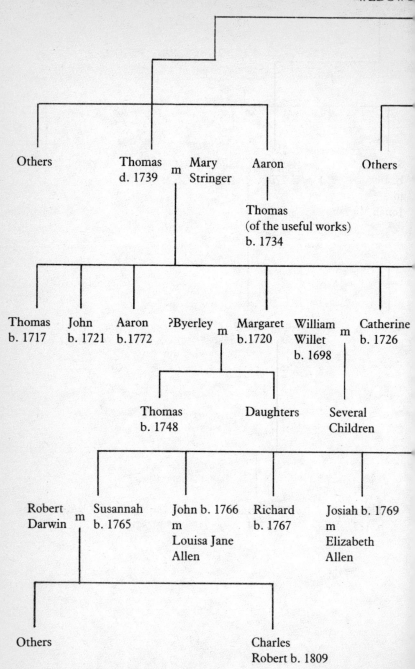

Others

Thomas
d. 1739 m Mary
Stringer

Aaron

Thomas
(of the useful works)
b. 1734

Others

Thomas
b. 1717

John
b. 1721

Aaron
b.1772

?Byerley m Margaret
b.1720

William
Willet
b. 1698 m Catherine
b. 1726

Thomas
b. 1748

Daughters

Several
Children

Robert
Darwin m Susannah
b. 1765

John b. 1766
m
Louisa Jane
Allen

Richard
b. 1767

Josiah b. 1769
m
Elizabeth
Allen

Others

Charles
Robert b. 1809

Sarah
b. 1695
m
Jonah Malkin

Richard   m   Susan
b. 1701   Irlam

Thomas
b. 1703

John
b.1705
m
Mary

Others

Josiah   m   Sarah
b. 1730   b. 1734

John

Thomas
b. 1771

Catherine
b. 1774

Sarah
b. 1776

Mary Ann
b. 1778

PREFACE

This is a novel and not a biography; but I have tried as far as possible to follow the events of the life of Josiah Wedgwood as they actually happened, filling in the gaps from my imagination.

Occasionally I have deliberately altered a fact for reasons of simplicity – for instance, the Big House at Burslem was not built until 1750; Bentley moved house again, from Chelsea to Turnham Green, in 1777; and William Blake was paid for 'painting on ceiling pictures' in 1785, not 1786. Also, faced with conflicting versions of the Etruria riot of 1783, I have opted for one of my own.

Since Sarah is known almost exclusively through Josiah's eyes – largely from his delightful letters to Bentley – there is little record of her life before her marriage, and in this book that period is imagined for the most part, as are her character and motivation throughout. This is particularly true of her relationship with Thomas Bentley.

Of the minor characters in the book, the following are invented, although someone must have filled their place in the story (even the broken dish is part of the Wedgwood legend): the Lathom family; Nan and Betty, and the servants at Spen Green; Sam Hunter; Billy; and Jane Hillyard. Everyone else has some basis in reality, if only as a name – even Taffy the horse!

Passages from the Wedgwood letters are quoted by courtesy of the Trustees of the Wedgwood Museum, Barlaston, Stoke on Trent, Staffordshire, England.

PROLOGUE

It was too quiet. Sarah moved uneasily in her high-backed chair, trying to bring some relief to her stiff limbs; and then stilled again, listening.

It must be close to dawn now, for it was long hours since the midnight silence had been broken by the distant clang of a bell, summoning help; the running of feet; urgent voices; the clatter, far off, of pots set on the fire. She had known the meaning of that last sound well enough: water set to boil, ready for the birth. No need to run for doctor or midwife in this house, for Dr Robert Darwin was already here, watching over his wife's bedside, the anxiety of the husband and father niggling beneath the calm competence of the experienced doctor.

But that had all been hours ago, and the sounds had long ceased, and now Sarah could hear nothing. She looked down at her hands, linked in her lap, edged with the fringe of the woollen shawl that wrapped her over the thick winter nightgown: bent crooked hands, lined, immobile, useless with the stiffness of age and rheumatism. Even the two rings, worn so long that they almost grew there, looked richly incongruous on the lined tired skin: the thin gold band of her wedding ring, the glowing ruby set with diamonds that Josiah had given her to mark the moment of their prosperity and fame. Once, long ago, these hands would have been busy, ceaselessly busy; once they had even been called beautiful – she remembered how deep and soft the voice had been that told her so, and how her wayward body had felt the resonance of it in every nerve and limb. For a moment now she saw her hands as they had been then – long, slender, not the white unmarked hands of a fine lady with no work to do more arduous than a little dainty sewing, but strong supple hands fit for any task, or almost any. They had never, after all, found the skill to shape a pot . . .

A long time ago. Strange, though, how the things that had happened years ago when she was young seemed nearer now in the solitude of old age than the events of these past few hours: the bell in the night, the running feet.

She moved again, impatience growing. What was going on? Why could she hear nothing? True, Susannah's room was on the far side of the house, well away from the nursery in which the children slept. Marianne, Caroline, Susan, Erasmus: Sarah herself had wanted to be near them – there was a joy in grandchildren no mother, burdened by responsibility, could ever quite hope to find. But if Susannah's room was far off, Sarah's hearing had always been keen – surely there should have been some sound?

She tried to pull herself together, force herself to be patient. After all, patience was something that, supremely, life had taught her, a lesson learnt in a hard school: so many years later it ought not to be beyond her to remember that lesson. And it was foolish to worry. It was not as if it was Susannah's first confinement. But when the others had been born Sarah had been many miles away, at her own home at Barlaston in Staffordshire; and it is always worse to be near at hand, sharing each moment but able to do nothing. And Susannah had never been strong.

If only her limbs were young again, and she could spring to her feet and run along the dark passages to that distant room and see for herself that all was well! But she was seventy-five, and racked with rheumatism, and if she were to reach for her stick and hobble her way to Susannah's bedside she would only be in the way. She had too much self-control to inflict that on her daughter.

If only someone would come . . .

A door slammed, far off. And into the still cold night a cry rose: high, thin, wailing.

Sarah began to tremble. She closed her eyes. 'Let all be well – with them both,' she prayed.

She realised suddenly how cold it was: the fire had burnt almost to nothing in the grate. She ought to go back to bed. But she knew she would not sleep, and it was worse lying down, waiting.

There were footsteps coming this way, nearer, nearer along the passage. Sarah sat very erect, brown eyes watching the door. 'Let it be news!'

There was a faint, very faint, tap on the door, little more

2

than a soft scratching. If she had been asleep she would not have heard it. But she was not asleep.

'Come in!' she called.

Her son-in-law's huge figure came in, stooping slightly beneath the lintel; and his face was lit with a smile.

'I thought you might be wakeful, Mama,' he said, bending to kiss her. 'We have a fine boy – and Susannah is well, tired but well. And when you've both slept, she and you, then I'll take you to see her, and the boy.'

Sarah gazed up at him, her mouth stretched wide in a foolish happy smile, and could think of nothing to say because there were too many emotions clamouring for release. Instead she clasped his hand and shook it gently.

'We're calling him Charles – Charles Robert,' said Dr Darwin. 'Robert for me, of course – and Charles – well, you know.'

She knew: the brother who had died, the brightest, most promising of the sons of eccentric Dr Erasmus Darwin. His loss had left a permanent scar upon his family, and on his father in particular; but that had been a long time ago, and there was no hurt now in the thought that a helpless infant, newly come into the world on this February morning of 1809, should also be called Charles Darwin.

'God bless you all,' Sarah whispered through that indelible smile.

'And you, Mama,' returned Robert, his voice a whisper too; and he kissed her again. 'And now you get back to bed.'

'Doctor's orders?'

'Doctor's orders,' he agreed firmly.

'How like your father you are,' she told him; and as she spoke she almost believed she could see the big ungainly frame of Erasmus Darwin grinning at her from the shadows, as if he had not after all been dead for seven years. Yes, Robert was like him, but in a curiously one-dimensional way. Or was that because her old woman's memory was playing tricks with her again, so that the dead seemed somehow more real than the living? No, she decided, it wasn't simply that. It was rather that there were no true eccentrics left these days. Men and women seemed more uniform, respectable, conforming, like goods made to a pattern in a factory; whereas the men and women of her youth had been gloriously and

3

inescapably individual, like the old-fashioned pots, clumsy, diverse, inimitable, every garish colour and lopsided pattern echoing the whimsical personality of their separate creators. She smiled wryly at the foolish fancy: after all, Robert Darwin was no pattern doctor but a forthright warm-hearted man respected by his patients. If he was not an eccentric he was no worse for that. And she had never been much of an admirer of old-fashioned pots.

Now he helped her to bed, and made up the fire and turned out the lamp, and then he left her. Sarah lay back on the high pillows and watched the leaping pattern of gold and rose on the ceiling, and smiled on with contentment.

Charles Robert Darwin – new born into the world, a hard uneasy world of revolution and war and rapid change. A world scarcely the same in any way as that into which his mother had been born forty-four years ago. Strange how when one was a part of it one did not see it change until, looking back, one realised that the things accepted in girlhood had all gone, for good or ill. What were those words, spoken to the girl of seventeen, excited, a little frightened? 'In these hands you hold the power to change the world' – a wild, grandiose, impossible claim, yet there had been truth in it, of a kind. Could one not say the same in a very real sense of every human being? Could one not say it perhaps tonight of the newly born infant asleep in his cradle at his mother's bedside?

Easier, perhaps, to say of a man: they were expected to do great things. The major events of the world – wars, inventions, the impulse to create or destroy – were all supposed to stem from them. For a woman it was different: her part was to wait – to be patient, to serve, to give birth. She, Sarah, had done all these things. She had loved – quietly, deeply, with passion. She had worked, kept house, made her home a pleasant place for the men in her life – brother, father, husband, sons. She had borne eight children, nursed and cherished them, seen three of them die and wept for them, guided the others to happy adulthood.

And now she was an old woman: Josiah Wedgwood's widow, Dr Darwin's mother-in-law. Here in Shrewsbury very few even knew of her existence, much less cared. Very likely even those who had once known her, in Spen Green or

4

Burslem or Etruria, thought she had died long since. Her life was over, leaving her nothing but memories to fill the days that were leading inexorably towards death. And many of those memories were peculiar to her alone, shared by no one now living, for though the name of Josiah Wedgwood was known and recognised in every corner of the globe very few indeed knew that she too had her place in the story, that without her there might even have been no story.

Strange, she thought, how the choices we make lead us along one certain steady path, and it is only when we look back that we realise how different everything might have been if we had gone another way. There had been so many choices in her own life, and the first that she could remember, made in childhood, was perhaps the one that mattered most because it had linked her for ever to Jos, and from it every other choice she had ever made had inevitably flowed. Because of it, years afterwards, she had made another painful choice, though it had taken every last tiny shred of her willpower to do so. Or had there in fact been no real choice? Her thoughts lingered on the question now as they had not done for a long time. After all, it hardly mattered any more, when the two men who once had meant everything to her were both long dead. She wondered momentarily, with a wry smile, if Jos now knew the truth. And if he minded.

Then she thought, 'If I were young again, if I could go back and face all those choices again, one by one, would I still take the same path? And if I did not, would I be able now, an old woman looking back, to do so without regret, or shame, or bitterness?'

'No,' she thought sensibly, 'I think I would have done the same, in almost everything. I am Sarah Wedgwood, and that is how I must behave, just because of what I am. Only a different person could have made a different choice.'

She turned her head a little to the side, and looked across the room to where Jos's portrait hung just above the fireplace. The grey eyes studied her kindly from beneath the dark brows, full of understanding, though he had never quite understood in life. Perhaps now he did. Sarah believed very firmly that somewhere, somehow, he was still alive, that they would meet again – all three.

Her eyes moved on, down to the mantelpiece where stood a

handsome pair of vases, blue jasperware decorated with pale graceful dancing figures and wreathed with a pattern of oak leaves. Jos had thought that ware the crowning glory of his life, but she was not so sure. Was it not a greater glory that the families of England, from the wealthiest almost to the poorest, dined on plates that bore the proud name of Wedgwood stamped upon them? And that the graceful simplicity of those dishes and plates, tureens and teapots, was as acceptable to the most refined taste as to the most rigid demands of fashion? Pale creamware, patterned delicately with a fine edging of brown or blue or mulberry, with only now and then a subtle touch of gold – perfectly shaped, perfect to their use. Could any potter ask for a greater monument than this, to know that king and commoner alike could use it with delight? Could she, Sarah Wedgwood, ask for more? If jasperware was Josiah's monument, then she could surely claim some at least of the glory for the queen's ware, for her taste and her knowledge had played a vital part in its creation.

It was all so long ago. She could almost believe that the old woman lying in bed dreaming away the dawn hours on the night of her grandson's birth had nothing to do with the young woman who over half a century ago, dimly and imperfectly but with conviction, had understood where her destiny lay. Could she still be the same woman?

Of course, she thought, smiling at her foolishness, we are always the same, deep down. It is only the surface that changes: the little light-footed girl becomes the weary, lined, rheumatic old woman. Yet perhaps it is not as simple as that. The fires die too: passion and pain, the power to hurt and to be hurt. The longer one lives, the slighter seem the griefs and joys that once filled every pulse with their torment or their ecstasy, as if somehow the vastness of the years swallows them up, until they become at last mere pinpricks in the scheme of things, like stars in a night sky.

She shut her eyes, and thought, 'But they say that the stars, close to, are as great as our world here on earth.' And as if to belie her thoughts of a moment ago she was all at once transported back to that lost past, swallowed up in it, as much a part of it as if she were not simply remembering but living it again, moment by intense moment. Reliving the night by the

6

canal, the torchlight leaping in deep-shadowed brilliance on faces filled with hate, the air heavy with smoke and shrill strident cries that set her stomach churning so that only her fierce will kept the coolness in her voice and her bearing. Living the joy of Susannah's birth, the bitterness as she carried Tom – and the sweetness of his growing, that lost fourth son of hers. Living again the moment beneath the trees where the night shadows were deepest, and her lover's arms warm about her, and heaven within her grasp, or so it seemed – only she had realised all too soon that heaven cannot be built on another's pain.

So many moments in a long life . . . the first grandchild, and Jos's wondering joy as he held the infant in his arms . . . the long weary years of grief, and their ending . . . the moment when the Queen, smiling and gracious, stepped from the sunlit street into the showroom, and she, Sarah Wedgwood, came forward to greet her . . . the stench of the slave ship, where first and for all time she had looked into the mouth of hell . . . Jos tenderly smiling on the hillside beneath the flowering gorse . . .

And then once more she was little Sarah Wedgwood, seven years old and riding pillion to Burslem behind her father with the icy December wind sharp on her nose, and the mare's hoofs ringing on the hard ground; and a fierce wild dancing excitement at her heart.

CHAPTER ONE

1741

Only the tip of Sarah Wedgwood's nose was exposed to the full iciness of the December morning. She was very glad that the rest of her, from her red gold hair to her narrow feet, was thoroughly enveloped in a full complement of winter garments: heavy linen chemise, stout woollen stockings, sturdy shoes, a warm gown of wool-lined damask laced over a quilted petticoat, and the thick red cloak, lavishly trimmed with fox fur, from whose wide hood her brown eyes looked brightly out on the frosty countryside. When she crossed her eyes – as she did once or twice – she could see how red and shiny the tip of her nose had become. But she was cautious about doing that, just in case the wind should change and make her eyes stick for ever and ever in that alarming position, as cook had warned her they would.

She could, of course, have pressed her tingling face against her father's long hard back, so that the folds of his cloak could warm it: she would only have had to lean forward very slightly to do so. But then she might have missed something, and that would have been a terrible waste of a journey. They had very nearly not come at all. If last week's drenching rain had not given way to a hard frost the road would have been impassable except to the most intrepid traveller, and her father's business with her uncles at Burslem, though important, was not so urgent as that. But, happily, the weather had turned cold, and the ruts in the road were frozen hard, and here she was, riding pillion behind her father on to the high moors of Staffordshire, far above the fertile Cheshire countryside of their home.

Her mother, as usual, had stayed behind. Only the sternest calls of family duty would drag her, distaste in every severe line of her mouth, to Burslem. She hated her husband's birthplace: a dirty poor little place, without beauty or dignity, so she said. She had said it again this morning as she came, hooped skirts swaying, to bid them a frosty goodbye at the front door. As she watched them leave she had thanked God yet again that her husband had chosen to turn his back on the place, wisely seeing the possibilities of the market in Cheshire cheese, a product much in demand in London and other important cities. As a consequence he had prospered, invested in rich Cheshire land, and risen sufficiently in the world to aspire to the hand of Susan Irlam, almost a gentleman's daughter, who would certainly not otherwise have considered marrying a mere Burslem man.

For Burslem meant two things: Wedgwoods, and pots. And these two (Richard Wedgwood excepted) were as a general rule inseparably bound up together.

Unfortunately even Richard Wedgwood had not succeeded in severing the family ties completely: the Wedgwoods were all, in Susan's eyes, regrettably family-minded. So Richard Wedgwood, having acquired a considerable understanding of financial matters, acted as agent and banker to his brothers John and Thomas, which was why he was riding to Burslem on this bright cold morning two weeks before Christmas.

There was no good reason at all why Sarah should ride with him: in fact her mother had come as close as she dared to forbidding her to do so, the day being so cold, and the roads so rough. But her father always had the last word, and he had said peaceably, 'Let her come: she loves to see her uncles, and they'll be glad of her company.' Sarah had smiled to herself with a delight that held her secret close and safe – for though she did indeed love her uncles, and gentle Aunt Sarah who kept house for them, it was not because of them that she went so eagerly to Burslem, nor yet for love of her father's company, nor for the ride in the fresh air. It was for the one thing her mother so deeply despised: the potworks.

Until her last visit, two or three months ago, Sarah had never seen inside a potworks. She had known that her uncles' business was housed somewhere in the untidy sprawl of buildings behind the house, but she had never given it a second thought, until on that memorable visit her Uncle Thomas, beaming with pride, had taken her on a personal guided tour: and she had been enthralled, utterly and completely enthralled by all she had seen.

Since then she had forgotten nothing: not the way the

10

young apprentices – some no bigger than herself – slapped and banged the clay together until it was smooth and dense for the potter (wedging, they called it); nor the concentrated care with which men glazed and painted and stouked (that, she learned, meant to put the handles on the unbaked pots); nor the sight – and heat – of the great domed hovels which surrounded the kilns stacked high with the round saggars in which the pots were held for firing. Nor would she ever forget the moment when Uncle Thomas had thrown a pot himself, seated at the treadle-turned wheel by the window in the throwing shed; and she had watched with a wondering delight as whole and complete as any she had ever known as the shapeless mass moved beneath his great hands – a touch here, a crook of the finger there – and suddenly before her eyes a bowl stood, perfect, symmetrical, ordered, formed in those few brief moments from what was little more than a clod of earth.

She could still feel the excitement of it, quivering somewhere in the pit of her stomach. From that moment on her mental image of God would for ever bear a close resemblance to Uncle Thomas. For had the rector not begun his sermon one Sunday in Astbury church by addressing God in the words of Isaiah, 'We are the clay, and thou our potter'? She had thought at once of Uncle Thomas in the throwing shed at Burslem. She prayed that he would let her see him do it again this time.

The ten miles from their home at Spen Green seemed long today, much longer than usual. But at last they reached the little hamlet of Tunstall on its ridge above the valley, and came to the brow of the hill beyond, and could see on the slope just below the muddled scattering of smoke-shrouded buildings which was Burslem.

It was not a beautiful place, certainly not if you compared it with the prosperous villages and farmsteads of the Cheshire plain. They could see a network of muddy lanes, raggedly hedged, beside which straggled haphazardly a few low thatched cottages intermingled here and there with makeshift sheds and the domed smoking shapes of the kilns that marked the many potworks. There was a windmill over to the east, and a distant scarring of coal pits, and to the south an undistinguished and dilapidated church, and two or three ponds

11

fed by sluggish streams, and almost as many inns and alehouses as there were potworks; and that was it. But today, knowing better what promise it held, Sarah felt her excitement rise as they rode steadily down the hill.

She knew the way very well by now – first, down the lane they called the Sytch, past the Hill Top houses and the Jolly Potters inn, and the sherd pile where broken pots were dumped; and the patch of ill-kept green where the maypole stood, and geese waddled and hissed; and then at last to the turning left between the Turk's Head and the Red Lion (another Wedgwood property) where her uncles' Big House marked the way to their extensive works. It was not perhaps a particularly big house by Cheshire standards, but it was built of brick and stone, and slated, and stood out like a Chinese porcelain plate on a fairground pot stall in what Sarah's mother called the squalor of Burslem.

Uncle Thomas was in the yard to greet them almost before they drew rein. Beaming, eager, his welcoming smile almost as wide as his outstretched arms, he came towards them and lifted Sarah down to receive his bearlike hug and harsh bristly kiss.

'You brought the little maid after all! John swore she'd not venture so far in this weather – but I knew she'd come and cheer our poor old bachelor hearts – eh, Sally my girl?' And he set her down and teasingly pinched her cheek.

'She'd not be left behind,' Richard explained, dismounting with the careful dignity which always seemed a little like a reproach for his brother's jovial familiarity.

They went inside, Sarah's small hand clasped in the enveloping warmth of her uncle's great paw; and in the snug parlour, carpeted and curtained and firelit, her aunt brought tea in blue-and-white Delft cups, and a plate of cakes which Sarah, mindful of her manners, handed round to the vigorously talking men.

'Quite the little housewife, eh Sal?' said Uncle Thomas indulgently. 'Will you come and look after your poor uncles when your aunt weds, little maid?'

'They've fixed a day at last then?' Richard asked, for all the world, Sarah thought, as if her aunt were not in the room to answer for herself.

'Aye, it looks like it – after Christmas, it seems. We'll miss her.'

12

'Then I'll come and keep house, Uncle Thomas,' put in Sarah. She spoke in such a tone of deadly earnest that for a moment her uncle was startled; and then he threw back his head and roared with laughter.

Sarah stared at him, and the sudden glow of delight which had lit her was doused in a moment. She had thought he meant it, that he wanted her to come and live here and take Aunt Sarah's place.

'I can sew very well, Uncle Thomas,' she said with a gravity which should have told him how offended she was. 'And I can make rose-petal preserve almost as well as Mama does. And I can cook quite a lot of things – and spin, and milk a cow, and play on the spinet – and I can read and write and add up quite big numbers, can't I, Papa?'

The laughter grew, while her father smiled and patted her head, and she reddened with hurt and anger that they should value her so little. For she could think of nothing she would like more than to live here, not just to care for her uncles and carry out all those necessary tasks, though she would do that too of course, and well – but to be near the potworks, near enough to see and smell and touch, to wander through the sheds when she wished, and watch the men at work; even, perhaps, one day, to shape a pot with her own hands or paint a sprig of flowers on the rough unglazed side of a jug or bowl. If only Richard Wedgwood had been a potter like all the other Wedgwoods!

But he was not, and she was his daughter and only seven years old, and they were laughing at her. She felt tears rise to her eyes and bit her lip fiercely: they would think her all the more of a baby if they saw her cry. But quiet Uncle John must have noticed her hurt, for he took her hand in his and pressed it, and said kindly, 'When you're older, my dear, then if you're not wed yourself you can come and keep house for us.'

'But a pretty maid like you will be snapped up, if I know young men,' said Uncle Thomas. 'With all those accomplishments too – what more could a husband want? And you'll have a home of your own and little ones to raise and wonder that you ever gave a thought to your dull old uncles.'

Sarah smiled politely, took one of her aunt's small almond cakes, and sat down on the little footstool beside her father's chair to eat it, aware young as she was that her uncle's flattery had been designed – successfully – to put her firmly in her place, which was that of a very small and unimportant female. One could hardly fall lower.

Her aunt took up her sewing and sat in silence while the men talked of Walpole's government, and war with Spain and France, and other important adult and largely masculine concerns; and very soon, Sarah knew, she would be told to run along and play. She knew where she would go then . . .

But this time the expected command did not come. Instead, when there was at last a pause in the talk, she heard Uncle Thomas say to her father, 'Young Tom over at the churchyard's in trouble again. Never could manage money of course – but he'd be glad of a word of advice from you if you can spare the time.'

'Always said he'd no head for business,' commented Richard unsympathetically. But he did spare the time since, as he explained to Sarah as they walked there a little later, young Tom was a Wedgwood and some kind of distant cousin. Fatherless for some years now, he had a mother and twelve brothers and sisters to support, a formidable enough task for a more able man.

Picking their way with great care – the road was full of holes where the Burslem potters helped themselves to the convenient clay by their front doors when their more orthodox supplies ran out – they made their way down the hill and almost out of the town, across the ford at the stepping stones, and very slightly uphill again towards the squat thatched church, beside which young Tom had his potworks. It was less curiosity about these as yet unknown relations than the prospect of seeing another potworks which had persuaded Sarah to keep her father company.

But as they drew nearer to the church she began to regret her impulse. A horrible smell grew ever thicker and more unbearable with every step, a sickening sweetish stench like that of rotting meat, which swiftly overlaid the familiar and exciting Burslem odours of smoke and clay and baking pots. Sarah screwed up her face and held her handkerchief to her nose.

'The churchyard's been overcrowded for years,' explained her father. 'Most disagreeable – no place to raise a family either, but beggars can't be choosers I suppose. You keep out of the churchyard, if you want to stay healthy that is.'

14

Sarah felt that his warning was hardly necessary, to say the least. She glanced over the wall as they passed, at the graveyard lumpy with graves scattered higgledy piggledy in every available space, and shivered, and wondered if even the lure of a potworks was strong enough to draw her near this horrible place.

But she had come, and the next moment they had reached the house, and, as the wind was blowing the other way today, the smell was not quite so bad from here.

The house was low, half-timbered and thatched and in a poor state of repair, with a jumble of sheds and kilns behind it, and a small field beyond in which grazed a lean house cow. The churchyard wall bordered one side of the field, and on the near side was a yard in which hens scratched among the potsherds.

The Churchyard Wedgwoods did not rise to a parlour: Sarah and her father were welcomed – warmly enough – into a draughty houseplace entered straight from the narrow frozen garden. There was a good fire in the hearth though, and the worn stone-slabbed floor was scrubbed clean and there was a polished high-backed settle pulled close to the fire away from the worst of the draughts. Mary Wedgwood, a pale weary-looking woman who was Tom Wedgwood's mother, brought ale and bread and c eese to refresh her guests; and Sarah sat in a corner of the settle and looked about her.

The room reminded her of the kitchen at home, with herbs and bacon hanging from the ceiling, a cat asleep by the fire, a large table occupying one end with benches ranged alongside. On the wall beside her, high up, was chalked a series of numbers, some faded and illegible with age, the lower ones as clear as if they had been marked only a moment ago. To her whispered question, when politeness allowed, her father told her they recorded the goods sold to the cratemen who carried the pots to markets and fairs in the district: Uncle Thomas, she knew, had great leather-bound books for such records, for she had seen them when he showed her into the shed he used as an office.

Cousin Tom, a stolid undistinguished-looking young man in his twenties, gave as little time as he decently could to the courtesies; and then said to Sarah, 'Go and play if you like – you'll find young Jos somewhere about. He'll look after you.'

15

Jos, she supposed, must be another of her relations; but she did not mind whether she found him or not. It was enough to be given the freedom to explore. She set off, happily, by way of the back kitchen – in which the womenfolk were too busy to notice her passing – into the yard beyond.

She had expected to find something much like her uncles' potworks – untidy, exciting, yet with its own fascinating order. But instead she could see at once why her father had that note of disdain in his voice when he spoke of the Churchyard Wedgwoods. The Big House works were conspicuously more advanced than those of their neighbours: larger, better built, more organised. This was like all the others in Burslem: a jumble of assorted buildings, the frozen earth between them scattered with broken pots and discarded clay, all filmed with a fine dust which gave it a look of uniform greyness. It was as if whoever was in charge had long since given up hope. Clearly the hand that kept the house neat and clean had no jurisdiction out here.

For all that, it was still unmistakably a potworks. There were two main sheds, dim and dusty, in one of which the wheel lay idle at the elbow of a man talking animatedly to another standing nearby, who turned and shouted, 'Clear off, you!' when she put her head round the door; in the other there seemed to be a great deal of activity – a game of cards accompanied by much drinking, even a noisy scuffle – but little actual work in progress, though one man was mixing glaze in a vat with a large stick, pausing now and then to scatter in a handful of grey powder from a nearby sack, or, more often, simply to watch the fight. She was not tempted to stay.

She found the kilns, one closed and smoking, one cold and in the process of being emptied: the door was open and she could see a man carrying out the saggars which had protected the pots from the fire. Not wanting to risk another rebuke she avoided him and wandered instead towards a small lean-to building propped against the wall of one of the sheds: its door stood slightly open, giving a glimpse of a clean bare little room.

She stepped inside, and then jumped, startled, as she pushed shut the door and came face to face with a boy. He

16

was a little older than herself, but not very much taller, sturdy, with thick brown hair framing a broad good-humoured face. But after the first surprise had subsided it was his eyes which held her attention. They were remarkable eyes, wide and clear and grey, set beneath heavy dark brows, and they had a look of lively intelligence which was instantly and overwhelmingly attractive. Sarah succumbed to the attraction and smiled.

'Hello,' she said. 'I'm Sarah Wedgwood. Who are you?'

'Josiah,' he said. He studied her with interest, but kindly. 'Are you a cousin?'

'I expect so.'

There was a brief silence while they both tried to think of something to say, all at once a little shy; but it was not a hostile silence, nor even a very uncomfortable one. Sarah's gaze wandered past her companion's shoulder in search of something of interest. There was a bench beneath the little window, at which he had been standing when she came in. On it was ranged a motley assortment of objects – stones for the most part, of various shapes and sizes, but set out in what was clearly some kind of deliberate order.

'What are those?' she asked. She moved closer, and could see now that each stone was marked fascinatingly with the detailed pattern of some living organism, so accurate that it might have been stamped upon it: here a shell, there a fern, frozen forever in unchanging immortality.

'They're fossils,' explained Josiah, lifting one out of the orderly row so that she could see it more clearly. 'Look – that fern grew thousands and thousands of years ago, and it turned to stone deep in the ground, and it was buried all that long time until I found it. I've got lots of different ones.'

Sarah moved from one to another, touching and gazing in wonder. 'Where did you find them?'

'Oh, lying about. If you keep your eyes open it's easy enough. Stone quarries are the best places.'

Just then Sarah came upon an object which was not a stone but unmistakably a piece of broken pot, of a colour and glaze unlike any she had seen anywhere before. It was smoothly curved, with a tiny portion of delicate pattern indented upon it, and all of one colour, a bright red-brown, with an even uncracked glaze. 'What's this?'

Jos's face lit with pride of ownership. 'They found it when they were digging for a new house over Newcastle way – the crateman brought it – he says the Romans left it behind. He often brings me things.'

Sarah turned and turned the fragment, her imagination straining in an effort to understand what it must have been like for those men of long ago who shaped the vessel from which this piece had come. Had they used a wheel, and a kiln, like the potters in Burslem? They were clever people the Romans, so the rector had said.

'I know about the Romans,' she told Jos. 'I learned about them in my lessons.'

'Do you go to school?'

She nodded. 'I go to the rector for lessons, with his girls and the squire's children. Where do you go?'

At that her cousin's expression took on a shuttered look, as if he would rather not discuss the matter, as being somehow too painful. 'I don't any more,' he said abruptly. 'Not since my dad died. That was two years ago, when I was nine. Now I work here, for Tom my brother.'

Envy, sharp and painful, gnawed at Sarah's heart. 'Are you an apprentice?'

'Sort of. They haven't drawn up the papers yet. I shall be when they do.'

'Will you throw pots then?'

A kind of inward happiness shone from his eyes, like the candle glowing inside a turnip lantern. 'I can throw a pot already,' he told her with an unmistakable note of pride in his voice, and she knew exactly why he had that look.

'Oh, I should like to see you!' Her voice emerged on a sigh of longing.

'Come on then,' he said, as casually as if she had asked to look at the cow.

The men in the throwing shed were still talking, or had been doing so: they were laughing now, probably, Sarah thought, at one of those obscure jokes which always made her father look greatly disapproving, for they broke off suddenly as she and Jos came in, clearly irritated at the interruption. 'Why aren't you wedging that clay, like Tom said you were to do?' the younger one greeted Jos.

Her cousin gave them a look that would have shrivelled

18

Sarah, but seemed to make no impression on them at all. 'I finished that long since. This is our cousin Sarah, and I'm going to show her how to throw a pot.'

So these young men were Josiah's brothers! Sarah stared at them, astonished that brothers could be so unalike, for the two stocky surly young men bore no apparent resemblance to Jos.

'Does Tom know?' one of them demanded.

'He wanted Jos to look after me,' Sarah broke in quickly, more to the astonishment of Jos than of his brothers, who accepted the information with a shrug. 'My father has business with him, you see,' she added helpfully.

After a moment during which the young men looked her over disparagingly, and shrugged again, they left the shed; and Jos sat at the wheel before the high window and set the treadle working, and took a ball of clay from the bench beside him and threw it with unerring precision right into the centre of the turning wheel.

Then, for the second time in her life, Sarah gazed in wonder as the miracle of creation unfolded before her – watched the broad supple hands, the sensitive fingers move with swift steady grace to mould and shape and control until, slowly, surely, the lump of clay grew: taller, narrower, hollowed and swelled into a rounded curve, swept in then flared out like a blossom opening to full splendour, and at last as the treadle ceased its rhythmic noise and the wheel slowed and came to rest a vessel stood before her, dark wet clay, unbaked, un-glazed, but already holding within its form all the essentials for ultimate perfection. It had been a wonder and a delight to watch Uncle Thomas at work; but somehow this was better still, in some way she could never have put into words. She only knew that she was, almost, supremely happy. 'I *wish* I could do that!' she whispered.

Jos grinned up at her, all at once no longer the creator of wonder but an ordinary mortal boy, and her cousin. 'It takes a lot of practice.'

'Uncle Thomas wouldn't let me try.'

'Is that Thomas Wedgwood of the Big House?'

She nodded, a little surprised by the sudden eager interest in his tone.

'I've heard they have invented a new device for measuring the heat of a kiln. Do you know about it?'

19

She smiled happily, and nodded again. 'They call them . . .' she wrinkled her forehead, struggling to think of the right words, 'pyro-metrical beads,' she said slowly; then added, 'Uncle Thomas showed me once.'

'I should like to see that!' It was his turn to be envious: Sarah, watching his brightly questioning eyes, felt an unaccustomed sense of importance. 'Tell me about them.'

'Well . . .' she began slowly, 'they look like this . . .' She cupped her hands like a half-closed flower. 'But very small – they're made of clay, but different colours – you put them in the kiln, and the colours show the heat.' She reddened slightly, regretfully aware of the inadequacy of her account. 'Uncle Thomas says they're not perfect, but better than nothing.' She saw that her companion was frowning, and feared that the poverty of her description had angered him; but then she realised he was simply thinking hard, trying from her clumsy account to visualise the device she was describing.

'You could go and see them,' she suggested; though she wondered, after the talk she had heard this morning, if a Churchyard Wedgwood would be welcome at the Big House. But her uncles were kindly and easy-going men: she did not think they were likely to turn a kinsman away.

'Perhaps I will,' he said. Very carefully, he slid a wire beneath the pot to detach it from the wheel and set it on the shelf where others stood drying; and then he rubbed his hands clean on a cloth.

'Can I try now?' asked Sarah, and held her breath with hope.

He looked at her with real compassion. 'I'm sorry. Tom wouldn't allow it . . .' Then, sensing the depth of her disappointment, he added quickly, 'When I'm a master potter, then you shall.'

She knew he was only humouring her, as everyone did; but she liked him all the same for his kindness. At least he did not laugh and remind her she was only a girl. She wondered, looking at him, what likelihood there was that he would one day become a master potter. He was after all merely one of the youngest members of a large and needy family. On the other hand he worked already in the potworks, and had begun to learn the essential skills – more than begun, she acknowledged, with a glance at the pot. She reached out now and touched it, very gently, reverently almost. 'I think it's beautiful,' she said.

He made a little mock bow, and grinned; then he said, 'I'll show you my best one, if it's not gone.'

He took her hand in his and led her at a run out of the door and over the yard towards a hut near the kilns, where the crateman's pony stood waiting with weary resignation while two men carried out pots to pack into the crates on its back: one was Josiah's brother Aaron (so he told her as they ran), the other the crateman himself, red-eyed and yawning after several congenial hours negotiating a price with Tom Wedgwood in the Shoulder of Mutton last night. It had not improved his temper.

But Josiah ignored the man and dived into the hut, and emerged in a moment carrying a graceful little pot of mottled blue. 'My first thrown pot,' he said proudly.

Sarah took it very gently into her hands, knowing instinctively how much it meant to him. And he was right to be proud. She had seen many pots in her life – she was a Wedgwood after all – but, she thought, never one so perfectly symmetrical in shape, so balanced and ordered, so satisfying in everything about it. She turned it in her hands, stroking the smooth glaze, enjoying the shape and feel of it; then she turned it over and saw scraped into the base the clear letters 'J.W.'

'I marked it as mine so whoever buys it will know,' said her cousin.

'Did you make all of it?' There was a note of awe in her voice at the possibility that so much artistry could be contained in one single human boy.

'Not quite. But I mixed the clay, and threw it, and I watched it through all the stages afterwards.'

'Your very first throw,' she said wonderingly. She had never thrown a pot, but she guessed that it was very much harder than it looked in the hands of an experienced potter.

'Not the very first,' he admitted. 'I tried lots of times: I had to throw the others out. This is the first good one. So it's sold and going off into the world.' Gently he took it from her, and himself encased it in straw and nestled it tenderly, like a child in a cradle, into the pony's crate. 'There – now it's safe.' He

21

straightened and turned back to her. 'Would you like to see the kittens? They were only born last week.'

Sarah loved kittens, but she felt it would be almost an anticlimax – so ordinary and mundane – after the wonders she had seen this morning. She smiled, however, and said yes, and Josiah took her hand again and they walked slowly back towards the house. Behind them the crateman closed the crates and set out on his way, leading the burdened pony. Josiah turned once to watch him go, and Sarah knew his thoughts were with his precious pot.

They were halfway to the house when there was a sudden shout, a long resounding rattling crash; a torrent of violent swearing. The cousins turned.

There on the road beyond the churchyard wall the crateman's pony was struggling to rise under a hail of lashes from his master's whip; and one crate fallen open lay askew with its contents spilling broken and damaged upon the ground.

A cry, sharp with anguish, broke from Josiah. He dropped Sarah's hand and sped out of the yard and along the road. Sarah stood staring after him, pity for the poor ill-used pony warring with her fear for Josiah, and for the pot he had made.

She watched him reach the crateman, who paused whip raised and glowered at the interruption. There was a brief and unfriendly exchange and then Jos bent down for a moment to examine the fallen goods; and afterwards rose and made his way swiftly back towards the works. Even from this distance she could see the grim pallor of his face.

A hand on her shoulder made her spin round with a startled cry. Her father stood there, smiling, with Tom Wedgwood at his side.

'I thought I'd find you somewhere hereabouts. Have you been behaving yourself?'

Sarah ignored the question and broke out in distress, 'Papa, the crateman's pony fell – and I think Jos's pot is broken!'

She was certain of it as her young cousin reached them, and she could read the full extent of the raw fury upon his face. He came to a halt and gazed mutely at his brother. Tom clapped a hand on his shoulder.

'Never mind, Jos lad. The pony stumbled in a hole, I

22

suppose? It happens – can't be helped. It's not the end of the world. At least they were paid for. Cheer up!'

Josiah drew in his breath sharply and raised eyes darkened with rage to Tom's face. 'How can you be so stupid?' he shouted, hands clenched tight at his sides, as if otherwise he might be tempted to hit his brother. He stood a moment longer, struggling vainly for words; and then he pushed roughly past Tom and away, somewhere beyond the furthermost building.

Tom shrugged. 'He'll get over it,' he said unconcernedly. 'He's a bit spoiled of course, being the youngest – gets his own way too much – but he'll learn.' He dismissed the matter from his thoughts, and turned to smile at Sarah. 'Well now, little cousin Sarah, are you going to come and see us again one day?'

Half an hour later as they walked back to the Big House, Sarah said to her father, 'I wish I could be apprenticed to a master potter like Uncle Thomas.'

Her father laughed, not even considering for a moment that she might be serious. 'Daft little lass! Whoever heard of a female potter?'

'Jos wouldn't think it was funny,' she told him reproachfully. Good humour instantly dispelled, her father grunted.

'Hmph! That's no recommendation. The runt of a poor litter that one. I'm sorry you were bothered with him.'

'Oh!' She bit her lip sharply, remembering just in time that well-bred girls did not argue with their fathers. Then she said carefully, 'I think he was nice.' It sounded totally inadequate as an expression of the warm feeling that filled her at the very thought of Jos.

'Even after that disgraceful display over the broken pot? I've never seen such a thing – speaking to his brother like that, when young Tom is the nearest he'll come to a father. A spoilt brat, that's quite clear.'

Sarah said nothing, because she could not find the words to say what she felt. But she was sure her father was wrong, and Churchyard Tom too: Jos was not spoilt. She knew about spoilt brats, for there was little brother John at home, four years old and from infancy indulged in every whim. There was perhaps some excuse for him, because he had always

23

been a sickly child; but that did not make it any easier for his older sister to be patient with his perpetual tears and tantrums. In some inarticulate way she knew that Jos's outburst today had been of quite another kind. His anger was not for himself, but for the stupidity and bad management that allowed a good pot to be smashed before it had been of any use to anyone, just by the simple accidents of an uneven road and an overburdened pony. He wanted perfection, and it angered him to find not only that it was beyond his reach, but that no one else cared that it was so. Only, from today, Sarah cared, as she knew she would always care about anything that mattered to him.

The next day Uncle Thomas granted what should have been her dearest wish and offered to show Sarah round the potworks: her father was busy with the account books and would be occupied all morning. Sarah, accepting the offer with a bright smile and a 'Thank you, Uncle Thomas', wished she did not feel just a little disappointed at the prospect. She did want to look round, of course she did: that was why she had come to Burslem in the first place. And Uncle Thomas promised to show her all the improvements that had been made since her last visit. It was just that, as she hurried along at his side, she could not help wishing that Jos could have been her companion instead. She had a growing suspicion that without Jos no potworks would ever have quite the same magic for her again.

She wondered if Uncle Thomas knew him. 'I met my cousin Josiah yesterday,' she said carefully, as they pulled their cloaks about them before stepping out into the yard from the throwing shed. She watched her uncle's face as she spoke, to see if it had the same look of disdain as had crossed her father's face yesterday when he spoke of Jos. But he merely looked blank.

'Josiah? Which is he now? One of the Churchyard family, I take it? There are so many, and I don't see much of them.'

'He's the youngest.'

'Ah yes, of course – long time since I've seen him. Bright little lad.'

Sarah's heart warmed still further towards Uncle Thomas; and she giggled. 'Little! He's older than me!'

Uncle Thomas grinned. 'Is he now? Then he must be a fine young man by now.' He pinched her cheek. 'How would you like to put a handle on a jug for me?'

So her disappointment was not so great after all. And in the afternoon while the men were closeted in the parlour, talking business, Sarah set out with a delightful sense of wickedness – since she had asked no one's permission – to run all the way to the Churchyard works. She took a long way round so as to avoid passing the church; and arrived very muddy and dishevelled from negotiating fields and hedgerows. But she found Jos without any difficulty: he was busy at the wheel, adding one by one to a neat row of pots set on the shelf, and he greeted her arrival with a smile of welcome which warmed her right through and set her skipping with joy as she went to his side.

It was an idyllic afternoon. He had work to do, but he let her stand and watch, explaining how different colours and textures could be achieved by varying the clays, demonstrating exactly how the clay must be centred on the wheel, and how it should be shaped; and listening with real interest to anything she had to say. After a while he led her to the kitchen, where his sisters Margaret and Kate were baking, and begged bread, warm and crusty from the oven, for the two of them. Kate, he had told Sarah, was his favourite sister, four years his senior and a pretty kind-hearted girl. Sarah, who had no sisters of her own, liked her at once.

Afterwards, for a little while, they played with the kittens, and then she realised it was already growing dark – though she felt she had only just this moment come – and Jos walked with her to the gate to see her on her way.

She came to a halt there, for in her happiness she had forgotten the churchyard. It was too dark already for her to consider trying to find her way again over the fields; but she felt a fluttering sense of panic at the thought of passing the wall and that horrible stench.

'I hate that place,' she said in a tight little voice. From here she could see a small knot of mourners standing about a grave. They were silent, dark, somehow adding to the sense of menace that hung over the place.

Jos, however, seemed quite unaware of anything abnormal. 'Do you?' he asked with a note of surprise. 'I never think about it – but then I've lived here all my life.' He glanced down at her, and must have read something of what she felt in her expression. 'I'll walk to the end of the wall with you if you like.'

Oh, the relief at being understood so well! Sarah smiled up at him, as close as she had ever come to adoring another human being. 'Thank you.'

They walked together, and Jos talked eagerly, not of pots or of fossils, but of the flowers he would grow in the little front garden when spring came. 'I'm the only one who ever does anything with it,' he told her. She was so fascinated by this new and unexpected side of her cousin that she did not even notice that they had passed the churchyard until Jos came to a sudden halt and she realised they had already reached the ford. 'You'd better hurry now,' he advised. 'It'll be dark soon. And I must hurry too – I've half a dozen more pots to make before supper. Tomorrow I'm coming to the Big House to ask about those beads. I'll see you then.'

Sarah ran up the hill with a light heart, singing a little song to herself as she went: and so heedlessly happy that she did not look where she was going, and collided with her father in the hallway of the Big House.

One look at his face warned her to subside into attentive silence; but she had forgotten her disreputable appearance. She saw his gaze travel stonily down her person, and decided against a smiling and cheerful greeting.

'Where have you been, Sarah?'

She was a truthful child, so she said with only a little tremor of apprehension, 'I went to see Jos, Papa.'

She waited for the chilly reprimand to fall upon her; but though Richard Wedgwood opened his mouth as if to speak, he closed it again, stared at her frowningly for a moment or two, and then said with icy precision, 'Go and tidy yourself. Supper has been ready this past hour. You must be in bed early tonight: we go home at dawn tomorrow.'

The world seemed suddenly submerged in cold dead greyness. Sarah stood motionless, her eyes on her father's stern face. Was this his punishment for her disobedience, in the spirit if not the letter?

'Tomorrow, Papa?' she stammered feebly. Framing the little question seemed to take a tremendous effort, as if it were almost more than she could manage. She had not known she was so tired.

'There's smallpox in Burslem,' he told her. 'I've no wish to risk infection.'

A tiny flame of hope sprang up again. 'But I've had smallpox, Papa.' Could he really have forgotten? They had all been so pleased that her soft pink-and-white complexion had emerged unscathed from the sickness.

'But John has not. We mustn't risk taking it home with us: you never know. Now don't argue. Go and do as you're told.'

She went, each footstep heavy and slow. She could not even remember how lightly and with what springy swiftness she had run here just a little while ago. John again; always John: 'Don't play the spinet so loudly, Sarah – John has a headache'; 'Let him play with your books, Sarah – he's only a baby'; and 'He couldn't help tearing them, Sarah – he's only a baby'. And the endless dreams and plans: 'Papa is going to buy the estate at Smallwood, so that when John grows up he will have a good-sized establishment to his name'; 'We must think of John's schooling – something better than the rector can do, of course'; 'John will not be a cheese merchant like Papa – he'll be a gentleman'. And now because of John she was to be dragged suddenly back to Spen Green away from the potworks and from Jos and all the new delights she had found. She did not hate John, not exactly; sometimes she was even quite fond of him. But there was a burning sense of anger and injustice in her heart at the way his needs, his desires, his interests, were always first in her parents' thoughts.

It was raining next day, a cold penetrating drizzle that only added to the misery of the journey. Once, as the mare plodded up the hill out of the town, Sarah looked back. There was the church, with its square tower and the scattering of buildings beyond; and a little gathering of mourners in the churchyard. She shivered, and quickly looked away again. She did not want to take that memory away with her.

At home they found John had a cold and was endlessly fretful, while his mother hung anxiously over him and could scarcely muster a greeting for the returned travellers. Richard Wedgwood had letters and business awaiting him; and Sarah found herself banished to her room to work on her sewing. As

27

she stabbed at the fabric with angry fingers she thought of Jos and his untidy disorderly home, and the potworks where he spent his days; and knew she would instantly have given up all the comforts of Spen Green to share them with him.

A month later, at dinner, her father observed, 'The Church-yard Wedgwoods are all down with smallpox, I gather – or most of them anyway. I'm surprised they didn't go down with it sooner, living where they do. They say three of the younger children are not expected to pull through – which I suppose will mean fewer mouths for young Thomas to feed.'

'The younger children' – and Josiah was the youngest of all! Sarah felt as if her heart had turned a painful somersault within her. The talk moved on uncaring around her; but she sat as if turned to stone, neither talking nor eating, all appetite gone. After the meal, as soon as she decently could, she fled upstairs, pulled a cloak about her, and ran out through the kitchen into the cold afternoon, grey and shot through with flurries of snow. She did not know why she had gone out, nor where she was going, only that she could not bear to stay indoors with them all.

And then she did know. She took the lane that led, after long windings, to Astbury church, the great medieval stone church in its carefully tended churchyard near which stood the fine Queen Anne rectory where this morning, as almost every morning, she had worked at her lessons.

Only she did not go to the rectory now. Instead, guided by some instinct deeper than anything she had ever been taught, she made her way to the church itself and with an effort turned the heavy iron ring and pushed open the great studded door.

For a moment she held her breath, standing quite still. Even on Sundays, busy with a well-dressed congregation, the church frightened her a little. Try as she might she could never quite put from her mind the weird carved gargoyles outside; or, worse still, the lurking multitude of devils which some long ago craftsman had worked into the ceiling of the south aisle – fifty-one in all it was said, although she had never dared to count them. There was a devil in the porch too, but he was set about with three angels playing musical instruments; and she set her mind firmly on their protective presence, pushed closed the door behind her, and ran below them into the wide high nave.

There all thought of her own fears left her. Only Jos mattered now, and his needs. She walked calmly, steadily down the long centre aisle to stand in the chill silence beneath the elaborate rood screen and gaze up at the delicate tracery of the east window, her hands clasped at her sides in tight little fists; and there she whispered in a small fierce voice as sharp and angry and challenging as the frown that drew her brows together over her brown eyes, 'Don't let him die, Lord! Don't let Josiah die!'

She did not dare to ask at home for news, though now and then her father went to meet her uncles at some safe distance from Burslem, and she was sure he must have heard something. When he returned, she would strain her ears to catch any passing reference to the fate of the Churchyard Wedgwoods, but none came, or not when she was within earshot. She could not say, 'Papa, how is Jos?' because she knew she would not be able to bear it if the news was bad and she had to endure her father's indifference. Through the rest of the winter, through spring and summer, the thought of Jos shadowed her every pleasure, a constant nagging ache somewhere deep inside her.

And then in September she went to Burslem at last, riding behind her father through the hazy autumn sunlight to the warm welcome of her uncles and their exclamations as to how she had grown.

They sat down as usual in the parlour, with tea brought by the servant who had replaced Aunt Sarah, happily married by now; and there, seated next to Uncle Thomas – who knew a little of what she felt for Jos – she was able to whisper her plea for news.

Her uncle looked down at her, and took her hand and patted it; and then he shook his head gravely, and she felt as if all her internal organs had, sickeningly, come adrift and tangled themselves in knots.

'Oh yes, your young friend – poor lad. The whole family were hit badly this time. Two of them dead – Jane and Abner. Did you know them? And poor Josiah was very ill, very ill indeed for a long time. Still is, come to that. He's not likely to leave his bed again. A severe inflammation of the knee, and great weakness – he'll be a cripple for the rest of his life.'

Sarah stared at him, her eyes wide and dark in a very white face. She felt cold, cold and stunned. She could think of nothing to say.

A cripple – Jos was a cripple. That sturdy healthy boy, with his bright eyes and his supple hands and his strong feet to work the treadle, who took care of her when she was afraid, and who hated any imperfection with all the fierceness of his soaring spirit, was a cripple; like poor Joey Foster at Astbury who lay day after day in a darkened room, motionless and in pain, a burden to everyone and most of all to himself. She could not imagine it. She only knew it was more terrible even than the nameless thing she had feared. Slowly, deep inside her, something stirred to life, uncoiling like a snake, growing and spreading, a terrible fierce consuming anger. 'That's not what I meant!' she cried within herself. 'I said let him live, God – being a cripple isn't the same thing at all!'

And then she remembered, she had not asked for life. It was what she had meant; but she had said, 'Don't let him die,' and God with all the lofty literalness of an unfeeling adult had taken her at her word. She bent her head, because the tears came springing to her eyes, and she thought, 'It's all my fault – I used the wrong words – but you should have known what I meant, Lord.'

Dimly, she became aware of her uncle's voice, gentle and anxious. 'Sarah . . .' and, more sharply, 'Sarah!'

Her gaze focussed on him at last, but for an instant only. The next moment she had jumped to her feet with an inarticulate little cry that explained nothing and run from the room, almost colliding in the doorway with the servant bringing more cakes.

She ran without pausing all the way to the Churchyard works and there did not wait to knock on the door but only thrust it open and stepped into the houseplace, coming face to face with Kate, vigorously scrubbing the table. The girl ceased her work. 'Sarah! What a surprise after all this time . . .'

Sarah had time, just, to notice that Kate's prettiness had gone, her face scarred by the sickness; but she only gasped breathlessly, 'Jos – I've come to see Jos . . .'

Kate laid down her brush, and carefully wiped her hands on her apron, and came to Sarah and put an arm about her. 'You know he's been ill?'

Sarah struggled to control her breathing, and nodded.

'You know he's left very weak – that he's still in bed . . .?'

Weak? Was that all perhaps? Had Uncle Thomas been wrong? Sarah looked up at Kate with a gleam of hope in her eyes. 'But he'll get better?' she asked eagerly. Kate destroyed that hope even before she replied: Sarah could read the answer in her sorrowful expression.

'If he does, it will take a long time – and he will never be as he was. It is his leg you see – his knee . . .'

Sarah stared blankly straight ahead of her, her face set hard. So she had been right: God had taken her at her word, granted her request not in the spirit in which she had made it but to the letter, so far and no further. She had got the words wrong, but she was only a child and knew no better: He should have known. Anger seared her, and she gave a little gasp, and then looked up at Kate. 'Where is he?'

Slowly, Kate led the way across the room to a door at the far side. 'He has a bed downstairs – it makes it easier.' She paused, one hand on the door. 'Don't tire him, Sarah – be calm and quiet.'

She opened the door then, and put her head round, saying, 'There's a visitor for you, Jos,' and Sarah walked past her into the little ill-lit room; and Kate gently closed the door behind her.

Sarah had come here without thinking, on impulse, driven by pity and grief and a burning sense of the unfairness of it all; but she had not given any thought to what she would find. Her imagination could not reach so far, and there had not been time. Jos would not be as she had seen him last, for he was a cripple now, bedridden and ill. She had a vague mental picture of her cousin lying still and pale and rather quiet; but that was all.

She had not for one instant conjured up what lay before her and kept her frozen to the spot, immobile and speechless and appalled. She could not have dreamed up the shrunken emaciated form stretched on the bed, mercifully part-concealed by the worn blankets: the eyes sunk deep in their shadowed sockets; the cheeks hollow beneath the broad

31

cheekbones, themselves sharp-edged now through the taut skin so that she could not even bring to mind any more how once the warm flesh had clothed them; and that skin unscarred, but grey and almost transparent; the wrists as thin and frail as dried sticks; and the hands – oh, that was worst of all! – the hands that once before her eyes had shaped a pot shrunk now to parchment- covered bone, thin, skeletal, lifeless where they lay pale on the brown blanket.

She stood unable to move her eyes from those hands, scarcely able to understand that this wasted creature – this corpse with glittering eyes – was Jos still; unaware that he was watching her, taking in every shade of her horror-struck expression. And then he laughed – actually laughed – faintly, so that she scarcely heard, but it was a laugh all the same, and her gaze shifted to his face, shocked by the sound.

'Am I so bad, Cousin Sarah?'

It was the voice she remembered, though sickness had weakened that too; and the light tone; and the smile, though it had a bitter edge to its sweetness. Most of all it was the eyes, bright within their shadows, that were just as she remembered them, and brought home to her sharply that this was still Jos, whom she loved.

She did not know what to say. She wanted to cry, or perhaps to shout in anger, but she did not know how. She stood twisting her hands before her, wishing she were anywhere but here, trying to force a smile and knowing she had not succeeded. Then she stumbled forward and sat down heavily and ungracefully on the stool at the bedside.

'Sick-visiting, Cousin Sarah? How gracious of you, I'm sure.' The voice was mocking, and the mouth had an odd wry bitter twist to it. The bitterness at least reached Sarah and stirred her anger to life.

'If that's what you think, I'll go!' she snapped at him; and was immediately horrified that she could have done so, for it was not really Jos who had angered her. Before she could move or think of anything else to say, one bony hand shot out and caught at her wrist, stronger by far than she would have thought possible. It even hurt her a little.

'No!' said Jos sharply. 'Don't go, Sarah! The days are so long, and the nights . . . and they all creep in and out again, but no one stays . . . and for God's sake don't look at me like that! I've had enough of pity.'

So she stayed – not in fact having thought seriously of doing anything else – and sat stupidly on at the bedside trying to think of something to say: something cheering, or common-place – anything at all but what she really thought or felt.

'You haven't brought any books, I suppose?' Jos asked wistfully. He gestured towards a pile of books on the chest beside the bed, arranged with mathematical neatness, not because they were untouched, but because for some time now he had found nothing else to do but set them in order. 'I've read all those.'

Sarah shook her head.

'Oh well – never mind.' He fell silent, frowning a little.

'I'll bring you some as soon as I can,' Sarah promised quickly, seizing with relief the opportunity to be practical. 'What kind of books do you like?'

'Any books – school books, story books, whatever you have. My body may not be much use, but my head's working still – I must have *something* to do.'

Sarah looked down at her hands, busily pleating the stiff folds of her pink damask skirts, restless with the awkwardness of it all. 'Uncle Thomas says,' she began carefully, 'that your knee's very bad . . .' She stopped. She did not need years of experience to know that she could not add, 'He says you will always be a cripple.' She looked up, and her eyes met Josiah's: they had a quiet steadiness in their expression which surprised her.

'It will get better,' he said, with such conviction that for the first time today she felt her spirits rise.

'Do you really think so?' She longed to believe him.

'Sometimes,' he admitted slowly, after a momentary hesita-tion, 'in the middle of the night when I can't sleep, and there's no one about – then sometimes, just a bit, I'm not sure . . .' For a moment, then, Sarah shared with him the lurking horror of the night hours, when he lay possessed by a cold dread at the thought that all his life might now for ever be limited, hemmed in, confined by the boundaries of the narrow bed and the four enclosing walls.

And then abruptly he grinned, and banished the shadows. 'In the daytime, when I can see things properly, then I *know* I shall get well.'

Sarah grinned too. 'Good,' she said, and added, 'you'll have to hurry up though. Mama says I'm not very good at sick-visiting. I don't sit still long enough.'

Josiah laughed with real amusement. 'Then you'd better come often so I get tired of lying here all the sooner.' He reached out and took her hand in his and gave it a squeeze. 'Sally,' was all he said, but she knew with a shock that he was telling her how much he needed her: Jos, the adored protective cousin, needed her.

She felt a little surge of pride at being so depended upon, so trusted; and a certain solemnity, as if this was in some sense a moment of dedication. Nothing would ever be quite the same again between them, for now she was the one who had to be strong. She must not turn to him for reassurance, but be ready always to be his friend, steadfastly believing that he would grow well even when doubt and fear threatened to destroy his own certainty. If ever she had doubts herself, then he must not know of them.

She folded her free hand about his, and smiled; and began to chatter easily about all the little homely things that had happened to her since they had last met, trying to bring something of the seasons, springtime and haymaking and harvest, into the dim little room.

CHAPTER TWO

1751

Burslem was like a place enchanted. Not a human creature stirred in its streets. Dogs lay panting in the shade; horses and cattle, sluggish with heat, hung drowsy heads low and bore with the plaguing flies until the last unendurable moment drove them to flick an exasperated tail or stamp a hoof. A relentless sun picked out every line of wall and hedgerow, kiln and roof with brilliant clarity, laying bare every hidden corner, every dusty hole in the road; giving the place an odd unfamiliar look, as if scrubbed bare, all its angular ugliness exposed.

But then in Wakes Week by long tradition all the potworks closed for the holiday, and for once in the year no haze of smoke hung above the town to throw a tactful veil over its blemishes.

Sarah had never seen it like this before; but the raw ugliness did not trouble her. Burslem had never been ugly to her, set about as it was with the warm glow of familiarity and happy memories, like an old friend so loved that the deformities become invisible. It was the one place where she felt she was ever fully alive; the only place where she could be truly at home. Today the way it dazzled in the sunlight answered some high note in her mood, buoyant and excited, full of vigorous springing energy. Besides, Jos was there, and where Jos was there could be no ugliness. Nowadays even the churchyard would only stir in her a sense of unease, overlaid by the knowledge that she was nearly at her destination.

As always, although it was Jos who drew her here, her ostensible reason for coming was quite different: Uncle John had been ill, and her mother had packed the saddle bags carried by Amos, the servant from Spen Green, with the most efficacious remedies to aid his recovery. Sarah urged her pony down the hill, Amos's horse plodding steadily behind, and let her imagination linger on the time, after dinner, when she would make her way to the Churchyard works.

Once in the narrow streets of Burslem it was clear that the air

35

of desertion that hung over the place was deceptive. A low murmur of talk, a whiff of pipe smoke reached her from alehouse and inn, where the older men gathered for peaceful drinking. Somewhere a woman sang as she clattered the cooking pots; and two children, heedless of the heat, played hopscotch in a potworks yard. But today most of the townsfolk had gone to the fair at Newcastle under Lyme and left Burslem to the sun, and the animals, the busy and the old.

The uncles at the Big House would by now have placed themselves in the last category. As if to prove the point they settled after dinner, as Sarah had known they would, to sleep away the afternoon, and left her free to go in search of Jos; who would never, she knew, allow a holiday to interrupt any work he had on hand. 'Take him off to the fair,' Uncle Thomas advised her. 'Do him good – do you both good.'

She thought he was probably right, and she was in the mood for a little unthinking enjoyment. She made her way on horseback – Jos found it easier to ride than to walk – along the familiar streets, scarcely changed since that memorable visit ten years ago, apart from a new building here, a kiln or two there.

The house and the works – and the pervasive smell from the churchyard – were almost exactly the same, no worse and no better, though the small front garden was bright with the nasturtiums and snapdragons sown and tended by Jos. For a little while about eight years ago the works had acquired, temporarily, what was almost an air of prosperity: that was when Tom Wedgwood had married a woman of modest but acknowledged means. But he was too poor a manager for the benefit to be more than temporary, and now his wife had died and her money gone. Perhaps without it the works would have failed completely; but certainly there was nothing to tell the passer-by that she had ever been.

Sarah did not call at the house: during the day Jos was only to be found indoors at mealtimes, or when he was ill. And today he must not be ill.

So, leaving her pony tethered by the gate – out of reach of the flowers – she made her way instead round the side of the house to the yard behind. There was no one about, no sound, no sign of life, except for a pair of hens flapping and

36

scrabbling in a dust bath in a shady spot beneath the trees at the far side. Sarah stood watching them for a moment, smiling at their obvious enjoyment; then, returning her thoughts to Jos, she looked about her.

The lean-to where once he had arranged his fossils was used as a storeroom now, full of unwanted oddments of all kinds: moulds no longer used, broken wheels, ineffective tools, a chair in need of repair; and the crutches which Jos – and Sarah – had prayed he would never need again. She did not look there nor in the throwing shed, for she was unlikely to find him in either place. The other shed then . . .

She paused, listening, her ear caught by some sound not heard before. Yes, there was someone there, more than one person, for she could hear voices. With a lift of the heart that brought a smile to her lips she crossed the yard and reached out to open the door, already in spirit greeting Jos.

'You've got to get it into your head, Jos – it wouldn't work!' Tom Wedgwood's voice was vibrating with anger, suppressed but very close to the surface.

Sarah stood quite still with her hand on the latch, wondering what to do. She did not want to go away, but if a quarrel was brewing it was none of her business: except that everything to do with Jos was her business.

'You owe it to me, Tom – you know you do!'

Sarah bit her lip: that was Jos, as furious as his brother. And even here outside the closed door she could hear Tom's enraged exclamation in response.

'I owe you nothing! God knows I've tried to do my best for you – taught you all I know, put up with your weakness, though it meant there was one thrower the less – oh, I know it's not your fault your knee's bad and you can't work the treadle. But I'm a man of business, and I've got to think of these things.'

'I've hardly been idle, now have I? When did you last find me taking time off to drink or play cards like the other men?'

'Sometimes,' Tom burst out with what was clearly a long-repressed exasperation, 'I've wished you would! I'm sick to death of your harebrained schemes – your "Won't you try this?" or "Why don't we do that?"' The mimicry was cruel, if not very accurate, and Sarah felt the hurt on Jos's behalf. 'You spend far too much time listening to that opinionated

Cousin Sarah – silly young baggage, putting ideas into your head, showing off to her poor relations. You should have more self respect than to go listening to her. Even mother wouldn't go poking her nose in where it's no business to be, and she's lived amongst pots most of her life. Sarah has no such excuse.'

Sarah could feel the indignant colour rising to her face. She itched to push open the door and confront Churchyard Tom, and defend herself against the slander. But Jos had already leapt to her defence.

'Sally's not opinionated, and nor does she poke her nose in. It's just that we think alike. She's got a good mind, and she uses it. And she knows more about pots than a good many who work here – she cares, and she takes the trouble to learn. And she's not showing off either. Besides, you know what I owe her . . .'

Tom's voice took on a note of angry derision. 'Oh, it's gratitude now, is it? Don't be a fool, Jos – I know what you want from her. You fancy yourself wed to her one day, don't you?' There was a tiny pause, while Sarah felt they must hear her heart beat, so loud did it sound. If only she could see Jos's face!

Tom must have read something there, for he said next, with a hint of sympathy softening his anger, 'You'd better rid yourself of that idea double quick. By the time she's ready to be wed she'll have found some other man to take her fancy – besides, you surely don't imagine her father would ever let her wed you? He knows you'll never have anything to offer a wife – and even if you had, he'll be setting his sights a deal higher than poor Cousin Josiah, you can be sure of that. She's out of your reach, Jos, and if you don't see it you'll only get hurt.'

'I'd have a good sight more chance of wedding her if you'd give me the partnership you owe me. It was always taken for granted, Tom, you know that . . .'

'Not by me – not once I knew what dreamy nonsense filled that head of yours.'

'I only want to make a success of the works, just as much as you do. After all, we're not exactly prospering, are we?'

'Who is, these days? Even the Big House folks are pulling in their belts, so I've heard. Times are hard. And at least I'm making a living: I want to keep it that way. What I don't need is a young whipper-snapper tied to my heels telling me I should try this new line or that, or find some fancy Liverpool merchant to sell my wares and look for new markets. I'm doing well enough thank you, and I intend to go on doing so, just as I have all along – go and find someone else to take you into partnership, someone who's got more money than sense and doesn't mind playing ducks and drakes with it to pay for your daydreams. And now I've better things to do with my time than stand here arguing with you, if you don't mind.'

Sarah stepped back quickly into a nearby doorway, just in time to be beyond Tom's line of vision as he flung wide the door and marched past, looking neither to right nor left. When he had gone she ran in to Josiah, pulling the door closed behind her.

'Oh, Jos, love . . .' She held out her hands to him, but he made no move to take them. He stood there, his brows drawn together in a frown, looking in her direction, though she felt that he did not really see her. 'Jos . . .' she said again, very gently. His gaze shifted slightly, the brows relaxed just a little, and he rested his hand on her shoulder for a moment before letting it fall again.

'Did you hear all that then?'

She nodded. 'It's so unfair, after all the years you've worked so hard – all you've done . . .' Unspoken was 'all you've suffered', but she did not say it. Jos rarely talked of the years of illness and disability, or of the struggle to return to some kind of normal life. He hoped the worst was past, but they both knew he would never wholly be free from pain and the constant fear of a relapse. He had thought once before that it was over, only to be struck down at fifteen years old with a terrible agonising return of the inflammation in his knee which even he and Sarah had come close to believing would be too much for him. He had come through that time, but it might happen again, and the shadow of that possibility hung over them always. Only they never spoke of it, as if by some long-made agreement.

Now, suddenly, he grinned, throwing off all the anger in a moment, with a little careless shrug. His rages were always like that, fierce but soon over. 'Never mind, Sally. Maybe he's right – we've never found it easy to work together. Brothers we may be, but we've precious little in common.'

'But what will you do?'

'There must be someone who wants a lame potter full of daft ideas.'

Sarah laughed, warmed by his cheerfulness, and gave him a sudden quick hug. 'Oh, Jos, you silly – *I* want you anyway.' Then she remembered what she had overheard, and blushed and drew back, suddenly serious. Would he remember too, and make the connection? She said hurriedly, 'Let's go to the fair.' In her embarrassment her tone was brusque, almost as if she hoped he would refuse.

'Do you want to?' he asked doubtfully. She smiled then, at the same time mentally rebuking herself for avoiding the subject uppermost in her mind, when she had come so close to speaking of it. She wanted to know how he had looked when Tom lectured him just now, and what he had felt and thought, and why he had said nothing; and if she did not ask she would never know. But the opportunity had gone now, for the moment at least.

'Yes, of course I want to, or I wouldn't ask.'

He grinned and took her hand in his. 'Then we'll go – I can think about little matters like employment tomorrow.'

'Do you think you can go on working for Tom in the meantime?' she asked as they crossed the yard: the hens had moved away now, leaving a new hollow in the already pitted ground.

'I suppose so, if I choose. But I don't choose to, any longer than I have to. This place,' he declared emphatically, 'drives out anyone with any kind of spirit. Look at John – he couldn't stand it either.' His brother John, nine years his senior, was now doing well for himself as a merchant of some standing in London: of all the Wedgwood brothers he was the only one with whom Jos felt any real kinship. They kept up a frequent correspondence, confiding griefs and troubles in one another: Jos had his leg, John an increasingly crippling tendency to severe depression. Sarah did not know John well, but what she did know she liked: at his best there was something in him of Jos's intelligence and imagination, though without the vitality and the stubborn spirit.

They reached the back door of the house, and Jos left Sarah while he went to change out of his dusty working clothes. 'Must be a credit to my company,' as he said with a grinning acknowledgement of her finery.

40

Sarah did not follow him into the house. She felt too restless to make the effort needed to sit down in the house-place and ask politely after this one and that, and listen in silence and without moving while they told her all the news. It was on the whole a happy restlessness, a mixture of enjoyment of the lovely day and excitement at the prospect of going to the fair with Jos, like any young girl with her sweetheart. It was so rarely that either of them enjoyed the more common pleasures of humanity, and it was not always possible to be satisfied only with the perfection of the shape of a jug, the colouring of new-fired clay, even when those joys were shared with her dearest friend. She was seventeen, and wearing her new riding habit of pale-blue camlet embroidered with silver, with a little tricorne hat tilted at a cheeky angle on her braided hair; and she knew she looked her best and longed for once to go out and show herself to the world.

Jos emerged a little later, neat and clean in his Sunday coat with his hair combed and tied back; and he was not alone.

'Kate's coming too,' he told Sarah cheerfully, apparently blind to the dismay which, for all her efforts to suppress it, she knew must have revealed itself on her face. She liked Kate, as no one could fail to like her, for she was gentle and sweet-natured, unfailingly kind and considerate; but she did not want to share today even with Kate. She stood feeling rather stupid – for she could think of nothing to say – while Jos went to saddle the old slow Churchyard horse.

'Jos has a book to return to Mr Willet, and I said I'd take it for him,' Kate explained quietly. 'I wanted to see him about something anyway. I don't want to go to the fair.'

William Willet, minister of the Unitarian meeting house at Newcastle for the past twenty-four years, was a man of learning and wide vision, and for some time now a firm friend of Josiah and his sister – and of their mother too, for she was herself the daughter of a Unitarian minister, and it was her influence which had drawn her children to the Newcastle chapel. Josiah, eager to extend the little education he had, turned to the minister for guidance in his reading; Kate, closely involved with classes for the children of the congregation, had another, deeper interest, so her family thought. Willet was over fifty, but he was a fine-looking man, thoughtful, eloquent, deeply compassionate, and unmarried;

41

and Kate's warmth and intelligence and good sense would make her an excellent minister's wife. Sarah knew what was being said, and softened a little towards Jos's sister. The glow in her face and eyes today did much to counter the effect of her ruined complexion: she looked almost pretty again. So she came with them, mounted behind Jos.

But her presence did take from Sarah much of her pleasure in the ride. All the things she had wanted to ask or tell to Jos seemed too personal for any ears but his, and she could think of nothing else to talk about. For some time Jos was quiet too, thinking perhaps of the quarrel with Tom and what it was going to mean to him; and Kate rarely had much to say, being essentially a good and sympathetic listener.

Rather than go by the road, unpleasantly dusty in this heat, they followed the track that led over the fields. 'We used to go this way to school,' Jos explained, as the horses plodded along the ridge above the valley, down a little and then gently uphill again. 'Though we walked then of course.'

They could see for miles around, back to Burslem on its hilltop, down to Stoke and Hanley, across the valley to Newcastle – all the little towns and villages of this pottery district. The heat was intense, pressing down from a blazingly blue sky. There were few trees here to shelter them, only a hawthorn or two, an occasional hedgerow enclosing one of the wide fields, and here and there thickets of gorse and broom and holly, against which the cattle huddled, seeking the thin bands of shade which were all that remained with the sun so high. Kate scanned the sky with anxious eyes. 'Do you think there'll be thunder later? It's so very hot.'

'There aren't any clouds,' Jos pointed out. 'If there is thunder coming it's a long way off yet.'

The track led them past the Ridge House, a low rambling half-timbered manor, with its ponds and barns and stables sheltered by trees and crowded on all sides by heather moorland: it had no near neighbours. The Ashenhursts, whose home it was, owned all the wide lands over which they rode. 'That,' Sarah thought, 'is what my parents want for me – to be mistress of such an estate, not a mere country girl riding on sufferance along a well-worn track.' They had not told her so, or not directly, but they had made it plain enough: Churchyard Tom had been quite right when he said they set

42

their sights, on her behalf, far higher than on Jos Wedgwood, lame and struggling potter. Even a prosperous potter would find himself beneath their consideration, for if her brother John were to be a gentleman, then his sister must not become less than a lady. 'Only,' she thought now, 'to do what they want I should have to cut myself off from Jos, from his friendship and companionship and the potworks which mean so much to us both. I could not do that.'

It was a relief when Jos's voice broke in on the gloomy flow of her thoughts. 'I used to love this part of the walk when we were children,' he said. 'It's all so open and wild – no people, no animals except a few sheep, just stillness and the larks singing.'

The larks were singing now, up and up in the bright hot air as if they could never quite reach the pitch of ecstasy that their spirits sought, but always went on trying and trying. Sarah felt her heart rise with them, and the tiny remaining traces of resentment at Kate's presence fell from her. She was here with Jos on this lovely day riding on top of the world, and she could not bear a grudge against anyone. She smiled across at Kate. 'Will you come to the fair and find us when you've seen Mr Willet?'

Kate shook her head. 'I'll make my own way back. I shall enjoy the walk.'

Sarah wondered if Jos was as aware as she of hidden meanings in the apparently harmless things people said in passing. Was he thinking now, 'Kate can enjoy a walk of three miles and more, as I did once; but I have to ride or I could not do it'? She glanced at him, but his face revealed nothing, or no more than a quiet interest in the sunlit landscape all around them. Perhaps he had long ago grown used to the contrast between the limitations of his disability and the careless ease with which everyone else seemed to manage their lives. Perhaps he no longer even noticed such remarks, as once he must have done.

The track reached the brow of the hill, and then dipped down the long slope to the green quiet valley, flooded sometimes in winter but dry now, its stream dwindled to a tiny trickle that scarcely raised a splash as they rode through. After that they joined the main road again for the last uphill mile to Newcastle.

They went first to leave Kate at the handsome house on the edge of the town where Mr Willet lived with a sister as house-keeper, waiting until the door had opened and Kate turned to wave them away before riding back to the High Street, where the fair crammed every inch of the wide thoroughfare before the stately Guildhall.

They left the horses well-stabled at an inn, Jos bringing with him the stick he always carried, even on horseback, in case he should need its support. As they walked together through the noisy colourful throng, Sarah could not prevent herself – young lady though she was – from giving a little skip with excitement. It was somehow intoxicating, the sprawl of colourful booths striped and fringed and topped with flags and pennants, their pinnacles emerging out of the jostling heads of the holiday crowd. There was laughter and music: a fiddler playing to one side, a ballad seller singing his wares to the other, so that halfway between them the disharmony was, to the musical like Sarah, appalling; and stallholders shouting for custom in a fluent dramatic rise and fall; and the full-throated cries of a crowd cheering on wrestlers and boxers and fighting cocks and dogs. Sarah linked her arm in Jos's and pulled him close to her side, with a little happy squeeze. He looked round at her and grinned. 'You look like a girl going to her first fair.'

'But I am,' Sarah told him. 'I've never been to a fair before.'

'Why ever not?'

'Papa thinks them haunts of lewdness and vice,' she explained, with mischief in her smile. 'And Mama thinks they're rather beneath her – noisy and vulgar. Just an excuse for drunkenness.'

'So they are,' agreed Jos, 'but tell me an event that *isn't* an excuse for drunkenness.' He came to a halt and looked at her with sudden gravity. 'Tell me now, Sarah, do you really think you ought to be here?'

The solemn tone shocked the smile from her face. 'Why not?' she asked with a faint note of defiance.

'Think what terrible ways you might fall into!' This time the sparkle in his eyes betrayed him. Laughing, Sarah gave him a little shake.

'Jos, you wretch! I'm glad I'm not your sister – poor Kate, having to put up with your teasing.'

He grinned. 'You get equal measure I should say.' He tucked

44

her arm more firmly under his. 'Now, to really serious matters. Margaret's coming home next week, and I want a present for little Tommy Byerley: a momentous decision, you must admit. Come and give me your advice.' Jos's sister Margaret had married four years ago and now lived at Welshpool, and when they came back to Burslem her little son was, Sarah knew, a constant source of delight to his uncle: Jos loved children, when he could tear himself from his pots long enough to notice their existence.

There were stalls selling every imaginable article – and some, Sarah told Jos with a laugh, that ought by rights to be unimaginable – and the crowd was so dense and so pressing that it took them a long time to find one that sold toys. But they did find it at last, and Jos bought a little brightly-painted wooden horse on wheels. 'Now you can tell your father you've been usefully employed today,' he said to Sarah, and he went on to buy her a length of blue ribbon as a reward. 'To tie up your bonny brown hair,' so he told her.

She took off her little hat and allowed him to thread his gift through her hair; and as he did so she realised they were being watched, by a man some distance away tall enough to see easily across the crowd. Or rather *she* was being watched, for Sarah realised with a little tingle of pleasure that his eyes were on her alone, on her bent head and her slender neck and the slope of shoulders and breast beneath the neat riding coat and waistcoat. He was, her covert observation told her, a good-looking young man, dark and handsome in the strikingly classical manner which would automatically draw any female eye in his direction. Feeling just a little guilty, she sent a tiny half-smile his way; and was obscurely disappointed when he turned and disappeared somewhere behind a distant booth, leaving an impression of broad shoulders in a well-made coat and a proudly held head covered with a mass of curly dark hair, short and unpowdered, as if he were used in more select company – and cooler weather – to wearing the wig required of a gentleman.

Inevitably, Jos went next to the pot stall: it was at such places as this that Churchyard Thomas sold many of his products, as did most of the local potters. Sarah stood looking on as Jos lifted plates and turned them in his hands, examined teapots with a critical eye, ran his finger around the rims of

45

bowls and cups. He was frowning as he did so, with all the disapproval of a perfectionist faced with the far from perfect. 'Would you buy things like this for your home, if you had the choice?' he asked Sarah.

'No,' she said with decision. 'Nor would my mother. She buys Delft or some other foreign ware for best – and goods from my uncles for everyday. Though even those are nothing special. You know, Jos, I've often thought that a potter who could make plates that were flat and even and would stack in a pile without wobbling or falling over; or cups and saucers fine enough to drink out of with pleasure and that matched each other; or bowls with a perfect even smooth glaze – a man like that would find a massive demand for his goods, and be doing a great service at the same time.'

Josiah lifted up a tureen whose pitted glaze, unevenly applied, and garish, clashing pattern made it stand out even in that undistinguished company; and he scowled at it, rather, Sarah thought with a moment of alarm, as if he were sorely tempted to throw it to the ground and grind it to pieces beneath his foot. But fortunately he did not, only saying disparagingly, 'It looks as if a drunkard made this – which maybe he did, knowing how many potters spend more than half their time drinking. You know how I've wished we had wider markets for our goods –' He paused, with a rueful grin, and corrected himself, 'No, not "we" any more is it? The Churchyard works then – I've wished they could sell further afield, like your uncles do, to Cheshire and Manchester, even to Liverpool; but as long as this is the kind of thing that's made, there's not even any point in trying to widen the sales. No person of taste would give something like this a second thought, unless he could afford nothing else – and that kind of sale doesn't make a master potter's name for him. But then of course Tom's not interested in making his name.'

'But you are,' Sarah reminded him; 'and you will. You care enough to try and produce the very best you can. After all, even while you've been at the Churchyard works you've brought about some changes for the better.'

'Not anywhere near what I'd like – and I had small thanks for it. In any case they were mostly just a matter of common sense – mixing clays and glazes carefully, cutting out waste of materials, keeping the rooms clean as far as possible so there

46

were fewer impurities brought in; just making sure that even if the glaze isn't up to much it's put on as well as it can be. But that's not going to get us very far. I need time to experiment with different materials, different clays and firing temperatures, different glazes and colours. And wanting to do it isn't enough if I have neither a job nor savings to help me.' He sighed; and then threw off the despondent mood as quickly as it had come, although Sarah recognised that it took some considerable reserves of willpower for him to do so. 'And I was going to put pots behind me! Look, there's the wrestling – and isn't that Harry Birchall from Hanley about to fight? I beat him once, when we were little boys at school. Let's go and watch.'

They joined the crowd gathered about a small roped-off area, in which two men stripped to the waist were circling each other, their muscled bodies gleaming and brown in the sun. Jos and Sarah watched as the slow preliminaries slid almost imperceptibly into the fight itself, the two men heaving and grunting and kicking up great whorls of dust with their heels, the thrashing struggling focus of every watcher in that wildly shouting crowd. They seemed, to Sarah's inexperienced eye, to be evenly matched: she feared it was likely to be a long bout. She was not very interested and would have preferred to move on somewhere else – but if Jos was enjoying it . . .

She glanced at him and surprised on his face a look so eloquent that it shot through her like a pain. She realised then that, coming here light-hearted to watch, he had been faced sharply with an unavoidable reminder of his weakness. There, admired, cheered at, applauded, two tough bull-like muscular bodies displayed physical perfection stretched to its limits. And meanwhile he, Jos Wedgwood, who once might have held his own in the ring and now could not even work the potter's wheel, leant his slight limping frame on a stick, because otherwise he would not have the endurance to stand so long. Sarah reached out a hand and laid it on his arm.

'Jos, love . . .' He heard her, though her voice was not very forceful against the surrounding noise; but the urgency of her tone reached him. With a visible effort, he forced a smile.

Sarah smiled back, assuming a sudden air of cheerfulness. 'I've had enough of this,' she said briskly.

At once he followed her, shoving through the crowd to a quieter space some way behind. Sarah linked her arm through his, glad that the watchers at the ringside had quickly moved back to fill the gap they had made, so they could no longer see the wrestlers. 'All brawn and no brain,' she said comfortably. 'No woman of sense would find them attractive. I'm starving – let's go and find something to eat.'

'Good idea.' His tone was as consciously cheerful as her own. 'My nose tells me there's food that way.'

They did not discover then if his nose was to be trusted, for just as they began to follow its guidance someone laid a hand on his shoulder, and said quickly, 'Josiah Wedgwood is it?'

They turned, and confronted a soberly dressed elderly man whom they had neither of them ever seen before, as far as they could remember. Jos frowned a little. 'Yes,' he said cautiously.

Sarah, with a stirring of anger, watched the man's eyes travel over her companion, up and down, but always coming back to the lame leg. Had someone said, 'You'll know him by the limp'?

When eventually the man ceased his scrutiny, his expression suggested that whatever the reason for it, he had answered some question to his satisfaction. 'I've had quite a hunt for you, I can tell you,' he explained. 'Mr Thomas Wedgwood of the Big House sent me off to your brother, and he sent me chasing off over here. I began to think I'd never find you . . .'

'But you have after all,' Jos broke in, a little impatiently. 'What can I do for you?'

Despite his confessed difficulties, the man had a look of someone with time to spare, ready to settle down and make the most of it. 'You won't know me,' he said unnecessarily, 'but my name's Alders, Thomas Alders of Harrison and Alders potworks in Stoke. I'm a plain no-nonsense potter who knows what he can do best and gets on with it. Mr Harrison, my partner in name, puts up the money, but he's no real knowledge of the trade. We agreed just lately that what we need is some new blood, someone with a bit of skill and imagination, a young man for preference – someone to take on most of the managing for me now I'm getting a bit long in the tooth. I had business at the Big House works today, so I let fall a word or two about how the land lay – word of mouth's the best way I know to do business. The upshot was Mr Thomas Wedgwood seemed to think you might just be what I was looking for. He had an idea you weren't settled at your brother's works; said you were hard-working, skilled, knowledgeable and so forth and showed me some of the marbled wares you'd been working on – said you'd a sound knowledge of the whole range of skills in a potworks, not like some potters who can throw right well but don't have the first idea how to mix a good glaze or choose their clay . . .'

'In the circumstances I had no choice,' Jos put in, his voice flat and unemotional. The man glanced again at his leg and shrugged.

'Well, yes, that's as maybe. Anyway, I'd a mind to seek you out, find out if we might suit together . . .' Once again he looked Jos over; rather like a bird assessing the possibilities of a particularly juicy worm, Sarah thought, amusement bubbling through her almost irrepressible excitement. She no longer saw anything offensive in his scrutiny: clearly the lame leg had not put him off or he would not have concluded as he did now, 'Well, what do you think, lad?'

Jos, high-coloured, silent, stared at him, opened his mouth as if to speak and closed it again abruptly when no words came. Sarah slid her hand down to clasp his, squeezing it encouragingly. He swallowed hard and said carefully, as if afraid to show how much it mattered to him, 'I *am* wanting a post of some kind – my brother and I don't suit too well – I would do my best to give satisfaction, of course.'

Alders nodded. 'Good. I hoped you'd be interested . . .' He stepped back hastily as a girl ran shrieking between them, hotly pursued by a tipsy young man. 'Let's find somewhere a bit quieter to talk.' He glanced uncomfortably at Sarah and added, 'Somewhere private like.'

Sarah slid her hand free. 'I'll meet you by the pot stall in an hour,' she said quickly. Whatever her private feelings might be, she would do nothing to stand in Josiah's way. She saw him hesitate, and gave him a little push. 'Don't be silly: I'll be all right. It's broad daylight, and there are lots of people about. I can look after myself. Now go on!'

But in spite of her brave words, she felt as she watched them go that she had somehow been brutally excluded from

Jos's life, just at the moment when it seemed that at last a turning point had come. There was Josiah, on the brink of deciding what might be his whole future, and to do so he had been forced to turn his back on her and walk away. Would it have been the same if his companion had been a man, one of his brothers perhaps? She doubted it. Something in Alders' expression had said as clearly as any words, 'This is men's talk – there's no place for you.'

She could not begrudge Jos his moment of triumph though; nor resent for long what could not be helped. At least Jos himself had never shut her out, or undervalued her. In fact, she thought with a rueful smile, in his brother's eyes he had always put far too high a value on her.

It was hotter than ever now, though the afternoon was nearing its end. The flags on the booths hung limp in the still air, the animals – dancing bear, stallholders' ponies, lean mangy dogs – flopped exhausted, in the shade when they could or, with weary resignation, in the full burdensome glare of the sun. The fiddler still played on, sweat rolling down his red face and agile arms, but few were dancing now; the ballad seller had long since ceased his singing and lay snoring by one of the ale booths, flat on his back with his hat over his eyes, like many of his erstwhile customers. Sarah picked her way carefully round the recumbent figures, reflecting ruefully that if her father were here he would feel that his worst fears had been amply justified; and found herself confronted by a crooked wooden sign stuck in the ground before a brightly coloured booth advertising in uneven lettering, 'Gipsy Petronella: fortune-teller'.

Sarah stood looking at the sign, smiling to herself. She had never had her fortune told, or even wanted to; but it might be fun, if rather silly.

What, though, if the woman were to say something alarming? Would her scepticism be proof against that? Perhaps it was foolish to take the risk. She wandered a little distance away, wondering what other as yet untried diversions the fair might offer. She was still hungry . . .

A tiny breeze had sprung up, though it did little to dispel the heat; there was a ridge of cloud massing above the hill. Had Kate been right, and was there a storm brewing? If so, it was still some way off.

50

Her gaze scanned the crowd and the booths beyond and then moved back in the direction of the fiddler and the dancers; and came to rest, involuntarily, on a tall figure standing watching the dancers – no, not watching them, for he was looking her way. And the next moment he had begun to move steadily towards her. It was the same young man who had watched her before, only this time she was without the protection of Jos's company.

That decided her: she turned quickly and pushed aside the fringed curtain of the fortune-teller's booth. As she did so, far off came the first warning rumble of thunder. She smiled to herself at the ominous appropriateness of its timing.

It was gloomy inside the booth, and for a moment or two after the curtain fell into place again she could see nothing at all; though a pungent smell of garlic, mingled with the odours of unwashed clothes and some forcefully exotic perfume, filled her senses. After a time, peering a little, she made out a shawled and beaded figure, seated facing her across a small table draped with a fringed cloth. Black eyes scrutinised her from a lined brown face framed in unnaturally black hair. Sarah wondered fleetingly how the gipsy attained that colour.

'My own recipe, lady.'

Sarah gave a little gasp, and then shivered. An apparent ability to read her thoughts was not what she had hoped to find: that would not be so easy to laugh about later.

'Sit down.' The deep voice, neither precisely feminine nor yet masculine, was given emphasis by the gesture of one ringed hand indicating a stool at Sarah's side of the table. With a steadily growing sense of reluctance, Sarah obeyed. Curiosity, rapidly evaporating, warred with an urge to turn and run away before it was too late.

'The money, lady.'

Sarah's hand was shaking as she laid a silver coin on the scarlet cloth: it disappeared so swiftly that she did not see it go.

'Your hands, my dear – lay them before me.'

She did so, very slowly. The gipsy reached out and grasped her wrists, turning the hands palms uppermost. For a long time, head bent, she studied them in silence. Sarah stared at her, wishing with all her heart that she had not yielded to her sudden foolish impulse. Out there in the sun it had seemed

51

like a game, but with that grave stern face bent over her hands it felt alarmingly serious. 'That's why she does it this way of course,' Sarah told herself sensibly. 'To make it seem a bit frightening – if it was bright and cheerful in here no one would ever believe her.' But she could not at present quite convince herself that she was right; and she almost expected the gipsy to rebuke her in the next breath for her unspoken scepticism.

Instead, the woman moved very slightly, and murmured, 'Ah! So: I see . . .'

Sarah held her breath, suddenly very afraid, abandoned by her protective shield of ironic detachment. She did not dare to ask what the gipsy had seen.

The woman raised a hand and slowly, carefully, ran a finger over the right palm, almost as if confirming some conclusion already reached. Then she raised her head and looked straight at Sarah. The faint light fell on the black eyes and glittered back again, finding no way through the smooth hard surface. Sarah could not draw her own eyes away, as if some will that was not hers held them there, in spite of herself. After what seemed a long interval, stretching out the tension between them, the gipsy spoke.

'I feel a great power in these hands: great power, for good or ill. It is for you to make the choice which it shall be. Only so much I see, not all.' She paused, and then continued, 'But I see great riches, greater than you dream of now; and fame – a great name, known over the whole wide world. Yes, that I see. In these hands you hold the power to change the world . . .'

Silence. A silence so complete, so alive with tension, that Sarah wanted to scream, shout, somehow destroy it. But she could do nothing. The eyes held her still, and the commanding hands.

Then at last, slowly, she felt herself set free, not just by the loosening grasp, but in some more intangible way. She had not been aware of holding her breath, but she released it now on a long ragged sigh, and carefully rose to her feet: her legs felt absurdly weak, and she was trembling. Not quite knowing what she was doing, she turned and walked out, stumbling, into the hot dazzling noisy sunlight of the summer fair.

It hit her like a blow in the face, after the quiet and the dark. Floundering, suddenly seized with panic, she forced her way through the crowd, seeking space and air, desperate to be alone.

She ran without stopping until she reached the tree-clad slopes either side of the Wolstanton road. Here it was green and cool and quiet, but for a few couples quite unaware of their surroundings. She sank down on the grass and bent her head on her knees and tried to gather herself together.

'Miss Wedgwood – Miss Wedgwood, are you ill?'

She raised a white face and stared at the tall figure standing over her. It was some little time before she recognised the young man whose apparent pursuit of her had driven her into the gipsy's tent. What had happened since then seemed temporarily to have obliterated the rest of the afternoon from her mind. But she did remember eventually; and realised too, after a little more reflection, that he must know who she was, for he had used her name. Was that why he had been watching her, and followed her here? She was sure she had never seen him before: he was not the kind of young man one would easily forget.

'Are you ill?' he repeated, clearly alarmed by her continued silence. She forced a rather tremulous smile, and shook her head.

'No – no thank you. Just the heat, that's all.' She could almost believe it, now she was beginning to feel a little better.

'It is damned hot,' he agreed, waving his hat to fan his face, as if she had reminded him how uncomfortable he was too. But he did not look particularly uncomfortable, Sarah thought, standing there in his fine riding clothes with a kind of indolent arrogance about him. He was, close to, irresistibly attractive. Sarah found herself smiling with what she recognised a little guiltily was a certain coquettishness: the confrontation with the gipsy was fast fading below the surface of her mind.

'Do I know you?' she asked.

The hat stilled and he raised surprised eyebrows. 'Surely, Miss Wedgwood – we were schoolfellows, after all.' He gave a little bow. 'George Lathom of High Newbold: you *cannot* have forgotten.'

Nor had she forgotten the big sullen boy who had sat at her

53

side in the rector's parlour all those years ago, resentful of the fact that a mere girl half his age should outshine him in almost everything; but she could see no trace of that unloved schoolfellow of her childhood in the handsome and charmingly smiling young man. She laughed. 'I'm afraid you've changed beyond all recognition, Mr Lathom,' she told him. 'I should not have known you.'

'On the other hand you have changed very little – except that now you are a young lady, and no longer a child – but still the pretty pink and white country lass I remember.'

She was doubtful if that was meant as a compliment, but she preferred to take it as such. She rose to her feet, George reaching out a hand to help her: even now he seemed to tower over her, though she was taller than the average herself. She had a curious quivering sensation in the pit of her stomach, set off by all that length of handsome masculinity: it was uncomfortable and yet agreeably exciting, giving an edge almost of danger to an unimportant chance meeting.

'You went away to school for a while, did you not?' she asked, her voice a little breathless and unsteady.

'I did – but that was not, I fear, a very successful experiment.' With a proprietary air which in spite of her excitement she found just a little irritating, he drew her arm through his and began to lead her back down the hill towards the town. 'Since then I have enjoyed a year or so of the Grand Tour. Very much more agreeable.'

'Oh, where did you go? Do tell me! I should love to see something of the world.'

'The power to change the world' half echoed the voice in her head, distancing her again from the happy everyday events of the fair and this unexpected encounter. Almost in anger she crushed it, forcing all her attention on her companion with what seemed to him a gratifying intensity.

'Oh, I went everywhere one is expected to go, of course – France, Italy, Austria and so on and so forth. At least now everyone does it one can always be sure of meeting one's own countrymen abroad and enjoying some good company. It must have been very tedious in the old days, with only foreigners around – foreigners and perhaps a few Jacobite exiles up to their necks in conspiracy. But these days there's quite a social life in Paris and Rome and Vienna and the other cities.'

It did not sound to Sarah as if his travels could have taught him much: it would not have satisfied her to meet only her compatriots abroad. But she asked a question or two more, listening politely to the not very informative answers; and was aware from time to time of the interested and envious glances thrown her way by many of the women they passed. It was undeniably pleasant to be walking along on the arm of the most handsome man for miles around, and that man a gentleman with manners polished beyond recognition by foreign travel.

The subject of his travels, his ambitions – limited to the family ambitions of land and politics – and his amusements, hunting for the most part, occupied George's conversation for some time. He told her that he had come through Newcastle today on his way to 'see a fellow about a horse', but finding the fair in progress had decided to stay awhile and 'see how the potters amuse themselves', as he put it, rather condescendingly, she thought. 'What are you doing all alone here today? I should have thought it rather a rough place for so cultivated a young lady as yourself.'

Was that a subtle thrust directed at her rather unfeminine abilities in Latin and Mathematics? If it was, she ignored it and took the question at its face value. 'Oh, I'm not alone – I came with my cousin Josiah.' Poor Jos, that George had apparently not even noticed him at her side in the crowd. George would never go unnoticed, tall and good-looking as he was.

'And he has deserted you? The wretch!' The accusation was made lightly, with a mocking smile, but all the same it brought Sarah quickly to Jos's defence.

'Oh no – he had to see someone, but we were to meet again – oh!' Her hand flew to her mouth. 'It must be time now. He'll be waiting I must go.'

She felt herself for a moment as disappointed as he looked; but she would not let him detain her any longer. And she left him with her spirits high, carrying with her the recollection of the deliciously flattering moment of parting when he had placed a kiss on her hand and promised to call at Spen Green when she was home again.

Jos was standing by the pot stall, and one glance at his smiling face told her all she needed to know.

'I start at Stoke after the summer,' he said happily, drawing

55

her to him in a hug, swiftly ended. 'Oh, Sally, isn't that good? I can hardly bear to wait!'

The fair had no more to offer now, except some gingerbread men and a portion of meat stuffed into bread from the sheep roasting a safe distance from the crowd: they carried the food with them while they retrieved the horses and rode out of the town.

'We'll eat on our way back, where it's quiet,' Jos said; then he glanced at the growing bank of cloud. 'And we'd better be quick, before the storm comes.'

As they went Sarah made Jos tell her all about the talk with Alders. She listened to him, interested and happy for him, but all the time at the back of her mind crowded the confused impressions of that hour of separation. The gipsy's prophecy meant nothing, of course: she had too much common sense to take it seriously. But at the time she had not doubted, had not dared to doubt.

Did Jos want to marry her one day? If she had ever thought of marriage, then Jos had been essential to that thought, for all that she knew her parents had other plans for her. But where, with Jos, struggling potter of Burslem, would be riches undreamed of and world-wide renown? Would she have to find them unaided, or would there have to be some other man to share her life – a George Lathom perhaps, heir to a prosperous Cheshire squire? She hated herself even for allowing such thoughts to come unbidden.

They went back the way they had come, over the little stream and along the track. Just below the brow of the hill they came to a disused stone pit, wide and tufted with fine soft grass patterned with daisies and tormentil and ladies' smocks, and shaded now that the sun was lower by a clump of gorse: she suggested that they stop there and eat their food.

They tethered the horses and pulled off their coats and spread themselves thankfully on the turf, and ate, realising all at once how very hungry they were; by the time they reached Burslem supper would be well past.

'Well,' said Jos, when the sharpness had gone from their appetites, and the food too had almost disappeared, 'how did you like your first fair?'

'Well enough,' thought Sarah, 'until I saw the gipsy.' Somehow she could not bring herself to tell Jos about it, which was odd, for as a general rule she told him everything. But somehow this was too intimate, too dark and secret to be told to anyone. So she said brightly, 'Very much,' and knew he was a little surprised that she was not more enthusiastic. She did not tell him about George either, feeling a little ashamed that she had found the meeting so pleasurable, since she suspected that George, grown-up, was for all his polish no more admirable than George the schoolboy.

The clouds were moving over them now, the thunder rumbling nearer; against the plum-dark sky the golden flowers of the gorse stood outlined brilliantly, a violent contrast of colour. Not really thinking, her eyes on the flowers, Sarah murmured, 'When gorse is not in blossom, then kissing's out of fashion.' The next moment she felt Jos's arm about her shoulder and he had drawn her close to him and brought his mouth down on hers, and was kissing her with a gentle thoroughness that astonished her. This was nothing like the cousinly peck on the cheek with which, now and then, he greeted her. It was exciting, as the meeting with George had been, answering a need in her which until today she had scarcely known was there.

There was a searing flash of lightning, and the thunder came crashing after it. Sarah's pony whinnied in terror, pulling at his tethering bridle. Jos rolled over and on to his feet. 'Quick, let's find shelter or we'll be soaked!' Sarah scrambled after him. There was a small wood close by but they knew better than to shelter there.

They ran to the horses, untied them, mounted. Below, a little way down the track, was a barn, empty now just before harvest. They rode there as fast as the frightened horses would go, and reached the arched doorway just as the first heavy drops began to fall. When a moment later the storm unleashed a fierce continuous sheet of rain they had soothed the horses and led them to a dim corner and left them there, and were standing side by side in the doorway, their arms about one another, safe, sheltered, protected.

Suddenly all Sarah's new-found doubts fell from her. What did a gipsy matter? Her fate was in her own hands, to make what she would of it. And if she chose to turn her back on all hope of fame and fortune, or even the lesser gentilities her parents sought for her, and commit herself for ever to Jos, then that was her decision. No gipsy could stop her.

57

But Jos, of course, could. She turned her head to look at him: he was watching the storm with an expression of exhilaration on his face. It seemed a pity to disturb him but she knew she had to speak. 'Tell me,' she said. 'What Tom said to you today, about wanting to wed me – was he right?'

Jos moved to lean back against the door post, facing her. 'What do you think?' he asked, and laid his hands on her shoulders, holding her so that their eyes were level. She studied his face, remembering the sturdy brown features of the boy she had met for the first time nearly ten years ago, and seeing them now contrasted with the face of the young man he had become. Still the broad cheekbones, though now they had no ounce of spare flesh upon them; and the brown skin – for he forced himself to take all the exercise he could, riding when he could not walk – though it was lined here and there like that of an older man. But it was the eyes, always the eyes, which drew her first, unchanged in their clarity and intelligence and directness of gaze beneath the heavy brows, and yet lacking now the unclouded brightness of boyhood, before he had suffered and struggled and won so many hard victories. Grey eyes, dark-lashed and steady: the eyes of a man she loved as she was never likely to love anyone else as long as she lived. It was not the love of poetry and pretty compliments, nor of ecstasy, but it was no less real for all that; and she saw its equal in his eyes. And in the next moment he had put it into words.

'I think you know there'll never be any other woman for me, as long as I live. I know I have nothing to offer now: Tom's right about that. But if you'll be patient and wait, and believe in me always, then one day . . .' He broke off, since there was no need to say any more. Sarah reached out and put her arms about him, and drew him close.

'One day,' she finished for him, 'I'll marry you – and that's a promise.'

He kissed her again then, and this time they were not interrupted. There was no disquieting turmoil inside her at his kiss; but nor was there uncertainty or guilt – only a sense of rightness, and of belonging.

CHAPTER THREE

1753–6

Sarah had spent a very trying afternoon in her mother's unalleviated company working at a seemingly endless set of tapestry seats for the parlour chairs whose existing covers had long since worn out. She had never much enjoyed sewing, and least of all this slow, repetitive, tedious work on an intricate pattern she did not like with colours she would never have chosen if left to herself. It did not help that her mother was unfailingly critical of her efforts; and that these days more and more the only exchanges between herself and Susan Wedgwood seemed to be of that kind: complaining, excusing; finding fault, defending herself.

Though not just these days, Sarah amended to herself as she bent over the hated work: it had always been like that to some extent, at least for as long as she could remember. Sometimes she wondered what it had been like before John had been born, if there had once been a time when she had known a full and generous share of her mother's love; but if so it was too long ago now for any trace of lost warmth to linger in her memory. And since his birth, her brother had been the centre of Susan Wedgwood's world, and would remain so now for ever. Sarah knew she could do nothing to change that particular disagreeable state of affairs, and so she had learned to live with it.

Which meant, on this cold grey November day, passing long hours battling with the hated rectangle of tapestry, enduring without comment her mother's periodic disparaging observations on her sewing; and when the time came folding her work neatly away and taking herself quietly and meekly to her room, there to change into a demure silk gown, all ruffles and hoops, ready for supper.

She had the more reason for resentment at present, for yesterday her father had ridden to Burslem on business, and she would dearly have loved to ride with him on the slight chance that she might see Jos, or at least have news of him. It was a long while since she had heard from him, though he had written from time to time telling her something of his life in Stoke. It was even longer since she had seen him, a year at least, for they had somehow managed to miss each other in the crowded noisy family gathering for Christmas at the Big House. Sarah suspected her parents of having a hand in that.

When at breakfast yesterday she had hinted that she might like to ride with her father, her mother had broken in swiftly, 'You're far too old to go riding about the countryside like a hoyden. Besides, the weather's most unfit, and I need your help at home. Why are you always so ready to take any excuse to neglect your duties?'

So she stayed, and her father had gone alone. These days he seemed much less her champion than he had once been, perhaps because, like her mother, he had begun to be alarmed at the closeness and durability of her friendship with Jos. As a child, though it might be regrettable that she loved to spend every spare moment of her time at Burslem in her cousin's company, it was at least acceptable. But when it began to dawn on her parents that the childish friendship showed no sign of ending, or of dwindling into a simple and occasionally indulged cousinly comradeship, they grew alarmed. They said very little of their feelings to Sarah – Jos was a cousin, after all – but they managed even so to make their disapproval abundantly clear. It had been a relief when Jos began work in Stoke, away from the possibility of chance meetings, though it would have been better if he had not now and then written to Sarah.

And then all at once George Lathom had appeared on the scene. Son and heir of one of the oldest of the local gentry families, he was everything Richard and Susan Wedgwood could have asked for in an admirer for their daughter. That he was an admirer was plain: he called at Spen Green with ever-increasing frequency, ready, with Sarah's apparent encouragement, to ride or talk or eat, or listen to music played on the spinet, if only he could be in her company. It seemed that an easy and very hopeful attachment was growing between them.

Sarah's parents were not to know that on their very first ride together after Sarah returned home from the eventful

Wakes Week fair, she had turned to George as they set out and said with astonishing frankness, 'I think you should know – I am going to marry my cousin Jos one day.'

He had stared at her for some time, amazed by this unconventional approach, and then asked with a somewhat grudging note in his voice, 'Does your father know?'

'No, but that makes no difference. *I* know, and when the time comes they'll make the best of it.' And then she had urged her horse into a canter and it had taken George, stunned into momentary immobility, some little while to catch her up. By which time, laughing and breathless, she had found quite another topic on which to converse.

That impulsive declaration, designed to make her position entirely clear and warn George that he could expect nothing from Sarah Wedgwood but friendship, had made no apparent difference to his attentions. He called often and they spent long hours together, and Sarah, secure in the certainty that he could have no doubt of the innocence of her intentions, nor she of his, had come to look forward to the diversion he offered and enjoy his company. He clearly admired her, in a light-hearted way; though he had no great intelligence, little sensitivity, and a marked inability to give serious thought to anything at all, his undeniable physical magnetism made up for that as far as Sarah was concerned, lending an edge of excitement and even of danger, fortunately never fulfilled, to his visits. And of course her parents, delighted to welcome so eligible an admirer for their daughter, completely forgot their apprehensions regarding Josiah. They were sure they had nothing to fear after all. How could anyone courted by George Lathom spare even a passing thought for a lame, half-educated, struggling young potter like Josiah?

Richard Wedgwood returned home that November day just in time for supper. 'Deplorable weather!' he exclaimed, as he took his seat at table. 'Scarcely seems to get light – and this cold fog chills you right through.'

The conversation wandered in an aimless manner for some time, while Sarah ate steadily and silently and wished her father would give her the news she wanted instead of the lengthy accounts of minor family tittle-tattle which could not interest her at all. Eventually, seeing that Rebecca had forgotten the apple sauce to go with the roast duck, Sarah

61

offered to go in search of it; and, returning, she heard her father say, just as she came in the door, 'Young fool can't even make the most of a golden opportunity.' The disparaging tone told her at once that he was speaking of Jos. She came to the table, very carefully laid down the sauce boat and, with equally slow precision, took her seat again.

'Oh?' she encouraged him, trying to make her tone as casual as possible. 'What's happened?'

'I was just saying – it's young Josiah from the churchyard. There he is, given a potworks of his own to manage, handed to him on a plate – and a good deal more than he could hope for, when you think his own brother wouldn't trust him enough to take him into partnership . . .'

'You always said Churchyard Thomas had no head for business,' Sarah reminded him quietly.

'Maybe not, but at least he doesn't go in for wild high-flown ideas with no sound basis. He knows that there's a limit to the risks you can take. Pity young Jos didn't learn that from him. Anyway, he's out of a job again, so maybe he'll learn this time.'

Sarah felt her heart contract. 'Oh, Papa – what happened?'

'Your Uncle Tom said Jos and Alders agreed to part on good terms, as not suited. But patch it up as they will, it comes to the same thing. They say he's tried other potworks, but no one wants to take him on. So young Jos will be home at the end of the month because he's not content to learn from his elders and betters like the rest of us. Thinks he knows it all already.'

Sarah could think of nothing to say that her father would not have seen as provocative or inappropriate; so she held her peace, and allowed her mother to move the conversation on to some topic of more interest to John, who saw little of his Burslem relations and dutifully shared her view of them; and was glad when the meal ended and she could make her way to her room, pleading a headache to excuse herself from the usual after-supper proprieties of music and talk. In her room she sat on the edge of her bed and stared into space, and thought, 'Oh Jos . . . oh Jos!'

What could she do? What could anyone do? There was little scope for a young potter with imagination and ambition, unless he had friends and money as well. The existing pot banks supplied most of the existing markets and – as Jos himself said so often – as long as the roads were so bad and transport so difficult there was little hope of finding new outlets. Unless you were in some way exceptional, offering something new and different . . . but for that you needed money, or a partner who believed in your gifts . . .

Sarah searched her mind for any avenue possibly unexplored. The uncles at the Big House, innovators once, had long since made all the living they required and were already half-retired. And none of the other Wedgwoods had anything like their flair for change and development. Nor did any of the other master potters of her acquaintance.

Except one – a business contact of her father, Thomas Wheildon. Richard Wedgwood had spoken of him approvingly as a man of large vision (that being an asset in his eyes, so long as it had proved its worth); and her uncles too had praised the superior quality of his wares. She had never met him, but she knew he lived at Fenton Hall just the other side of Stoke, and that he was perhaps the most prosperous master potter in the district.

'I *must* see Jos,' she thought urgently. 'He would lose nothing by going to see Wheildon – and Wheildon might, just might, be able or willing to take him on.' Then she thought, 'But what if Jos has already seen him, and asked for work? He must have heard of him, working so near. Perhaps Wheildon wouldn't see him – perhaps he has no need for new men and wouldn't consider him. Besides, what Jos needs is a partnership, or a position that will soon lead to one – something with responsibility, room to try out new things. And a man has to be convinced of someone's value to take him on that way. He needs to be sure that Jos is the man he's always been looking for – but how does one set about convincing Thomas Wheildon of that?'

She realised at last that though she was looking at nothing in particular her gaze was in fact resting on a small blue pot standing on her writing desk. Her eyes focussed on it, and she took in as if for the first time the satisfying balanced shape, the fine mottled-blue colouring and smooth shining glaze. It was almost exactly a replica of the pot broken long ago at Burslem on the day she and Jos had met; he had made it for her as a kind of gesture of gratitude for her loving support soon after he had returned to work on recovering from smallpox.

'I wonder . . .?' she thought, gazing at it. If a master potter were to see it would he recognise in its creator a man of great gifts, of promise? Might this treasured possession of hers speak more eloquently for Jos than any words which he or she could find?

But how could it be made to speak, from the pretty little room where she sat? She lay awake for much of the night, pondering the problem; and by morning was not much nearer solving it. She only knew that somehow she must make her way to Fenton, taking the pot with her, and seek an interview with Thomas Wheildon. It would be better if she could do so without provoking a conflict with her parents, or deceiving them; but if that was not possible she was sorry, only go she must.

As she climbed out of bed she prayed that it might be a fine day: if so, a ride would seem natural, the more so after so many days of being cooped up indoors. She could even invite John to ride with her, so long as he was well wrapped up against all possibility of a chill. Perhaps her parents would excuse him his lessons for once, for the sake of a healthy ride in the crisp sunny air.

But when she pulled the curtains aside she saw that the weather was, if anything, worse than yesterday's: it was a dark cold dank morning of dismal fog and rain, the sort of day when no sane person would stir from the fireside without very good cause. She had good cause, but she must keep it to herself.

At breakfast she said lightly, as if the thought had only just occurred to her, 'I think I'll ride this morning. Bess needs exercise, and I'm ready for some good fresh air after all this time indoors.'

'Good fresh air!' commented her father mockingly; and her mother said quickly, 'You'll do no such foolish thing. I need your help with the linen this morning. I told you we were to go through it and sort out the sheets that need mending.'

Sarah's heart sank, but she did not give up. 'Can't we do that this afternoon, Mama?' She knew full well that if she rode to Fenton she would be unlikely to arrive home again before nightfall; but by then her mission would have been

64

carried out and she could face the anger of her mother with complacency.

Unfortunately Mrs Wedgwood was unyielding. 'No, we may not. This afternoon we shall be mending the sheets – and for some days to come I should think. If we have a fine day, then you can consider a ride. But not today, on any account. I never heard such nonsense.'

Sarah, dejected, acknowledged defeat, for the moment at least. Short of direct disobedience she could do nothing else: and desperate though she was to go to Fenton she could not quite risk so drastic a course, or not yet at least, when there might perhaps be other possibilities.

So, after breakfast, with reluctance in every step, she followed her mother to the linen press on the landing and gave her critical attention to the bedlinen; or as much of her attention as she could prevent from straying after any distraction which offered itself. It was a relief when a knocking on the door and Rebecca's soft hurrying footsteps in reply gave her an excuse to turn and peer down into the hall. She could not quite see the front door from here, though she had a good view of the polished wooden floor; but she could hear very well as George Lathom stepped inside and asked for Miss Wedgwood.

Her mother made no murmur of protest when she laid down the sheets she held, lifted her hooped skirts high and clattered headlong down the stairs. In fact Mrs Wedgwood only smiled benevolently, shaking her head just a little at her daughter's impetuousness.

George too was gratified by Sarah's eager smiling arrival before him; though as she greeted him his own smile vanished in dismay.

'Oh, George, I'm so glad you've come! I'm tired of being cooped up indoors all this time and I've been so wishing there was someone else mad enough to want to ride on a day like this. Just wait while I change, then we can go – you *will* come, won't you?' She held out her hands appealingly, deliberately blind to the look of imminent protest on his face and the moves he had already made to discard his muddied cloak. With an obvious effort he forced a smile.

'If that's what you'd like, Sarah,' he agreed meekly.

'Oh, it is – it is!' And she ran up the stairs as swiftly as she had descended them, pausing in her flight across the landing to drop a light kiss on her mother's forehead. 'You don't mind if I don't help you now, do you, Mama? I will later, I promise.'

'No,' said her mother, startled by the unusual display of affection, 'that's all right if . . .' The rest of her words were lost on Sarah as she reached her room and began swiftly to pull off her morning gown and replace it with the dark severity of her winter riding habit. She knew that her mother was indeed happy for her to ride with George: there would be no talk of hoydenish behaviour now. She might have been better pleased had they stayed at home by the parlour fire – as doubtless George had intended they should – but so long as they were together then she was content. It was, in fact, all she could wish for.

Sarah took the pot, cocooned it in silk handkerchiefs and concealed it in the pocket of her gown, and then, plumed hat on her head, crop in hand, made her way more decorously back to where George waited at the hall fireside. Excitement and a slight sense of wickedness must have given an added sparkle to her eyes, for as she joined him she saw George look at her with what seemed a closer interest than usual: uncomfortably, she felt her colour rise under his scrutiny. She smiled to cover her confusion, and said quickly, 'I'm ready then – let's go.'

It *was* most unsuitable weather for riding, Sarah thought ruefully as she led the way at a brisk trot along the lane away from the house. In any other circumstances she would not for a moment have considered going for a ride. But she had come, and she did not regret it and merely urged her horse to greater speed, quickly leaving George behind. It was some time before he was able to catch up with her.

'Sarah!' he demanded then, with what was for him unaccustomed irritability – he was generally too indolent to waste his energy on anything so wearying as emotion. 'What is this? Why the sudden passion for fresh air?' She turned to look at him and slowed her pace just a little to allow him to catch up, and his tone softened slightly, though she realised with alarm that he had suddenly read something quite other than her intention into her action. 'Was there something you wanted to talk over – something private?'

The lowered voice and hint of shyness in his expression

brought the colour to her face. She shook her head vigorously, quick to put him right. 'No – no, not at all. But I must go to Fenton – you know, near Stoke – and I don't want my parents to know . . .'

He dragged his mare to a shuddering halt. 'Fenton! But it's two hours' ride or more, even in good weather – and another two back. We can't go all that way – we'll not be back for dinner, maybe even supper . . .!' He stared at her, as if he could not really believe that the slender graceful figure before him, tall and erect on her staid brown horse, could have spoken so wildly. She too reined in, since there seemed to be no choice in the matter.

'But I must,' she said quietly. 'You see I have urgent business there – something I can't tell my parents about, or not yet anyway. I shall when I get back of course.' She noted the dismay on his face, and went on a little ruefully, 'I'm sorry, George – I'm afraid I used you, coming so conveniently when you did. It must have seemed very cold-blooded of me – but I had to do it, you see.'

He continued to stare at her for some time, clearly seeing her in a new and not wholly agreeable light, and then said with a note of growing stubbornness, 'You might at least tell me why there's all this urgency. I can't see why anyone should want to go to Fenton, least of all in this weather.'

'There's someone I must see,' she said, and then, realising that the words sounded dismissive and that she did perhaps owe him the courtesy of some fuller explanation, went on, 'I want to see Mr Thomas Wheildon . . .' She had not thought it would be so difficult to keep her voice casual. 'He has a potworks there, as you may know. I thought he might be willing to employ a cousin of mine.' The careless tone did not deceive him at all.

'You mean your cousin Josiah.' She nodded, seeing him frown. 'Is this his idea?'

'No, he knows nothing of it.'

'And what's he going to think of your interference?'

She opened her mouth to say, 'Whatever concerns him concerns me too,' and then thought better of it. She had never considered that anything to do with Jos could be other than her business but she realised she did not want to say that to George. Instead, she said simply, 'We understand each

67

other,' and turned away and urged on her horse, calling out as a parting shot, 'You don't have to come with me – go home if you like . . .'

'As if I'd let you go all that way alone!' George called back, urging his horse after her. When he reached her again he found the breath to say with a note of fierce exasperation, 'I thought you so quiet and well-behaved!'

Sarah, who loved riding, found nothing pleasurable in the journey to Staffordshire that morning: they had too far to go in too short a time for that. When they came at last within sight of Stoke they were weary, wet, mud-spattered and dishevelled; and Sarah suddenly found that her certainty about the wisdom of her action had left her.

She slowed her horse to a walk, aware that in silence George had done the same. They rode side by side through the little town, through the market place busy with people hurrying on their way, eager to be indoors again – anywhere indoors, so long as it was out of the fog and the rain and the cold. Sarah knew they must have passed the house of Daniel Mayer, draper and Dissenter, where Josiah lodged; but she knew also that her cousin would not be there at this time of day, and she did not know where Harrison and Alders' potworks were to be found.

She rode slower and slower, lost in thought and quite unaware of the questioning looks George directed at her from time to time. And then as they began to leave Stoke behind them she suddenly drew rein and came to a complete halt. George did the same.

'What's wrong?'

She looked at him with a vagueness of expression, focussing on him only after several seconds, which suggested to him that she had until then completely forgotten that she was not alone. Then she said abruptly, 'I'm going to see Jos first.'

George sighed ostentatiously. 'I do wish you'd make up your mind!' he grumbled.

'Go home if you don't want to come,' Sarah returned, guiltily aware that she wished he would do exactly that. He had provided the excuse for her escape from her parents' vigilance, but that once done she would have preferred to carry out the rest of her mission without his company and his critical intruding presence. She did not now, for instance, want to admit to him that she had begun to doubt the rightness of acting on Jos's behalf without first consulting him. Nor did she intend to confide in George; but she did not like feeling burdened by the suspicion that perhaps he guessed very well why now she turned her horse and began to ride steadily back into the town.

They found Harrison and Alders' potworks without too much difficulty and there Sarah, ignoring as best she could the leering stares and appreciative shouts of the men busy in the sheds, left George outside and asked her way to where Jos was at work supervising the packing of the finished pots for transport and sale. She could see as she came nearer to him that he was in a far from genial mood; but then if he was merely working out his notice until the time came to leave the works that was hardly surprising. She thought with concern that he looked tired and a little drawn, as if perhaps his knee pained him today.

But as he raised his eyes and saw her coming all trouble left his face. He gazed at her, smiling, as he finished what he was saying to the man packing the crates; and then he came to her and took her hands in his, his eyes never leaving her face as if he found all the comfort and refreshment he needed in looking at her.

'I heard what happened,' she told him, when their silent smiling greeting was over. 'Papa said Uncle Thomas thinks you agreed to part.'

'So we did, though there were one or two storms on the way to that amicable arrangement, I'm sorry to say.' His grin was a little sheepish, and she grinned too, imagining the scene. 'The pity of it is that having burned my boats here I've no means of sailing on to new and greater things.' His gaze moved from her face at last, and took in her travel-stained appearance. 'Where have you ridden from, to get in that state? Further than Burslem by the look of you.'

'From home,' she admitted. 'I thought perhaps . . .' She paused, and started again. 'Have you tried Thomas Wheildon?'

'At Fenton Hall? I thought of him, of course – I called there first, but he was away when I called, and they told me he wasn't taking anyone on at present. So that was that. A pity, because he has quite a name, and if only I could have seen him and talked to him . . .' He shrugged. 'But there it is. It's the same story everywhere. No one's expanding at present, and there are no vacancies.'

Sarah frowned a little. 'Do you think Wheildon's home now?'

'I've no idea,' Jos replied in some surprise. 'I had the impression he was only away briefly on business, but I don't know. That was two weeks ago. Why?'

'My father knows him quite well – they do business together. I thought I might see him, put in a word for you . . .'

Jos laughed. 'Oh, Sally, so that's why you've come all this way!' He hugged her, drawing encouraging whoops and catcalls from his workmates. 'That's a piece of heroism indeed – but truly, love, I don't think it'll make a scrap of difference.'

'It would be very unheroic to go away without trying . . .' She reached into her pocket and struggled to pull out the pot, still mercifully intact after its journey. 'I thought I'd show him this.' She was alarmed to see Jos scowl as she unwrapped it.

'Oh, Sally, not that! Goodness knows I can do better than that. Wait here . . .' He hurried away, and returned a little later with an article in shining green and cream, shaped to look like a cauliflower. It was a moment or two before Sarah, staring at it appalled, recognised that it was a teapot.

'Jos, it's hideous!' she cried, though in an undertone for fear the men should hear. It astonished her that Jos could have made anything so ugly. To her surprise he grinned at her reaction.

'Yes, it is, isn't it? But I've heard this kind of thing sells well – I did a few experiments with the green glaze in my spare time, and I'd like to do more but Alders isn't interested. However, Wheildon has his ear to the ground as far as fashion goes – try it on him. He should be able to see the quality even if he doesn't care for the design.' He kissed her lightly. 'Go on your way then, and good luck to you.' Then he added more gravely, 'Only don't grieve too much if he says no. Something will turn up.'

She sensed that for all his cheerfully confident manner he

was depressed at his lack of prospects; and the knowledge sent her on her way all the more determined to win Thomas Wheildon to his side.

At Fenton George parted from her in scarcely disguised ill humour outside Thomas Wheildon's comfortable house, and went to fill the time until she should emerge again by seeking some kind of shelter and refreshment for the horses and for himself. Sarah, uneasily conscious in these orderly surroundings of her unappealing appearance, followed a brisk servant to a warm study which reminded her, in its look of slightly old-fashioned comfort, of one of the rooms at the Big House. Thomas Wheildon, a tall broad stern-looking man, greeted her with frowning puzzlement and asked her to be seated.

'And how can I help you?' he asked. Sarah was relieved that his tone was courteous; and she hoped that her own when she spoke would somehow belie the disreputable nature of her appearance. Apprehensively, she took the teapot from its wrappings and set it on the desk before the potter, reflecting dismally that it looked more vulgar and garish than ever. The making of it must have taken some considerable skill, for it had none of the rough crudity of a fairground pot; but she wondered if it had been worth the effort.

'What do you think of this?' she asked cautiously, watching the man's face for any trace of laughter, or horror.

But he merely looked at her with a kind of wary curiosity, and then lifted the teapot and turned it in his hands, raising the lid to look inside, examining it from every angle.

'Hm – very nice. We sell a lot of this kind of thing. But this isn't one of ours, is it? A neat piece of work though. Well thought out, pleasing shape – I like the glaze. Where did it come from?' His eyes widened suddenly, ran sharply over her. 'You didn't . . .? No, no, that's not possible. No way a young woman could learn a skill like this – takes a long apprenticeship, experience, training . . .'

'You think it could not be a *young* man's work then? That it's too good for that?'

He smiled at her eagerness. 'I think I'm beginning to see it all, young lady. No, I don't think it's too good to be a young man's work – if he were a skilled young man, that is. And clearly he has skills of other kinds, too, to charm his sweet-

71

heart into exerting herself so on his behalf. I've hit the nail on the head there haven't I?'

Sarah blushed. 'Almost,' she admitted. 'But it was my idea, not his. You see, he's already been here, and they told him you were taking no one on.'

'No more I am. I gather from that I didn't see him – generally I don't.' He linked his hands on the table before him and leaned forward, his expression intent. 'Perhaps you'd better tell me why I should consider making an exception for this young man – that's what you want me to do, isn't it?'

Sarah nodded, her eyes bright with hope.

'I think it most unlikely I shall,' Wheildon went on, dampeningly. 'But now, let's look at this pot. First, how much of it is your young man's handiwork? Did he do the moulding himself?'

'Everything,' said Sarah proudly. 'He prepared the clay, and moulded it and fired it, and mixed and applied the glaze – everything from start to finish.'

'Hm.' He was silent for a moment, thinking, and then he went on, 'Why, I ask myself, should a highly-skilled young man – he is out of his apprenticeship I take it?' She nodded again. 'Why then should he be in need of work?'

'Because,' Sarah burst out with all the intensity of her deepest convictions, 'because he's too good for all the dull plodding stupid potters who daren't take risks or try anything new – because he can see what might be done, and he must have the chance to explore his ideas, find out what is possible, experiment with new glazes and clays . . .'

'And you think I'm not a "dull plodding stupid potter who daren't take risks"? All very well, young lady – what is your name, by the way? I didn't catch what they said when you were shown in.'

'Sarah Wedgwood.' So it wasn't her name that had gained her admittance. She waited a little nervously for him to realise that she must be Richard Wedgwood's daughter: only it seemed it was other Wedgwoods who came to mind.

'Wedgwood, eh? There are potting Wedgwoods all over Staffordshire. Will none of them take on this young man?'

'"A prophet is without honour in his own country,"' Sarah quoted grandly.

Wheildon laughed. 'You mean he's a Wedgwood too and his own kin'll have none of him? So he's trying what Stoke can offer, since Burslem's spurned him. Hm . . .' He was silent again for a moment, then said, 'I do know Harrison and Alders need a new manager – they've just parted with the last. Come to think of it, he was a Wedgwood – oh!' He broke off and stared at her. 'It wouldn't by any chance . . .?'

Sarah nodded, suddenly sensing failure after all; but she could not leave without a last plea on Jos's behalf. 'But they wouldn't give him a chance – he's too good for them . . .'

Wheildon sighed. 'So you want me to take on this young man who may be too good for everyone, but seems to be singularly slow to convince anyone of it? Well, I'll tell you what I'll do – I'll see him, talk to him, find out for myself what he can do and why everyone seems so damned anxious to be rid of him. And that's all I undertake to do. I'll take a chance if my nose says it'll pay off – but I'm not a fool and I'm not a gambler. Well, will that do for you?'

Sarah could have leapt up and hugged him; but instead she kept herself firmly in check, and smiled broadly and said, 'Oh yes, sir – yes, indeed.'

'Then you get him to come and see me tomorrow morning before I start work.' He smiled, dispelling all the last traces of severity from his face. 'And now let us take a dish of tea together to seal our bargain.'

By the time Sarah and George – who was by now bored and impatient beyond words – reached Stoke again there was perhaps only an hour of daylight left, and Jos had already made his way back to his lodgings. They found him entertaining a voluble, excited and yet orderly gathering of young men in his room. He had told Sarah in his letters of the lively community of Dissenters in Stoke – nonconformists in religion (like his own family) whose refusal to subscribe to the doctrines of the Church of England excluded them from public life and from the universities. They would seize every excuse to meet, to talk and argue and exchange ideas; and she had been a little envious of the enthusiasm in Jos's tone, wishing she could be part of his new circle of friends. Now, actually finding herself amongst them, she was acutely aware that for all her warm welcome she was an intruder, the more so with the sullen George at her side.

73

But Jos did at least come with her to the waiting horses, once she had told him her news; and thanked her warmly and with delight for all she had done; and even seemed, just a little, to resent George's presence, though he parted from him with cool politeness.

There was no time now to linger, even had it been possible. It would be dark well before they reached home, and there was still her parents' fury to be faced. But Sarah felt she could bear anything now, knowing that she had opened a door for Jos and certain that his own abilities would take him safely through it.

It was just as well she had her buoyant mood to keep her spirits high on the uncomfortable journey home in the foggy dusk; for George, angry at what he regarded as a wasted day, sulked for the whole ten miles or so of the ride. He spoke only once, to say resentfully, 'I hope you're satisfied, dragging me all this way . . .'

'I did not ask you to come,' she reminded him. 'You could have stayed behind.'

'You surely don't think I would leave a young lady to ride alone all this way without an escort?'

Sarah bit back the further angry retort which sprang to mind, and said in a more conciliatory tone, 'Perhaps I should have thought of that. But truly there was no need. Still, thank you all the same. It's turned out very well in the end.'

George snorted. 'Just find a servant to ride with you next time, that's all I ask.'

'Don't worry,' said Sarah with asperity. 'You can be sure I shall.'

After that neither of them said anything until they reached Spen Green; and even then George spoke only, as courtesy demanded, to Sarah's parents.

She did not, after all, confess to them where she had been today. They greeted her return with a conflicting mixture of angry anxiety – which she had expected – and satisfaction that it should have been in George's company that she had been absent so long, and so inexplicably. It was too great a temptation; so she yielded to it and, feeling guilty and uncomfortable, allowed them to think that George alone had been the cause of her absence. She was relieved that he did not enlighten them himself; although, warmly pressed to stay to supper, he did so, and maintained a flow of generalised conversation throughout the meal. When, afterwards, he took his leave of them, he made no attempt to see her alone before he went, as he generally did: he had not, then, forgiven her for the day's events. She accepted, with a faint twinge of regret, that he would not come to Spen Green again for a very long time, if at all.

She was the more astonished then when, next morning, almost before breakfast was over, she saw him dismounting at the door. She was in her room at the time, gathering up her riding habit so as to take it downstairs for washing; and instead of going on her way she sat down and waited for someone to come in search of her. Intrigued though she was by George's arrival she did not want to risk a chance meeting in the hall.

But no word came, and she had almost given up, beginning to feel cold in the chill atmosphere of her unheated bedroom. In any case, surely by now George must have gone again? And then at that moment Rebecca arrived and summoned her, not, as she expected, to the parlour, but to her father's study. Greatly puzzled, she consigned the riding habit to the maid's arms and went on her way.

Richard Wedgwood sat gravely at his desk, but smiled as she came in. 'Sit down, Sarah.'

She did so, aware all the time of some undercurrent of excitement in the room, as if something important was about to happen.

'This is a very happy day for me,' her father went on, 'and for your mother – and for you too, I am sure.'

Sarah stared at him in uncomprehending bewilderment.

'Can't you guess what I'm talking about?' he continued, with a note of tender amusement that puzzled her still further. Sarah shook her head.

'No, Papa, not at all. I haven't the least idea.'

'Then I'll have to tell you, I can see. Mr George Lathom has asked for your hand in marriage.' His smile broadened: she had never seen him so alight with satisfaction and joy. 'It was not wholly a surprise to us, as you can imagine. And I'm glad to say that it seems his father has no objection – and nor have we, of course. And I've reason to believe you're not quite indifferent to him yourself, eh, Sally my girl?' The playful note in his voice, sharply at odds with her father's generally grave demeanour, grated painfully on Sarah's nerves and stirred her out of the state of numbed disbelief in which she had been listening to him.

'George? He's asked for my hand? You can't mean it, Papa – you must be mistaken!' Her voice held a note of undisguised horror, and she watched its effect on her father as a sense of unease began to steal into his satisfaction. Even allowing for some surprise on her part – though he could not understand how she could be surprised – her present white-faced dismay seemed a little excessive.

'It's hardly something I could make a mistake about, Sarah,' he told her a little drily. 'And why the surprise? His attentions have been clear enough, even to myself and your mother. They must have been even more marked to you.'

'But . . . but he knew . . .' she stammered, trying wildly to understand. 'I didn't – I told him right at the start . . .' She broke off and stared dumbly at her father, as if hoping that he might even now tell her it was all a mistake.

'Told him what?'

'That I'm to marry Jos.'

There was a tiny moment of utter silence, an icy, chilling, appalled silence; and then her father broke out with a note of cold fury in his voice which she had never heard in it before. 'You *what*?'

It was no light thing to risk adding to that already explosive anger. Quietly, but with a steady firmness which masked the frightened beating of her heart, Sarah said, 'I told George Lathom at the outset that one day I should marry Jos. For it's true.'

'It is most assuredly not true, as long as I have any say in the matter! And I trust that, though you seem to have lost all sense of duty and respect and every trace of common sense you ever had, you do still acknowledge my right to some say as to who you marry. You cannot seriously have considered for one moment that I or your mother would allow you to tie yourself for life to a penniless cripple.'

'He is not a cripple,' Sarah corrected him indignantly. 'And if he's poor now it won't be for long. With his gifts he will be able to make a name for himself.'

76

Richard Wedgwood exploded into a sound which in a less dignified man would have been termed a snort. 'He's shown precious little sign of doing so for one supposedly so talented. I didn't think you were such a fool, Sarah. It was all very well to have a liking for your cousin when you were both little more than babes. But you're nineteen now, and I thought you had more than your share of good sense. Clearly I was wrong –' He broke off, staring at her as if trying to understand how his own daughter could behave so inexplicably.

'I don't want to hurt you, Papa, or Mama either . . .' Sarah began, trying to soften his mood. But the words had quite the opposite effect, for he snapped, 'You won't, Sarah, believe me. If you've taken leave of your senses we have not. You marry Josiah Wedgwood over my dead body, and that's my last word on the matter. So you can put him out of your head from now on and give some attention to making a good match with a young man who has something to offer. Even you must see that George Lathom is all you could wish for: an excellent prospect, certain to ensure a comfortable place for you in the world.'

'Except that I don't want to marry him.'

'Only because you've had your head stuffed full of nonsense about wedding your cousin.' Her father paused for a moment, and then went on more calmly, 'Fair enough, maybe you need time to get used to the way things are. I'll not ask you to make a rushed decision. That you like young George is clear enough: I suspect time will do the rest, now you know you must not think of your cousin. I'll ask him to be patient, and we'll say no more for the present. I think he cares for you enough to take the advice.'

'Papa, I don't *want* to marry him, and I never shall want to,' Sarah repeated, with a floundering sense that there was no obvious way in which she could reach him or make him understand. That she must not repeat that she would one day marry Jos was obvious: her father would not give the matter a moment's serious consideration. But that did not mean that she had accepted his decree. Some day, somehow, she and Jos would be married: every instinct told her so. But it could not be for a long time yet, and meanwhile she had to live at peace with her parents. She did not, however, feel that humouring them in every other aspect of life was necessary to keep the peace. But she did recognise that for the moment at least her father was immovable. She said mildly, 'Tell him what you please, Papa; but I know I shall not change my mind.'

Her father gave one of those infuriating half-smiles which indicate that the hearer knows better than the speaker but is too tactful to say so, and then brought the uncomfortable interview to a conclusion. 'I'll have a word with young Lathom, and let him know how things stand at present; and then I think you must speak to him yourself. You owe him that at least. He's very fond of you, you know.'

Richard Wedgwood left Sarah in his study – 'to think things over a little,' as he put it – while he went to convey his disappointing news to George Lathom. What passed between them Sarah had no means of knowing, though she could guess; and she had plenty of time for speculation, for her father was absent for a long while.

'Think things over a little,' he had commanded her; and she did so, though not exactly on the lines he might have hoped. Her first instinctive reaction was one of anger; anger that George should not have taken her at her word, accepted her assurance that she was, in spirit at least, promised to Jos; and so left her in peace to enjoy his friendship, and the complacent approval of her parents. If only he had not called today, everything could have gone on as before!

But she knew it was not as simple as that. A sense of guilt stirred uneasily through her consciousness, bringing sharply into focus first this and then that: things she had done, and said, showing her for the first time where those innocent unthinking actions had led.

She had deceived her parents yesterday, and made use of George for her own ends: she had been ashamed of that even before this morning's visit. But she could see now only too clearly that yesterday was nothing, set against the rest. There was no excuse: she was not a schoolgirl, unable to read the signs. She should have known that George would not have been so attentive all this time unless he had expected it to lead somewhere. There had been no kisses, except that chaste caress on the hand at their first meeting, but there had been looks, and light compliments, and an occasional lingering touch: enough to tell her, if she had not chosen to shut her eyes to the truth. And who but a man besotted with her would have allowed himself so to be made use of yesterday?

For a moment, a little glow of delight lit her, that she had been able to awaken such devotion in so eligible a young man. But then she took herself sternly in hand, and reflected how much she must have hurt him, and how much more, now, he would be hurt; and she felt only thoroughly ashamed of herself.

It was a very subdued Sarah who some time later went meekly in to where George waited in the parlour, lowering her eyes quickly when he scrambled clumsily to his feet at her entrance, blushing and awkward and quite unlike himself. She closed the door, and tried to think of something to say that might soothe him; and then forced herself to look up at him and say gravely, 'I'm sorry. I didn't want things to turn out like this. But I thought I made it clear enough that it was Jos I would marry.'

George shrugged and said nothing, as if emotion would not let him speak. In spite of herself, Sarah felt irritation rise in her.

'Why did you come like this? I didn't deceive you, did I?'

'But in a way I did,' she thought, 'because I let you dance attendance on me, and liked it, and you too in a way. It is not your fault that I thought you could not feel deeply.'

'I suppose not,' he admitted, with a rough edge to his voice. 'But I knew your father wouldn't see things the way you did. And I thought perhaps you weren't sure of your own feelings – that you mistook them a bit . . .'

'I don't make mistakes of that kind,' she said severely. 'Besides, how could you think that, after yesterday? I *know* I used you dreadfully . . .'

'I thought if you knew I cared for you . . .' He reddened further. 'You may have thought I would think you weren't good enough for me – that I couldn't be interested.' And then, abruptly, he regained his assurance, clearing his throat and beginning again as if on a speech long-rehearsed. 'As far as I can see it's only your passion for pots and potworks that stands in the way. You're always talking about them. If your cousin was – say – a blacksmith you'd not look at him twice. Admit it now: it's true.' He did not wait for her answer, however, but beamed at her with an expression that suggested a sudden inspiration. 'When we're married I'll buy you a potworks of your very own – set one up in the grounds at High Newbold if you like – there's plenty of room. Then you can have it all to yourself, do just what you like.'

Sarah stared at him, shakily close to laughter, and yet filled even more with a kind of disgust which effectively obliterated her own sense of shame. 'It's not a game, George. I don't want a potworks as a plaything. For me Jos and pots go together: I love them because they're a part of him. I want neither without the other.' Yet, she thought fleetingly, it had been her passion for the potworks which had drawn her first to Jos, not the other way about. Would the one have endured without the other, or would it have gone the way of all childish enthusiasms, and come to nothing? She had of course no means of knowing; she could only accept things as they were.

She could see, however, that George was entirely unconvinced by her argument. 'We shall see,' he said, with an echo of her father's knowing smile. 'I think you deceive yourself. Sometimes others know us better than we do ourselves. But time will tell. We shall of course continue to be friends.'

Irritation, anger, shame, pity mingled in Sarah and exploded in an outburst of exasperation. 'Oh *George*! What can I say to make you believe me?'

Unruffled, by now entirely in command of himself again, he stepped nearer and pinched her cheek, in a manner disturbingly unlike that of Uncle Thomas with his habitual playful caress. 'Come now, Sarah – you don't find me unattractive do you? Admit it now.'

Just the touch of his hand had brought the colour to her face and set her heart beating faster. She could not deny the truth of what he said; but she knew that particular truth was irrelevant, a distraction, of no importance at all. She said nothing, though, only gazing at him puzzled to know what to say; and he took her bewilderment for something else and pulled her into his arms and began to kiss her with a passion which was at once unrestrained and yet thoroughly practised and controlled. For a moment she yielded to it, and wanted to yield; and then she came to her senses and struggled to free herself from his embrace.

He released her, eventually, apparently quite undisturbed

by this further rejection, which clearly he did not see as such. 'You don't know your own feelings, you know,' he assured her. 'You'll see. I shall continue to come—'

'Then I'll refuse to see you!'

'Then I'll visit your parents, and go on doing so until you admit I was right.' He kissed her again, but lightly and with no other touch; and then he reached for his hat and whip, laid aside on a chair, and, smiling still, took his leave of her.

Two days later she had a bubbling, excited letter from Jos, telling her that in a few days he was to begin work at Fenton Hall, with the distinct possibility of an early partnership on favourable terms.

At last, as the weeks passed, it seemed that Jos had found what he was looking for: a congenial employer, soon a partner, who invited and encouraged experiment and innovation. Jos developed new lines, found his horizons widened by rides on business to places never visited before – to the growing town of Birmingham for instance, where he made a number of useful contacts and new friends – and was more settled and happy than Sarah had ever known him to be.

Then one day, three years later, she received an anguished note from Jos's sister Kate, now married to William Willet: Jos was dangerously ill.

It had begun with a minor bruise on the right shin which, in anyone else, would have cleared up within a matter of days; but for Jos with his disabled knee no bruise was a minor one. The knee became agonisingly inflamed, and the fever which followed brought him close to death. It was a measure of the danger that threatened him that Sarah's parents let her go to him at once.

Throughout the terrible days while his life hung in the balance and the doctors, called in succession to his bedside, alternately bled and purged him to the point of emaciation, Sarah and Kate together nursed him, and watched, and prayed; and when at last they knew that in spite of everything he was going to live, it was on Sarah's shoulder that Kate wept out her relief and thankfulness.

But Sarah knew that simply to live was not enough. Ahead lay the struggle to regain his strength and the use of his limbs, and then take up the threads again where they had been so cruelly broken off; and before that stage could be reached there would be the long weary months of convalescence while he fretted because work at Fenton Hall was going on without him, and in his weakness was tempted to despair of his eventual recovery.

'*Use* the time!' urged Sarah fiercely one day, terrified by the bleak look in his eyes. 'Until you grow stronger, do what you are still able to do – read and talk and think.'

She brought him books from her small resources; but better still she encouraged his friends to do the same. William Willet came often, made suggestions, prodded him into argument and discussion, and sent the most educated and thoughtful men of his acquaintance to provide stimulating company. Jos read widely and avidly as never before, in particular the scientific works that gave him an understanding of the processes used in his work, but also literature, both modern and classical, philosophy, anything and everything that came his way.

And when at last he was able to return to Fenton Hall he found that somehow what it offered was no longer enough: Wheildon's wide vision seemed narrower than before, too restricted by caution and the daily demands of profit and loss. Jos renewed his experiments with greater understanding and a fresh enthusiasm, and worked in a new and methodical manner: he began to keep notes of his findings in a ledger, in a code of his own devising. He saw opportunities never visible before and longed to seize them; and discovered very quickly that Thomas Wheildon was frightened by the change in his partner.

In a few months, Wheildon reminded him gravely one day, the partnership agreement would be at an end: perhaps it was time to think of something else . . .

CHAPTER FOUR

1759

'Well,' said Josiah, looking round the bare little room, 'here we are at last.' His bright happy grey eyes came briefly to rest on Sarah; and then he reached out and threw his arms about her and folded her into a delighted hug. 'Oh my Sally, I don't know where I'd have been without you – not here, that I do know.'

Sarah clung to him in a state of silent happiness which for this tiny fraction of time was complete. They were together, sharing their moment of triumph, looking forward to a future full of opportunity. If time did not move on, however full of uncertainties the days ahead, then this moment would have lost most of its joy and its purpose, for after all it was the hope it held out to them which made it so important; yet Sarah could not help wishing just a little that it would not end, that they could somehow stay for ever held together by love and achievement and happiness.

But of course they could not; and after a while Jos drew back and looked into her smiling face.

'This is the very beginning of the firm of Josiah Wedgwood,' he declared, as if making an important announcement; though his voice was quiet, for her alone. 'Now at last we shall show them – and no one ever again will tell me what to do – except you, I suppose,' he added with a laugh. 'You always were a bossy managing lass, my Sally.' He slid his hand down to hold hers, and swung her arm gently. 'Now, I have a promise to fulfil. Remember?'

She looked at him blankly, not understanding; and then, slowly, shook her head. 'I remember no promise – only that we're to be married one day – and I know that can't be yet awhile.'

'It won't be all that long, not now,' he assured her. 'Then Miss Sarah Wedgwood will become Mrs Sarah Wedgwood, and we won't have to go to such great lengths every time we want to see one another. But no, that wasn't the promise I meant. Do you really not remember?' He grinned impishly, in the way she loved. 'Well! – then you wouldn't have held me to it after all – I never thought of that! I might have got away with it if only I'd realised.'

'Jos, give over teasing and tell me what you mean!'

He held both her hands, looking at her, and said solemnly, 'One day, the very first day we met, when you were just a little girl, and I not much older and still hale and hearty, you had one single passionate wish—'

'Oh! – Oh yes, I *do* remember.'

'And I made a promise, Sarah Wedgwood, didn't I? I told you that when I was a master potter myself, then you should throw a pot.' Sarah saw again the dusty throwing shed of the Churchyard works, and the little girl standing in breathless wonder as the budding craftsman unfolded the small miracle of creation before her eyes; and she nodded, smiling in silent delight. 'So you see,' Jos went on, 'I am a man of my word. Today I have signed all the papers, and thanks to Aunt Egerton's legacy I've paid my first £10-a-year rent, and I am now from this moment Josiah Wedgwood, Master Potter of the Ivy House works. And I am going to take you this very minute to the throwing shed and you shall throw a pot . . .' He hesitated: his eyes ran over her flowered silk gown with its wide hoop and lace flounces; and a moment of doubt shadowed his face. 'Unless you're too fine for such a murky job . . .'

Sarah laughed, excitement bubbling up in her. 'What do you think, Jos Wedgwood?' she demanded. 'You don't get out of your promise that easily you know.'

He kissed her lightly and tenderly, and led her out of the as yet unfurnished office and into the empty sunlit courtyard. Distantly the sounds of merrymaking reached them: laughter; the inexpert scraping of a fiddle; a small crowd cheering on a favourite wrestler. They were sounds that, fleetingly, took Sarah back to the Wakes fair – Jos at her side, George Lathom, handsome and commanding (better not to think of him), the gipsy and her prophecy. She could smile now at that last. The world had not changed yet that she could see, whether at her hands or those of anyone else. Today was May Day and as usual a general holiday to be

84

celebrated in the usual ways; but what the world did with its time was at the moment of no interest at all to Sarah. All that mattered was that at last Jos was standing alone, ready with her loving help to make his mark upon that unheeding world. And, of course, that she was today to feel the clay beneath her hands, and to begin perhaps to be a potter too.

'A female potter'. They had laughed at the very idea. But why not? To throw a pot did not ask for brute strength, but skill, control, delicacy of touch. A woman as much as a man could have those qualities. Why not Sarah Wedgwood? One day perhaps she would see her own pots packed in the crates, ready for sale.

With her hand in his Jos led her across the yard and through a low doorway into the throwing shed, scrubbed clean – Jos was very particular about cleanliness in the work-rooms – wheel and bench already in place. Sarah smiled to herself: how like Jos, and how right, that this corner of the works should be ready for use when as yet even his few personal belongings had only been dumped unceremoniously in the tiny living room of Ivy House. He knew, as she did, that though his infirmity might often exclude him from it this was the heart of the works; and to that heart Sarah was at last to be admitted. There was a painful constriction in her throat now, from the emotion of the moment; she clutched Jos's hand tight and did not even try to speak.

On the bench lay a thick damp piece of cloth wrapped about some shapeless object; and a coarse workman's apron, clean and neatly folded.

'Put this about you and roll up your sleeves,' Jos said, handing the apron to her; and as she did so he unwrapped the cloth to disclose four or five neat balls of clay; red-brown and moist and heavy, the raw material from which so often she had seen such splendour take shape. 'There you are – all ready for you.' So he had planned this moment, even before they met this morning at the Big House for the signing of the lease: she smiled at him, and he smiled back, standing there with a ball of clay held in his hand. Then he said, 'Now, let's see you set the wheel turning – though I think it best if you don't try and throw, not the first time.'

'I thought that was why you brought me here!' She stared at him in dismay, but he only laughed.

85

'Don't worry, Sally – you shall make a pot on the wheel – but for the first time it's easier if you begin with the wheel at rest. It takes a lot of practice to throw accurately, and there's no point in making it harder for yourself than need be. But let me see that you can get the wheel moving first.'

She went to take her seat at the wheel; and then stopped, with a laughing glance at Jos. 'You'll have to excuse my immodesty, if you're going to make a potter of me.' She pulled up her skirts, fumbled at her waist to find the strings that tied her hooped petticoat, and let it collapse with a swish in a circular heap about her feet. 'I'd not get near the wheel with that on,' she explained to Jos's scandalised face.

'It's a good thing Burslem doesn't know how you're celebrating the founding of the pottery – my reputation would never stand it.' He put his arms about her. 'Now I can hug you better, without that thing swaying up behind every time I come near.'

She laughed, and kissed him briskly, and then pushed him away. 'Don't distract me now – I'm here to work, remember.'

She perched on the high seat before the wheel, her silken skirts hanging in long soft folds to the floor, and rested her foot on the treadle; and after a while found the movement she needed and saw the wheel begin, a little hesitantly, to turn. It was harder to find the right rhythm so that it turned smoothly, with the gentle monotonous even bumping noise she had heard so often; and it made her leg ache, even after so short a time. It was this simple task from which Jos's diseased knee had excluded him: she understood a little better now, and was glad that she did so.

'That's it,' he said approvingly, wholly matter of fact. 'Now, stop it again, and then slap the clay down in the centre.'

That, so she thought, was easy enough. She smiled to think that the unappealing object lying there could be turned at her hands into something fine.

'Now, firm hands, but most of all steady ones. Take it slowly – don't try and go as fast as you've seen me do it, or your uncles. And keep your hands wet from the bowl there – now, rest your arms on the side to steady them; and set the wheel turning. What you must aim to do first is to get the clay completely centred.'

She sat as she had seen him do so often, and crooked her wet hands about the clay: she felt its roughness, cold, hard, yet pliable.

'Firmer now, Sally – don't let it fight you or you'll lose it. Press down more.'

She moved her fingers, and the clay shot suddenly sideways, landing half off the wheel, lumps flying all over the place. 'Oh!' She stared at it in panic.

'Stop the wheel,' said Jos calmly.

'What did I do wrong?' she wailed.

'Just got your hands wrong, that's all. It went off centre. Don't worry – it happens to all of us at the start.' He tidied up the wheel, and banged and pummelled the clay back into shape, and replaced it. 'Now, try again.' He reached over her shoulders and placed her hands about the clay. 'Like that: steady now, and firm – don't let it get away.'

This time he guided her, his hands over hers, centring the clay, and then letting her feel how each movement of the strong fingers shaped it, drew it up, hollowed, curved, flared it at the lip. When at last he told her to bring the wheel to rest a small pot stood there, a little uneven (despite Jos's help), not quite symmetrical, but not bad, she felt, for a first attempt: except that it was not, precisely, her own first attempt.

'Now let me try alone.'

Jos stood back. 'Of course.' He slid a wire beneath the pot to loosen it from the wheel and set it on the bench, wiped over the wheel with a cloth, and then handed her a second ball of clay. 'Try a small dish – you'll find that easiest.'

She set to work this time with confidence, her hands steady, firm, moving exactly, she felt, as she wanted them to move. The clay was not quite in the centre, she could see that; but when after trying this way and that she seemed able only to push it off centre another way she gave up trying to remedy the situation and set to work to create her dish. The sides moved up and out from a narrow base, almost as her imagination wanted them to do. She smiled to herself, a happy secret smile, and moved her fingers again, just a little, to bring the sides up a fraction more. She felt the clay give, like over-wet pastry; her thumb moved too far; and the whole thing flopped into an ungainly heap. It was all she could do not to weep as the wheel stilled and revealed the full ugliness of what she had made. She had waited nearly all her life for this moment and now this – this horrible object – was the result. She felt sick. 'Look at it!' she cried in disgust.

Jos laid his hands on her shoulders, gripping them in a firm warm clasp, trying, she knew, to allow some consolation to flow into her. 'You're only a beginner, remember. That's not bad for a first attempt – only you brought the sides out too fast and too far, and let it get over wet. You'll learn very quickly. Take it off and try again with some fresh clay.'

They must have stayed there in the throwing shed for several hours, while Sarah shaped, and poked, and touched, and pulled, and time after time began all over again; and always ended, even at best, with something so far from the perfection she longed for that her frustration and misery grew and grew. In the end she took her last hideous attempt and flung it furiously on the bench, and rose to her feet, knocking the treadle so that the wheel gave a last frantic spin.

'You do it, Jos – show me it can be done!' There was a desperate note in her voice, a plea for him to prove that the miracle was possible; that what she had done was indeed a caricature of the least efforts of a skilled potter. The wearying failures of the past hours seemed to have shrivelled all her joy in the potworks, all her sense of wonder, all her belief even that this was the centre and purpose of her life. Yet if it was not, why was she here at all?

She had not considered the diseased knee; nor did Jos, now, understanding her need. He sat down and set the treadle working, and reached for a ball of clay he had prepared while she was busy; a little frown of concentration creased his brow, hinting at the will power which ignored the discomfort. Holding her breath Sarah watched as with a swiftness that dazzled her as never before he threw the clay surely on the centre of the turning wheel and with all the delicacy and dexterity she had come close to forgetting, and more, shaped a pot as perfect and flawless as all her own had been the opposite.

When the wheel came to rest and Jos turned in silence to look at her, Sarah stared down at the pot; and all at once burst into tears. 'Oh, Jos – I wanted to do it so much – and I can't! I can't!'

She felt his arms close about her, strong and comforting, and he drew her head down to rest against his shoulder, rough with the harshness of his homespun coat. 'Never mind, lass – it takes practice, lots of practice. I've been doing it nearly all my life, remember . . .'

'I bet your first attempt was better than any of mine!'

He laughed gently, not unkindly. 'What if it was? That doesn't mean you wouldn't make a potter in the end. We'll stop now, for today – but you can try again another day. It'll come in time.'

Sarah drew back from his arms and gazed soberly at the sorry-looking object which was her most successful pot, the one Jos had helped her with; and then looked again at the lovely thing he had just made with such fluent ease. And she shook her head. 'No, Jos. It was a dream, that's all. I'll never be able to do what you can, and it's no good pretending anything else.' She felt her lip tremble and bit it sharply, forcing a smile as she turned to look at him. 'I don't know what I'm meant to do, but it's not this I'm sure.'

He pulled her to him again, his hand running soothingly over her hair. 'That's as you wish, love – but never think there aren't so many countless things you can do so much better than I ever will . . .'

'Tell me one!' she challenged him; and he grinned, and then was instantly deeply serious, looking intently into her face.

'You're my joy and my comfort, my help and my hope and my inspiration . . .' He paused while, awed into silence, she stood trembling in the circle of his arms. 'Without you,' he went on in the same grave undertone, 'I would be nothing today. I could never find the strength to fight without you at my side; or the will to improve my mind when my body lets me down. I think even you don't know how easy it is to despair when you're ill and everything seems hopeless. I thought it was the end for me when I was laid up so long in Stoke – I'd given up hope – but you were there to make me turn it to good. Do you think I'd have done all that heavy reading without you? Do you think I'd have started up here today without you?'

'That was my uncles, not needing these works any more – and Aunt Catherine's legacy,' she reminded him gently.

'Oh, those were the little things, the means, that's all – it was you first, as always. Never forget that, love – never . . .' He held her to him, and she clung there, moved beyond words. It was quite some time before he drew away, and became practical again.

'I tell you what else you're good at, and I'm not: keeping accounts. Uncle Thomas says you've a great head for figures. I was going to ask you, if you wouldn't mind, if you'd keep an eye on the books for me here – once I've anything to enter in them, that is. You know I've no head for that kind of thing – not that I can't add up, but I always seem to find some other little thing to do when I should be going over them. If you could look them over now and then and keep me on my toes, I'd be grateful. Will you do that?'

'You know I will.'

'And if you want another job you can tell all your fine rich friends what a clever young potter Josiah Wedgwood of the Ivy House, Burslem is, and how they must all buy my wares.'

Sarah smiled. 'Of course I will, Jos – you know that.'

He kissed her again, thoroughly and full on the mouth. She slid her arms about his neck and hugged him.

'Jos, I love you – and if you couldn't do without me, then neither could I without you. Don't let it be too long before you make your fortune and we can be wed!'

He laughed and freed himself. 'Then I'd better get to work at once. Come and tell me how I should arrange the office – after all, I have three whole articles of furniture to grace it with . . .!'

Sarah understood Jos well enough to know that the joyous buoyant optimism of that first day would not last. It was an odd quirk of his character that he could bear physical pain and the restrictions of his disability with constant courage and even cheerfulness; but that the most trivial setback or reverse would at other times plunge him into the deepest of depressions. 'Perhaps,' Sarah thought, 'no human being can be expected to have enough courage to cope with all of life's troubles; and goodness knows, Jos already has more than his share of courage and troubles alike.' She was not surprised then that it took barely a month for the bright hopes of that May Day to darken into doubt and, soon after, despair.

This time, though, Sarah had to acknowledge that Jos was not without good cause for despondency. Despite all her recommendations, despite all his hopes and plans and the limited but real reputation he had built up for himself at Fenton Hall, the world did not flock to the Ivy House works to buy his wares; did not even trickle that way. By now the house had a trim and welcoming look, its little garden bright with summer flowers; but in the office there was nothing to match that cheerful exterior.

'Wheildon would say, "I told you so!"' said Jos gloomily, as Sarah shook her head over the books in which very few entries had been made since her last visit two weeks ago. 'He said it wasn't the moment for trying out new lines or seeking new markets. He said if I wanted to take risks that was my affair, but I'd have to do it alone.'

Sarah rose swiftly to her feet and linked her arms loosely about his neck. 'And you know that if you were not ready to take risks now and then you would never be anything but mediocre: a dull plodding potter like your brother. You said that yourself when you decided to leave Wheildon, and you were right, Jos – of course you were.'

He gave a wry smile which was without cheerfulness. 'Then where are my customers, Sally?'

'They'll come, Jos, you'll see – give it time, love . . .'

'You've seen the books: you know how little time I have. Each week I fear I'll not be able to pay the men's wages – each week it gets harder. I've already laid some off – and I can't make pots without men.'

His face, she saw, had a grey pinched look and there was a hopeless note in his voice which clutched at her heart. But she knew she must not let him guess for a moment that she shared any of his misgivings. She gave his arm an encouraging squeeze.

'You've a fine stock of pots already made, love. We must make sure they are seen and sold as soon as possible. What does Cousin Tom think of all this?' Cousin Tom was another Wedgwood relation who had been taken on as journeyman when the works opened: a tall dark dour man, hard working and totally loyal.

'Ask him,' Jos said, rather as if he no longer cared very much what she did since he did not believe she could work

91

miracles; and he was by now convinced that nothing less could save the works.

She gave Jos a light kiss on the cheek by way of consolation and set out in search of Tom. He shook his head at her in answer to her questioning.

'He's right enough, Sarah – things couldn't be much worse. What's more, I'm glad you've come today, for it's my belief he's stinting himself to pay the wages – I can't see how he's doing it else. Not that he'd admit it to anyone; but he might just to you. Ask him what he's had to eat today.'

Tom was right: Jos's dark little larder held a drying crust of bread, all that remained of the loaf which had been his only food for five days. Sarah scolded him roundly and bore him off without delay to the Big House just in time to ensure an invitation to supper; she also had a quiet word with her uncles so that Jos, too proud to ask for help, might be guaranteed an open invitation to eat with his relations whenever he wished. And then, that minor problem solved, she set herself to worry over the much more difficult one of finding customers for the Ivy House works.

It would have been so much easier, she felt, if she could have confided in her parents; then she would not have had to return home burdened by an anxiety she could not share. But even her uncles could offer no more than sympathy – and that, she sensed, was tinged with a feeling that Jos had at last overreached himself, that this time he could not succeed. Certainly they would hold out no hope, nor make any suggestions which might help. It was a simple – if painful – fact that until and unless Jos made a name for himself the customers would not come; but until they came in any number he would have no hope of making a name for himself. And there were already potters enough in Staffordshire to supply all the needs of the district, and more.

So much for their dreams; so much for the plans to experiment and develop a fine household ware, something to tempt the customer away from the popular Delft and other imported products. So much, Sarah thought as she rode home, her spirits lower than they had been for a very long time, for the hope of winning her parents' consent to their marriage.

Not, of course, that her hopes for this last had been based

on anything more tangible than her belief that, once Jos had established himself, then her parents' objections would fall away without any further persuasion on her part being necessary. She knew that this was all that could offer her such hope. Her parents were as disapproving as ever of her friendship with Jos and put every possible obstacle (short of outright prohibition) in the way of her visits to Burslem. Her uncles, though more sympathetic, would not openly defy their brother, so she could find few incontestable reasons these days to take her within reach of Jos. Time and again she felt a longing to defy them all, to tell her parents her mind was made up and nothing could make her change it; even to leave home. But what good would that do? Not one of her relations would encourage such disobedience by taking her in; Jos was in no position to support a wife; besides, for all her anger and their disapproval, she did not want to break for ever with her parents or cause them the grief that must result from such defiance.

In any case, she thought now with a rueful smile, what would such behaviour do to John's prospects? A wayward sister, gone to the bad – no, that would never do in the respectable gentlemanly circles in which he moved; though, joking apart, that consideration could never weigh very heavily with her. John at twenty-one had grown into a gentle pliable young man, devoted to his mother, easily swayed by her ambitions for him and content to let her rule his life. Often ill, he was rarely away from home, though his own house at nearby Smallwood was comfortably furnished and equipped with servants and stables and a good-sized estate requiring able management: for the most part it was Richard Wedgwood who did the managing. Sarah, fond of John in a slightly pitying way, suspected that such a degree of responsibility would never be to her brother's taste; and she knew that he cared very little what position he held in the world, so long as it demanded no great exertion from him.

At Spen Green today she found that her mother was in an unusually light-hearted mood: there was none of the carping fault-finding that generally greeted her return from Burslem. Instead she was welcomed with a smile of rare warmth and an air of suppressed excitement, which intrigued her while it filled her with misgiving.

At supper she learned the reason: the family had been invited to dinner at High Newbold the very next day. And High Newbold was the home of the Lathom family.

'It all came about quite by accident,' Mrs Wedgwood explained. 'I was on my way to Congleton and called on the rector in passing, and Mrs Lathom chanced to be there. We fell to talking of this and that, and I don't quite know how it was but Mrs Lathom at last expressed an interest in seeing the house at Smallwood – so kind of her – and the upshot was that John and your father were invited for the hunting tomorrow, and we are all to dine there afterwards. Is that not wonderful?'

Sarah wondered exactly what her father's reaction had been, when faced with this plan for tomorrow: he had no interest whatsoever in hunting. Nor, for that matter, had John; but presumably both men had been brought to see that it would be socially to their advantage to hunt in such company.

But it was not, of course, the discomfiture of her father and brother which primarily occupied her mind at the prospect. It was a long time since she had seen George Lathom. He had, as he had promised, come often to Spen Green following the proposal, the recollection of which still made Sarah feel painfully guilty. Since she would not ride with him again, or allow herself to be left alone with him, he had been forced to content himself with enjoying her company as one of the family; though perhaps enjoying was hardly the word, for though she was always polite, she was also cool and distant, constructing an invisible barrier between them which he was never allowed to cross. If he showed any sign of warmth, or of trying to manoeuvre the conversation towards personal matters, then Sarah would immediately rebuff him. Whatever his intentions, he had not proposed again.

At last, after more than a year, the visits had become less and less frequent and in due course ceased altogether. Once, for a little while, there were rumours of his imminent marriage to some local landowner's daughter; but if they had any truth in them nothing had come of it. He was, as far as Sarah knew, still single. And she knew only too well that her mother's jubilation stemmed from a sudden hope that George might be tempted to renew his suit; and might this time even succeed. After all, very soon her daughter would be beyond marriageable age, at least as far as that kind of genteel marriage was concerned. Sarah, unmoved at the possibility of another proposal (which she thought most unlikely), wondered only how it would feel to see George again.

She had often ridden through High Newbold and past the handsome park gates of the Hall, glimpsing its rambling half-timbered frontage from the road. This afternoon though she and her mother drove in at those gates in the carriage sent by Mrs Lathom to bring them, and stepped out on the gravelled drive beneath the ancient yew trees to the cool welcome of the servant waiting to take their outdoor clothes and the more robust greeting of Mrs Lathom herself. She was a tall handsome woman in purple, with a brisk manner which had in it more than a hint of condescension. 'Why did she ask us here, if she so clearly thinks us beneath her?' wondered Sarah, uncomfortably aware of her mother's breathless affected volubility, and even more of the distaste in Mrs Lathom's expression as she listened to it. Sarah had an uneasy suspicion that Mrs Lathom could only have invited them to please her son; and because, with a substantial dowry to her name, Sarah Wedgwood would make an acceptable bride for George Lathom, if not perhaps a wholly desirable one.

They were led into a panelled hall gleaming with polish and warmed, like all the rooms, by a blazing fire, although there was no one here to sit beside it. From there they were taken up wide stairs, lit by long mullioned windows looking on to the exquisite formal garden, and into the long gallery – and as they went Mrs Wedgwood exclaimed rapturously at the beauty of ornately plastered ceilings, ancient tapestries, family portraits, furniture of such fragile elegance that Sarah wondered fleetingly whether it was strong enough to support the weight of portly Squire Lathom and his hunting friends. She knew what her mother was thinking: 'How could any girl fail to be impressed by all this? Now at last Sarah will see sense! If only George is still of the same mind . . .'

In the long gallery the hunting party – among them, Sarah noticed, George's sister and a number of other ladies – was already settled about the fire. Her father looked stiff and disapproving, standing a little apart as if disassociating himself from the ribald talk which was causing such uninhibited laughter. John, on the other hand, his face flushed to an unaccustomed rosiness, was equally anxious to appear completely at home amongst the other men: he looked tired, but was laughing and joking with the best of them. George, seated a little sullenly in a chair near the hearth with his long legs stretched towards the flames, looked bored and uninterested. He had put on weight and no longer had the power at a glance to set Sarah's pulses racing. But in some things he had not changed: as soon as he saw her he jumped to his feet and came to greet her, smiling brightly.

'Sarah – Miss Wedgwood! Mama said you would be here . . .' He took her hand, and she allowed him to do so though her smile was restrained. 'I'd hoped perhaps you'd come hunting – I know how you used to like a good fast ride.'

She ignored the sly allusion to that eventful ride to Fenton, and said quietly, 'I like riding, yes, but hunting does not interest me. I feel too sorry for the hare.'

'Still,' George went on, 'you're here now, and that's what matters. How are you? You look very well.'

Mechanically she answered his questions and allowed him to lead her to the fireside (where it was much too hot) and even made the effort to ask him about himself, drawing from him the inevitable monologue. It seemed that hunting played an inordinately large part in his life these days, and clearly he was trying to make sure he left out no detail of his experiences in the hunting field during the past months. Listening to him with only half her attention, Sarah wondered that she could ever have found his company exciting.

Then it was dinner time and George led her downstairs again to the dining hall, talking still; and Sarah caught a glimpse of her mother's face with a smugly jubilant expression upon it. 'Now,' Mrs Wedgwood would be thinking, 'she is in George's company, and he is most attentive, and she has only to look about her to see what marriage to him would bring her.' She did not know that all this ostentatious luxury only brought more sharply to mind what she had seen yesterday: Jos's little house at Burslem, with its four cold scarcely furnished rooms darkened by the ivy that grew close to its windows, cheerless and unadorned by anything but his precious collection of books and the lovingly preserved fossils which once, long ago, she had admired. When, very soon, they sat down to eat at a table crowded with dishes – fresh salmon with fennel sauce, roast veal, chickens and ham, pigeon pie, peas and beans, roast pork with gooseberry sauce, strawberry tarts lavishly crowned with cream – she thought only of the stale crust in Jos's larder which, without her help, would have continued to provide the only food he ate in his lonely poverty. The thought spoiled her appetite and she sat eating little and absorbed by her anxieties, while George talked on, and on.

Now and then a shout of laughter broke into her thoughts, or a remark tossed loudly across the table, dragging her attention back to the present. But there was little to hold her interest. It was all noise and laughter: gossip about neighbours, and hunting exploits, and political scandals, as if everything was a joke. Not that Sarah wanted a life without light-heartedness and laughter; but she had felt often that George was incapable of seriousness, and now she saw why. He had never known any other kind of talk, or learned how to think. In a happier frame of mind she might have been able to join in the laughter, and muster a mood of light-heartedness for these few hours. But tonight she could not do it. Bored, impatient for the meal to end, she sat with the waves of talk and laughter washing over her and an expression of unconvincing attentiveness on her face.

'Fine dinner service, Sophy!' boomed a woman two seats away on her right. Across the table Mrs Lathom smiled and bowed her head. The woman lifted a bowl holding fruit and held it admiringly against the light of one of the branching candlesticks. 'You can see the light through porcelain, you know.'

'Ah,' said Mrs Lathom, 'but that isn't porcelain – has all the look of it though.'

Her guest exclaimed and carefully put down the bowl. 'I'll say it has – quite deceived me. Where did you get it? It's never English ware!'

Mrs Lathom looked close to laughter at the very idea. 'Lord no! It's oriental Delft, from Holland. You won't find an English potter making anything that good.'

'Oh!' Sarah, instantly forgetful of rank and manners alike, broke in on the exchange. 'I can't agree. I admit I've seen nothing quite like this in Staffordshire – but there are wares as good, of their kind. Our English potters at their best can stand comparison with any Dutchman.'

Mrs Lathom stared at Sarah, with a hauteur quite unlike her former bluff heartiness of manner. She did not like to be contradicted; but worse, Sarah had by implication reminded the company of connections which would be better forgotten. Sarah knew her mother was holding her breath, fearful that all her hopes of a good marriage for her daughter were about to crumble into dust. But she cared not one jot.

'You are partial, Miss Wedgwood – but in error.' Mrs Lathom's voice was cold. 'Where is the English potter whose plates match one another or stack without falling over? Fairground pots, yes – but not the kind of thing I'd give houseroom to.'

Her heart beating fast, Sarah seized her opportunity. 'I know a potter who makes wares as good as any Delft,' she said staunchly. There was a small disapproving silence broken by an embarrassed titter, hastily extinguished. Mrs Lathom stared at her for a moment, saying nothing, and then turned pointedly to speak to her neighbour.

Sarah glanced at George: he was scowling ferociously beside her. 'How could you, Sarah?' he whispered under cover of the flow of relieved talk about them. 'The first time we've met in months, and you still can't leave those damned pots behind – nor that dusty potting cousin of yours. What do you suppose they'll all think of you now? I'd wager anything my mother's regretting she ever asked any of you here tonight. Your brother may think himself a gentleman, but with you around he's going to find it hard to convince anyone else of it.'

'Then let *him* worry about that,' Sarah retorted softly. 'I can only be myself – I've never pretended to be anything else but what I am.'

'And what is that?' George asked, though still in an undertone. 'A respectable young lady of decent well-to-do yeoman stock, well brought up, accomplished – or a potter's woman, all dust and drudgery?'

'If I must have dust and drudgery to be Jos's wife, then so be it,' she assured him proudly. 'You know that's what I want.'

'Then you're a fool. And I don't think you've really

thought about it. You'd hate it, giving up all your comforts, slaving away day and night, spinning, brewing, baking, scrubbing floors, carrying coals – no time for cards, or riding, or music – nothing but toil.'

In spite of herself she laughed. 'What do you know about it, George Lathom? Besides, I can spin wool with the best of them, and do all those dirty jobs if I have to. I've never been afraid of hard work. Better surely to endure drudgery in the company of someone you love than luxury with anyone else.'

'You only say that because you know you're safe. There's no chance of you wedding your cousin so long as your parents oppose it.'

'Then,' she said, her eyes unwaveringly on his face, 'I shall wed no one.' But for all her confident tone she felt her spirit shrink at the bleakness of the prospect.

It was a relief when at last Mrs Lathom rose to signal the moment for the ladies to withdraw to the gallery and leave the men to their drinking and smoking. George, sunk in sullen silence by now, did not even look round as Sarah left her seat.

The ladies settled themselves, laughing and chattering, to play cards and sew, and talk of servant problems and London fashions and the latest scandals. In due course Mrs Lathom would make the tea, and the men would join them, and there might be more card playing and perhaps some music, and dancing late into the night; and not until supper was served would they be free to go home.

Sarah, ignoring a glance of exceptional severity directed at her by her mother, sat on a window seat apart from the company and gazed out on the still sunlit garden. If this was indeed her natural environment – as even George seemed to think – why did she feel so acutely uncomfortable in it? On the other hand, could she be sure that she would feel more at home with the dust and drudgery George had promised her with Jos? Certainly if she were to marry him as things stood now, defying her parents and so losing any chance of a dowry, they could have at best only a precarious existence in which any small change – poor trade, the birth of a child – would leave them destitute and thrown on the cold mercy of parish charity.

Would she mind a life like that, if it brought her Jos and the potworks? But that was fruitless speculation, for – as

George had said – so long as Jos was in such circumstances then she could not marry him, not least because he would not consider the possibility. She could only wait, rent with anxiety on his behalf, and try hopelessly to think of some way to help, knowing that even her little effort this evening had been utterly in vain.

'You play, I gather, Miss Wedgwood – pray do so.'

The command was insulting in its complete disregard for her own wishes, but Mrs Lathom was clearly intent on exacting her revenge for Sarah's lack of breeding. There was nothing Sarah herself could do either but take her seat at the beautiful inlaid harpsichord, search through the music upon it for something she could play, and begin at once. She was angry at Mrs Lathom's behaviour, but glad all the same to have something to do which she enjoyed. The notes tinkled trippingly beneath her fingers, and for the first time that evening she was, briefly, a centre of approval.

But not for very long. In a moment or two the chatter had begun again, and she knew she was playing for herself alone. It was one of the things she found hardest to endure about music in company, that for the most part everyone seemed to regard it as a pleasing background, like a picture or a figured wallpaper, and not as something to be enjoyed with every ounce of one's being. It was good to be playing though, letting the music flow on so that for a little while she could forget the chattering silliness of the company. She could forget everything, even her anxiety about Jos.

Downstairs the men had reached a state of boisterous good humour: ragged cheering, laughter, stumbling feet on the stairs signalled their coming. In the gallery there was a murmuring rustle of heavy silken skirts carefully arranged, a stir of focussed attention, a self-conscious resumption of talk.

The door opened – or rather was flung wide with a flourish by one of the men – and into the room marched unsteadily first Squire Lathom, by now thoroughly drunk, and then at the head of a motley procession the equally drunk George himself, bearing aloft his mother's favourite Delft bowl out of which a red-brown liquid splashed spasmodically. He crossed the room, came to a rocking halt before his mother and stood looking up at the bowl, as if puzzled as to what it was and why it should be there. Sarah glimpsed her father at the rear of the procession, trying to look as if he had no connection with it whatsoever; though John, his arm draped about the shoulders of the young man next to him, had clearly no such reservations.

At last, very slowly, George managed to lower the bowl to the level of his mother's eyes, though he tipped a considerable quantity of its contents over her brocaded skirts in the process. A strong smell of what Sarah thought might be brandy (at least in part) filled the room. Mrs Lathom rose furiously to her feet, pulling in her skirts.

'Better than tea,' George told her, unperturbed, and nodding emphatically. 'Besht punch – all good thingsh—' He thrust the bowl at his mother, slopping the contents still further; and then as she drew back again he looked about for some surface on which to lay the bowl, stumbled, lost his footing, and fell flat on his face on the carpet sending the bowl crashing on to the hearth.

The liquid spilled, spreading, over the carpet, soaking slowly into the rich coloured silks of its surface, and the bowl fell apart in three fragments and lay still.

A howl of anguish and fury broke from Mrs Lathom. 'George, you careless drunken fool – my best bowl!'

George lay where he was, laughing foolishly, quite beyond being troubled by his mother's anger. Then he moved a little and stretched out an arm: with a prickle of embarrassment Sarah saw his bloodshot gaze settle on her, his finger point her way.

'Sharah –' he said, grinning inanely, 'she'sh the one for potsh . . . mend it for you, yesh – Sharah knowsh all about potsh . . . potsh . . . potsh . . . potsh . . .' and he bent his face to the floor and began to drum out the repetitious rhythm of the words with his fists. Sarah felt that every part of her must be glowing crimson with shame, and she knew they were all looking at her, but she saw only the hard angry eyes of Mrs Lathom. She felt her heart throb chokingly fast – if only the floor would open and swallow her up . . .

Mrs Lathom turned back to George, calmer again, but no less angry. 'Have the mess cleared up – there's nothing to be done.' Someone – not George, who was wholly incapable – hurried to call a servant; and Sarah realised suddenly with the force of a revelation that here within her grasp was not a disaster but the very opportunity for which she had prayed. She ran to Mrs Lathom.

'Madam, George is right – I do know someone who will mend the bowl.'

Mrs Lathom stared at her for a moment, and then snapped, 'Rubbish, Miss Wedgwood – it's broken beyond repair. Don't try and tell me it can be put back as it was.'

'Not quite perhaps – but near enough, so that only you will ever know the difference.'

Again that stare, hostile, disapproving, utterly sceptical; and then giving way just a little to hesitation. Sarah seized on it.

'Let me take it for you. I'll ask my – kinsman – to mend it. After all, even if it isn't perfect afterwards you've nothing to lose by it – but I promise you won't be disappointed.'

Mrs Lathom gave a barely perceptible nod, and then turned to the newly-come servant to give orders that George should be carried to bed (he seemed to be already asleep), the floor cleaned up, and the pieces of the bowl packed ready for Miss Wedgwood to take with her when she left.

Next day Mrs Wedgwood was, for once, full of approval as Sarah set off for Burslem with the broken dish packed with extreme care in a basket at her saddle. 'You will give such pleasure to Mrs Lathom if the bowl can be mended well: it should make up a little for your behaviour last night. Make sure young Jos doesn't let you down.'

'He won't,' said Sarah, relieved that her mother seemed to regard the whole episode as a device to reinstate herself with Mrs Lathom. But of course her mother did not know of Jos's present plight, and seemed blithely unaware of any other possible motive for her daughter's action; or perhaps she chose to shut her eyes to it. Either way, Sarah thought, it was just as well.

She rode through the summer rain in a mood of happy confidence such as she had not known for weeks. Here at her saddle was the chance for which Jos had waited so long. She imagined how it would be: the pleasure lighting his face as she told him what had happened and placed the dish in his hands; the delicate craftsmanship with which those two beloved hands would piece together the shattered fragments, repair paint and glaze, and restore the dish in all its perfection to a delighted Mrs Lathom. In no time at all word of his consummate skill would have reached all the wealthy families for miles around, and customers would flock to the Ivy House works.

Her dream held until Jos took the pieces from her; and then it was shattered as abruptly as the bowl itself had been. She saw Jos frown, and her heart seemed to turn an anxious somersault.

'You will mend it, won't you? I promised you would.' She did not say, 'I never doubted you,' for some instinct was already warning her of what he was about to say.

He raised his eyes from the bowl: their expression was quiet but grave, like his voice. 'This can't be mended, Sarah – or not in any way I'd be happy with, or you either, come to that.'

She felt cold and knew the colour had drained from her face. 'I told her you would,' she whispered through a dry mouth – thinking all the while, 'What have I done? Have I destroyed his good name for ever?'

He smiled wryly. 'I'm not a miracle worker, Sally.' Carefully he laid the pieces on a table nearby, and then turned back to her. 'What I can do is copy it.'

'Copy? But that wouldn't be the same!'

'Oh, Sally, you thought I could do the impossible – and now suddenly you don't even believe me capable of doing something a little difficult but still within my powers – that's not like you!' He put an arm about her. 'I must admit it's not the kind of work I'd choose to do. It means tying up men and materials in a single project; and it's going to take time, a fair bit of time. But I'm in no position to be choosy – and besides you gave your word, so there it is.'

Still Sarah gazed at him with doubt in her eyes. 'But a copy – that's not what I told her.'

He turned her to face him, his hands on her shoulders, and said earnestly, 'I promise you it will be as fine as the original – she won't know the difference. We'll confess of course, but only when she's seen it and said how pleased she is. Does that make you feel better?'

She smiled faintly and nodded, and told herself that she must trust Jos in this, for where his craft was concerned he had no equal.

He started at once, working night and day, and barely pausing to eat the food Sarah brought him from the Big House where she was staying: Uncle John had surprised them all last year by marrying, and his wife Mary was a splendid cook. By day Sarah worked with Jos, helping to mix clays, making a careful note of what had already been tried and failed, so that they should not waste time doing the same work twice.

'The problem is,' Jos told her, 'that I know the Delft potters mix marl and sand with their clay, but I must get the proportions right, otherwise it won't work.' He showed her the small tablets of newly fired clay – the most recent batch of experimental mixtures – laid on the table beside him. 'See, this one's far too coarse; and this cracked badly in the firing; but this one, the last we tried – what do you think of that?'

Sarah took the hard square of clay in her hand and examined it carefully. It was smooth, firm, strong, yet as thin and fragile-looking as one of Aunt Sarah's delicate almond biscuits.

'It looks about right.'

'That's what I thought. Let's try a larger piece and see what to do about the glaze.' He held out a fragment of the original dish. 'See the bluish tint in the enamelling – it's no more than a tint, but very distinctive. We must get that right.'

It took eight weeks of constant laborious work before at last they could stand aside and gaze in triumph at the completed bowl, delicate, shining, as beautiful as the other once had been.

'I don't think even Mrs Lathom will know the difference. . .' said Sarah. 'No, I'm sure of it.' She linked her arm through Jos's. 'Do you want me to deliver it? Though I think perhaps it would look more businesslike if one of your men took it.'

Jos nodded. 'Yes, you're right – it would. Will Moore's a reliable sort of man, and careful too – he can ride Taffy.'

Next morning they stood side by side in the yard to watch the man go, mounted on Jos's sturdy brown horse with the precious bowl thoroughly packed with straw and held on the saddle before him. And then they settled down to wait for his return.

104

'It can't take him more than two days,' said Sarah. 'The roads are dry and it's only a few hours' ride to High Newbold.'

Ten days later there was still no sign of Will Moore, and no word had come, no message been sent. Sarah and Jos said nothing but read the same terrible vision in each other's eyes: the shattered bowl beside the road; Will taken flight, drowning his fears of his master's wrath in some distant inn, terrified to come back and confess. Perhaps they would never know.

Sarah settled down for what seemed the hundredth time to look over Jos's haphazard accounting. By now every possible correction had been made, and the books were more in order than they had ever been; but the pretence that she was working helped to occupy her mind a little. She was halfway through when someone called from outside, and Jos flung open the door to admit a Will Moore whose round rosy face was momentarily transformed by a grin which threatened to disappear either side of his ears so wide was it.

'Will! Where in God's name have you been? We've been sick with worry – what happened?'

'I've been livin' like a lord, master,' said Will with defiant cheerfulness. Sarah, watching, thought Jos looked in danger of exploding.

'The dish – what of the dish?'

'That's just it, master – I've been at High Newbold all this time, and I've never had such feastin' in all my life. You'd never believe the food. Grand young kitchen wench they have too – mind, dunna tell my Bess that—'

'Will, the dish!'

'I said, master – that's why. You shoulda seen the lady's face when I told her it was a copy – she wouldna believe it till I showed her the piece of the old one. And she was that pleased she said I could have the best the house could offer. Oh, and she's comin' here to see what your own wares are like – happen she'll buy a dinner service – an' has a friend goin' to marry off a daughter who's comin' with her – Friday, she said.'

'Friday! That's today!'

Will scratched his head. 'Aye, it is that. I've had that good a time I'd forgotten what day it is.'

Jos clapped him on the back. 'Never mind, Will – go and tell your Bess all about it – leaving out the kitchen maid that is . . .'

He watched the man go and then turned to Sarah, his eyes alight with excitement. 'Sally my girl, what do you think of that?'

Sarah linked her arms about his neck and kissed him tenderly, and then stood gazing into his eyes.

'I think, Jos love, that you are the most wonderful, clever, dear Jos there has ever been – and all you need is a sensible young woman to set you on the right path for your fortune to be made.'

He laughed. 'Then you'd best get busy at once, or I'll not have my best pots set out before my rich customers arrive.'

CHAPTER FIVE

1760

Overhead the arching branches were already glowing with the tints of autumn: gold and red and bronze and yellow and copper and a thousand unnameable shades between. The sun lit them, the wind stirred them to set an intricate dappled pattern dancing on the grassy rock-strewn path up which Sarah walked, her head bent, her cloak pulled tight about her, the wide brim of her beribboned milkmaid hat shutting out any view of the myriad fire colours over and around her. She walked on in the same heedless manner, shut in with her thoughts, until the path turned a corner and widened suddenly into a glade on a kind of natural shelf in the hillside; and here at last she came to a halt, raised her head and gazed back the way she had come.

She had not realised she was so high up, so far above the small spa town of Buxton nestling below within its circling hills. She could look down on it now, on the new and fine houses many of which were still in the process of being built, and the colourful cluster of people about the health-giving St Anne's well, where this morning (as every morning this week) her mother, leaning heavily and complainingly on her arm, had taken the waters; and then, further afield, to the high green Derbyshire hills, patterned with stone walls, which stretched to the borders of Staffordshire and Cheshire somewhere to her right in the hazy blue distance. Now, as if released all at once from some kind of bondage, she drew a deep slow breath, and threw back her head and closed her eyes, feeling the wind fresh on her face and the sweet fragrant moorland air clean in her lungs, which had been for so long clogged with the stuffy air and stale odours of the sickroom.

She was not sure why she loved the Derbyshire hills so much but she had always done so, ever since the first of many family outings when she was a very small girl. She was undeterred by the bleakness of the moors, the untamed landscape scarred by quarries and lead mines, dotted with lonely farmhouses, populated by a dogged primitive withdrawn people. She loved the high places, and she loved the deep secret dales with their sparkling rivers, their caverns and sheltering trees. No other landscape had quite the power to move her as this did, as if some deep desire of her spirit found fulfilment here. 'When Jos and I are married,' she thought now, 'then we shall come here often, to refresh ourselves for the next stage of our work.'

'*Our* work,' she had thought; yet the words brought a sickening lurch to her stomach. The future, once stretching before her calm and bright, beckoning her on to certain happiness, had a different aspect now: the past weeks had made sure of that. She dared not look ahead, for it was as if a dark swirling mist hid the path from view, and she knew that what lay beyond, unseen, was grim and gloomy and menacing.

She hated herself for such thoughts even as she was thinking them. It was not her mother's fault that the long feverish cold of last winter had hung about her; that now, several months later, she was still far from well – or rather, very much worse. And it was, of course, Sarah's duty as the only daughter to care for her mother, to keep house for her father and brother, to devote her life to those nearest to her. It was not her mother's fault that these ties kept her from Burslem, from the Ivy House, from Jos.

But it might have been easier to bear if her mother had not been openly so glad that she was kept at home. 'Do you good not to be for ever hanging around your cousin Jos. Time you got him out of your system,' Mrs Wedgwood had said one day, and the sharp pain in Sarah's breast had almost driven her to make a harsh retort. She had choked it back just in time, out of respect for the sick woman: only the pain had lingered long afterwards. As it had that other time when she supposed some of her impatience – for all her efforts to control it – must have shown, for her mother had said, 'If you think life's passing you by, then remember you spoiled your own chances. It's not everyone who's given a second chance – and I know George Lathom would have had you that day the dish was broken. You could have been wed by now, maybe have a babe on the way. But you always were a stubborn contrary girl.'

It was not that, ever, she regretted that lost opportunity – if

108

such it had been – or had since given a second thought to George, beyond being relieved to hear that he was at last about to be married to some eligible girl she did not know. But the thought of children was quite another matter; and of being mistress of her own household; and of having some purpose to her life, other than this. None of those things would have taken from her the duty to her mother, but they might have sweetened it, and rid her of the fear that often kept her sleepless.

Yes, it was the fear that was the worst thing – fear of the future. What if her mother were to be ill for a long time, years perhaps? What if Sarah were to be kept at home, tied to the sickroom for what was left of her youth and through middle age, until it was too late to pick up the threads which bound her to Jos? Would he be able to go on without her – or she without him?

She tried to reason herself out of her despondent mood. Jos was doing well now, so she heard. Very likely his books would be in a terrible muddle by the time she saw him again, but at least they would be full. He was overflowing with ideas too, and had sent word to her that he had a host of new designs and she must come soon and advise him on which would sell best to his rich customers. If things continued as they were now it might not be very long before they would be able to marry.

And surely Mrs Wedgwood would soon be well. They had come to Buxton to see what its healing waters could do for her health, and today there had been a marked improvement. She had eaten a good dinner for once, and afterwards, instead of lying restlessly on a couch as Sarah tried to amuse her, had announced that she would go to bed and sleep, and that her daughter might consider herself free for the afternoon. She had indeed fallen into the first deep refreshing sleep she had known for a long time, and so Sarah had gone out with a clear conscience and a sense of liberation to enjoy what was left of the day.

She had come alone, refusing to bring a servant for company: it was not perhaps a very wise move, but the need for solitude was greater than prudence or common sense. She was glad to find the woods deserted, and to know that only she was there to send birds fluttering startled from the branches or small animals scuttling for safety. Her mother was not an easy woman at the best of times, but in the irritable, complaining, exacting mood which afflicted her when she was ill she was doubly difficult: Sarah realised only now, when she was briefly free of them, how the demands of the past weeks had drawn on her reserves of patience and how thoroughly weary she was.

She was the more annoyed then to realise on reaching her viewpoint that her precious privacy was about to be invaded: someone was coming towards her up the path from the town. The agitated chattering of a jay drew her attention to him first, and looking towards the source of the disturbance she glimpsed the dark cloth of a man's coat appearing and disappearing through the trees as its wearer came steadily uphill.

She was not frightened exactly, but to be a woman alone in a wood with a strange man was hardly the most desirable of situations; and as he came more into view she saw that his walk had something dogged and purposeful about it, which was not reassuring, though his head was bent and she did not think he had seen her yet. She looked round quickly for some way of avoiding him. She could hide herself in a clump of hollies at the edge of the clearing but that, she felt, would be both uncomfortable and a little silly. She could hurry on up the hill where the path wound its way through more thickly growing trees to the summit; but the denser woodland meant greater concealment not only for her but for any man with dubious intentions, and she did not think she could walk quickly enough, tired as she was, to escape a determined pursuer. Besides, safety lay down there in the town, and she could not reach it without passing him.

In the end she decided to stay where she was, enjoying her view and hoping he might pass her by without seeing her. She was carrying nothing and wore no jewellery, and in her plain blue unhooped gown should not attract attention; and as the man came nearer still she saw he was soberly but respectably, even expensively, dressed. He did not look like a footpad.

Then, as he reached the clearing and paused, seeing her, all her fears dissolved in compassion. She did not think she had ever seen a look of anguish so intense as was exposed now on the face of this stranger. For a moment she wanted to run to him, hands held out to comfort; and the exclamation that sprang to her lips forced its way from her as a murmur, just loud enough for him to hear.

Almost at once he seemed to take himself in hand. He drew himself up to his full height – which was a little over the average – and removed his hat to uncover his dark hair; and though he did not smile he made a little inclination of the head which was not quite a bow.

'Good afternoon, ma'am.' His voice was deep, with an attractive resonance, though the unhappiness was still there. 'I had not thought to find anyone else here at this time of day.'

It was, quite simply, an observation; but Sarah felt uncomfortable, as if he had reproached her for an intrusion. 'I was just going,' she lied, colouring a little.

He seemed instantly to regret his words. 'I beg your pardon – that was very rude of me – please stay. If my presence is an infliction I am happy to leave you in peace.'

There was such a winning charm in his manner that Sarah smiled, suddenly wanting him to stay. 'Not at all. No one able to enjoy a view like this should be selfish about it.' He had beautiful dark eyes, she saw – though their expression was sad – and his graceful ease of bearing combined with a quiet elegance of dress to suggest a cultivated and well-educated gentleman. Fine hands too, she noticed absently, the long fingers bent around the brim of his hat . . .

'It is a favourite view of yours, too, then?'

'Not until now. I have never been up here before. But you obviously knew what to expect.'

His eyes seemed more deeply shadowed than ever. 'It was our – my wife – it was her favourite walk, when we came here together.' Then, clearly feeling that an explanation of his stumbling speech was required, 'She died a year ago, in childbirth. Our little girl died too.'

'Oh, I'm so sorry.' He could not be much older than she was, about Jos's age perhaps. Very likely his wife would have been younger. Perhaps they had married late, after long waiting. She felt a surge of panic: what if she and Jos did not live to marry? Trying to turn the fear aside she said without really thinking, 'You must find it a comfort to remember her here'; and then was afraid she had said completely the wrong thing.

The next moment she was sure of it, for there was a break

111

in his voice. 'I think it was too soon – they tell me I should be over it by now, whatever that means – but . . .' He broke off as if he could not trust himself to go on.

'A year is not very long,' she said gently, with a poignant insight into what it must be like to know you will never see the one you love in this life again. If it were Jos and she were left . . . Even lesser griefs left their scars; and that total separation must be beyond bearing. It hurt her even to try and imagine it.

'No: it is nothing.' He turned to look away from her at the view, as if he did not want her to see how near he was to breaking down. 'We were very close – so many interests shared, painting, music, poetry. She had such gentleness, such a loving heart – no one in trouble was ever turned away . . .'

Sarah had often suspected that there was something in her face that invited confidences. People she hardly knew had been known to unburden themselves to her at length and without hesitation. But she had never before felt so moved by anything she heard, nor so warmed by the speaker. She listened, saying little, while he talked of the wife he had loved and what she had meant to him; and how unbearable it had been to lose her, the more so because he had come to her bedside too late to be with her when she died.

Sarah wondered if she ought to say more, if she should do something other than stand here at his side, simply listening: she had no real experience of grief herself, close though she had come to it, and she did not know what would be helpful. But when at last he had finished he brought to an end the little silence that followed by saying, 'Thank you for listening so patiently. Most people seem to think it harmful to allow a mourner to talk of his loss – as if you should cut yourself off from the past the moment the person you love has died. But I know – and I've heard so from others too – that the greatest need is to talk. I am sorry you should have had to suffer it.'

She smiled a little. 'It is not difficult to listen.'

It seemed as if he had indeed found some comfort in talking, for almost at once he lost much of the haunted look which had so struck her when she first saw him, and which had lingered even afterwards in his eyes and voice. 'Tell me,' he said now, quite calmly, 'are you too a visitor to Buxton? I

112

think perhaps I saw you in church yesterday morning, with an elderly lady.'

'My mother – we are here for her health. She likes to be seen at morning worship. I'm afraid I don't share her sentiments.' She instantly regretted the slightly acid note in her voice: it sounded ill-natured, and she strongly suspected that her companion would have no liking for sneering remarks of that kind. There was about his face – about the mobile mouth in particular – a gentleness unusual in a man; although that he was wholly masculine she had no doubt, for she was already aware of a strong attraction.

Fortunately perhaps he read something quite other than unkindness into her words. 'You are not a devoted daughter of the church then?' There was even a hint of amusement in the dark eyes.

'Not of the established church, no,' she admitted, 'though I was brought up largely in its fold. But I think so many of the clergy follow what should be a sacred calling for entirely worldly reasons, and that so often shows in their lives, and in the emptiness of the worship in their churches. It touches neither the heart nor the mind.'

She thought there was something guarded in his expression. 'You are perhaps a follower of John Wesley – a Methodist?'

She laughed. 'Goodness me no!' Then thinking that might sound appallingly rude, added quickly, 'Forgive me – I did not mean to offend. Perhaps you are a Methodist?'

He smiled then, and it was as if he had struck her, so devastating was the sweetness of that smile. She felt breathless, hearing his next words through a sensation close to that of intoxication

'Indeed no. I'm afraid the Reverend Mr Wesley, whatever his estimable qualities, plays too much on the emotions of his hearers – on their fear of damnation, their superstitions. But then I do not believe in damnation, nor do I believe true religion lies in hysteria. That is, I think, only for unbalanced minds. Have you heard him preach?'

She shook her head, feeling a little unbalanced herself. She had found George Lathom attractive, in a superficial way, but she had never before known this disturbing total awareness of another person, as if her whole self – mind as well as body –

113

had been suddenly awakened. It seemed odd to be talking of something so separate, so outside her deepest concerns, as the doings of an itinerant preacher. Yet somehow everything had become of the deepest importance to her. 'A cousin of mine heard him recently, when he came to his town. He thought him sincere but misguided. But he won a large following by his preaching, amongst men and women who until then had lived very rough irreligious lives. The effect he had is already very marked – you have to admit that many people do change their lives completely for the better after hearing him.'

'But for the wrong reasons, don't you agree? Or rather for no *reason* at all, for it is wholly irrational.'

'Yes, I suppose that's true. And I suppose in the end it does matter *why* you do right, as well as that you should do it.' She smiled reflectively. 'I remember some visiting parson when I was a child telling us how all our sufferings in this life were a punishment for our sins, and if we didn't repent at once the Lord would hand us over to a thousand tormenting devils when we were dead. I was terrified – our church had little devils carved on its ceiling, and for a long time afterwards I had nightmares that they were coming for me. But I fear it made no difference to my behaviour: I think perhaps even then I didn't really believe it at heart. Now I find myself more and more attracted to the Unitarian way of things – I have kinsfolk of that persuasion. I like the calmness and reason and benevolence of their teachings. But perhaps most people need some emotion in their religion if it is going to move them to follow its teachings wholeheartedly.'

'Because they lack education,' said her companion earnestly. 'Give them education, teach them to use their minds and you would, I think, find that reason would lead them into the right path without recourse to fears and passions that could as easily be swayed another more dangerous way. Don't you agree?'

'You would need universal education to bring that about – and much better teachers than the general run.'

'Why not? It would be difficult but not impossible. Nothing is impossible.'

She smiled ruefully. 'I see there is no limit to your ambitions for mankind. And womankind too, I suppose . . .'

'Of course – if women are seen as the least rational part of

114

humanity, then that is surely because their education has always been the less. Or do you think I'm talking nonsense?'

'I think if it could be done it would make for a revolution, in everything.'

'Exactly.' Again that smile. 'Look about you – at the corruption of our political life, the cruelty and injustice of our laws, the immorality and self seeking of those in high places, the squalid struggle for survival which is the life of the poor . . . Can you doubt that a revolution is what is needed?'

She laughed, releasing some of the excitement bubbling through her. 'You are a dangerous man, I can see.' Dangerous, yes, for she could feel it in her racing pulses, the tremors that ran through her whenever he smiled or turned those long-lashed dark eyes upon her. Yet he was gentle, quiet, courteous, and mourning for his lost wife: what possible danger was there in that, what attraction even? He was perhaps, superficially, the least threatening man she had ever met. It could be, she thought, that the danger lay in her, or in the power he had to attract.

Now, as her eyes sparkling with laughter met his, something caught and held her. She felt a kind of stillness, as if everything for a tiny fraction of time held its breath. Yet she was breathing; and so was he, though something in his expression told her that he felt the strangeness too. She shivered and said quickly, looking about her, 'It will be dark soon. It's time I went back.'

'Then I will see you safely home, if you will permit it.' Had she imagined that there had been anything out of the ordinary? – for he was matter of fact, calm, offering her his arm.

She laid her hand upon it, and they turned in silence and began slowly to make their way down through the trees towards the town. The fabric of his coat beneath her fingers was smooth and fine, she noticed, and through it his warmth reached her, comforting against the chillness of the wind that had sprung up with the failing light and set the dried leaves rattling and rustling over their heads. She could feel still that odd kind of tension, not unpleasant exactly, but disturbing. Her intense awareness of the man at her side threw him into sharp focus, blurring everything around him.

'Do you like music?' she asked suddenly. She did not quite know why she asked, only that it seemed important.

He turned to look at her. 'Yes, very much. Or I did before –

115

last year. Since then I have not found it possible to sing. She used to play while we sang, you see.' He gave a rueful half-smile. 'Once I would have thought it impossible that I could have lived a whole year without music, but there it is. One day it will come back, I'm sure of that. What of you? Do you play or sing?'

'A little of each, though I play more than I sing. I love music but I find there are very few people who care for it as I do.'

'To most people I'm afraid it's simply a useful social asset, like playing cards or dancing,' he agreed. 'If that were all it meant to me then I should be singing still. Tell me, what music do you like best?'

'Oh, all kinds. I think, for singing, Handel is unsurpassable – his death last year was a great loss. But there is so much else I like too. I am working through a new book of sonatas by Dr Arne at present – new to me anyway. I like them very much: the second one in E minor in particular.'

She saw with delight that there was a smile of recognition on his face.

'Yes, that's very fine – I know it well.'

It seemed almost too good to be true and she found herself laughing with happiness. A chance meeting like this, beginning so strangely and unpropitiously – yet it had brought her here through talk that excited and exhilarated her to a sense that she had found a friend, a kindred spirit. He laughed too, all at once far removed from the grief-stricken man who had come on her in the glade. They talked of music with delight and enthusiasm all the way down the hill and through the town and to the door of Sarah's lodgings.

And then, suddenly, there was constraint between them. He turned to face her and raised her hand briefly to his lips, and then said a little awkwardly, 'Goodnight, and thank you,' and then he waited while she went into the house and closed the door behind her.

It was only afterwards, when it was too late, that she realised she had not asked his name. Nor, she thought with shame, had she once – or not for more than an instant – thought of Jos during the hour or so that they had spent together. What had come over her, to be so unsettled by a chance encounter

116

that for the remainder of the day and much of the night she felt restless, excited, impatient for the morning to come? And it was cruelly disloyal of her to wonder if tomorrow they might meet again somewhere in the little town.

But they did not meet, though wherever she went her eyes searched for him. There were few people in Buxton at this time of year, and it was a small place. Perhaps, she thought, he was deliberately avoiding her, embarrassed because he had revealed his deepest feelings to a total stranger; perhaps he had simply left the town. Probably she would never know, for they were unlikely ever to meet again; but she wished she did not feel quite so depressed at the prospect.

'It's just like George Lathom,' she told herself sternly. 'I'm flattered because he's attractive, and he spoke to me – that's all.' But she knew it was not like that. She knew, though she did not want to face the knowledge, that physical attraction had been only a tiny part of it, strong and real though it was. She knew that the sense of excitement had stemmed as much from a mutual attraction of minds as of bodies. She had never before met a man who gave her – even for a moment – such a sense of opening up new worlds, of limitless possibilities for the intellect and the imagination. She had never before, even with Jos, felt that she could have talked of anything at all and he would have understood. Yet she had little enough on which to base her conviction of this. After a few days she began to believe she had imagined it was anything but an unimportant interlude; or she thought she believed it.

She was glad when at last her mother seemed on the way to recovery and they could go home. If, now and then, thoughts of the man at Buxton still troubled her, she tried not to let it worry her. He meant nothing and could have no part in her life. She had other concerns and problems and anxieties in plenty without adding him to them.

Just before Christmas her mother grew suddenly worse and died, and she had for a time to give all her attention to comforting her father and her brother who were overwhelmed by a shattering grief she could not share. And then, as life slowly settled into a new and quieter routine, she had time again for Jos and found that no longer did she have to fight for every moment spent with him. Her father did not approve, but Jos was his kin and he put no great obstacles in her way.

So she went often to Burslem, and together, absorbed and happy, they worked on the creamware Jos was developing as his principal product. He experimented with clays and glazes and firing temperatures, trying to achieve a fine creamy-white tableware of uniform colour and smoothness, while Sarah advised and criticized, and suggested how best to design a teapot or plate, pointed out that this shape of handle was most comfortable to hold, this curve of spout best for pouring, that size and design of plate most useful and practical as well as most pleasing to the eye. They laughed at their mistakes, and shared their delight when things went well, and found the days too short for all they wanted to do. And Sarah found there was, through her working hours, no room for any thought in her head but of Jos and all they were doing together, and at night no need for anything but sleep, the deep dreamless sleep of the woman who is happy at last.

CHAPTER SIX

1763-4

It had all sounded so innocent, a casual aside in a cheerful and reassuring letter: 'Dr Turner, the surgeon, brought a neighbour of his, one Thomas Bentley, to cheer my confinement – you know how irksome I would find it – and the remedy worked better than any medicine . . .'

Sarah had been enormously relieved when the letter came. Jos had ridden to Liverpool on business in the spring of 1762, anxious to find a merchant to deal with his increasing trade in the port where clays from Cornwall and America were brought in and completed wares shipped to other parts of the kingdom. But four weeks had gone by, and Sarah, asked to keep an eye on things in his expected five-day absence, had been sick with worry at the lack of news. The potworks had run smoothly enough – in fact lately Jos had become so prosperous that he was looking seriously for larger premises – and there had been little more for Sarah to do than compare notes with Cousin Tom and cast a quick eye over the books.

Only there had been that terrible vacuum, with no news, no hint of what had happened.

'We'd have heard soon enough if he'd met with an accident,' Tom said cheerfully. 'He was carrying papers with his name on them. They'd be able to trace his relatives.'

But she knew that Tom was trying as much to convince himself as to reassure her, and she was not cheered by the words. She had grown very fond of Tom: his silent gravity made an odd foil for Jos's ebullient enthusiasm and swiftly changing moods, but he was hard-working, conscientious and utterly trustworthy. They had become firm friends.

And now, daily, when Sarah came to the Ivy House works from the Big House where she was staying with her uncles, they tried to console each other while all the time seeing in the other's eyes how far they were from succeeding.

119

Then, at long last, the letter came, addressed to Sarah at the Big House, a brief, cheerful, matter-of-fact letter, Jos's tones in every line. He had, he told her, injured his disabled knee as he rode to Liverpool. With great difficulty he had arrived at his destination and there become very ill indeed. Now convalescent, he apologised for the anxiety his silence must have caused, told how well he was being entertained – and since this friend of the surgeon's, Mr Thomas Bentley, was a prosperous merchant, he had also inadvertently found someone to handle his affairs in Liverpool. Greatly relieved, Sarah was glad it had been no worse, worried a little about the number of times his knee had laid him low, and bore the letter off to Tom Wedgwood to cheer him in his turn.

It all seemed so insignificant at the time, the illness the only aspect of the affair which might have consequences for the future. Sarah did not give a second thought to Liverpool merchant Thomas Bentley.

Not, that is, until Jos came home and she saw the change in him. There was a new light in his eyes, a new excited glow as he limped haltingly about the office and told her all that had happened; and the name Bentley was in every sentence.

'And Bentley said . . . Bentley knows Joseph Priestley – you know William Willet's mentioned him, a delightful man. Bentley took me to see him at Warrington – Bentley had a hand in setting up the Academy there, of course. Bentley says he will do this . . . do that . . .'

She had listened patiently, aware of a little envy of the new friend but telling herself that this was the first flush of enthusiasm and would not last. She had been wrong. That had been over a year ago and still Bentley's name was almost never out of Jos's talk. Bentley and Jos wrote long confiding letters to one another, and Jos had even risked the journey to Liverpool again, taking with him this time his nephew Tom Byerley, his sister Margaret's wayward and difficult youngster, who had returned to Burslem where his widowed mother now lived, almost as besotted with the famous Bentley as was Jos himself.

Sarah tried to reason with herself. After all, she and Jos had known each other from childhood; their love for one another, their mutual understanding was as close and real and as much a part of them as their heart and lungs – and as necessary.

120

Or was it any longer? Had this new friend, this smooth Liverpool merchant with his persuasive tongue and influential friends done the one thing she would have thought impossible and driven a wedge between herself and Jos? He did not even seem to come to her for advice any more, or not often; and she had to make a deliberate effort to find out how he was faring. And always, always it seemed as if, when they were together, Bentley stood there with them, an insurmountable barrier.

Bentley was a well-read man and his favourite poet was James Thomson; so Jos, hitherto indifferent to poetry, must needs rush at once to acquire copies of Thomson's poems. He read some to Sarah, who thought them stilted and pompous but was too wise to say so.

Bentley had decided opinions about the education of women: so that 'when we have a daughter he will be just the man to advise us.' Sarah was too relieved to find that their eventual marriage still seemed to play a part in Jos's scheme of things to protest at the assumption behind the words.

Bentley was as eager for improved roads and turnpike projects as Jos; and what was more had an impressive idea for a network of canals to aid trade to the north-west.

Bentley contributed occasional articles to various radical periodicals in Liverpool and London; so Jos became a regular subscriber to many of them, eagerly reading to Sarah whole paragraphs of elegant prose on political or philosophical matters.

Bentley longed to see an end to religious divisions and was closely involved in the setting up of a chapel in Liverpool for worshippers eager for a new and more rational creed. Jos spent hours discussing the project with Kate's husband, William Willet, who had long ago attended the Academy at Findern where Bentley, himself the son of a Derbyshire squire, had been educated: it was one of the many establishments set up privately to provide higher education for young Dissenters.

Bentley knew exactly how sales of Wedgwood wares should be handled in Liverpool and had many lofty ideas for new products.

This last hurt Sarah most of all, for here was the greatest threat to herself, until now Jos's adviser in everything. Each day she felt more shut out, more unwanted. She began to think that very soon Jos would have no further use for her at all.

Yet the goal towards which they had worked for so long seemed so near. At last Jos had begun to make a secure living for himself. Not long after that fateful visit to Liverpool he had leased the Brick House works in Burslem, increased his workforce, and just before Christmas 1762 had moved to the new and larger house that went with the works. The new range of creamware, the simple, functional everyday ware on which they had worked so hard together, was already finding a market and selling well. Daily, it seemed, he made improvements to glazes, clays, moulds, decoration. At long last all the promise she had seen in him was beginning to become visible to everyone, to be recognised for what it was not only in Staffordshire but also further afield: in Liverpool, Birmingham, even London, where Jos's brother John acted as agent for the firm.

And now in what should have been a time of triumph – was indeed so for Jos – she found herself shut out. She was twenty-nine, well past the age when a man like George Lathom would consider her for a wife; he was himself long since married to a wealthy girl very much younger than herself. She had heard of the marriage without regret, for her regrets were of another kind.

Steadily, with a growing sense of despair, she saw her dreams fade away to nothing. She found herself shut up at Spen Green, increasingly bitter, dried up, lonely, a spinster daughter keeping house for father and brother with an empty unfulfilled future stretching before her. She looked back and wondered whether she could have made a different life for herself if she had chosen to do so – not by marrying George, but perhaps by mixing more in the kind of society her parents had wanted her to enjoy. She might then have met some truly congenial man who could offer her a life richer and more fulfilled than now seemed likely to be her lot – someone like the man she had met so briefly in Buxton, whom she still remembered occasionally with a fleeting sense of excitement and of opportunities lost. If Jos were not to be hers then perhaps there was not after all any disloyalty in that memory. But it did not comfort her.

That a woman could live a fulfilled and happy life without a man she did not doubt; but then she must have some other purpose, some goal towards which to work. Keeping house for her father and brother was not enough, or at least not for her. There was always something to be done even when the house was spotless, and the fruit preserved, the meals planned, the shopping completed: there was always some garment in need of mending, a sick servant or neighbour to be visited, the garden to be weeded and planted. For recreation she had music and books, walking and riding; for company servants and friends, her father and John. And yet she felt empty, restless, increasingly irritable and embittered. She found herself looking with a curious urgent hunger into cradles in the houses she visited, achingly longing to hold a child in her arms. She found herself lying wakeful at night, her body tense and unsatisfied in some way she only half understood, though she had worked all day to what she had thought was the point of physical exhaustion. When she did sleep, she found herself troubled by dreams that left her shamed and disturbed, in which once or twice the man at Buxton played a part he had never played in life. Most of all she missed the potworks, the excitement over each new development, all the planning and dreaming. And Jos.

Every month brought back memories of times shared, perhaps never to come again: spring, and the bright May Day opening of the Ivy House works; summer, and memories of the Wakes fair; autumn, rides to Burslem and the days of work on the broken bowl. Pride would not let her ride there now when she sensed that Jos had no need of her; this time she would not go until he sought her out. But pride was a cheerless friend and brought her no comfort, for Jos did not seek her out.

The weeks passed. The gold and bronze and copper and flame of the trees sheltering the house at Spen Green faded and dimmed to brown, beige, grey; and gently, slowly, the leaves drifted down to lie silent on the earth, beaten there to a sodden pulp by the winter rains. Darkness came early and left late, as if reluctant to go away at all.

Christmas drew near, and the house at Spen Green was warm and perfumed with spices and fruit and roasting meat. Visitors came and took tea, or sipped mulled wine. Sarah entertained them on the spinet, or with talk that had no life in it. Two days before Christmas, bearing gifts, they went to Burslem.

As always for the whole Christmas season the Big House was crowded and full from dawn to dusk, and for half the night as well, with the uproarious good fellowship of the Wedgwood family Christmas. Aunt Mary – a full-blown Wedgwood after five years of marriage to Sarah's Uncle John – made very sure that no aspect of the hospitality should let down the family honour. 'You never know who might just drop in,' she was always saying, and so pies and jellies and hams, great joints of beef, lavish puddings – food for ten times the number of guests – were set before them at every meal, covering every inch of the vast cloth-spread surface of the great dining table. Fires roared, brass and furniture gleamed, the best porcelain and pottery and silver set off the splendour of the food, the air was heavy and scented with wood smoke and evergreen boughs. There were games and songs and music and dancing and laughter, and a constant succession of Wedgwood friends and relations coming and going. But no Jos.

And then on the evening of Christmas Day itself Sarah came downstairs to supper a little late, delayed by a finally uncontrollable burst of weeping of which she was thoroughly ashamed; and standing in the doorway to draw breath and smooth the skirts of her flowered silk gown and still the trembling of her mouth, she looked across the room and saw him.

He had his back to her and was deep in animated conversation with his brother Aaron and Sarah's uncle (by marriage), Jonah Malkin. Sarah's heart seemed to turn a somersault inside her and then steady a little to a quick frightened rhythm. She stood quite still, staring at his back, very fine in wine-coloured velvet: he was wearing a wig too in honour of the occasion. She wondered fleetingly if her own observations some while ago on the elegance of dress necessary to a rising master potter had taken effect at last; or whether it was rather the result of some other influence, some more recent advisor – some smooth polished gentleman of fashion perhaps? Suppressing the thought, because it would take her nowhere she wanted to go, she wondered what she

124

should do now. Go straight to him and greet him as if they had never been apart? Or go instead to help Aunt Mary at the table and wait until he should happen to notice her? What then if he did not; or, worse still, did so but ignored her afterwards?

She was still hesitating when he turned as if in answer to her doubt. There was no surprise on his face, no shame, no coolness: just his dear old familiar smile, as warm and light-hearted as if they had last met only yesterday. Then he gestured to her to join him. For a moment, hurt at his casual manner, she toyed with the thought of turning away as if she had not seen him; but her need for him was too great, and so she crossed the room to his side.

He did not seem to notice the severity of her expression. He simply reached out an arm and slid it about her waist, drawing her near, into the little circle about him. 'Here, Sally, come and tell Jonah I'm right about the turnpike road. I can't make him see that without good roads business can't grow as it should.'

No apology, no anger, no coolness – not only that, but Sarah realised with a little shock that Jos was completely unaware of the possibility that anything might have come between them at all. He had not even noticed their separation; or if he had it had seemed of no particular significance to him. Sarah tried just for a moment to feel indignant at being so taken for granted; but somehow she could not do so. He was Jos, and that was the way he was made, and she could do nothing to change it. Nor, now she stood near him with his arm warm on her waist, and very soon with her arm also about his slight body, would she have wished to do so. She realised with a force stronger than any she had known before how much she had missed him. Now that they were together, and she was complete again, she understood in full what absence from him had meant, how empty life had been without him. She would not let it happen again.

Later, when the other two men began to tire of turnpike roads, Jos led her to supper, talking still, and said as they ate, 'Come to the works after – I've something you must see.'

Her heart was singing as they walked through the empty streets in the windy darkness, the air chill on their glowing faces. She could almost believe that she had imagined they had been apart so long, so little did Jos himself seem to be aware of it. Yet, she thought, it was – perhaps – worth all the anguish to be so happy now.

The Brick House works had been closed down for Christmas; the buildings were dark and silent and deserted, the ovens cold. But Jos had a lantern and guided her through the silent yard to the shed nearest his own house. There he held the lantern high so that its glow fell on a shining new machine, set at a convenient height against the wall for a seated man to work it, its cogs and wheels gleaming and well-oiled, ready for use.

'There!' he said triumphantly. 'You weren't too sure about Cox, were you? But I told you he was full of ideas for improving the turning lathe.'

'But you took him on for his book-keeping,' Sarah reminded him; 'and it was that I was worried about.'

'I've not found any problems with that either,' Jos told her airily, which in view of his own deficiencies in that respect she did not find very reassuring; but she did not risk deflating him by commenting on it. He had in any case already put the weaknesses of William Cox out of his mind, and was moving closer to the machine. 'Look what we've done so far – it's a great step forward. You'll remember the problems with the old model?' Sarah nodded, for he had explained them to her in detail the last time they met, all those months ago. 'See here now—' He set the treadle working and the lathe began to turn smoothly, with the minimum of noise. Jos talked eagerly as he demonstrated with lavish gestures of the hands how the machine could be used to hold an unbaked pot whilst a precise pattern was incised upon it. Sarah watched intently, greatly impressed by the work that had been done at a time when she knew Jos had been more busy than ever in the potworks themselves. She could only guess at the night hours that must have been occupied with work on the machine; and be thankful that William Cox had after all proved of use.

The demonstration over, Jos ended more soberly, 'But there's work to be done on it still, a great deal of work – see how it needs attention at this joint.'

Sarah examined the faulty connection with interest, and then smiled. 'I'm sure you'll find a solution. You've done so much already.'

126

'I've sent for a French work on engine-turning, by one Plumier – would you have enough French to translate it for me?'

'I'd have to see it first,' said Sarah doubtfully. 'It depends how difficult it is. I didn't learn much about pots and machinery in my lessons.'

'There's always Bentley then,' said Jos, unconcerned, though Sarah felt a pang shoot through her. She was tempted to cry out, 'I'll do it however hard!' But she knew that was silly. Jos needed the best work, and if she could not supply that herself then she must be content for him to seek help elsewhere. She had other gifts to give in plenty.

'That's the least of my worries though,' Jos went on. 'The trouble is that every improvement costs so much, and there's so little capital to spare.'

'I thought business was good.' Her voice was calm, warmed with friendly interest; but an inescapable and yet startling thought was beginning to take shape in her head, crystallising into a curious sense of inevitability.

'So it is, and getting better. But if I'm really to expand as I should, I need to spend – and spend quite widely, on new equipment, new men, new clays. It all costs money. It's a vicious circle, Sally.'

'Then isn't it time we married, and you had my dowry at your disposal?'

The cheerfully matter-of-fact words fell at the last into silence, a silence so complete that Sarah began to be afraid at the effect they might have had. She stood watching Jos. He was half-turned away from her, one hand resting on the lathe; and he had become very still, as frozen and motionless as the now idle machine. She could not see his expression.

Then all at once he turned to look at her and he was trembling. 'Sally—' he murmured unsteadily, half-whispering, 'I . . . you . . .'

Sarah felt panic rise in her. It had seemed so natural to say what she had, the right and obvious solution to Jos's predicament. After all, they had always known that in time it would come to this, that one day her father's objections would have to be faced and overcome. Or had she been wrong and did Jos no longer see the necessity for it at all?

'I'm right, aren't I?' she asked quickly. 'Isn't that the sensible thing to do?'

'Sensible . . .!' He laughed suddenly, and flung his arms about her and enveloped her in a warm fierce hug, laughing and talking all at once in an outpouring of delight. 'Oh, Sally, what a fool I am – all this time, and we could have been wed long since. There's nothing to wait for now – we'll wear your Dad down soon enough, you'll see – and we can be together, always. I've wanted you that much these past months, and there was never time to ride and see you – yet I never thought – oh, Sally, I *do* love you . . .!' And as words failed him he kissed her.

All her fears slid from her. Joy bubbled through her, overflowing, warm, dancing in her eyes and her smile and her heart. She reached out and linked her arms about him and closed her eyes to savour better every sweet sensation of his embrace, strong and warm and safe, the one place where above all she was meant to be.

After a moment, suddenly, he drew back and seized her hand. 'We won't waste any more time – let's go and find your Dad now.'

Sarah gave a gurgle of laughter. 'On Christmas Day?'

'What better day, may I ask? "Good will to all men" – he *can't* turn us down today!' He reached for the lantern and they ran together, laughing, breathless, through the works, along the streets, past the brightly-lit festive houses to the open door of the Big House. There he paused and slid his arm about her to hug her quickly to him and smile, a warm secret smile, sharing delight and hope; and then they went in.

Uncle Thomas was crossing the hall. 'So that's where you two are! Don't tell me – you can't keep away from those works even on Christmas Day! We've been wanting you – come on now, or the dancing will be done before you've so much as tripped a measure.'

Sarah broke in on his hospitable chatter. 'Where's my father?'

'In there somewhere,' said Uncle Thomas vaguely, gesturing towards the parlour. 'What . . .'

But they did not pause to hear what else he had to say. When he looked round they had gone and were already halfway across the parlour, making their way towards the point where Richard Wedgwood stood in grave conversation with Aunt Mary. He looked round as they reached him, with

128

an unsmiling nod of acknowledgement. Jos laid a hand on his arm, quite unconcerned by the cool welcome, the presence of Aunt Mary and the crowding relatives about them.

'Sir – we want to be wed, Sally and I – and soon, very soon . . .'

Richard Wedgwood's shocked silence seemed to spread, sending out ripples into the company; the cheerful noise fell to a whisper and then faded to nothing, creating a circle of quiet about them. Sarah's father stared at the pair for a long time, as if trying to convince himself that they were indeed the daughter and cousin he knew, his eyes as cold and hard as pebbles. Then he said slowly, 'We shall be at home again in three days' time, on the twenty-eighth of December. I shall expect you on Thursday the twenty-ninth, at ten o'clock. We can discuss the matter then.' His tone implied only too clearly that his readiness to discuss the matter conceded nothing: the battle still lay ahead.

Jos, certain of ultimate victory, was unperturbed. He beamed and clasped the hand of his reluctant father-in-law-to-be and said, 'Thank you, sir – I shall be there.' And then, as Richard Wedgwood returned pointedly to his interrupted conversation, Jos smiled at Sarah and without warning suddenly pulled her after him, through the grinning throng of relations and into the hall, to where, just outside the parlour door and in full view of everyone, hung the great kissing bunch of holly, mistletoe and scarlet ribbons. And beneath it, in a public declaration of intent, Jos gathered Sarah into his arms and kissed her long and thoroughly.

It took two weeks to talk Richard Wedgwood into a grudging acceptance that if his daughter was ever to marry – a prospect which he did not welcome but which he was fond enough of her to realise was desirable – then her cousin Josiah must be her husband.

Sarah, knowing her father too well, left all the talking to Jos but gave him the full benefit of her advice as to the tactics most likely to succeed. And so Jos cajoled and argued and finally negotiated with a stubborn shrewdness which startled his future father-in-law and in time brought the two men to a considerable degree of understanding. Richard Wedgwood was forced to admit that despite all his predictions Jos had

129

eventually made something of his life and was no longer the totally ineligible suitor which Richard had for so long believed him to be. He was not in any sense well-to-do, his health was unreliable and he showed no signs of ever being more than a competent master potter – and Richard had never envisaged Sarah married to a master potter. But if that was what she wanted she could do worse, he had to acknowledge: Jos was making enough to keep himself and a wife – and any children – in reasonable security; and Sarah's dowry, used wisely (Sarah, he knew, would see to that), would help to expand an already prospering business. In an uncertain world a slump in trade, a misjudgement, an accident unforeseen and unplanned for, could easily overthrow any gains made in years of struggle, but it was not possible to cushion Sarah against every contingency. Besides, it had become transparently obvious that Jos cared for Sarah and valued her as highly as he did himself, and that he could be trusted to look after her as well as lay within his power. Once he accepted the situation, Richard Wedgwood's only concern was to strike the best bargain he could with the young man.

Wednesday, 25 January 1764, was a cold crisp bright day. Sarah had trimmed her best gold brocade gown with amber ribbon, and made a pretty lace cap to cover her bound-up hair. With a posy of holly and Christmas roses in her hand she walked up the aisle of Astbury church on her father's arm to where Jos waited in his Christmas coat and fine new bob wig. He turned to smile at her as she came to stand beside him in all her bridal festiveness.

The ceremony was quiet, solemn and soon over. After wards they rode back to Spen Green across the snowy fields together with the now noisy congregation of Wedgwood friends and relations for feasting and dancing until close on nightfall. And then Sarah changed into her riding habit and mounted pillion behind Jos on the faithful Taffy for the journey to Burslem. Those guests who were going home that way – which was the majority – formed a noisy and convivial escort all the way to the sober tidy front of the Brick House. For a little while, there was jostling and joking and a ribald song or two, sung in teasing snatches; and then at last the door closed and Jos turned to face her, and they were alone. It seemed all at once very quiet.

Sarah felt her heart beat fiercely, not with fear, but with a sudden strangeness, excitement, anticipation. She knew, without a clear understanding, that they stood at a turning point, that this moment along with the vows exchanged this morning marked the beginning of their married life. Other women in her position would already have received a word or two of advice from their mothers, but Sarah's mother was dead so there had been no one to give her advice. She knew that marriage meant some union closer than the brief sweetness of kissing, something that led often if not inevitably to the birth of children. She had seen how the animals in the fields mated and produced their young. She sensed that somehow tonight with Jos she would bring to an end all the undefined longings that had so often tormented her, the restlessness, the uneasy dreams. She felt suddenly shy and stood, head bent, waiting for what would come.

Jos reached out and drew her into his arms. She could feel his breathing quicken, knew that he was trembling a little. He too was shy then, unsure of himself.

'Sally – my wife . . .' he whispered, his mouth warm on her hair. 'Come upstairs now.'

They went together to the room where someone had lit a fire and turned back the sheets on the square curtained bed. There was ale and bread and cheese on a table, but neither of them was hungry. Instead Jos held her again and began to kiss her fiercely, with a need that stirred all the passion in her to life. She felt his hands move down her body, tugging with clumsy eagerness at the hooks of her bodice, steering her gently back towards the bed until they half-fell on to it. With her arms about him she pulled him closer to her, instinct and passion supplying the knowledge she lacked of what her body needed now. She whispered his name again and again, full of longing and love.

And then, somehow, it was over, almost it seemed to her before it had begun. Contented, relaxed, smiling, he had drawn away to lie at her side with his arm about her, lazily stroking her hair. 'My Sally . . . my dear wife . . . my dearest and only love . . .' his voice murmured soothingly in her ear. 'You are the first, you know, and always will be.' But

131

she was not soothed, only a little comforted for what had not in the event brought her to the completion she had longed for. She felt disappointed in some way she could not have defined. She felt, obscurely, that this union of their bodies should have meant more to her, should have brought her to some kind of joy: he had cried out as if in ecstasy, but for her there had been none. For a moment she had felt it was near, just out of reach , but if so it had in the end eluded her.

But they were together now, man and wife at last after the long years of hope and struggle and patient waiting. Nothing could take that from them; and as they drifted into sleep held in one another's arms it was that sense of homecoming, however incomplete, which consoled Sarah and let her rest.

CHAPTER SEVEN

1765 (I)

For five days Jos had been wild with excitement, as restless and exhilarated as the hares leaping on the moors in the March winds. Sarah bore his mood with patience, suppressing her irritation and concealing too the lesser tumult of her own emotions.

It would have been so much easier to bear if little Susannah, until now the sunniest and most peaceful of infants, had not coincidentally taken it into her head to lie wakeful and crying for half of each night. Perhaps it was not wholly a coincidence; perhaps she sensed that there was something in the air and was making sure that she would not be forgotten in the excitement. Whatever the reason, she had chosen this time of all times to change her orderly routine to a new and disruptive pattern.

By day, of course, she slept soundly, waking only with admirable regularity for the necessary feeds; but no sooner were Jos and Sarah stretched exhausted on their bed and the candle extinguished than their first-born – three months old by now – would begin to wail loudly into the night. She was not hungry – that was always Sarah's first thought; nor wet – the second possibility; nor, as far as her mother could see, in any pain or discomfort. On the contrary, the moment an anxious face appeared above her carved wooden cradle she would close her mouth, open her blue eyes wider than ever and give a crow of delight, reaching tiny hands happily towards the candlelit face.

'Bless my little Sukey – she only wants to play!' Jos had cooed at her, when one night her crying had woken him too. It was all right for him, Sarah thought with the sourness of exhaustion. For the most part he slept through the cries of rage which ensued when Susannah, fed and changed and rocked and sung to, and apparently sleeping at last, was left alone as her weary mother crept back to bed.

It was not as if Sarah could make up for the wakeful nights by resting during the day, for she was far too busy. Not that she had many domestic duties to perform: very early in their marriage Jos had made sure of that. She had been concerned that her dowry should be used only for the expansion of the potworks and not to provide any comforts for herself. She would spin wool for their clothes, she insisted, brew the beer, bake their bread, prepare their meals from the simplest of ingredients, clean the house, grow the vegetables, care for the hens, milk the cow, gather kindling for the fires and so on and so on. But after a month of this Jos stormed in as she sat at her spinning wheel and said firmly, 'Into the lumber room with that thing, Sally – I need a wife, not a maid-of-all-work, and you're never free when I want you. We can get servants to do all this – we're not quite paupers you know.'

When she tried to protest that paupers or not they needed every penny they could spare for the works he hugged her and said, 'Sally love, the works won't thrive without you, however much is spent on them, so we'll have no more argument about it.'

Since what he said was exactly in tune with her inclinations, Sarah consigned most of the domestic tasks to Nan Povey and Betty Wood, two Burslem girls newly employed to run the house and look after the livestock, and confined herself to little more than supervising them when necessary. And for the rest of the time she devoted herself to the work she loved best, as Jos's friend and helpmate and partner. He taught her the code in which he recorded the results of his experiments (to prevent anyone from carrying details of his findings to a rival potworks, as he explained to Sarah), and she installed herself at his side as he worked, noting every detail in the ledger and giving her opinion when asked.

When Jos was not experimenting there were accounts to be kept, bills to be sent out or paid, orders taken. And on the many occasions when Jos was busy with plans to open a new turnpike road between Leek and Newcastle, or with his newer grander scheme for a canal system to link the Trent to the Mersey, for which he was trying to raise support amongst the gentry and manufacturers, then Sarah was needed at the works to supervise Tom Byerley in the office – or, as Jos grandly called it, the counting house. His nephew, seventeen

134

now, was proving a source of anxiety both to his doting mother Margaret, running her own little milliner's shop in Newcastle under Lyme, and to his uncle whose high hopes for him had consistently failed to be realised. The boy was lively, intelligent and good-natured, and Jos thought it natural and right that he should be groomed for a responsible position within the expanding pottery business. His more prosperous uncles had seen that he was well-educated, and on leaving school it was intended that he should begin work at Burslem.

Unfortunately young Tom, returning from a visit to Bentley in Liverpool with his imagination set alight, had decided he was to be a writer – poetry, novels, he did not mind what, but he had dreams of going to London and setting up in some attic lodging, working away through the night by the dim glow of a single candle stub. Jos was horrified and told him so in no uncertain terms. Bentley cast a calmer eye over some examples of Tom's work sent to him by his friend, counselled patience, and very gently and kindly suggested to Tom that from the evidence he had seen a literary future was not perhaps one he ought to consider. After a little while, his dreams abandoned, Tom settled down in the counting house to learn his trade under Sarah's guidance. 'He's doing well,' said Jos happily. 'He's seen the sense of it at last.'

He spoke too soon. Anxious that the boy should see how John Wedgwood worked on behalf of the pottery in London, Jos sent him to stay with his other uncle there. Tom returned two months after Susannah's birth with his head full of the excitements of London. And of one in particular.

'You should have seen Powell as King Lear, Aunt Sarah,' he would say. 'Such anguish, such heart rending grief. You should have heard him say, "We two alone will sing like birds i' the cage."' He declaimed the words with such emphasis that Sarah had to repress a giggle.

Another day it was, 'Oh, Aunt Sarah, Miss Pope is the most delightful actress there ever was – sweet and sprightly and so alive – and she's only twenty-two even now. She was on the stage first at fourteen – just think of it!' Or else, 'There is nothing like the theatre you know, Aunt Sarah.'

It was Sarah's unspoken opinion that he had seen rather too

many plays whilst in London; but then perhaps no one had been able to prevent him from doing so. Certainly his mind was on little else at present. She would go into the counting house and find him deep in thought, gazing absently into some visionary distance, very far away indeed from mundane considerations of income and expenditure. It was hard to make him give any attention to his work at all. Sarah, trying to be patient and remembering what it was like to be seventeen and full of dreams, listened to his raptures and did most of the work herself. So much, she thought, for young Tom being trained to fill the place left vacant by William Cox, now – to her relief – too busy elsewhere in the works to be spared for book-keeping. Tom Wedgwood too had no time to give to office work; and when business called him away from Burslem, Sarah would find herself with the men to supervise as well.

Then on a cold day in early January this new living creature had come into their lives and brought inexpressible joy and yet another complicated strand to be woven into the days which were never long enough.

And now, just when Susannah had taken it into that little golden downy head of hers to keep her Mama wakeful all night, they had news that at long last Mr Thomas Bentley, merchant of Liverpool, was to visit them. He planned to stay one night at Burslem on his way home from a trip to London as representative to parliament for the Liverpool corporation.

'I don't want to meet him!' Sarah thought resentfully, as she helped Nan clean and polish the spare bedroom, and went over the meals with Betty, and listened endlessly to Jos's flow of talk – plans for them to do this, talk of that. 'Oh, and he will like to see the lathe – we've talked of it so much. And you must tell him what you said to me about his draft for the canal pamphlet – there wasn't time to write it all.' No time, Sarah thought, when he seemed to do nothing but write, sitting at his desk long into the night or before dawn writing and writing his thoughts to that distant friend. Their marriage had changed nothing; Bentley was still between them.

No, thought Sarah with compunction, that's not fair. She herself was at last where she had always longed to be, a partner with Jos in the great enterprise of his life, sharing with him the experiences of every working day. Whatever little disappointments there might be she knew she could ask little more of marriage than she had already; and since perfection was not possible in this life then she was as near to it as she was ever likely to come, with the added consolation that Jos clearly thought they had achieved it. 'Accept the best respects of two married lovers, happy as this world can make them,' he had ended one of his letters to Bentley not long after their marriage. Even his troublesome knee, which seemed these days to be never without pain and was often inflamed enough to prevent him from walking on it at all, did not seem to mar his happiness.

And now that his best friend and his wife were to meet at last he felt that his cup was overflowing with delight. He could ask for no more; and he could scarcely contain himself for excitement.

The night before their guest's arrival Jos slept like a child – or like most children, with the exception of his own daughter who kept her mother hanging over the cradle until dawn and ensured that Sarah faced that important day in a haze of weariness.

Jos, excited and preoccupied, seemed to notice nothing, and hurried away after breakfast to give what remained of his attention to the works. Sarah swallowed as much of her breakfast as she could, a little bread and ale – only occasionally did they begin the day with the more fashionable (and expensive) tea which she had been used to at Spen Green – and then she made her way to the kitchen to make sure that everything was progressing as it should.

She found Betty at the pump just outside the kitchen door, vigorously filling a bucket. The girl smiled as she came nearer and straightened, pausing for a moment 'I've got the pies done already, madam,' she said cheerfully, 'and there's just the fish to clean, and then it's all done that can be until it's time to put the meat on to roast.' Her round rosy face beamed reassurance and youthful competence. Betty was only fourteen and orphaned – and therefore little burden on their slender resources since the parish authorities had been only too glad to find her a position – but she loved cooking, and if the results were not always entirely successful they were rarely completely disastrous, and she was improving all the time. They had been amazingly fortunate in finding her; just as they had been with Nan, who was good-natured and willing and loved small children. Sarah always knew Susannah was in good hands when she herself was busy.

Since the house did not seem to need her supervision, Sarah pulled on her cloak and set out for the office. Tom Byerley had gone on business to Birmingham today, a little resentful that he would thus have no chance of seeing again his hero Bentley; but Sarah was relieved that she would not have his theatrical raptures to contend with on top of everything else.

Somewhere above the choking smoke of Burslem's forty or so potworks the sun was shining. Now and then a stronger gust of the frisky wind let in a gleam of light through the gloom, silvering the puddles in the holes in the solid clay surface of the road, and the shine like the slip that the potters used which coated the cobbles in the yard: Jos had seen that the cobbles were laid so that, when one day improved roads allowed wheeled traffic into the town, the carts and wagons would be able to drive comfortably right up to the Wedgwood works. The tiny occasional shafts of light were all that brightened the grey gloom of the day, letting in a breath of freshness to counter the gritty dust that seemed to fill nose and throat and lungs; and to counter too the smell which was always there underlying all the other smells of the town, the stench of death and decay from the churchyard. It was the one disadvantage the Brick House works had over Jos's first inadequate establishment at Ivy House – they were further down the hill, almost on a level with the church whose squat tower was just visible over the roof tops between.

Before she came to live here, loving the place so much for all it had to offer, Sarah had not realised how much time Burslem spent in a self-induced twilight. Dreaming only of being here with Jos she had not guessed how much she would find herself longing for clear air and blue skies, for summer sun and the crisp bright winter days; and for the feel of something else underfoot than the heavy clay which stuck in great wedges to every kind of footwear. She did not even now wish herself elsewhere, for where Jos was, and the works, was her home; but she did regret sometimes that there was hardly ever time to ride out on the hills or in the woods away from the smoke and the grime.

Today she wondered fleetingly what Jos's fine gentleman of a friend would make of this place: she imagined him picking his way with shuddering horror through the mud, a scented handkerchief held to his painfully assaulted nose. But that vision could not somehow be made to fit with Jos – how could any friend of his be affected or over-fastidious? Except that Jos in his warmth and simplicity of character was too ready to trust, too slow to see the faults which he did not share in other men. It was she who had the experience and subtlety and a certain necessary cynicism.

Some faults though Jos did see, and with them he had no patience at all. His voice reached her now, raised in fury at some recalcitrant workman in the shed where the pots were glazed. Perhaps the man had dipped a pot unevenly; perhaps he had come late to work, long after the bell had rung to summon him – the bell in its turret above the works had been Jos's contribution to punctuality, as something more readily audible than the customary horn; perhaps he had been absent yesterday, celebrating 'St Monday' as did workmen all over England, extending the Sunday break from work as the mood took them; perhaps he had muddied the vats of glaze with clay or dirt, or failed to wash his hands afterwards at the bucket placed by the door – Jos had so many rules for his works, and most of them quite alien to the men who worked for him, used as they were to the old easy-going haphazard ways which had been good enough for generations of men before them. When Jos was present – or they thought he might be – the rules were for the most part obeyed: Jos's anger was already legendary, and feared. In his absence things reverted almost wholly to normal, despite all Tom Wedgwood's efforts to the contrary. Tom or Sarah herself had then to stand over a man to make sure that he kept to the rules, and of course they could not be everywhere at once.

Sarah felt too tired today to face any unpleasantness. She had wanted to ask Jos about an account which she thought he had told her was paid, though no one seemed to have recorded the payment, but instead she went to the office and closed the door and tried to concentrate on the bills and letters and columns of figures.

In the end though, the other tasks done and that uncompleted matter shouting at her for attention, she did go in search of Jos. She found him in the throwing shed, standing by the wheel watching Sam Hunter, a young man recently employed, as he worked on a vase: there was, she thought, both approval and envy in his expression. She laid a hand on his arm. 'Jos, that account . . .'

He turned sharply, as if she had startled him, looked puzzled for a moment and then nodded. 'I'll come.'

They walked together to the office. 'Bit of a know-all that one,' he commented as they went. 'Thinks he can improve on my designs – and only just out of his apprenticeship himself. A good craftsman, but he'll need some watching.'

Sarah, smiling to herself, wondered if once Thomas Alders had spoken in just such terms of Jos; but she said nothing. After all, Jos had never had Samuel Hunter's truculent nature, which made him a difficult man to handle in spite of his gifts. Jos needed men like Hunter, but if they would not work his way he could achieve nothing.

The question of the account was quickly settled and Jos, anxious to check that Sam was now following his instructions to the letter, turned to go: but at the door he paused and glanced round. 'You look tired, Sally,' he said, as if the realization had only just penetrated his consciousness.

'Of course I do,' she retorted rather crossly. 'I was up all night with Susannah.'

He came back to her and laid a hand on her shoulder. 'You lie down a little this afternoon. I'm not going for Bentley until seven – that gives you plenty of time to rest.'

'But there's the dinner service to be packed for Sir William Meredith – you know there's likely to be damage if the men aren't supervised, and Tom's got enough to do without that.'

'Then I'll see to it, of course. I can spare a moment or two.'

Sarah frowned worriedly. 'I don't want you on your feet longer than need be. You've had more than your share of trouble with that knee lately. I don't want it to flare up again.'

Jos grinned. 'Nor do I – but it's behaving itself at present. It left me alone all night, unlike our Sukey. Now don't argue – you go and rest.' Having decided the matter he once more turned to go, but Sarah called after him.

'Jos—' He looked round. 'What did Dr Darwin say to you the other day?' Erasmus Darwin was a fellow enthusiast for the projected Grand Trunk canal, a warm, lively, opinionated man who experimented with mechanical devices and wrote poetry with the same enthusiasm as he chased after any interesting idea; but it was for his unquestioned skill as a doctor that Jos had visited their new friend at his Lichfield home a week ago.

'I told you didn't I?'

'You were very evasive,' Sarah said severely. 'You fobbed me off with some nonsense or other. But I know you better than that. I'd have pursued the matter then if there hadn't been so many other things to do.'

'If you must know then, he said the only final and certain cure was amputation.'

There was a little silence. Sarah knew she had gone white. 'Jos, that's terrible . . .' she whispered after a moment. Jos shrugged; if he had felt the shock of it at first it had passed by now.

'I don't give up hope of something a bit less drastic. Nor to be fair does Darwin. Don't let it trouble you – go and rest.'

'As if I could rest after that,' Sarah thought as she made her way obediently to the bedroom. But perhaps Jos's nonchalance had reassured her more than she knew, for it was not his problems which kept her tense and wakeful. She worried instead about the supper, under preparation downstairs (Jos would mind so much if it was not of the very best); and she kept remembering small tasks not done. There would be ample time and there was nothing vital requiring her attention, but her restless body would not be made to believe it and relax.

At last, hot, tired and uncomfortable, she gave up the attempt to sleep, fed the wailing Susannah, and began to dress. By now, she realised, Jos would already have left for Newcastle to meet the London coach. He would probably not be home for an hour yet, but she felt she would need all that time if she was to make herself presentable. Looking in the mirror she gazed ruefully at the face pallid with exhaustion, the shadowed eyes and discontented mouth: so much for the happy bride, the fulfilled young mother.

She selected a gown of soft blue wool, a simple countrified garment without hoops which she often wore when working in house or garden or about the works; its colour suited her and would help to emphasise any little warmth left in her complexion. She had intended to wear her best gown of gold brocade but, although magnificent when happiness and health gave life to her face, it would today only have aged her, drawing attention to the lines of exhaustion and the haggard greyness.

She brushed her red-brown hair and pinned it close to her head, and put in place the little matronly white lace cap she kept for Sundays and holidays: and then she looked again in the mirror. The unsophisticated creature (nose too long, mouth too wide) looking back at her bore little resemblance to the bride that Jos would want his friend to see as he stepped over the threshold, but it would have to do. She could not bring herself to care very much how she looked.

Once ready, she made her way to the kitchen to see how Betty was faring. She was relieved to find that all was going smoothly there, the smell of roasting meat flowing appetisingly from the spit over the fire, pies and jellies at exactly the right stage of preparation, an air of unhurried efficiency filling the room. In the dining room, too, Nan had seen that everything was exactly as it should be: the table set with one of Jos's finest creamware services, and the silver which had been a wedding gift from the Big House uncles, new candles set in the sconces, tinder box ready by the door.

Upstairs, Susannah, as if repenting her misdeeds of last night, was sleeping soundly, the picture of angelic innocence in her cradle by the big bed. 'Without doubt,' thought Sarah with a wry smile, 'she's making sure of her sleep now so that she'll be really wide awake through the night hours.'

She cast a final housewifely eye over the guest room – fresh primroses on the mantelpiece above the log fire cheerfully burning, the best embroidered bedspread upon the bed, the simple furniture gleaming with polish.

What *was* he like, this friend the thought of whom filled so many of Jos's waking hours? She knew all at once that she had been wrong: she did after all want to meet him. Not because Jos wanted it, not because it was her duty to do so, but simply from curiosity to know what manner of man could so have charmed Jos that three years after their first meeting his feelings were, if anything, warmer and deeper than ever.

The clatter of hooves on cobbles reached her ears at last: two riders coming to a halt in the yard beside the house. She was suddenly as nervous as a young girl at her first meeting with strangers, her heart thudding furiously against her ribs, her hands trembling. She smoothed an imaginary stray wisp of hair and pulled her skirts into shape, and drew a deep steadying breath before setting off slowly down the stairs.

She heard Jos's voice just outside the front door, excited, in full flow; and a quieter voice replying with necessary brevity. She halted halfway down the stairs, her eyes on the door, waiting. She heard the handle turn, saw it pushed wide, letting in the last soft daylight; and Jos ushered in his friend.

He was about medium height, though beside Jos he looked taller; a prosperous young man whose well-made dark travelling cloak half concealed a coat of some rich red material. From the cloak's heavy folds emerged the pale outline of a hand, long fine fingers holding a hat. For an instant Sarah had one of those curious, inexplicable sensations of recognition: this is a repetition, I have seen this before, the hand and the hat. But then it was gone and the man moved forward into the light of the hall candle. She looked down on dark hair, unpowdered, receding a little from a high forehead – then he raised his head and smiled, a swift warm smile that lit his whole face to the depths of his dark eyes.

'I *have* seen him before,' she thought. 'Now where – where?' She wondered if she saw in his expression some similar thought pass briefly; but he simply bowed, while behind him Jos said, 'My wife – my Sally . . .'

'Your servant, Mrs Wedgwood. I have long wanted to meet you. Your husband has told me so much . . .' The voice was deep, quiet but well-modulated; a musical voice, resonant and educated.

'A smooth polished sort of man,' thought Sarah behind her polite smile, as she completed her descent of the stairs. 'Just as I thought – he knows how to charm, after a fashion. But I know more than Jos about smooth charmers – I shan't be taken in.' And all the time behind her resolution not to be won over lurked the incessant niggling question, 'Where have we met before?'

'You are welcome, Mr Bentley,' she said, her voice cool and a little clipped: she sensed that Jos was disappointed at its lack of warmth. 'Please come into the parlour – Nan here will

143

take your cloak . . .' The maid stepped forward from where she had been hovering in the shadows. 'There is a good fire in here – come in and warm yourself. I know how cold one becomes, sitting a long time in a coach, and the wind is chilly today . . .'

She led the way, every inch the courteous hostess; but with the polite words forming an impenetrable shield against the charm which had so won Jos, and which already she knew was real enough, almost tangible.

And behind the shield the flocking questions worried at her consciousness, 'Where have we met? Did he come to Spen Green once to see my father – a business friend perhaps? I've never been to Liverpool, so it couldn't have been there. Or am I wrong, and we haven't met at all – perhaps I'm mistaken . . .'

She glanced at him, standing now by the fire, and found that he was watching her with the same furtively questioning expression that she knew she must have. As their eyes met he looked away again, and made some inconsequential remark to Jos. She was not mistaken then – only it seemed he was as puzzled as she. She was almost tempted to question him, claiming some prior acquaintance; but that would be tantamount to a friendly approach, and she had resolved to keep her distance. Instead she busied herself pouring wine for the men, and then left them together while she went to supervise the final preparations for supper.

Torn between curiosity and mistrust, Sarah found herself reduced almost to silence while they ate. The food was perfectly cooked, the setting cheerful, and Jos talked happily of the mutual friends Bentley had met in London; the longer visit he must pay them very soon; the progress of the canal scheme; and he vainly tried to draw Sarah out, make her take some part in a conversation which became steadily more one-sided, for even Bentley seemed to have little to say. Jos, who had hoped for so much from this meeting between the two people – as he told Sarah – whom he loved best in all the world, struggled with his disappointment and beneath his cheerful flow of talk cast an occasional covert disapproving glance at his wife.

At last, to Sarah's relief, the moment came for her to retire to the parlour and leave the men to their drinking; or more particularly, in this case, their pipes of tobacco. She murmured her excuses, and rose to her feet; and as she did so Bentley broke in swiftly, 'Please, Mrs Wedgwood, don't so break up our little gathering – if you must retire, then let us come with you. What do you say, Josiah?'

'I'm all for it,' said Jos, cheered by this indication that his wife had made a better impression on his friend than seemed possible; and perhaps hoping that in the greater comfort and informality of the parlour Sarah's inexplicable mood might evaporate.

The parlour was small, but furnished with several comfortable chairs, a little table, a writing desk, and Sarah's spinet, firmly closed since she had little time to play these days. It was towards that favourite instrument that Bentley moved as soon as he entered the room, appreciatively fingering the smooth inlaid wood.

'Ah now, Mrs Wedgwood, I'm sure you play . . .' The words fell away into silence. His eyes met Sarah's, and Sarah felt a fiery colour flood her face. So that was it!

'I *knew* we had met before!' Bentley exclaimed. 'I was sure of it, but I could not for the life of me remember. That was it, wasn't it? Buxton, four – no five years ago. We talked of music then – that's what brought it back. Music,' he added, suddenly grave, 'and much else.'

Steadily she returned his gaze, caught in a momentary stillness not unlike that – she remembered now – which had held her in the wood all those years ago. 'Yes,' she said quietly.

They stood looking at one another, saying nothing; but the barriers had gone. He was Jos's friend, but hers first. When Jos had come home from Liverpool with a glow in his eyes and talked of Bentley, then that was only to be expected for she had felt it too – the excitement, the sense of kinship and for her, as a woman, something more. Thomas Bentley, who could stir the heart and at the same time lead the imagination out beyond any point it had reached before – yes, she understood Jos, and Tom Byerley – and she was just a little afraid.

What Jos thought of the silence between them, or if he noticed it, she did not know; for he broke in on it joyfully, 'So you know each other already! What a strange thing! Tell me how it happened . . .'

His eyes never leaving Sarah, though with her head bent she

145

only felt them there, Bentley explained, 'It was the year after Hannah died, my first visit to Buxton since then. The day before I left I took a walk to a place we had both once loved. I was in a black despairing mood, seeking only solitude; but I found – your wife – there. We somehow never thought to exchange names. But she – oh, I can never fully explain – she was more than a friend to that stranger intruding on her peace. For that I can never thank her enough.'

Jos beamed delightedly. 'That's my Sally, bless her. There's no one like her in trouble.' Sarah felt Jos's arm slide about her and looked round at him, grateful for the diversion. 'So you had a good talk, like all the talks we've had so often?'

'Something like,' said Bentley with a smile; but also, Sarah thought, with a hint of reserve.

Jos drew Sarah to the fireside, reaching out a hand to summon his friend to come too. 'This is all I could wish – that you two should love each other as I love you both. It's what I've always wanted, more than anything.'

Bentley smiled. 'That calls for a song then, does it not. Will you play, Mrs Wedgwood?'

'Of course she will,' Jos agreed happily; and so Sarah went to the spinet, and opened it, and conferred with Bentley over the pile of music upon it; and they chose – or he chose, for she left the choice to him – Handel's lovely 'Where'er you walk'. He sang to her accompaniment in a warm rich baritone, the kind of voice she would have expected from hearing him speak. As he sang he looked at her, as if he meant to say that it was she who brightened the paths along which she walked. George Lathom used to watch her meaningfully while he sang – something he did only as a means to an end, and then not well – but Bentley's manner was nothing like that; rather it was tender, that of a man making a graceful compliment to a woman he could only respect and honour. Jos watched them, clearly delighted that they should be suddenly so at ease together. Humbly, Sarah realised there was no trace of jealousy in his expression; loving, he wanted only to share that love. So for him it was the greatest joy that he could share Bentley's friendship with Sarah, as he had always shared everything. Perhaps, she thought, that was why the two of them had been brought together at Buxton, to make it possible for them to be friends now.

They sang two or three more songs with Jos as an approving if uncritical audience, and then returned to the fireside and talked. Sarah had never known such talk or felt time pass so quickly. There was no sense that she as a woman must have no part in it, for she was accepted as one of them, without whom the company would have been incomplete. All the things Jos had told her about, the subjects dear to Bentley's heart and so also to his, were discussed: harmony in religion and the non-denominational chapel for which he was working; the importance of education for women as well as men; the need for integrity and independence in public life; the possibility of reclaiming wasteland so that the unemployed could work and support themselves by growing food; the evil of wealth and prosperity founded on the obscenity of the slave trade.

'But does not Liverpool owe its very existence almost to the slave trade?' Sarah asked, moved by the vehemence of his argument.

'Certainly it does – but better to be poor than rich by such means, don't you agree?'

'I'm sure you're right, though I know very little about it, I'm afraid.' She smiled. 'I can't imagine you're the most popular man in Liverpool.'

'Ah, but he is, amongst the people who matter,' Jos put in. 'When the corporation wants a spokesman in London it sends Bentley, as you see. And even his enemies can't help liking him.' Bentley laughed and repudiated the compliment, but Sarah thought it was probably true. She had found him attractive at Buxton, wrapped up though he was in his grief for his wife. Now, the worst pain over, himself again, his charm was almost overwhelming. There was the grace of bearing and manner, the courtesy, the sweetness of his smile, the genuine modesty that went with a breadth of knowledge and intellect which was exhilarating. He talked of things of which she knew nothing, and she learned from him; but there was neither pomposity nor arrogance in his manner, and nothing to make her feel inadequate.

They lost all sense of time passing, so much indeed that when Susannah's wailing reached them from upstairs it took them by surprise for they had not realised it was so late.

'Bless her little heart, she doesn't want to be left out of our good company!' said Jos.

'At least she hasn't waited until we'd gone to bed,' commented Sarah, glancing at the grandfather clock in the corner of the room. 'Good gracious me, she has after all – she's right on time. I hadn't realised it was so late. It's one o'clock.' She rose to her feet. 'Excuse me, gentlemen.'

'Bring her down, Sally. I'm sure Bentley would like to see the little maid – and maybe she'll sleep the better for it afterwards.'

'At least he'll know who to blame if she keeps him awake for the rest of the night,' Sarah retorted with a laugh as she left the room.

As usual, Susannah greeted her arrival with a beatific smile and an entrancing gurgle. 'Little monkey that you are!' Sarah told her as she lifted her from the cradle and wrapped her in a shawl.

Downstairs Bentley came to meet her holding out his hands. 'Let me take the child – if you'll trust her to me that is.'

It was neither courtesy nor a wish to flatter her that made him ask so eagerly. Sarah remembered the baby who had died with its mother and was touched by the emotion on Bentley's face. Very gently, carefully, he took Susannah into his arms and stood smiling down at her, wholly absorbed as if he had forgotten everything else.

After a time he looked up, remembering where he was, and then, still carrying the child, sat down again near the fire. 'She is beautiful, a credit to you both.'

Jos reached over and held out his forefinger, so that his daughter's tiny fist closed about it. 'The best little girl there ever was,' he agreed happily.

Sarah, standing by the door, watched the two men bent dotingly over the smiling child. She felt a sudden twist of fear; Susannah was so tiny, so vulnerable. So many things could happen to a child long before it grew to adulthood – if it grew up at all – and even then there was so much that could hurt and maim and destroy. The whole of life was fraught with danger – the more so if one loved so generously, so freely, so trustingly as did Jos. She knew then that it was for him she feared, more than any of them: which was strange, tonight, when he seemed so very secure in his happiness.

She went to them and reached down to take the child. 'I

148

must go and feed her now, and see if she'll sleep, or we'll none of us be up in the morning.' As Bentley returned Susannah to her his eyes met hers for a moment, steadily. She felt again that heightened awareness of him and that sense of all else fading to nothing. She said quickly, 'I'll say goodnight then – I trust you'll sleep well.'

'Thank you – and goodnight.' He stood up and held the door open for her, and as she passed said, 'Josiah is a fortunate man.'

'So are we both, in our friend,' she returned. But she knew as she mounted the stairs in the dim light of the hall candles that she had spoken almost defensively, because she wanted the words to be true, so far and no further; and because she did not want to look below the surface to the unease that lay there.

She sat in the dark in their bedroom with Susannah sucking noisily at her breast and kneading with contented little hands, and told herself it had been a good evening, the first she hoped of many. No longer would she feel that Jos's friend stood between them, for now she knew he was her friend too: that chance meeting in Buxton had made it possible. No longer was any part of Jos's life closed to her, for they shared everything.

Susannah had been asleep for some time when Jos came to bed at last, though Sarah was still lying wakeful in the dark. She heard him undress without lighting the candle, felt the chill draught of air as he slid carefully beneath the blankets and turned on his side facing her. 'I'm awake,' she whispered, and he drew her into his arms. She nestled close, her head bent beneath his chin; she felt the need tonight for a safe refuge.

'That was a good evening,' he murmured into her hair. 'Though you were very quiet at supper – trying to remember where you'd met, I suppose.'

'Yes.'

'Strange, that – and we none of us guessed. I'm glad though. I did so want you to be friends. You do like him don't you?'

'Yes, of course.'

He began sleepily to make love to her. Sarah, sleepy too, found her mind wandering into dreams. The man warm between her thighs was watching her with dark eyes, the hand on her breast was pale, long-fingered, fine; passion caught her up, carried her towards a goal long sought and never found – and then with a jolt she came back to reality, and to a shameful realisation of where her imagination was leading her. She laid her hands on Jos's warm brown hair, and knew he had once again reached that unknown, undiscovered place and left her outside its closed door.

But he was her dear and she loved him. As he moved aside she kissed him and murmured goodnight, and lay for a long time with closed eyes, listening as his breathing settled into the deep even rhythm of a man soundly asleep. She found herself wishing that Susannah would wake and so give her some excuse to get up and walk about, and try through activity to still the restlessness that kept her wakeful. But tonight Susannah slept on in her cradle and it was Sarah alone who saw the dawn light creep into the room.

CHAPTER EIGHT

1765 (II)

'Mr Smallwood?' The stocky little man turned from the window and stared at her, as if her arrival was not wholly welcome. 'I'm afraid my husband is away from home today, and so is Mr Thomas Wedgwood. How can I help you?'

'When'll he be back then?' the man asked testily.

Sarah was tired, very tired. Susannah had not yet outgrown her wakeful nights; she had kept it up now for three months, and in her most gloomy moments Sarah feared she might do so for ever. And Sarah had been up early today to see Jos on his way. She had then at last found time to spend with Tom Byerley and his accounts – a thankless task at the best of times; and to lock away the newly fired clay samples which Jos had been working on a week ago; and had been about to arrange for the carrier to take two large orders to London when she was told that Mr Smallwood of Newcastle was in the office asking for Jos. Smallwood was, she knew, a relatively well-to-do potter himself – just the kind of man Jos needed on his side at the moment. So she tidied herself, forced a welcoming smile and went to see him. The smile did not waver even in the face of his obvious ill- humour.

'Not until late – perhaps not until tomorrow. He's at Worsley Hall.' She saw interest and a spark of curiosity gleam in the man's eyes. 'He is calling on his grace the Duke of Bridgewater,' she added with studied nonchalance. 'They are to discuss the plan for a canal to link the Trent and the Mersey. You know it's proposed to take it close by us here?'

The man nodded. 'Aye, I'd heard as much. I'd heard as well that the great folks want us potters to put our money into the scheme. All right for them, I'd say.'

'Oh, but surely you must see how useful it would be. A canal barge is ideal for transporting pots – smooth, swift, undisturbed by the weather for most of the year. Just think what a direct route to Liverpool could mean for foreign

151

trade . . .' She had all the arguments to hand, for she had gone over them often in just such circumstances as these.

Mr Smallwood gave the matter a little thought and then said, 'I don't have that much trade overseas.'

'But you could! The problem until now has been the transporting of pots safely to the ports. After all, the sea is often the most convenient route even to London and the south. And the cheapest.'

'Aye, mebbe. But it'd be a lot of money down and a long time before there's any return – if at all. How do we know it'll come to anything in the end? It'd take some building.'

'So it would. But if my husband believes in it then it will succeed, you can be sure of that. And the best men will be involved. You must know Mr James Brindley – he built the flint mill for my uncles at the Big House here at Burslem.'

'Aye, I know – a good man, I'll grant you. Has he a hand in it then?'

'He's to be the engineer and oversee the work. He's had experience on the Duke of Bridgewater's estate of course – you'll know of the skill it took to build that canal, being the first of its kind. As I said, the best men . . .'

'Well, we'll see – besides, I didn't come here to chat about canals. I'll give it some thought, but we'll let it be for now if you don't mind. It was your husband I came to see, and if he's not here then I'll be on my way.'

'If it was a matter of business,' Sarah broke in, 'you can safely leave it with me. I am responsible in his absence.'

The man hesitated for a moment, and then shrugged. 'Very well then – it's this I came about.' He held out a letter, a little stained and dirty by now but with the remains of an elaborate seal still attached. Sarah took it and unfolded it. 'The Palace of St James' – the phrase seemed to leap out of the page at her. With a sudden sense of excitement she read quickly.

It was indeed from the court, from a Miss Chetwynd, sempstress and laundress to Queen Charlotte, ordering for the royal household a tea service of Staffordshire ware to a design set out in detail in the letter, which was very clearly addressed to Mr Smallwood himself. Sarah read it through carefully twice, and then looked at the potter with an expression of puzzlement. 'I don't understand – why have you brought this to us? I can see you would be pleased to be honoured like this, but . . .'

'Honoured? Pah! Nothing but trouble that I can see – all that gold, fancy patterns. We don't make stuff like that in Staffordshire – if the Queen wants that sort of thing she should find some fancy foreign pottery. And even if we could do it, just think how many men would need to be tied up in a job like that, for goodness knows how long. And the expense – can you see them paying what it really costs? No, I make my living from good solid ware that sells well and that I can make in quantities worth the effort. I don't want my works put out for some fancy affair like this, Queen or no Queen. And that's what they all say – I've trailed this order round half Staffordshire and no one will touch it with a pair of tongs. I don't doubt Mr Wedgwood will say the same when he's told – but I thought it worth a try. There's not many left, but the small men who couldn't make a watertight chamber pot.'

'My husband will do it: you can be sure of that,' Sarah said with confidence, and watched the amazement spread over Mr Smallwood's face, qualified by a marked scepticism.

'Mebbe,' he said. 'I'll leave that with you – see what he says. If he doesn't fancy the work he can pass it on to someone else – I'll be going then. Good day to you.'

It seemed hours, long interminable hours, until there could be any expectation of Jos's return. Sarah propped the letter on the parlour mantelpiece and tried to occupy her mind with the many jobs to be done. It was not difficult to find work to do, but very hard to suppress the excitement bubbling through her and the impatience to be talking of it with Jos.

But when Jos did come home, close on midnight, he too was overflowing with eagerness to talk of the day's events. 'His grace thought as we did about everything, Sally,' he told her between mouthfuls of a belated supper. 'He'll give us every help – we couldn't have asked for a better reception . . . You know he has a gondola on his canal at Worsley? We had a nine-mile trip on it today, all the way to Manchester for our meeting – what a way to travel! . . . His grace has a Roman urn, found when they dug for the canal – 1500 years old, he says – red Etruscan ware, and very fine: I've a mind to try and copy it. Do you remember the fragments I had years ago? I'll still have them somewhere, I

153

suppose . . . And what's more, Sally, he's ordered a complete table service in creamware – how's that for an order?'

Sarah smiled and took the letter from the mantelpiece. 'You're going to be busy then – listen to this.' She began to read aloud the details of the Queen's order: '". . . twelve cups for tea, with saucers, slop basin, sugar dish with cover and stand, teapot and so forth . . . all with a gold ground and raised flowers in green – six green fruit baskets and stands edged with gold."'

Jos's good humour was dispersed by a frown. 'Who's wanting that ugly-sounding ware? I hope you didn't say we'd do it – I've more than enough to do just now, and you know what I think of special commissions – nothing but trouble.'

'Even if they're *royal* commissions?'

Jos stared at her. 'What?'

'See for yourself. Mr Smallwood brought it. It seems he doesn't like special commissions either, nor does anyone else. He clearly thought even you wouldn't be mad enough to undertake it. But I assured him you would.'

Jos took the letter, but gazed at Sarah in dismay. 'Oh, Sally, you didn't did you? He's quite right, it doesn't make sense – and all that gilding – I haven't the materials or the men to take it on, let alone the experience.'

'Jos, it's from the *Queen*. Miss Chetwynd there is one of the royal ladies.'

Jos read the letter then; and afterwards looked up at Sarah with a quizzical little smile. 'Well now, I'm a cautious man you know – a potter could get his fingers burnt with orders like this. One can't be too careful . . .'

Sarah gave him an exasperated shake. 'Jos, give over now! I'd not have wed you if you were like that, you know I wouldn't.'

'So you wed me for my rashness, is that it? Or,' he added with a glance at the letter, 'my bad taste, being able to concoct a tea service like this.'

'Do it, however ugly. 'But while it's in the making send a sample or two of creamware to court, and some patterns. Then maybe you'll have royal orders for the things you do best. Just think: "Josiah Wedgwood, Potter to the Queen". How does that sound?'

Jos shook his head gravely. 'Very grand, Sally. But there

was I just getting used to "Josiah Wedgwood, Potter to his grace the Duke of Bridgewater". It's all too hasty for me.'

'But you'll do it, Jos, won't you?' She could hear the teasing note in his voice, but she was still not sure that it did not hide an element of seriousness.

'Maybe, Sally, maybe.' For all the hesitant words she could see clearly now the sparkle in his eyes. 'But wherever do you think I'm going to find the time?'

'*We're* going to find the time, remember. Let Tom keep on with the creamware and the like – and you and I can work on this order. And write to John in London. He's just the man to send to court with the patterns – he'd do it for you gladly.'

'There's the gold too – he'll need to make inquiries for me about that. I've used it so rarely – and in this quantity it's quite an undertaking. We had the name of a supplier once, didn't we? We'll need leaf gold, and the powdered sort . . .' He broke off and grinned suddenly. 'Slave-driver, Sally – Bentley should be agitating for your abolition. What with canals and turnpikes and now this – there's not a moment's peace for a poor potter.' He paused again. 'Talking of peace, is our little Sukey not going to wake up to greet her Papa?'

Sarah glanced at the clock and back at Jos, and they both stood listening. Not for months now had these hours passed without their daughter's wailing accompaniment. Together they crept up the stairs and gazed, candle held high, into the cradle. Susannah slept on, her quiet breathing the only disturbance she made.

Jos put his arm about his wife. 'Well, there's a sight to gladden the heart. Do you think she's decided to mend her ways?'

'I do hope so,' said Sarah fervently. And then she smiled, 'I know I'm partial, but sometimes I think she's the most beautiful child there ever was.'

'Of course she is – she's just like her Dad.'

Sarah gave him a little shove. 'Jos Wedgwood, you vain old thing!' Laughing, he turned and folded her into his arms.

From that moment onwards neither Jos nor Sarah found themselves with time enough on their hands to wonder if they had been foolish to take on the royal order. All they knew was that – hard workers both – they had never worked so hard in all their lives before. And it was not as if the canal scheme suddenly made less demands on Jos than before: on the contrary the need to muster every ounce of support he could took him away from home for days together. On his return he and Sarah would retreat to the locked room in the works to experiment with the gold that was facing them with such difficulties. Jos had never liked gaudy decoration and as a result made little use of it; but to win the Queen's patronage her first order must be met to the letter, so gold it must have, whatever the cost and difficulty. 'No expense spared,' said Jos cheerfully. 'Her Majesty can afford to pay.'

He was in a buoyantly happy mood which kept him afloat on a wave of enthusiasm through the busy days and almost as busy nights of that summer. In fact Sarah thought that it was at night he was most happy, working by candlelight on his experiments with gilding and green glaze and clays, once his committee meetings and her office work were done; while she sat recording all he did and giving the criticisms which now and then he demanded. Watching him one night, perched on his stool at the table, head bent intently over a small sample of gold work, turning it this way and that so that its rich sheen caught the candle flame, Sarah was struck by his look of total happy absorption.

'Sometimes I think you're never happier than when you're experimenting away,' she said. 'I wonder if you don't really like that better than making pots.'

'It's all part of it,' Jos murmured abstractedly; and then he laid down the sample and looked up with a smile. 'But perhaps you're right in a way. If I'd never been lamed I suppose I'd have gone on potting in the same old way and thought no more of it. But lying in bed set me reading and thinking and that's how I got interested in experimenting. Perhaps if I'd been a man of means and leisure like that fellow who wanted to wed you once, I might have given all my time to science. But I have to earn a living, and I don't know much about anything but pots, so here we are. As it is at least I can do both the things I love best.'

Sarah grinned. 'And all the other things that take your fancy on the way.'

Perhaps if it had not been for the 'other things' Jos might have become aware rather sooner than he did of the growing

156

difficulties amongst the men at the works. He and Tom between them had selected certain more able men and set them to work on the Queen's order, leaving the others to continue to produce the creamware to meet the outstanding orders.

'We could do with taking on more hands,' Jos said as he sat at dinner with Sarah on the day work began on the royal order, 'but there just aren't the skilled men we need. Besides there's nowhere to put them if we had them. As it is they're all going to have to work in together. I've cleared that storeroom off the throwing shed for the gilders. After all, I don't want the men seeing how the gold work's done – the next thing we know they'll be off to some other potter trying to sell their knowledge.'

'Knowing how little the other potters wanted to tackle the work I doubt if they'd get far,' Sarah soothed him. 'But space is a problem. There's nowhere to store the orders before they're packed to be sent off either – and the men are all falling over one another. Any more orders and they'll be having to stand in line to use the wheel and the lathe.'

'If you could get them to do anything so orderly,' commented Jos gruffly. 'But you're right. We can maybe build on a shed here and there, but there's not much scope for expansion. It's time we looked for new premises – or better still land on which to build our own.'

Sarah gazed at him, eyes shining. 'And start from scratch, everything planned just as we want it – that would be wonderful!'

'Separate rooms for each process, with their own doors, no going from one room to another traipsing all the dust through. And when there's a new process only the men working on it would know what it was.'

'I think you'd find it very difficult to stop them wandering from room to room – they like to meet up and talk, especially in the breaks.'

'Unruly lot that they are! What we need is a complete reformation in our men – each one giving all his time to the job he has to do and nothing else; like the cogs in a machine, working away smoothly and quietly and in perfect order.'

When she went into the works next day Sarah almost laughed aloud at the contrast between Jos's dream, and the scene before

157

her eyes. Man the machine, efficient, orderly, the vital part in a smooth process by which a perfect pot was to be made – the vision faded and died as she stood in the doorway of the throwing and modelling shed and looked about her.

It was a fair-sized room, opening at one end into the dipping shed, at the other, through an archway rather than a door, into the room where stouking and drying were carried out. There were benches and tables and shelves, clean and neat by the standards the men were used to but unbelievably cluttered and dusty and disorganised if looked at with Jos's dream as a guide. The water in the bucket placed by the door of the dipping shed was murky, the towel grey, the soap looked as if it had been trodden underfoot by some unwary workman, for it was gritty with dirt. The floor was scattered already with broken pieces of disused moulds and fragments of wet clay, though she knew that last night Jos had personally supervised its cleaning; he had doubtless ordered that the bucket should be emptied too, but it did not look as if that instruction had been obeyed. The men looked more at home in their setting than would have pleased Jos: three stood chatting by the window, doing nothing at all, one sat slumped on a stool clearly suffering from a hangover, while several of them appeared to be half-inebriated already – they had clearly drunk well at their breakfast break. Only two men were doing anything at all, one clumsily repairing the clay about a mould which had been too dry when applied and so was cracking, the other carrying a tray of newly made pots through to the drying area next door.

Sarah made her way to the group of talking men: they barely paused as she came near. 'Where's Master Tom?' she demanded.

One of them shrugged carelessly, his gaze shifting only momentarily in her direction. His whole manner had a studied insolence which infuriated her, whilst at the same time it puzzled her. She had never before met with anything but respect here, as Jos's wife and a Wedgwood herself, as if in acknowledgement that though she was a woman her name and her status somehow set her apart as having a rightful place within the works.

'I dunna know. Happen in packin' shed,' said the man, and at once turned back to resume his conversation.

'And what should you three be doing?' Sarah pursued crisply. 'I can't believe the work's all done.'

The man – self-appointed spokesman perhaps – looked at her again, as if to express a resentful astonishment that she should still be there. 'Mindin' us own business. Them as thinks us can work wi'out a break had best think again.'

'Them' Sarah suspected was probably Jos himself, a reference put in the plural for reasons of self protection rather than accuracy.

'You have breaks allowed you already, and this isn't one of them,' Sarah pointed out. 'You're paid to work – and if the orders aren't met you'll be the first to suffer.'

'Like us is first to benefit when they are?' he asked mockingly. 'Oh aye, I like that.'

'If the works prosper then everyone does well.'

He raised an eyebrow and then slowly, precisely, he spat. He turned his head away to do so and aimed carefully and accurately at a spot on his far side, as if trying to minimise the offence, but Sarah knew that was not his motive. To spit at her feet would have been an unpardonable rudeness; he had in fact come as near to that as he dared.

One of his fellows, uneasy, broke in quickly, 'Happen we'd best get on, Will.' But though they did at last return to their tasks they waited until Sarah had moved away before doing so.

She made her way then towards the packing shed, increasingly disturbed by a sense that the atmosphere of resentment was not peculiar to these three men. To find men talking, or drunk, or fighting, or working with less than full enthusiasm was usual, almost to be expected; but this air of discontent, even of bitterness, was new and a little frightening.

Sarah found Tom quickly; he was indeed in the packing shed, helping to set two dinner services safely on their way to London. It was an almost impossible task, packing pots so that whether on horseback or in a wagon they should suffer no harm on the rough roads. Perhaps when Jos's turnpike was done it would all be different; then at least there would be no need for the first stage of any journey to be carried out on horseback. Better still would be the canal – smooth water and wide safe barges. She wondered where exactly it would run, and how far the pots would have to be carried to the barges.

Tom, pushing straw into place about two soup tureens,

straightened himself and nodded as Sarah came in, a little grimly she thought. At her signal he followed her into the office beside the packing shed, where they could be alone.

'You've noticed it then,' he said, before she could say anything.

'You could cut the air with a knife. How long's it been like this?'

'Oh, it's been building up bit by bit – since the men were set on the Queen's order anyway.'

'But why? You'd have thought they'd be proud to do it.'

'They just complain there's more work than they can cope with. They don't care a jot who the work's for, so long as it doesn't mean they've to put themselves out more than usual.'

'Does Jos know?' He had not mentioned it and, since putting the men to their tasks at the outset, had scarcely been at home. There had been last night, but then she knew he had descended on the works at the end of the day furiously creating order from chaos and not pausing to allow any murmur of discontent to reach him. He would have noticed nothing then, beyond the usual disorder which he found so distasteful.

'Josiah hasn't had time to know – nor I to tell him about it. Besides there's not much I can put my finger on. The work's being done, after a fashion. There's as much coming out at the end as usual, I'd say. It's just the mood of the men – and that I don't like. But they stop their talking and get back to work when I'm there, all silent like. I can't get a word out of them for the most part, though I've tried. I don't rightly know what's at the bottom of it and I wish I did.' It was the longest speech Sarah had ever heard from Tom Wedgwood and a measure, she thought, of his anxiety that he should be driven to make it.

He took her then through each room, so she saw for herself how the men turned back to their work at his coming with a silent hostility which was quite unlike their usual noisy chaffing good humour. Not quite everyone seemed to be affected – one or two greeted them with a grin and a cheerful remark, a few worked on away from the others with quiet good humour – but for all that the unpleasantness prevailed. Sarah had often taken charge at the works, giving orders, seeing they were carried out, but she had never had to con-

160

tend with anything like this. Feeling a little out of her depth she mentioned the problem to Jos when he came home that night.

It was not, as it happened, the ideal moment for such a disclosure, if there could have been such a thing. He had been at Trentham Hall, home of Lord Gower, Lord Lieutenant of the county, an influential politician and relation by marriage of the Duke of Bridgewater, that enthusiast for canal building whose help was so much sought for this new scheme. The Duke himself had been at Trentham today, and Jos had met them both.

'What we really have hopes of is Lord Gower's public support. If we can get a meeting together with all the gentry who might help us – and he would lead it, tell everyone how greatly he recommends our scheme and so forth – then we'd have no difficulty raising funds, or getting the project through parliament. He was most affable today – I think we'll be able to win him over . . .'

'I hope so,' Sarah put in absently, wondering how she could possibly tell him about her anxieties without deflating his present optimistic mood.

'He wants a copy of Bentley's pamphlet as soon as possible – I must write at once. And,' he went on with a surge of pride in his voice, 'what is more I had a little triumph all of my own. You know Dr Swann's tale of when he was at supper at Trentham and his lordship spoke of how our creamware had a glaze like no other for fineness? He said the very same to me today, and asked many questions about the works and the wares we make and so forth. And then he said he had other kinsfolk of his staying at Trentham and he'd a mind to bring them over here one day next week to see what we have to offer. So we can confidently expect a visit from his lordship himself, his grace the Duke of Marlborough and Lord Spencer, to name but three. We'll have to make sure everything's in order – set the office out as a showroom perhaps. You'll see, Sally, we'll have Wedgwood wares at Blenheim and Althorp as well as Trentham – and the court of St James. Before we know where we are no gentleman in the land will consider his home complete without its Wedgwood dinner service.'

It was then, because there was no putting it off, that Sarah told him.

Jos stared at her in silence for some time after she had finished speaking. She watched the frown gather on his brow and his mouth harden; and then he cried, 'What have I done to be saddled with such men?' He crashed one clenched fist down on his other palm. 'I've had nothing but trouble from start to finish – idle, drunken, good-for-nothing, disobedient. Goodness knows how I'm ever going to get anywhere with men like that!'

'You've got quite a long way already,' Sarah pointed out quietly; and then added without thinking, 'After all, not many potters could expect a visit from lords and dukes and the like . . .'

'And what do you suppose they'll think when they see the sort of men I have to depend on? They'll be expecting a decent orderly work place, all peace and quiet and industry – and instead they're going to be faced with that unruly rabble . . .' He rose to his feet and began to hobble painfully about the room. 'They've been nothing but trouble from start to finish, the whole pack of them.'

Sarah laid a gently restraining hand on his arm. 'Jos, whatever their shortcomings you need them if you're ever to do anything worth while – just as they need you . . .'

'Then I wish to goodness they'd realise it! I need good honest useful tools, not disorderly layabouts who can't be trusted for a moment.'

'Jos, you're being unfair!'

'Am I?' He settled his gaze on her, the anger subsiding a little. 'Maybe. We shall see.'

She kept her hand where it lay for a moment longer. 'Jos – don't go to the works in that mood tomorrow, not in anger. You need to try and find out what's wrong, try to understand, put it right if you can.'

'Put it right!' He flared up again in an instant. 'Put what right, pray? I know what's wrong well enough. Those lazy good-for-nothings who call themselves workmen don't like to have anything the least bit hard to do, anything that needs a bit more effort than usual – they might just find themselves having to get there on time and keep at it without a break for a drink here and a gossip there, just to get the work done. Tell me, were they all on time today? Were they all working hard? Had they got the fruit baskets ready for biscuit firing,

162

as I ordered? No,' he added before she could reply, 'there's
no need to say anything – I know the answer for myself, only
too well. And what about the water for washing? Had they
made sure it was clean, and put out a clean towel?' Again he
did not wait for her answer. 'Why can't they see it's for their
own good? I've told them often enough about the dust, and
the lead in the glaze – you'd think at the very least they'd
mind their own health. Sometimes I wonder what it is they
have in their skulls – not brains I'm sure, or none you and I
would recognise.'

'They just don't like change – at least not all at once.'

'Not all at once! Most of them have been with me for years
– months anyway. How long does it take, pray?'

There was no soothing him that night. Sarah knew he slept
very little, and next day he scarcely paused for breakfast
before bursting explosively on the works, just as the bell sent
its resonant note chiming over Burslem.

Any workman not at the next moment seated busily at his
bench was greeted with a torrent of fury; and every man, old
or young, highly skilled or the newest of apprentices, was
subjected that day to a ferocious and blisteringly critical
scrutiny. If anyone had thought of giving voice to discontent,
he soon thought better of it, confronted by the scowl of Jos's
dark brows and the savagery of his tongue. Jos never swore,
never used the kind of language common amongst both the
workmen and the gentry who hunted with George Lathom,
and he did not waste the words he used; but he left no one in
any doubt as to what he thought of anything other than total
obedience and absolute efficiency.

Sarah – observant of every sullen expression on the face of a
man bent dutifully to his work, every resentful glance exchanged when Jos's back was turned – supervised more
quietly the cleaning (with wet mops, to keep down the dust)
and tidying of the works, the bringing of chairs and cushions
and other adornments and comforts into the office, the
setting out on the office shelves (cleared temporarily of books
and ledgers) of a few choice specimens of the very best wares
that Josiah Wedgwood, potter, could produce, arranged so as
to catch the eye and attract the interest of the would be
purchaser, whenever he should arrive.

By the time the bell rang again to mark the end of the

163

working day the sheds were tidier than they had ever been before, the office had all the welcoming appearance of a fashionable London shop (so said Jos, who had been to London) and the men, going home, were cowed into meekness.

Every day for the next week Jos never left the works during daylight hours, incessantly observing, commanding, making sure the men did not for a moment forget that his eye was upon them. But even he knew that the battle was not yet wholly won. The works might present the busy quiet orderly appearance he had hoped for; but only on the surface. No man dared arrive late, but a good many failed to turn up at all, especially on the Monday; and though they all kept to their work, it was grudgingly and sometimes at the expense of the quality of the goods produced.

'The Queen's service will never be finished if they go on like this,' Jos raged. And Tom, very grave, said in an undertone to Sarah as she came (as she did daily) to bring flowers for the office, 'The ill feeling's still there, even if no one dares say anything. It's my belief that'll have to be put right before things will get any better.'

It was Sarah's belief too, but she knew it was not the right time to point that out to Jos, who was concerned first of all with providing a smooth appearance to impress the visitors when they should come. Besides, she suspected that his way of 'putting things right' would not be hers.

The guests came at last exactly a week after Jos's visit to Trentham. Sarah saw them from the landing window, riding past the house with an accompanying train of grooms: a laughing group of young men in riding clothes, heedless of the mud and the dirt, enjoying the novelty of this visit to the unprepossessing little pottery town. Among them, an older man taller and graver than the rest, was Lord Gower, whom Sarah knew by sight.

She waited until they had disappeared into the works yard, and then hurried downstairs to put ready the cakes and wine which Jos had said she should bring to the office as soon as he had sent a man to say it was time.

The servants from Trentham had already been dispatched to the kitchen of the Brick House, to refresh themselves with ale and set Nan and Betty in a flutter, by the time Sarah

164

crossed the yard carrying with great care a tray on which stood a bottle and glasses and a plate of Betty's best honey cakes.

The little office seemed amazingly crowded today with all those men – so tall beside Jos's slight form – standing about, lounging in the chairs, talking loudly and animatedly. But it had gone well so far, she could see that: Jos, reaching a vase of printed creamware down from the shelf, had a glow of happy pride about him which she could almost feel from across the room. He looked round and smiled as she came in.

'Ah, Sarah . . .' He took the tray from her and set it on the desk; and then laid his hand on her arm to guide her towards Lord Gower. 'My lord, may I present my wife.'

Her mother would have been proud of her elegant little curtsey, and of the modestly smiling manner in which she received the Earl's compliments and went on to exchange courtesies with the youthful Duke of Marlborough.

'Mr Wedgwood tells me you plan a visit to London in the autumn,' said the Duke. Sarah glanced swiftly at Jos, who gave a faint apologetic smile at her surprise. She felt a little stir of indignation that he should spring the plan on her like this; and then remembered what she should have told him by now, and tried to put it out of her mind. 'You must call at Blenheim on your way – I can arrange for you to be shown round. In fact you could break your journey there: my steward would be happy to accommodate you.' Sarah murmured their thanks.

The Duke's cousin Lord Spencer was equally gracious. 'I have great plans for Althorp – I know now where to come for the best English tableware.' He glanced approvingly at the fruit dish held in his hands. 'I have been telling your husband he should make tiles – good quality tiles – for a dairy, for instance, or a washroom – they are hard to come by . . .' Smiling, Sarah noted the observation for future reference, as doubtless Jos had too. 'Your husband is to show us around the works shortly.'

'And I trust you will delight us with your company during our tour, ma'am,' Lord Gower put in. Sarah thanked him and went to pour the wine and hand round the cakes.

The working sheds had just the air of industrious orderliness which Jos had hoped for. On the surface there was no no sign at all that here was anything but a smoothly running pottery, each man busy at his allotted task. 'This is a marvel,' Lord Gower said; and Sarah knew that in a way he was right. She had a sudden fleeting recollection of the Churchyard works, the mess and muddle, the rough homely wares; and of her uncles' pottery, where they had always worked as the men did, not minding too much if there was drinking or an unscheduled break for a wakes or a wedding, or if the clay was wasted or spoiled. Very likely even they thought it all part of the natural order of things. She saw suddenly how very far Jos had come in a few short years; how his energy, his striving for perfection had transformed an untidy haphazard Burslem potworks into this large and growing enterprise which men of fashion chose to visit. It might be very far from the ideal, might perhaps never become what Jos wanted it to be, but she saw as if with new eyes what a change he had made. And she thought she understood suddenly just what the men must feel, faced with this overturning of everything that was known and familiar.

It was in the throwing and modelling shed that all was not exactly as it should have been. The wheel stood motionless and no one was making any move to work it. Samuel Hunter was standing nearby, talking in a low voice to the three men who worked with him on the Queen's order, and he broke off abruptly as the door opened. With a churning of her stomach Sarah realised that he was coming towards them, intent on speaking to Jos; and some sure instinct told her that to let him speak now would only mean disaster, for Jos perhaps, but even more for himself. She sprang forward, smiling. 'Ah, Mr Hunter, you were going to show me the teapot so I could make sure it poured well. How scatter-brained of me to forget all about it! Forgive me, your grace, my lords – poor Mr Hunter cannot get on with his work until I've passed the teapot. Come and show me now – it's in the dipping room, I suppose?' She saw the man hesitate, looking from her to Jos and back again. She clenched her fists at her sides. 'Let him take the hint!' she prayed. Unfortunately the Duke took it himself and only too well.

'Then do let us see, ma'am,' he broke in. 'Show us how you test a teapot.'

166

Sarah smiled on through her alarm, trying not to look at Jos, who was gazing at her, utterly bewildered by her astonishing behaviour. He would be angry with her later she knew, but for the present that did not worry her at all.

'Ah no, your grace – I'm sorry, but we let no one outside the works see the wares before they are passed as perfect. If the teapot passes the test, then I will show you. Excuse us now . . .' She moved across the room, away from the guests. 'Mr Hunter!' she called over her shoulder; and to her relief after a moment more of hesitation he followed her.

She led the way to the dipping room, and to a far corner where no one was about; and then she turned to face him. He looked down at her and there was almost a smile on his face, beneath the customary truculence.

'What's that for?' he demanded. 'Happen ye'll have to find a teapot now.'

'Or it's failed the test and I smashed it,' she suggested. 'But you knew well enough why I did it, don't you? You were going to speak to Mr Wedgwood.'

'And show him up in front o' those grand gentlemen? That wunna do now, would it? But it might ha' made him hear what I had to say.'

'It would have made quite sure you were out of a job,' Sarah retorted. 'You must have known that.'

The man shrugged. 'Good trained potters anna that thick on th' ground. He'd be pushed to replace me.'

'Don't be so sure. He can offer secure steady work, good wages . . .' Hunter exclaimed under his breath, and Sarah broke off and looked about her. The men dipping plates in the glaze at the other end of the room had ceased their work and were watching the little scene with interest. 'Come to the storeroom. We can talk better there.'

The storeroom attached to the packing shed was large and empty, but for a few completed articles ranged on its shelves; the visitors were unlikely to come in here. Sarah closed the door behind them, shutting them into a dimness lit only by one, high, barred window. She imagined what the comments would have been had anyone seen them come in here, but fortunately (she hoped) no one had. And whatever was on Samuel Hunter's mind, it was not anything which could justifiably have given rise to ribald comment.

'Now,' she said, turning once more to face him. 'What exactly were you going to say to Mr Wedgwood?'

'I'll say it to his face if you dunna mind.'

'I'm trying to help, can't you see that? It would suit neither you nor Mr Wedgwood if you were to lose your job.'

'Aye, it's another story wi' me, isn't it? Not like poor old Harry Shaw. You didn't trouble to speak up for him. Just a jack of all trades, poor lad, fit for no more than mixin' glazes – never mind that he's gone through his 'prenticeship like everyone else.'

'What has Harry Shaw to do with all this?'

Hunter regarded her with an ironic half smile. 'Nowt, Mrs Wedgwood, nowt at all – except that I'm the only one can speak up for him. The rest are feared they'll be thrown out o' work too.'

Sarah began to remember: Jos had been saying something to her last night about being forced to dismiss one of the men, but Susannah had woken before she could question him further, and she had forgotten about it afterwards. She tried now to remember some of the details of what he had said and fit them together with what she knew already.

She did not remind Sam that a moment before he had been boasting of the shortage of trained potters. Instead she said, 'Why exactly was Harry Shaw dismissed?'

Hunter shrugged. 'Didna come in to work Monday.'

'Don't you think that's fair?'

'Course it's not fair! There's any number o' us has Monday off now and then – always has been, so long as there's been potbanks in Burslem.'

'As I remember it wasn't just the "odd Monday" where Harry Shaw was concerned.'

'So what? He's not the only one. Where I served my time you was lucky to find anyone in on Monday at all. But the work got done.'

'Ah, but what work, Sam? There is a difference, isn't there?'

'I dunna see why. We're all potters, even Harry Shaw. We all has us own way of doin' things. Just because it's not Mr Wedgwood's way it's no worse for that.'

Harry Shaw, Sarah remembered, had not even been able to mix the glazes efficiently: Jos had complained of it more than

168

once, and spoken of it to the man himself as well. Sam must know that, for though Jos always intended to administer his rebukes in private his voice when angry carried only too clearly; and in the open working sheds there was little privacy.

'You know the glaze was spoiled more than once. Two whole orders were ruined because he failed to follow Mr Wedgwood's instructions about weighing the materials, and missed out some vital ingredients.' It was the kaolin he had omitted, Sarah knew, but Jos made sure none of the men knew by name what ingredients they were using for fear they might take word of it elsewhere.

'They weren't ruined at all. They'da done fine for any other potter.'

'Because any other potter would have been content to have his glaze cracking. But Mr Wedgwood has spent hours finding out how to stop that happening – he already has a reputation for the finest glaze there is – he can't afford to have incompetent workmen destroying it.'

'Oh, an' he's the only one knows what's best! What about Harry Shaw? He does things the way they've always been done, an' takes the holidays we've always had, an' he finds himself out o' work. It's not right. You can tell Mr Wedgwood that if Harry Shaw dunna get his job back then we'll none of us be workin'.'

Sarah sighed with exasperation. 'Sam, listen to me. I *know* Mr Wedgwood expects different ways from you. I *know* it's hard to accept change – though it shouldn't be that hard for a young man like yourself. But just think what will happen if things don't change. We'll be back to sending a few poor pots to fairs and markets, and most of you will find yourselves out of work. The old chancy ways of doing things were fine when there was only a little local demand for the pots – but they won't do now the goods are going to all the big houses round about, to Liverpool and London, even overseas. If the quality falls, or the output, even those markets will be lost.'

'How many people see the odd crack in a glaze?'

'More than you think, I suspect. And there's more to it than that, as you'd know if you thought about it. You all have different tasks to do about the works, according to what you do best – but if the man who mixes the glaze misses a day's work, then everything's held up in the dipping room – or if the lads doing the wedging are slow in their work, then the throwers are held up for want of clay – as has happened to you, hasn't it? I've heard you grumble about it, more than once. Even old widow Warburton in Hot Lane has to get her painting done in time for the final firing, so that the orders can be ready to be sent off by the date they're needed. And *she* knows that better than a good many of you men here in the works. No one's ever had to wait for her. If Harry Shaw felt put upon because he was set on mixing glazes, then he shouldn't have done – he was every bit as important as everyone else, which is why when he didn't do his work well, or worse still not at all, he had to go. Don't you see that?'

She could see that her words had made some kind of impression on him, for he was gazing at her with a speculative expression; but if he was in any way convinced by her argument he was not yet ready to admit it, for he said grudgingly, 'All I see is that we've got all the changes to put up with, all the extra work, while Mr Wedgwood has the glory and the profit.'

'Oh that's nonsense! He works harder than any of you.'

'Not in here he doesna. Where I was apprentice the master worked alongside us – he would talk to us and listen to what was said. We hardly see Mr Wedgwood except when he comes flyin' in to shout at us. Master Tom's all right – he does his bit I'll grant you. But all Mr Wedgwood thinks about is turnpikes and canals and what have you.'

'Do you think the wares we make would have the reputation they do if that were true? Think of all the hours he spends working on improvements – often through the night, when you're all fast asleep in bed. And however little you see him he does care for your welfare. You may not like all the rules but a fair number of them are for your own good, not his – like washing after dipping and keeping the dust down. What's more, he'll give praise where it's due and acknowledge skill. It's you he chose for the throwing of the Queen's order, not anyone else. You should be proud and pleased.'

'Happen I would, if I got paid any more for the extra work.'

'You're on piece work over and above your basic wage – do more work and you're paid more.'

'I can only do so much. And dunna tell me we'll see much of

170

what Mr Wedgwood makes on this order because I'll not believe you.'

'Most of the profit will go into improving and expanding the works and its products, as it always has. But you already earn more than men in other potworks around here. And there'll doubtless be more pay rises as demand grows. But not,' she concluded, 'if men like Harry Shaw go on living in the past. The old days are over, at least as far as these works are concerned. Accept that and there's a future of unlimited opportunity for all of us. But I'm afraid there's no place in it for men like Harry Shaw.'

She could see now that he was moved by her appeal; but at the same time he had decided to take a stand, and he would not abandon his position without a last blow on its behalf.

'So they starve – right?'

She thought of Harry Shaw, not as a troublesome incompetent workman, too slow witted to understand what was asked of him, but as the father of a grown son with the mind of a child and as the husband of an ailing wife; and she softened. 'Of course not. I'll make sure he has some kind of work to go to – not here, because even if he wanted it I don't think that would be fair to anyone. But something to give him a living. I give you my word on that.'

Hunter nodded, satisfied at last. 'Good,' he said, which, she supposed, was the nearest he was likely to come to thanking her.

'And, Sam Hunter . . .'

'Aye?'

'Next time you have something on your mind, choose a better time to bring it up – or, better still, come to me with it first.'

He nodded again and grinned, a little sheepishly. 'Aye, Mrs Wedgwood, that I will.'

By now the visitors had returned to the office to conclude their tour by making a gratifying number of purchases. Jos glanced round as Sarah came in and then looked quickly away again, as if he did not – yet – want to face the question of what she had been doing. The Duke of Marlborough greeted her cheerfully, 'Ah, Mrs Wedgwood, how was the teapot?'

For a tiny embarrassing instant Sarah could not remember what he was talking about; then she said hastily, hoping she had succeeded in covering her hesitation, 'Oh, I'm afraid it was not good enough. It has been smashed. It will have to be done again.'

'What admirably high standards you have here,' commented Lord Spencer, his approving gaze moving from Jos to Sarah and back again. Then he added, 'You know, Mr Wedgwood, you should have some kind of London warehouse, then the fashionable world would more easily be able to see your wares – you could have your patterns and designs displayed there, too, for a choice to be made and orders taken. I'm sure you would find it to your advantage.'

Later, with several new items added to the order book and the office shelves all but emptied of pots, Jos and Sarah stood in the gateway of the works to watch their guests ride away; and then at last Jos confronted Sarah. 'What was all that nonsense about a teapot?' he demanded as they made their way towards the house. 'There was no teapot ready, and if there had been you'd have left it until after they'd gone. What were you doing?' He was clearly annoyed, but more than that he was puzzled by such inexplicable conduct.

'I could see Samuel Hunter was spoiling for a fight with you.'

'What, there and then, in front of everyone? Even he wouldn't be so foolish. Whatever gave you that idea?'

'Instinct, I suppose: I was right you know. That's why I had to get him away quickly.'

Jos stared at her, absorbing what she said with growing distaste. 'Whatever's got into the man to think of behaving like that? I've put great trust in him, acknowledging his skill and reliability. He's one of the best men I've got – or I thought he was. How *could* he let me down?'

'Oh, I think it was just because he knows you value him. He was acting as spokesman for them all – or rather for Harry Shaw. They wanted him to have his job back.'

'Then he *has* gone mad! I can see no reason whatsoever to keep on a man who's proved himself over and over again to be totally and incorrigibly incompetent. I can't see why anyone should want to speak up for him.'

'Because he's old and poor and has heavy responsibilities.'

'I'm not running a charitable institution, Sally. A few more like him in the works and I'll be needing charity too. Sam should be ashamed of himself. I hope you told him so.'

172

'Not in so many words,' Sarah admitted. 'Oh, don't worry, I gave him no reason to think you'd reinstate Harry Shaw. But I think there was really more to it than just that one grievance.'

'I'm sure there was – it's quite clear that Sam Hunter's one of those born troublemakers. If he's not careful he'll find himself out of work too. He may be a good workman, but there's no room in my works for men who go round stirring up trouble.'

'It's not just him, Jos. As I said before, they don't like change and you've altered a great many things. They'll come round, in time, bit by bit – but don't expect miracles. They resented Harry Shaw's sacking because he was only carrying on in the old time-honoured way . . .'

'But they *know* that's not my way – they know they can't go on like that here.'

'Perhaps if you'd tried to explain why you were making all the changes, instead of just laying down the law and leaving it at that – perhaps then they'd have been more ready to accept it.'

'I'm the master, they're the men. It's my job to give orders, not to tiptoe around trying not to ruffle any feathers. If they don't like it they know what they can do. Besides, most of them wouldn't understand what I was on about if I did try to explain what I was trying to do.'

'Sam Hunter did.'

He halted and looked round at her. 'Oh? So you explained it to him did you? What did he say? "Thank you kindly, Mrs Wedgwood, and maybe I'll think about doing as I'm told"?'

'Not exactly. But I think now he understands he'll be happier with the changes, and maybe the others will take a lead from him. I made him a promise though.'

Jos scowled. 'What was that?'

'I said I'd find some kind of work for Harry Shaw, somehow – so he won't starve, or be thrown on the parish.'

'Did you now?' said Jos caustically. 'Then you'd better get busy or you might find you've let him down.' And he walked briskly on ahead and into the house.

By bedtime Jos's ill humour had evaporated. He drew Sarah into his arms and said, 'You can tell Harry Shaw that my brother Thomas wants a new man at his works, since old

173

Ben Simpson died. I'll not recommend him, mind – but Tom knows him well enough, and I reckon they'll suit.'

'So that's where you went after dinner! Oh Jos!' She snuggled closer, resting her head in the hollow of his shoulder.

'I'm not quite heartless, you know.'

'I never thought you were,' she said. 'Just a bit impatient sometimes.' Then, after a moment, she went on, 'Jos, what was all that about going to London? That was the first I heard of it.'

'Oh the idea came to me this morning. The Queen's order should be ready by October. I thought once it was sent off I ought to go to London anyway – there are any number of people I ought to see. And Sukey's weaned now so you can come too – Nan can be trusted to look after her, or better still Kate will have her. We can make a little holiday of it. How would you like that?'

'Very much,' she murmured. 'And, Jos . . .'

'Yes?'

'By this time next year Susannah will have company.'

'You mean . . .?'

'Yes, I'm expecting another baby. In March I think.'

After that, Jos forgot all about the works and its problems, and about holidays and everything else, until they fell asleep in one another's arms.

The first thing that struck Sarah about London was the noise. They arrived in the evening at the Bull and Black Swan in Holborn, where John Wedgwood met them with a carriage to convey them and their luggage to their lodgings in Lawrence Lane, close by where he himself lived. The inn – one of the major coaching inns in an area dense with such establishments – was filled with the thunderous rumble of wheels on cobbles, the clatter of hooves, the shouting of waiters, servants and ostlers, coachmen and irate travellers, the crying of children and, horribly, the whining of beggars from the shadowed corners by the entrance to the inn yard. To Sarah, her head spinning with weariness after the days of travel, it was overpowering and intolerable. She had only a dim dazed impression of the short rattling journey to Lawrence Lane; of the meal, hot and savoury, waiting for them, which she could

174

not eat; and of the bed in the austere little room between whose warmed sheets she slid at last to fall into an exhausted sleep, which even the night sounds could not penetrate.

It was however the noise which woke her next morning, a relentless crescendo of noise reaching a level of intensity by daybreak which she was to learn would last until darkness fell. She had thought it bad last night, but she knew now that last night had been almost an interval of quiet in the ceaseless activity of the city. Below her window rumbled and rattled the carts and wagons and coaches, like a sudden deafening clap of thunder endlessly prolonged. Now and then a louder crash proclaimed a collision, and a torrent of shouted abuse – mostly mercifully incomprehensible to the ears of someone unused to London speech – would follow after it. Through the din the street sellers shouted their wares: fresh milk, eggs from the country, flowers and oysters – every conceivable product in an almost indistinguishable cacophony. Cans and buckets clanged and clashed, voices shouted from windows, doors slammed, dogs barked; somewhere, even, a raucous male voice roared out a defiant ballad.

Next day, when John Wedgwood took them on a modest tour of the most essential sights – St Paul's, the Tower, with a walk along the quieter riverside areas to watch the ships pass – there were other sensations, other impressions. The smells, first: the stench of horse dung piled deep in the streets and household rubbish thrown anyhow in alleys and even from windows overhead; the stink near the butchers' shops, and the evil waters of the Fleet River and of the Thames itself; the choking smoke of a thousand coal fires pouring their sooty waste from the densely packed houses and tenements. It was worse than anything Sarah had ever known in Burslem, even at its busiest.

And there were so many contradictions and contrasts too. London seemed to be a city at once renewing itself and decaying. In one street there would be fine new stones being laid, with pavements raised and fenced to protect the passers-by from the wheeled traffic; and the dangerous colourful creaking signs that swung ominously in every little wind, and often crashed into the street, were being replaced by a simple system of numbering – so that John Wedgwood's address 'At the Sign of the Artichoke, Cateaton Street', might one day become something like 'Number Seven, Cateaton Street', or whatever was appropriate.

In places, too, there were fine oil lamps on standards to light the streets; quiet alleys with trees and little gardens; and parks with cows grazing, like a glimpse of the countryside in the heart of the city. Yet turn away for a moment from this busy scene of rebuilding and improving, and you might find yourself at once in a nightmare: rickety tumbledown houses so roughly built that the crash of falling masonry was yet another of London's familiar sounds; cobbled streets shiny with filth and so narrow that anyone on foot risked being mown down by a cart or a carriage and with no room for two vehicles, if they met, to pass; ragged scrawny barefoot children grey with dirt and sickness diving through crowds and traffic in search of whatever pickings they could find; men and women alike sunk in a drunken stupor in the gutter, slumped miserably in doorways, fighting and shouting from alleys and windows. Sarah had seen poverty in Burslem, even in Spen Green, but nothing like this in all its raw horror. These people were not, she thought, like human beings at all, but subhuman, degraded, struggling not to live but simply to exist.

'It's better than it used to be,' John reassured her, seeing her dismay. 'Since they restricted the sale of gin there's a good deal less crime and sickness.'

Sarah could think of nothing to say to that. She felt crushed by the hideousness of the poor streets, bewildered by the contradictions, above all overwhelmed by the sheer scale of the city, its thousands of people of whom almost none were known to her, its crowded cramped buildings, its harshness and carelessness of life.

Yet at the same time something about it all set her pulses racing, thrilled and excited her. To see those splendid wonderful buildings of which she had heard so much, to walk amongst politicians and celebrities in the park, and even glimpse Queen Charlotte passing in a coach with her ladies, to feel that she was here at the heart of the kingdom where momentous decisions were made – all that was heady stuff, which made her feel both insignificant and important all at once.

Jos, who had been to London before, was excited too, but

mostly because of the possibilities it offered him. An intro-
duction to the Duke of Bedford led to several mornings spent
taking patterns from a magnificent service of French china
at the Duke's mansion. A day at Turnham Green with Ralph
Griffiths, a Staffordshire friend of the Wedgwoods and now
the prosperous owner and editor of the *Monthly Review*, led
to a round of visits on behalf of a leaflet by Dr Joseph
Priestley on 'Liberal Education', which for political reasons
most editors – and even the generally radical Griffiths – were
wary of publishing; and there were further visits, on
Bentley's behalf, to arrange for the printing of a plan to
accompany the final version of his canal pamphlet. And of
course there were patrons to be won over to the cause of the
canal – Jos had come to London well armed with intro-
ductions from Gower and Bridgewater to their connections in
the capital, men like the influential Lord Cathcart.

Last but not least, Jos had an appointment one morning at
Buckingham House, the Queen's London residence in St
James's park, to see Miss Chetwynd, the lady responsible for
placing the order for the tea service which had now been
safely delivered.

'Let's hope the Queen liked it,' Jos said as he left Sarah in
his brother's care for the day. 'John sent a pair of vases with
the service just to show what we can do, but he's heard
nothing yet.'

Sarah, missing Susannah, shut out from most of Jos's
activities – though she enjoyed the bustle and talk at
Turnham Green – might have found herself bored and miserable as never before had it not been for John. She liked
him. He was a slight dark man, with a cultivated manner of
speech and dress which would have been startlingly out of
place in Burslem, and he neglected his own business to show
her the sights and entertain her as best he could – and his best
was very good when, as now, he was in excellent health and
spirits.

Today, while Jos was at Buckingham House, he took her
on the river to Richmond to enjoy a morning of country quiet
which exactly suited her mood, restoring her to calmness. But
they returned to find that the following days were unlikely to
bring them any more such interludes.

'Sally – John . . .' Jos greeted them, more voluble than

usual with excitement. 'The Queen wants me to attend upon her in person with more samples of my ware, so she can place an order for something in the creamware – she was delighted with the service, Miss Chetwynd says. I'm to see her on Thursday morning . . .'

'Then we'll have to go shopping tomorrow,' John told him. 'You'll need the correct court dress.'

Jos stared at his brother, his enthusiasm momentarily dampened. 'I hadn't thought of that. What is the correct court dress?'

'A sword, for one thing – every well-dressed courtier must have a sword.'

Jos gulped, and then laughed suddenly. 'What do I want with a sword? I've never even held one, let alone used it.'

'That doesn't matter. It's the correct dress.'

The look of half-humorous dismay Jos cast at her set Sarah laughing too. 'You'll be Sir Jos yet, my love!' He grinned and took her hand in his.

'You must come as well, Sally. I am to bring someone with me to help carry the wares. Why not my wife and best partner?'

'Then we'll need two court dresses,' said John. 'Though I imagine Sarah won't actually be presented.'

For Sarah, court dress meant a low-necked gown of figured silk, wide-hooped and rigidly boned at the bodice with the long flowing sacque at the back ending in a little train; for Jos there was a waistcoat lavishly patterned with silver lace, a damask coat and breeches, a new wig and of course the sword, bought at the fashionable Sign of the Flaming Sword in Great Newport Street – it was small, as inoffensive looking as a sword could possibly be, and caused both Sarah and Jos a disproportionate amount of amusement.

'You're like a pair of children,' John commented as Jos strutted unevenly about their lodgings with the weapon at his waist. 'It's not so very out of the way, you know.'

Somehow on the following Thursday morning as Jos crossed the shining length of floor towards the waiting figure of the Queen the sword did not look ridiculous any more, and nor did the elaborate court dress – perhaps because everyone else in that hot sunny room was similarly over-dressed.

Sarah, watching Jos from where she had been instructed to

178

wait between two footmen in the doorway, was a little fearful for him, willing him not to do or say anything which might draw a sneer or a laugh from the disdainful-looking gathering of ladies-in-waiting clustered about the Queen.

As it was late in the year a fire had been lit, but outside it was unseasonably warm, the sunlight falling through long windows to focus, as if by prior arrangement, on the stiffly gowned young woman seated at the far end, her expression a little severe. Sarah thought Jos must be very hot and uncomfortable in his fine court clothes, for she was herself and she did not have to walk across that room between all those critical watching eyes.

Halfway across the room one of the Queen's ladies – Miss Chetwynd, Sarah supposed – came to meet Jos and lead him forward the last few yards to introduce him to the Queen in a low voice which Sarah could not quite hear. She saw the Queen smile, however; and then Jos bowed. It was not a courtier's bow, flourishing, simpering or extravagant, but a simple dignified gesture of greeting from a man to a woman who deserved his respect. Sarah felt a surge of pride.

She saw him move on again at the Queen's command, answering her questions with calmness and fluency, looking not awkward, over-dressed or out of place, but quietly at ease despite his slightness of build and halting step, as if such splendid surroundings were as natural to him as the throwing shed at the Brick House works.

After a short exchange of talk – which again Sarah was too far off to hear – Miss Chetwynd turned with a signal and the footmen at Sarah's side gathered up the two boxes of sample wares which they had brought with them and carried them to set them before the Queen; and then Jos took each piece in turn to show it to her.

It grew hotter with each moment that passed. Sarah was glad that she was in the shade, but poor Jos had the sun full on his back, though he seemed unaware of it. The Queen looked even more uncomfortable, for the light shone full in her eyes, so that now and then she put up a hand to shade them; and even from here Sarah could see the little beads of perspiration gleaming on her pale skin.

'Why doesn't someone do something?' Sarah thought with irritation. There were blinds at the windows but no one made

179

any move to pull them down. It was possible that the Queen did not want to interrupt her talk with Jos by asking for some shade, but surely one of the watching ladies could have taken some action? Perhaps, Sarah thought with a wry little smile, common sense is in short supply at court; or perhaps it is beneath the dignity of one of those fine ladies to do anything so lowly as pull down a blind – and presumably a footman would not dare to do such a thing without instruction. It must, she thought, be very unpleasant to live so surrounded by etiquette and ceremonial.

Then she heard Jos say,' Excuse me, ma'am', and the next moment he had stepped quickly across to the offending window and pulled down the blind. Shade covered the Queen's face as he returned to his place.

There was a rustle and murmur amongst the ladies and a look of astonished disapproval on one or two faces; but the Queen smiled with manifest delight and the next moment said with an approving clarity intended for all to hear, 'Ladies, Mr Wedgwood is, you see, already an accomplished courtier.' And then she returned with more warmth than before to her examination of the wares.

The little incident caused a sensation out of all proportion to its significance; within a matter of hours news of it seemed to have spread throughout London society, for they heard of it wherever they went. Jos was amused. 'What a comment on court ways, that common sense is so out of the ordinary!' He was more impressed by the order for a dinner service which the Queen had placed with him, and her promise to interest the King in ordering Wedgwood wares for his own household. But Sarah hugged the memory to her, knowing that it was Jos's own staunch simplicity of character which had made the morning such a triumph.

After that, almost everything must seem a little like an anticlimax, but John did his best to ensure that it was not, as far as possible. When Jos was not busy elsewhere – and in particular in the evenings – John arranged as many varied outings as he could to show off the splendours of his city and delight his guests.

They went to Vauxhall Gardens, and Sarah was enchanted by the little alcoves in the trees strung with lamps, the food and talk, the company, above all the music. Another evening, at Ranelagh, the music was more splendid still. And – to round off their stay in style – John hired a box for them at Drury Lane so they could see David Garrick's opening performance in Shakespeare's *Much Ado about Nothing* after a long absence from the stage, and be delighted by the acting and fascinated by the new lighting system installed by the celebrated actor manager which illuminated the stage from the wings by some means invisible to the audience.

'Hm,' commented Jos as the first act came to an end, 'the theatre may not offer much prospect for a lad like Tom Byerley, but I can see the attraction.' Sarah agreed, smiling happily and looking about her with lively interest at the noisy overcrowded pit and the boxes opposite filled with the fashionable, all silks and brocades and frothing lace. One young man caught her eye particularly, richly dressed but with his darkly handsome face lined and shadowed by age or experience, or sorrow perhaps: there was something intriguingly familiar about him. It was only as the second act began, and she caught his eye and saw an answering gleam of recognition, that she realised it was George Lathom.

At the end of the next act she saw that he had disappeared; and a moment later he was there, behind her, asking Jos politely for the favour of a word with his wife, 'for old times' sake'. Jos was enjoying himself too much to feel any resentment at the request, and shortly afterwards George was bending over Sarah's outstretched hand with all the studied negligence of a gentleman of the world. She saw his eyes take in the elegance of her court gown, with its décolletage, its flounces and quilting, and the little ruffled ribbon band about her neck, and her hair dressed high and illuminated with a pompom knot of flowers. She saw with undeniable pleasure both admiration and respect in his expression.

'How delightful to see you again,' he said. 'And how well you look.' That, she thought, studying him through her smile, was more than she could truthfully have said of him. He looked much older than his thirty-nine years, careworn, even a little dissipated. She noticed too that his skin beneath its scattering of powder was not over-clean, his wig was a little askew, and he had clearly been drinking rather heavily.

'You are well, I hope? And your wife?' Her eyes strayed

181

across to his box, wondering which of the three ladies there was the one he had married.

Seeing where she looked he said, 'Oh, she is well enough: she chose to stay at home . . .' He paused, and she had a sudden fear that he was about to strike a more intimate note, even to talk of the feelings he had once had for her, but he only said, 'I can see you are happy. And your husband has done well – I hear him spoken of everywhere. He seems to have caused quite a sensation at court . . .' He glanced, smiling slightly, at Jos, who joined them, the conversation at once becoming general. Later, Jos told Sarah that it was said George Lathom had lost a large part of his fortune in reckless living. A sudden reformation in his style of life might still save the situation if he put his mind to it, but it was also said that his wife, weary of his unkindness and extravagance, was almost wholly estranged from him.

Sarah, listening to all this as they rode in the coach back to their lodgings, slipped her hand into Jos's. 'There, love – see what you saved me from.'

He grinned. 'If you'd had the managing of him he'd not be in this state now – but, mind, that's not a recommendation for you to go taking him in hand.'

Sarah laughed and kissed him. He looked tired, she thought, but then he had been ceaselessly busy since they came to London, so it was hardly surprising.

'I was going to write to Bentley tonight,' he said when they reached their bedroom, 'but I think I'm too tired – I'll write in the morning.' His need to write so often to his friend no longer troubled Sarah, for she understood it. She found herself wishing that she could see Bentley again herself, now, at this very minute, so that she could share with him her many crowding impressions of London, and hear what he thought of them. Jos was too full of his own concerns to want to talk of hers; and besides he was too weary.

It was not until next morning, when after a restless night Jos woke heavy-eyed with a headache and a searing pain in his leg, that Sarah realised he was more than just tired.

'I'm in for another bout, I'm afraid, love,' he said, with a hint of a smile, mirthless enough, for these familiar bouts of pain and fever came ever more frequently, and each time his knee took longer to regain some degree of strength. By now he knew that the days when he used, sometimes, to be altogether free from pain had gone for good.

Sarah sent word to John, who came full of concern and summoned a surgeon to the bedside. While the surgeon examined Jos, Sarah stood with John by the window looking out on the noisy street, and said softly, 'Sometimes I'm afraid it will lay him low for good. He seems to be worse after each attack – and they happen so often now.'

'Do you want me to bring in one of the fashionable physicians to advise? I'm not sure who would be best – though the best of all of course is Erasmus Darwin, and you know him I think. You know he's had every possible inducement held out to him to settle in London?'

Sarah smiled, remembering Darwin's own colourful observations on the subject when he came once to dine at the Brick House. 'He hates London. I think he's rooted for ever in Lichfield.'

'Ah well, there we are: he'll never make his fortune in Lichfield, that's for sure. But our loss is your gain. I should ask his advice when you're home again.'

Once, during the next long night as she lay at Jos's side in the dark, kept wakeful by his restless feverish stirrings in search of ease from pain, Sarah found herself dreading the possibility that they might not reach home, that Jos might never again be well enough to travel. But that was perhaps the lowest point of his illness. Slowly, day by day, the fever lessened, and though it left him weak and easily tired he was only the more eager to set off for home as soon as he could hobble round a little on Sarah's arm.

They took the journey slowly, staying one night at Bleinheim where they admired the splendours of the Duke of Marlborough's mansion – 'Just about a fit setting,' so Jos said laughingly, 'for the best Wedgwood ware' – and spent an evening with the Duke's steward at a theatrical performance at Woodstock, which only served to remind them of the splendours they had seen in London.

But all the way home it was Burslem that was in Sarah's thoughts: the little brick house, the works; and Susannah. They had been gone nearly a month now: would the baby still remember her after so long? Would the little girl herself have changed beyond all recognition?

They reached home in the dark, taking the last part of the journey of necessity on horseback though the ride left Jos white and shivering with pain and exhaustion. The first – the only – essential was to see him safely to bed, with a good fire in the grate and a hot brick wrapped in flannel at his feet. And only then was Sarah free to make her way to where Susannah slept in her cradle in the bedroom across the landing.

She stood looking down at the rosy slumbering infant, thankful that this was still recognisably the Susannah she knew, alive and well and content. But she had changed during the weeks in the care of her aunt and Nan: her cheeks were more rounded, her hair a little longer, curling at the ends, and she had grown.

'She's been as good as gold, Mrs Wedgwood,' Nan told her. Sarah knew she ought to leave the child to sleep but she could not bear to do so after so long. She bent down and lifted Susannah into her arms.

The blue eyes opened wide, studying the face above them with steady gravity; and then a small hand reached up, fingers spread wide, and Susannah smiled and crowed with laughter. Sarah laughed too, though there were tears in her eyes.

It was strange to be home, after so much time away and so many new experiences. In some ways everything was familiar, exactly as it had always been; and yet in another way it was curiously unfamiliar, as if some kind of invisible barrier had fallen into place to cut her off from everything she knew so well, so that she was no longer quite a part of it. The works were just the same; and the men working there; and Tom Wedgwood and Tom Byerley, glad to see her back again. She had a great deal to do for Jos became very ill again, and it fell to her to pick up all the threads left by their absence. But she felt restless, unsettled, as if her travels had made her unable any longer to be contented with the narrow horizons of her home. Burslem seemed smaller than before, a little mean, a dirty mediocre place, matching London neither in splendour – of course – nor even in degradation.

She took John Wedgwood's advice and sent word to Dr Darwin, who clicked his tongue over Jos's condition and ordered her to make up the spare bed to accommodate him. 'I want to k-keep a close eye on him for a d-day or two,' he said, thus succeeding in both alarming and reassuring her at the same time. In the end, because she trusted him, the reassurance won; and as it happened by the next day Jos was already clearly on the way to recovery.

'Is there any way of guarding against these terrible bouts of illness? Each one seems to leave him worse than ever,' she asked the doctor before he left.

'N-no way that he d-doesn't know about already,' said Darwin gruffly. 'But don't worry. He's no weakling, or he'd n-never have lasted so long. He'll d-do now – but s-send word at once if you're worried.'

Sarah found when she went in to Jos that Dr Darwin had left more than medicine behind: he had also dispensed a piece of gossip which he thought might interest his patient.

'You know old Mrs Ashenhurst?' Sarah looked puzzled. 'At Ridge House – the large estate on the hill on the way to Newcastle.' Sarah did remember then. She remembered the heat of a summer day, heavy with thunder, the distant views, the brilliant gorse; and Jos telling her that this was his favourite spot. She had rarely been that way since.

'Yes, I remember,' she said quietly.

'It seems her only son is in the army and settled in Ireland. Darwin says the estate will be sold on her death, and he wonders if she would sell before then, if it were made worth her while.' He smiled at the excitement in Sarah's eyes. 'The canal is planned to pass just at the foot of the hill there, clear through the estate,' he added casually.

Sarah reached out and took his hand in hers. 'Oh, Jos – if only . . .' she whispered, hardly daring to breathe her hope out loud.

CHAPTER NINE

1766–7

On the 14th May 1766, the Bill approving the construction of a Grand Trunk Canal from the Trent to the Mersey ended its passage through parliament, and three weeks later at the Crown Inn at Stone the proprietors of the scheme met to set up a committee and appoint its officers.

Jos came home next day with his own personal triumph to report. 'They've made me Treasurer,' he said proudly; and then grinned at the look on Sarah's face. 'Don't worry, it'll probably be more a case of raising money than keeping accounts, and besides everything has to be approved and scrutinized by the committee. You can keep an eye on me too if you feel the need.'

Sarah came and slid her arm through his, and kissed him. 'I'm sure you'll do very well. They couldn't have found a more honest and trustworthy man for the post, as I don't doubt they know full well. Do you pay yourself a salary for your pains?'

He laughed. 'I have to bear my own expenses from my nothing-a-year you know – but I shall enjoy having a part in such a fine scheme . . .'

'As if you haven't had a part all along! There would have been no scheme without you, now would there?'

He would not agree; but she knew that when, on 26 July that year, every one of the potters closed his works and came to celebrate the opening of the enterprise, they all knew it was more than anything Jos's day of glory. And in acknowledgement of that fact, Jos himself was asked to cut the first turf at the Brownhills near Tunstall, close to the point where, one day, the canal would run into the projected tunnel through Harecastle Hill.

'I wish Bentley could have been here,' Jos said as they rode into the green valley; and Sarah thought he must be the only man connected with the scheme not to be present on this historic occasion. She saw Lord Gower and the other aristocratic patrons in a little group just slightly aloof from the rest of the gathering; Thomas Wheildon and her uncle John Wedgwood, prominent among the potters; the imposing figure of Matthew Boulton, metal manufacturer from Birmingham whose energy and enterprise matched Jos's own and who hoped that there might in due course be a further canal link with the Severn passing his own works; John Sparrow, Jos's lawyer, who was clerk to the proprietors of the scheme; Erasmus Darwin, over from Lichfield for the day and already deep in argumentative discussion with the big awkward ungainly figure of James Brindley, the engineer, whose own side of the conversation was conducted in gruff monosyllables; and a whole host of ordinary happy people – wives, workmen, children – enjoying the holiday atmosphere and the promised feasting to follow.

They had of course to endure a cluster of speeches beforehand, beginning with Lord Gower and ending at last with Jos, each recounting at length the difficulties that had beset the path that brought them at last to this day – rival schemes, reluctant landowners, political manoeuvring. But Jos's speech was the briefest and most humorous and ended with a flourish as he thrust a spade into the turf and set the canal work on its way.

They cheered as he lifted the neat square of earth – red-brown beneath, tufted above with grass and summer flowers – on to the barrow held ready at his elbow by Brindley; and then at last, after one concluding speech, the expected barrel of ale was rolled in for toasts to be drunk to anyone and everyone who had anything to do with the scheme.

Sarah, with something of a sense of duty, braced herself to go and talk to Brindley. She liked him, and welcomed him often to eat at their table at the Brick House, but he was so inarticulate that conversation with him was difficult in the extreme. He seemed to come to life only when canals or engineering problems were mentioned, and even then the words did not come easily. He always carried chalk in his pocket, so that when language failed him he could clear a space on the nearest available floor and draw a diagram there: Sarah's kitchen flagstones had suffered several times already in the cause of the canal. She would love to have been present

187

in the House of Commons when he and Jos put the case for the scheme before the parliamentary committee.

This time though she did not have to struggle for very long to elicit some kind of response to her inquiries after his health and that of his young wife, for Lord Gower came to join them, bowing to her and skilfully drawing them both into conversation about the course of the canal. Brindley's face lit up, and when Gower asked him what problems he would face in tunnelling through the great mass of Harecastle Hill, the engineer impulsively reached for a cheese from an adjoining table laden with food, cut it up, and crouching on the grass arranged the pieces about an ant heap to demonstrate exactly how it was much easier to go through the hill – using miners skilled in tunnelling – than to construct an elaborate system of locks to take the canal over the top. Sarah watched in fascination as the great hands sliced and moved the cheese about, and the ants ran over the creamy yellow surface; and she was sure that Brindley saw only the long rocky hill, the valleys on either side, and the straight beautiful tunnel that would one day run through it.

'R-remarkable man,' Dr Darwin commented to her later, when she had at last extricated herself from the fascinated little crowd that had gathered about Brindley. 'N-no book learning to s-speak of, yet he s-solves problems n-no one's ever thought of before.'

Sarah smiled. 'Jos says he takes himself to bed in a darkened room when he can't see a way out of a difficulty. A day or two like that, he says, and it all comes clear!'

They stood in silence watching Brindley from a distance, seeing Jos come limping, stick in hand, to join the spectators: his leg must be tiring him after all the exertion of the day. The same thought must have struck Darwin, reminding him too how Jos had come by his disability, for he said suddenly, 'Did Wedgwood tell you? I suggested inoculating your little ones against s-smallpox.'

Sarah looked round at him. 'But John's only four months old! Wouldn't it be dangerous?'

'Of course it would be d-dangerous – it'll be d-dangerous at any age. But not as d-dangerous as a full dose of s-smallpox caught by chance when maybe they're n-not so fit to throw it off. I know what I'm t-talking about you know – I inoculated

188

my own b-boys. Think about it – n-next spring m-maybe. You d-don't want them going through what that m-man of yours has suffered.'

'No.' She frowned. 'We'll see – I don't know . . .'

But Jos himself had no doubts, and early the next year Susannah and John were inoculated with a slight dose of the deadly disease that had so scarred Jos's life; and at the same time Kate Willets' two little girls underwent the same ordeal. At Kate's suggestion Susannah was sent to stay at Newcastle, where the company of the cousins she loved might distract her from the discomforts of the sickness.

It was a harrowingly anxious time for the parents of the four children. Jos rode almost daily to Newcastle to see how Susannah was faring, but Sarah was kept at home by her fretful feverish son, unable to leave him, wearied by the sickness of a new pregnancy, and yet desperate to see her daughter again.

In the end John recovered more quickly than any of them; and on the Sunday following, Sarah and Jos rode to Newcastle to join in morning worship at the meeting house with a fervent thankfulness, for Kate had told them that Susannah too was over the worst. When they went afterwards for dinner at the Willets' house they found their daughter playing happily with her cousins Jenny and Katt, the marks of the sickness already almost gone from her skin; she was a little thinner than before but bright-eyed and happy.

Jos left Sarah at Newcastle to spend the rest of the afternoon with the little girl and see her safely tucked up in bed with her cousins after supper, and then to stay overnight himself before coming home in the morning.

Once Susannah was asleep, Sarah made her way down to the kitchen where she was surprised to find Kate lining a pie dish with pastry for an apple pie. Kate looked up as Sarah came in. 'Now do you believe she's going to be all right?'

Sarah nodded. 'I believe it – thank God.' She pulled a stool from beneath the table and sat facing Kate, reaching out to take an apple from the bowl, and a knife, and setting to work to peel and slice.

'You don't really need to sit here with me you know,' Kate said. 'There's a good fire in the parlour, and the cat just longing to curl up on someone's knee. It's only my whim to

spend my Sunday evening pottering in the kitchen when I
know there'll be no superior disapproving looks from cook.'

Sarah laughed. 'I'd much rather be here with you than
cosseting your fat cat upstairs.' Then she grew grave again. 'I
don't know how I can ever thank you for your care of
Susannah.'

'Don't speak of it – you'd have had more than you could
manage with Sukey and baby Jack sick together, and you
with another on the way. It was the best thing for her to be
here – in any case she kept my little rogues company, and
they could all be sick and ill-tempered together.' She took the
slices as they fell from the knife and swiftly began to fill the
pie. 'You know what I think, Sarah?'

Sarah smiled. 'A hundred and one good things, I know.
What is it this time?'

Kate sat down suddenly, her eyes bright in her rosy face. 'I
think we need a holiday, you and I.'

Sarah laughed, taken aback. 'Oh, Kate, what would our
husbands say? Don't they deserve a rest too?'

'Oh, those two can't bear to leave their work for five
minutes, you know that. William frets terribly if he's not
within reach of his flock and his study meetings and his books
– and as for Jos he lives for his pots and his canal and his
committees and so on. No, what I had in mind was a nice
female jaunt – shops and a little social life, just to set us up
again – but if we leave it too long you'll be in no condition to
go jaunting.'

'And where do you suggest we go?' Sarah demanded,
suddenly catching some of Kate's enthusiasm. It had been a
long winter, and the past weeks had told on her terribly, and
on Kate too.

'Liverpool, of course – a nice short journey, and Miss
Oates is always pressing us to stay. What could be better? I
must have new curtains for William's study, and Margaret
will give us some commissions, I'm sure. And wouldn't you
like to get some ideas for furnishing your fine new house,
when it's built? What do you say?'

Miss Elizabeth Oates was Bentley's housekeeper – older
sister of his dead wife – a plain sensible woman who had
visited Burslem once with Bentley, and made a favourable
impression on her hosts. Sarah felt the colour creep into her

face, but hoped that in the dim candlelight Kate had not seen it. 'What do you think Jos will say if we propose going to visit his dear Bentley without him?'

'Why should he have all the pleasure of the great man's company all the time? I think it's our turn, don't you? Besides, we'll be visiting Miss Oates not Mr Bentley. Don't you think she deserves visitors in her own right? You know how she'll love to show us the sights of Liverpool.'

Sarah tried not to think how pleasant it would be to see Bentley again. Jos had seen him several times since that momentous first visit to Burslem, but she only once; and she found herself longing to talk to him, sing with him. But she said cautiously, 'I don't know. I don't like to leave Jos when he's had so much on his mind.'

'But his worries are over now. You said yourself his leg's not been too troublesome lately. He's got Peter Swift to help him – Mr Bentley knows a good man when he meets one, doesn't he? – and you said you thought Tom Byerley was settling down (which I doubt, but never mind). No, there couldn't be a better time to leave Jos – do you both good. Besides, we can be there and back within the week.'

'And what about the children?'

'Oh, Sarah, stop making difficulties! We both have excellent girls to care for our children. Make the most of it while you can leave them – when there are three you'll not find it so easy you know.'

Sarah was convinced, because she wanted to be, and rode home next day in high spirits, ready to tackle Jos.

It was a bright gusty March morning, with a sense of bubbling life about it that exactly matched her mood. She rode steadily enough down the long hill from Newcastle into the shelter of the valley, where work had already begun on the canal; then on a sudden impulse turned her plodding mount off the road and on to the track that led up over the hill to Burslem, and urged the reluctant beast into a fast trot – a canter was beyond him.

She did not often come this way, even though it held such happy memories of that long ago day at the fair. But soon, if all went well, this sheltered sunny hillside with its trees and clumps of gorse and little stony fields would belong to them. The negotiations were already under way – if slowly, for Mrs

Ashenhurst was proving a difficult woman – and they had begun to plan both the works and the house. The 'useful' part of the works, where the everyday domestic items, including the creamware (now called queen's ware by royal consent) were made, would remain at Burslem under Tom Wedgwood's direction; while here the new works would concentrate on the classical-style vases and other ornamental items which were becoming increasingly popular – their production and development had been Bentley's idea, to a large extent.

Sarah looked about her as she rode, imagining how this quiet hillside might look one day if all went well. It was to be called Etruria, after the Italian province where, it was said, the best pottery of ancient times had been made. Recently Jos's imagination had been fired by copies of drawings sent to him by Lord Cathcart; they were designed as illustrations for a book on classical antiquities, and had been done by Cathcart's kinsman William Hamilton, Ambassador to Naples, who was a noted collector of Greek and Roman objects and of vases in particular. Jos had dreams of making vases as fine – and as renowned – as those he had seen so lovingly depicted.

Then she reached the brow of the hill, and Burslem rose before her, a scar of clay and smoke on the green slopes.

In the hall of the Brick House she came face to face with Tom Byerley. What he had been doing she did not know but he started as she came in, stared at her, mumbled something about being in a hurry, and before she could close the door or ask any questions had pushed past her out of the house. She watched him go, a little puzzled; and then put him out of her mind and went in search of Jos.

She ran Jos to earth at last in the hovel surrounding one of the kilns, discussing firing temperatures with the fireman, looking rather small and fragile beside the other man's great bulk; seeing him like that always frightened her a little. Jos, though, was more concerned about Susannah than anything else, and only when Sarah had assured him that their daughter was still making excellent progress and would soon be fit to come home (if she could be persuaded to leave her cousins) was she able to put forward Kate's proposal. 'A grand idea,' he nodded approvingly. 'So long as I can come in

192

person to fetch you back here afterwards.' She laughed, and they linked arms and walked back to the house together, discussing the arrangements for the trip.

It was only then that they discovered the reason for Byerley's odd behaviour. On the table in the hall, half concealed in the dimness beneath a candlestick, lay a folded piece of paper; and opening it they found it was a note from the young man. Jos read it aloud: "'Uncle – forgive me – I *must* try what I can do on the stage. I hear they want players in Dublin – I beg you to tell my mother I shall write as soon as I have news. Your dutiful nephew, Tom Byerley."'

"'Dutiful nephew" forsooth!' He gazed in exasperation at Sarah, 'What shall we do? I wonder how long he's been gone?'

'About two hours, I should think. I met him as I came home – he must have been leaving the note then.'

'And he rode over from Newcastle this morning as usual, so he'll have been mounted. We could go after him.'

'Perhaps,' suggested Sarah, 'he should be allowed to try the stage. He's thought of nothing else for months – and you said yourself it was preventing him from giving his mind to his work. Very likely a few weeks as a poor player will show him what a fool he's been, and he'll come home determined to settle to a useful trade.'

Jos sighed. 'I hope so, Sally. Sometimes I despair of him. And what are we going to tell his mother?'

Margaret Byerley was distressed at her son's departure, but hardly surprised. 'I never thought he'd settle while he had all that play-acting nonsense in his head,' was her resigned observation on the matter. It seemed that he had for the past months been saving carefully from the small wage his uncle paid him – hence Sarah's impression that he was settling down, for he allowed himself few pleasures. Clearly he had been saving for just such an escapade as this; but at least they need not worry that he would not be able to keep himself, for a little time at least.

But for Sarah and Kate, Byerley's flight presented a further difficulty. 'There'll be one pair of hands the less here at the works,' Sarah said anxiously to Jos. 'I think our trip to Liverpool will have to wait.'

'Nonsense! Not having Tom do the accounts is a positive

advantage – Peter Swift will do much better if he hasn't to keep an eye on the lad. No, you go – after all, I want an excuse to come to Liverpool too, you know.'

Smiling, Sarah kissed him. 'Since when did you need an excuse?'

Just before they left, Margaret Byerley heard from her son. He had never reached Dublin, for at Chester he had learned, somehow, that there were no openings there for a stage-struck lad with no experience whatever. But as chance would have it a band of strolling players was performing in Chester just at the very moment of his arrival in the city, and he had managed to persuade them to take him on. He had been with them only a day, so he could not tell his mother yet what success he had met with.

'Foolish lad!' was Jos's only comment. 'I shall be surprised if he's not home again by the summer.'

Kate and Sarah took the stage coach from Newcastle to Warrington, and there stayed for one night at the recently founded Warrington Academy with Joseph Priestley – minister, lecturer, and old friend of William Willet – and his young wife. They arrived tired after their journey, but still somehow found themselves sitting up until well after midnight deep in theological discussion with their hosts. 'Sometimes,' said Kate, when at last she stretched thankfully out on the bed she was sharing with Sarah, 'I think it would be so restful to be surrounded by men who think only of hunting and drinking.'

'But how dull,' Sarah pointed out, and Kate laughed.

In Liverpool Bentley came with Miss Oates to meet their coach. 'Welcome to our fine town,' he greeted them, holding out a hand to help them down. Kate stepped out first, with a kiss for both their hosts, warm and natural and unaffected in a way that Sarah envied. She herself was acutely self-conscious as she laid her hand on Bentley's outstretched palm, and stepped out into the inn yard. She had forgotten how very dark his eyes were, and what a disturbing effect they had on her, and she felt herself blushing as he kissed her, though it was no more than the customary greeting between friends.

She liked Liverpool. It had none of the dirt and poverty and degradation of London, though there were poorer areas near the docks. There were potworks to the east of the town, but little else to taint an atmosphere freshened by winds blowing along the Mersey from the sea. Most of its population was prosperous, tempted there by just that clear air and the open sea views and pleasant countryside around. There were public gardens and tree-lined walks, and large fine houses set about with flower gardens and fruit trees, churches and a public library (one of the very few in the country), bowling greens and a theatre, fine shops and inns and coffee houses, and the bustling river full of shipping.

Perhaps the finest street of all in this town of wide clean streets was the one where Bentley lived – the aptly named Paradise Street. His house was spacious, and provided not only with comfortable furniture but a fine collection of books and pictures, many painted by close friends, and set about with a large and lovely garden. As Bentley ushered them inside Sarah was struck by the atmosphere of cultivated good taste which filled the house, a sense that here was the home of a civilised man, a fit setting for the gathering together of congenial friends.

They had music that day after dinner – with two or three light-hearted satirical songs of Bentley's own – and good talk, not too demanding on their tired brains; and after an ample supper they went to bed. 'You'll need to gather your strength for tomorrow's assault on our shops,' Bentley told them teasingly as Miss Oates led them up the stairs to their room.

It was not just the shopping that demanded all the stamina they had. Every one of the five days in Liverpool was filled with activity of mind and body. They shopped, certainly, enjoying the unaccustomed luxury of being able to choose from a wide range of goods; they explored the fine gardens, named Ranelagh after their London model – though Sarah thought (and told Bentley so) that they were finer than Ranelagh, less showy, more countrified and restful; they called on acquaintances and friends; and they went, on Sunday, to swell the little congregation at the splendid new Octagon Chapel in Temple Court, so enthusiastically established by Bentley and his friends for the practice of 'rational religion', with its simple set form of worship, and an eloquent thoughtful sermon from its respected minister, Dr Nicholas Clayton.

On Monday Kate was anxious to visit the shops again, with

a number of commissions to carry out for Margaret Byerley for goods to supply her little milliner's shop in Newcastle. But Sarah felt disinclined for shopping – for which her enthusiasm was always limited – and in the end Kate and Miss Oates agreed amicably to keep one another company, and Sarah prepared to spend a day quietly in the house and garden, sampling Bentley's well-stocked library or wandering along the grassy paths edged with spring flowers. Bentley, unaware of these arrangements, had left the house before breakfast, to work at his office or warehouse, Sarah supposed – she had no very clear idea what his business entailed.

'No wonder Jos likes coming here so much,' she thought as she studied the titles of the long rows of books. There was everything here: novels, plays, poetry, scientific works, books on antiquities or theology or philosophy, classical works in Greek and Latin, and a considerable number of volumes in Italian and French, in which two languages the well-travelled Bentley was fluent. She had taken down one or two books, dipped into them and returned them to the shelves, but made no final choice, when she turned at the sound of the door opening to see Bentley himself standing there.

For a moment she felt absurdly guilty, like a schoolgirl discovered in some misdemeanour; she could see that Bentley was surprised to see her. But he simply smiled comfortably, setting her at her ease. 'Were you daunted by the prospect of yet more shopping? Very wise – a necessary evil at the best of times. A library provides much pleasanter recreation.'

'Especially one such as this,' Sarah returned, wishing she did not sound quite so much like a simpering society woman; she had meant the compliment to come from the heart.

Bentley stepped towards her. 'Have you found anything to your taste?'

'So much that I don't know what to choose.' She was very aware of him at her side, as if some electrical impulse was running between them. She wondered if he felt it too, but she could see no sign in his face that he did. He reached past her to take a book from the shelf, almost brushing her shoulder with his arm, so that she shivered a little. 'Have you read this?'

She looked at the title. '*The Divina Commedia of Dante* – but isn't that in Italian?'

'This is a translation, though I have the Italian. You have

some Latin, I believe – you might find you could understand it. It's better in the original – much of the poetry is lost in the English.' He reached down the first of three leather-bound volumes from another shelf. 'Here is the *Inferno* in the Italian – see if you can make sense of it. I've heard it said that the vision of hell has the most drama – but for myself I think the *Paradiso* the finest, so long as one first progresses through the whole.'

She opened the book, smiling at him. 'Don't you find it all popish nonsense, the idea of damnation and purgatory and so forth? It hardly accords with your views on rational religion.'

'Ah, but it's poetry – and besides, Dante seems to me to imply that hell is rather the natural consequence of the wrong we do than an externally applied punishment. That seems right somehow. I think that in every philosophy there is some truth – and, talking of truth, what did you think of our Octagonal worship yesterday?'

'I found it pleased the mind, a more formal version of the worship at our Newcastle meeting house perhaps – but I wonder if in the end worship needs to reach the emotions as well as the reason – I don't know . . .' She broke off, her ear caught by some distant sound carried on the wind. 'Church bells, on a Monday? Is there some festival?'

She thought his face had an odd expression – a little taut, with a hint of grimness about it. 'Simply a ship returning safe to harbour, after a long voyage.'

She smiled. 'That's a pleasant custom, to welcome it with bells. Will it be one of the ships you trade with? Or do you not know?'

She had not imagined the grimness then, for it deepened now and spread to his voice, giving it an unaccustomed hardness of tone. 'I know. And I have no commercial interest in it. I don't trade with slavers.'

'Oh!' She was intrigued, knowing his views. 'Will it be carrying slaves then?'

He shook his head. 'No, not now. Very occasionally slaves are brought here for sale, but for the most part they are sold in the West Indies.'

'I know very little about the trade.' She smiled faintly. 'We don't see slaves in Burslem you know.'

'You are fortunate.' He was not smiling, and she wondered

if she had offended him; she had never seen him angry, so she could not be sure. But after a moment he asked hesitantly, 'Are you tired? Have you decided firmly on a quiet day?'

'No – not necessarily. Have you an alternative to offer?'

'Please say if you would rather not – but if you wish to know something of the slave trade I can appoint myself your instructor. You would have to give me a little time to make some arrangements, but it is not far to the docks. We can walk there in a few minutes – I know how you enjoy walking!'

She smiled warmly. 'I should like that. Shall we see the ship come in?'

'No, we should be too late. Besides, I wouldn't encourage you to greet a newly arrived slave ship in my company – I am not exactly popular amongst slave traders. However, there is another ship which arrived last week – and while everyone's busy elsewhere . . .' He broke off, and then added briskly, 'If you would like to come, make yourself ready – I'll be gone for a few minutes, but not long. Wrap up warmly – the wind can be cold at the riverside.'

There was an agreeable, slightly conspiratorial atmosphere about the whole business which excited Sarah. She changed from her loose morning gown into the serviceable riding habit of dark blue cloth – let out a little at the waist – in which she had travelled to Liverpool, and filled the time she had left in the garden, enjoying the warmth inside its sheltering walls.

Later, out in the street, walking along with her arm in Bentley's, she realised that the wind had a keen edge to it, setting the feathers dancing in her hat, tugging Bentley's dark hair free from its confining ribbon.

'What arrangements did you have to make?' she asked him.

'I have found a seaman prepared to show us over his ship.'

'I thought you weren't popular with slave traders.'

He gave her a quiet sideways smile. 'He didn't know me – and I'm afraid I did offer a small inducement.'

'A bribe? Oh, fie, Mr Bentley, to think of you stooping to corruption!'

He laughed, but she thought it touching that he also coloured a little. 'In a good cause, Mrs Wedgwood – I have every excuse.'

'Then you must be forgiven.'

They emerged from a narrow alley into the full sharp wind

198

blowing from the river and across the wharves of the Salthouse dock. Where it opened into the river the tall-masted outline of a ship moved black against the shining water, coming slowly their way, and cheered and waved in its passing by an enthusiastic crowd. Sarah had seen a scattering of black faces in the Liverpool streets, but there were none here today, she noticed.

Bentley led her quickly in the opposite direction, towards a ship rocking quietly at anchor. The wharf alongside it was deserted, except for a single seaman, stocky and bronzed, wandering aimlessly about. It was to him that Bentley went now, whispering quickly to Sarah, 'I must beg you – show no emotion, keep your opinions to yourself. He thinks us only ordinary visitors taking an interest in the shipping.' And then he called to the man.

Close to, the ship seemed huge, with great high black wooden sides towering over them. Sarah gazed up at it, and wondered if Bentley had really intended that they should board it. She could not believe that she would ever be able to climb up there.

At a shout from the sailor a rope ladder slithered and dangled its way down towards them. 'Can you manage the climb? I'll come behind, in case you fear to lose your footing.'

She had no wish to appear cowardly, and so she reached up and pulled herself on to the first swaying rung, her hands gripping fast to the harsh tarred rope. 'I can do it,' she said as if to convince herself, and began to edge her way, step by step, up to the high rim of the deck. Thank goodness she had worn neither hoop nor train today!

After what seemed a very long time, a great arm shot out from above, emerging apparently from a broad bearded face; and in a moment, somehow, she was standing on the scrubbed deck, buffeted by the wind and watching Bentley scramble after her over the side, followed by the seaman from below. Once he had recovered his breath, Bentley was cool but smoothly affable. 'Now,' he said to the sailors, 'before you show us your fine ship, please to tell us exactly how the trade works – my companion here is most anxious to know, being a stranger to Liverpool.'

The big bearded man grinned, and Sarah assumed an expression of attentiveness. 'Well, suppose I tell you how it

199

was with the voyage just ended. We loaded up here with a good cargo – now, let's see, what did we carry this last time? Malt, spirits,' he began to check the items off on his fingers as he spoke, 'muskets, knives, gunpowder; brass ware; cotton goods; pots, good earthenware pots . . .'

'Ah,' put in Sarah brightly, 'my husband is a potter. I wonder if you carried any of his goods?' She saw Bentley shoot a startled look in her direction.

'Very likely, ma'am – very likely.' The sailor was clearly not much interested in the matter. 'That would be about all, I reckon. Then we set sail – and a rough passage it is to the Gold Coast, I can tell you. I've done it more times than I can remember, and I'm lucky to be alive to tell the tale.'

'The Gold Coast – where's that?'

'Africa, of course – where the black gold comes from, good healthy slaves, men and women and children. We trade our goods with the chiefs and the white traders, and we get slaves in return.'

'How do you get them? Do they come willingly?' It was a stupid question, asked in a tone of fatuous innocence. The smaller seaman gave a snort of laughter, and the bearded man grinned with a flash of white teeth.

'Aye, willingly enough with a gun at their backs and shackles to their arms. This last voyage was a good one – a full ship. She's 150 tons, and we carried 400 slaves and got 370 odd clear to Barbados in nine weeks.'

'And what happens to the slaves in Barbados?'

'Sold in the market – the buyers come and look at their teeth, general health and what have you, much like buying a horse – and then it's work on the sugar plantations, hard work in hot sun – only negroes can stand it, and then they need a good overseer to keep them at it. Even then there's a high death rate – but that keeps the trade going, so who am I to complain?'

She looked away so that he should not read in her face what she thought of that remark. 'You say there are women and children amongst the slaves. Do they come as families with their menfolk?'

The man shrugged. 'Who knows? Sometimes maybe. But we don't trouble about that – they don't have feelings like us white men you know. Think of them as cattle like – so long as

200

they get food and exercise on the voyage that's all they mind about.'

Sarah looked about her at the empty deck, imagining it peopled with seamen, and four hundred slaves; it seemed suddenly very small. 'How can they exercise?'

'Dance,' said the other man laconically. 'You should see them.'

'Do they like dancing?' Sarah asked in astonishment, trying to understand how anyone in such bleak circumstances – even with few human feelings – could bear to dance. After all, even animals moped if they were unhappy. She had heard cows cry when their calves were taken away.

The man smiled. 'Aye, that they do – and if they don't they change their minds with a cat o' nine tails at their backs. Got to keep them healthy, you see. Mind, that's when the weather's fair. They're all snug below when it's bad.'

The bearded man led them to the hatchway set in the deck. 'Here's where we stow the cargo, for safe travelling.' He lifted it, and bent to hook a narrow wooden ladder on to the edge. 'Want to take a look?'

Sarah came nearer and then recoiled, holding her hand to her nose.

'Aye, smells bad, doesn't it? Smell of negroes, that – can't get rid of it, though we'd none on the way back.'

She felt Bentley's hand on her elbow. 'Do you want to go now?' he asked softly. Turning, she saw he was concerned, but she shook her head.

'No, I want to see,' she said with determination.

She took a deep breath and followed the bearded seaman into the hold, Bentley following.

Even breathing as little as she could the stench was dreadful, an ugly lingering smell of decay and excrement that reminded her forcibly of the stink of the churchyard at Burslem, though it was not quite the same. It was dark too, lit only by tiny holes at intervals along the sides, so that it was a while before she could make out any detail.

She saw at last that she stood in a kind of narrow passage running down the spine of the ship, though not for its full length. Once away from the hatchway she could not quite stand upright, but had to bend her head a little. On either side a shelf ran, evenly dividing the space in the hold.

'This is where the males are carried – there's another hold that way for the females, and another for the boys, all with their own hatches. This last trip we carried two hundred males in here, stacked on the shelves – shackled, of course, in case of trouble. We get mutinies sometimes.'

Two hundred men. Sarah looked from side to side, trying to imagine even one man travelling for nine weeks on that narrow shelf where there was scarcely room to sit in comfort, none at all to stand. No air, no light to speak of – and two hundred here in a space at the best no larger or wider than the dipping shed at the Brick House works, which Jos considered too small for five men not always working together.

Bentley asked some question which she did not quite catch; and she heard the seaman explain, 'Oh, if they don't eat we force feed – there's an instrument for that. Can't risk losing slaves through starvation. They do it for spite sometimes.'

'Spite?' thought Sarah. 'Or is it rather heartsickness? How must it feel to be carried by force from all you know and love, shackled in this tiny space with brutal men to guard you – no privacy, no quiet, no air, nowhere even to perform the natural functions but where you sit? And for a woman, torn from her family? Or a child from its mother? I could not eat if it were me. I should want to die.'

All of a sudden she thought the hold was full, the shelves crammed with dim shapes, dark anguished faces peering out at her, eyes pleading for help. She seemed to hear cries echoing in her ears, stifled weeping, moans of pain and desolation. The stench swamped her, seeping through ears and mouth and nostrils. The darkness deepened, closing in on her, horrible, full of terrors, fear and loneliness and deep despair.

She swayed and a hand closed on her arm. 'Sarah – Mrs Wedgwood . . .!' The hand steered her towards the gleam of light from the hatchway, and the phantom shapes faded into silence. 'Help me – she's feeling faint – there's so little air in here.'

Somehow – she didn't quite know how – she found herself at last back on the deck, drawing in great gulps of the clear sunny Liverpool air, looking round at the palatial warehouses, the distant bright-coloured crowd, the seagulls wheeling against the blue sky, and telling herself that this was real and not the weird nightmare that had overcome her just now.

Someone brought a stool and she sat down on it, aware of Bentley hovering anxiously over her; but already she felt better. She smiled at him reassuringly. 'Just the stuffiness – and my condition,' she lied.

The rope ladder safely negotiated once more, Bentley drew her arm through his and they set out along the wharf away from the ship. 'We'll go home now, as quickly as we can.'

'No – no, not yet.' She looked up at him. 'I want to walk a little – blow away that stink – please, if you don't mind.'

'Of course, if you're sure. We'll go to the Ladies' Walk.'

The Ladies' Walk was a beautiful avenue of trees to the north of the town, with a fine view across to the sea; and though it was some distance away Sarah walked quickly, as if trying somehow to leave behind the haunting impressions of the slave ship. They said nothing until they reached the walk, empty and sunlit and blessedly tranquil; and there slowed their pace at last.

'You'll wear me out!' Bentley said teasingly; and then, after a moment, he halted and turned to face her, laying his hand over hers where it rested on his arm. He looked troubled. 'I was wrong to take you there – it was thoughtless of me. It is no place for a lady of any feeling.'

She smiled ruefully. 'You would have us women educated, yet you are afraid of hurt feelings – it won't do, you know. I am *glad* to have seen it – everyone ought to see, and then perhaps there would be such anger it would not be allowed any more. And we call this a Christian country!' She paused, as if too moved to say any more, but after a time went on earnestly, 'I do not believe that slaves have different feelings – Mr Bentley, I *felt* the despair in that place!'

'I know: I also felt it, and not for the first time. And you are right, they have feelings as do the rest of us – more I think than those brutes who were our guides today. I have a friend who has a freed slave as his servant, and often at his house I have talked to the man – he thinks and feels as deeply as anyone I know, with a great understanding of humanity learned, I fear, in a hard school. He is only one, but not unique in that, I am sure.'

'Then what can be done? Is there any hope of ending the trade?'

'There's always hope – but I fear far more people regard it as necessary, even desirable, than would wish to abolish it.'

'Then they must be taught what kind of trade it is.'

'So they ought, but I doubt if they would care much if they were. If you look on the negroes as so many cattle, then I suppose they are not too badly used, considering – on the best of the ships, that is, like the one we saw today.'

'Best!'

He nodded gravely. 'Oh yes – there are much worse – greater overcrowding, terrible cruelty, poor food, a much greater mortality. That was a good slave ship.'

She stood still, facing him, looking up into his sombre face, and burst out with vehemence, 'There is no such thing! How can you talk of good slave ships, as if to give the slaves more space, more air, more of anything would make it right? If they lived like kings it would still be wrong, for they are not free and that is the evil!'

His eyes were bright with a kind of recognition, as if she had put into words all he felt. Suddenly, on impulse, he raised her hand and put it to his lips; and then stood holding it in a steady clasp, returning her gaze. At last he said, his voice husky with emotion, 'One day, please God, men will wonder that we ever stooped to enslave our fellows.'

He patted her hand then, suddenly brisk again, and drew it once more through his arm. 'We must be going home.' They turned and began to walk slowly back towards the town.

After a time, Sarah said, 'Mr Bentley, you don't think any of Jos's pots *do* go to Africa, do you?'

He shook his head emphatically. 'Certainly not. He would not allow it – and I act as his agent in Liverpool, remember. I am very particular who I do business with.'

'He wants you so much to be his partner you know.'

'Yes, I know.' He walked on in silence for a moment, deep in thought, and then said, 'But how can I leave all this? You see some of the work that needs to be done. There will be no hope for the slaves if the few of us who understand how evil the trade is fail to do what little we can. Here there are influential men who can be won over, newspapers that will publish articles on matters of concern, coffee houses where we can gather and talk – it may not be a great deal, but it is a beginning, and the only one possible at present.'

'And all Jos has to offer is the inducement of a fine house for you on our grand Etruria estate, when it's ours at last. Yes, I can see it's not much.'

He smiled a little wistfully. 'It's a great deal – not the house, of course, but the rest of it. Josiah is like no one else I know – I would give up a great deal to share in his enterprise; but some things – no, I cannot. It is not just the slave trade – there are other things too: the Octagon Chapel, for example. Besides, I know nothing about pot-making.'

'You'd soon learn; but yes, I can see Staffordshire has little to offer, set against Liverpool. You are needed here. Poor Jos.'

That evening, after supper, Sarah took the volume of Dante which Bentley had shown her that morning and sat quietly trying to make out the Italian. She was reluctant to go to bed too early, with this morning's impressions still fresh in her mind; nor did she want to talk about them to Kate, whom she had told only the essentials of her day's activities. Jos's sister, tired but happy after her shopping, nodded occasionally over her sewing, and Miss Oates was openly snoring. Bentley, seated a little apart in a corner of the room, appeared to be absorbed in his own reading, but after a time he edged his chair closer to Sarah's. 'How are you getting on?'

She smiled. 'Not very well, I'm afraid. I can make out bits here and there. This, for instance . . .' She pointed to the passage before her. 'Is that "Lancelot"? And "diletto" – delight perhaps? I wish I knew how it should be pronounced. Would you read some of it to me, in Italian?'

He did so, his deep gentle voice somehow richer, more gentle in those lovely lilting words. She did not need to understand; she could feel the poetry running through her veins, in her pulses, her whole self. She sat looking down at her hands, absorbed in the reading, but turned with a small cry of protest when he came to an end, rather suddenly she thought. She found that he was looking at her with a curious intentness.

'What does it mean? Will you translate it for me?'

'Perhaps it's better left untranslated,' he said lightly. 'I couldn't compete with the poetry.'

'Oh, please do – it did sound beautiful, but I should like to understand it too.'

He began, hesitantly, explaining, 'The poet in Hell has come on the souls of the lovers Paolo and Francesca . . .' He looked down at the book, translating smoothly: 'Francesca tells how they two "read one day, to amuse themselves, of Lancelot and the love that bound him; we were alone," she says, "and with no suspicion. That reading caused our eyes to meet, our faces to colour, but it was one moment only that vanquished us."' He broke off, and then went on in a hurried tone, rough-edged and a little breathless, 'They read how Lancelot kissed – and then they did the same. The passage ends, "that day we read no further". She was married, you see, but to Paolo's brother – just as Guinevere was the wife of Lancelot's dearest friend.' With a snap, abruptly, he closed the book and laid it aside. 'Josiah comes for you tomorrow, does he not?' His voice was almost curt in its crispness. Sarah nodded, unable to speak. She found that she was trembling.

Jos did come, limping into the house with his face aglow, to embrace the two people he loved best in all the world; and Kate too, for she was almost as loved. Sarah clung to him a moment longer than he expected, as if trying to reassure herself of something, though she was not quite sure what.

He was full of excitement over a new discovery. 'Yesterday I rode over to see how the work was going on the Harecastle tunnel,' he told them as they sat down to drink tea in the parlour. 'Brindley's taken on a huge task there, running the canal through the hill.'

'Why did he decide to go through and not over?' Kate asked. 'I was never quite sure.'

'He'd have needed a complicated system of locks to take it over the top – he thinks the tunnel simpler, and better for the barges. And of course it means the coal mines through the hill will have direct access to the canal. But there's a long way to go still – many years certainly. He asked to be remembered to you, Bentley – I told him I'd see you today.' The almost illiterate engineer was another of the many who held Bentley in the greatest admiration, a respect which was fully returned, though Bentley had all the education that Brindley lacked. 'They've made some finds,' Jos went on, '. . . the

206

backbone of a great whale, buried five yards down in the clay . . . and at the north side of the hill they found a layer of sandstone, enclosing small bits of coal and other minerals, and impressions of ferns, vetches, hawthorn – all kinds of plants and trees, and all shivering to atoms when they reached the open air. Darwin is to come over and see all our wonders – you should come too.'

The two men began eagerly to discuss Jos's theory that the fascinating strata might have originated as a liquid outpouring, something like the lava flowing from Vesuvius. Sarah, watching them, was struck at once by a new light-heartedness in Jos's friend, as if he were released from some constraint. He talked more than she had ever known him talk before, with wit and laughter and a gaiety that had a kind of wildness about it. 'He is glad Jos has come,' she thought. 'Perhaps he was growing bored with my company, and Kate's.'

Later, after supper, she asked Jos if there was any news of his nephew.

'I'm afraid not. His poor mother's very worried but there's little we can do.' He turned to Bentley. 'You heard of Tom Byerley's latest escapade, I suppose?'

'I did. I gather you decided to let him have a taste of the stage and see for himself if it would suit?'

'That was Sally's suggestion.'

'A wise woman, your wife.'

She coloured a little at his approval, but he did not look at her.

'I know,' said Jos cheerfully. 'You know, you should find yourself a wife, Bentley – with such a fine example of marriage before you, how can you fail to be tempted?'

'Ah,' returned Bentley quietly, 'but where would I find another such as Sarah?' He spoke lightly, but Sarah thought there was a tremor in his voice; only she could not be sure.

They left for home next day, and Sarah felt that these last few days had changed her for ever. She was sure of one thing: the memory of the slave ship would stay with her all her life. She would see Liverpool always with different eyes because of it; the clean wide streets, the fine buildings, the clear air, the bustling atmosphere were somehow all tainted by what she had felt that March morning. It was a relief to return to the honest dirt and smoke of Burslem; even, a little, to catch the smell from the churchyard, though it brought to mind only too readily the stench of the slave ship. But the churchyard smell was of the dead, speaking only of man's incompetence and carelessness; the ship stank of a living hell, made by man for man.

Once she was safely back home, caught up again in the routine – erratic as it sometimes was – of house and works, Jos felt it was his turn to go on his travels. He was anxious to go to London and investigate the possibility of setting up a warehouse there. 'I can't leave it all to John,' he explained. 'Besides, he won't know everything to look for – but I don't want to leave you for long in your condition.'

'Jos, the baby's not due until June at the earliest. I'm very well, and I had no difficulties with either of the other two. Go now, and you can be back long before this one's born.'

So he went, leaving Sarah in charge; and three weeks afterwards, while he was still away, Tom Byerley appeared one morning in the doorway of the throwing shed, looking tired and sheepish and thoroughly miserable. It had been raining since dawn, and he was soaked through and lavishly coated with mud.

Sarah exclaimed, gave a final hurried instruction to the lad wedging the clay, who had left several air pockets in his previous batch so ruining an entire firing of pots, and hurried to Byerley. 'Have you just got back? Have you been home?'

She thought simple practical questions were best; but even so as he shook his head she could see that his mouth was trembling. 'I don't suppose you've eaten lately either, or rested. Come to the house.' She steered him firmly out into the rain, across the yard and into the kitchen, warm and glowing and smelling of new bread. Glancing at Tom's face, she sent Betty on some lengthy errand upstairs, sat the boy at the table, made him take off his wet coat, and brought food for him.

But he did not begin to eat; he simply sat staring at her, quite clearly very near to tears, and then at last he growled, 'I'm not cut out for the stage,' sniffed loudly, and glowered down at the food.

Sarah laid a hand on his wet hair. 'Never mind. You gave it

a try. Sometimes you just have to accept that you can't be good at what you'd most like to do. I'll tell you something . . .' She pulled a stool from under the table and sat on it, her hand over his. 'More than anything else in all the world I would like to be able to throw a pot, just an ordinary pot – I don't aim to compete with your uncle. But I can't – I've tried, and I just haven't the gift for it. I have to be content with other things that I can do. Still, it's hard to accept. And in any case,' she added ruefully, 'I don't imagine you find my disappointments any comfort to you.'

He raised his eyes to her face. 'At least you can work in the pottery.' He sniffed again. 'They didn't want me at all.'

'But we do, if you'll have us.'

He tried to smile, but without much success. 'I don't want to be a clerk. I want to go on the stage.'

'I know. But you're here now – make the most of it for the moment. We can think what's best for you when your uncle's home. You might like to go and visit your father's people in Durham, to see if they have anything to offer. Or go and talk to Mr Bentley – he's a man of the world.'

Tom's face brightened slightly. 'Yes, I might do that.'

'Then you shall. But for now you ought to go and see your mother as soon as possible and let her know you're safe. So eat up, and then you can be on your way.'

He ate then, hungrily, and with each mouthful looked a little more cheerful. She helped him into his coat – warm, if not thoroughly dry – and saw him to the door. 'At least the rain's eased.'

He turned once before he left, to thank her; and added suddenly, 'I think I'll go to America. They won't expect the *best actors there.*'

'Maybe – but for now you're going no further than Newcastle, so on your way, lad!'

He laughed and went to the stable to saddle up his horse.

By the time Jos came home his nephew was resigned to trying again to find some sober and respectable post, in London perhaps this time – but with America as an alluring alternative should London fail to hold him. Jos, full of the possibilities of the various vacant buildings he had viewed in the capital, had little time to spare for the lad's troubles; and two days later a far graver trouble of his own put all else out of his mind.

Following him from London came a letter from John Wedgwood's business partner: Jos's brother was dead.

The very day of Jos's departure, the letter said, John had gone to Ranelagh to see the fireworks, and afterwards made his way to a favourite inn near Westminster bridge to eat, hoping also to spend the night there. But they had no bed and so, after midnight, he had set out alone to look elsewhere. At dawn they found his body in the river.

Grey-faced, Jos finished reading and stared at Sarah. 'Do you think he took his own life?' he whispered in horror.

Sarah put her arms about him. 'No, love, I don't. He had been enjoying himself – fireworks, good company I don't doubt – no, surely it was an accident. You know how dark the streets can be . . .' And how infested with rogues, she thought, lurking in alleyways to rob an innocent passer-by and push him to his death in the river. But she did not speak of that possibility; nor, again, of the other, darker one, which she had denied to Jos. What if John had gone alone to Ranelagh, seeking solace for one of his black moods – there was no mention in the letter of any company, and if he had been with others, why should he have gone on without them? Had he found no help for his despair amongst the lights and fireworks of the pleasure gardens, no cheer in the solitary meal at the inn where they had no bed to spare – and walked out into the night in a bitter desolation of spirit which had led him at last to the black waters of the river? She hoped she was wrong – she hoped Jos was reassured – but the possibility haunted her for a long time. They would never know the truth.

Jos, grief-stricken, poured out his heart to Bentley. 'Let us now be dearer to each other if possible than ever,' he wrote, 'let me adopt you for my brother . . .'

The plea must have moved Bentley as nothing else could, for by the time, soon afterwards, that their second son Richard was born, he had agreed to become Jos's partner in the new works; and Jos was already making plans for the house where, one day, Bentley would come to live as their near neighbour.

CHAPTER TEN

1768

Sarah was halfway downstairs when she heard the knock on the door. 'It's all right, Nan,' she called. 'I'll go.' Nan was nursing Richard who was quiet for the moment, and Sarah did not want to risk setting him crying again.

It was Peter Swift at the door, thin and tall and awkward. 'Good morning, ma'am,' he said, removing his hat. Sarah stood gazing blankly up at him, almost as if, with one thing and another, she had forgotten who he was. After an uncomfortable moment or two he said hesitantly, 'Mr Wedgwood said to come at ten.'

Sarah gave a little gasp. 'Is it ten already? Oh my goodness! I'm so sorry, Peter – come in and I'll tell Mr Wedgwood you're here.'

She showed him into the parlour, stooping quickly to retrieve Susannah's doll and a spinning top left lying on the floor. It was high time they had somewhere more fitting for conducting matters of business – though, 'please God,' she thought, 'it won't be long now, if only the weather improves so the builders can make some progress.'

Outside in the hall again, with the door closed behind her, Sarah paused. She had known Swift was expected: Jos had wanted to discuss the possibility of financing Tom Byerley's passage to America. But she had been so busy this morning that she had not realised how quickly time was passing – what with baby Richard grizzling and fretful (why did he always catch every cold that was going?); and Susannah in an awkward mood, squabbling with John over every little thing; and the new cow about to calve, and instructions to be sent to the works for a batch of vases to be packed for the new London warehouse; and then – her thoughts came to a standstill, halted by an abrupt question, 'Has Jos been down to breakfast yet?'

She put her head round the dining room door. Her own

211

plate and cup had been cleared long since. She had eaten alone, creeping softly out of bed so as not to wake Jos, asleep at last after a restless night. The table looked exactly as it had when she left it five hours ago, Jos's plate and cup set neatly in place, clean and untouched. She turned and ran quickly up stairs and pushed wide the bedroom door. 'Jos . . .' she murmured softly.

He had got as far as the edge of the bed and was sitting there dressed only in his shirt and breeches, making no move to put on his other clothes. She thought he must have been there for some time, for his eyes met hers in a kind of mute appeal, sharpened with desperation. It was a long time since he had looked really well; but this morning his face had a dreadful greyness, every line of it taut with pain.

'Jos love,' she said, coming quickly to sit beside him. 'Peter Swift's here. Shall I tell him you're not well and can't see him today?'

Jos shifted his position slightly, caught his breath, and was still again. 'No – yes – oh, Sally, I don't know . . .' He turned his head to look at her, but with great care, as if every movement however slight hurt him unbearably. 'I can't go on like this.'

Sarah thought of the countless pain-racked nights and the hobbling tormented days that were the best Jos seemed able to hope for now; and the ever shorter intervals between the bouts of fever that wholly incapacitated him. She thought of the visit to London ended just a month ago which should have been such a triumph – he had gone there, after all, to arrange for the opening of their very first warehouse, at the junction of Newport Street and St Martin's Lane on the edge of fashionable London to the north of Charing Cross, but he had come home exhausted and ill, though refusing to give in to his weakness. Now, it seemed, it had at last exacted its revenge.

Gently she ran her hand down his cheek. 'I know, love. Shall I send for Dr Darwin?'

Jos reached out and gripped her shoulder and very slowly raised himself on to his feet. He stood looking down at her with a frown of concentration, willing himself to stay where he was. 'Yes, Sally, you send for him. I've made up my mind – it's coming off.'

Sarah stared at him, not understanding – or, more truthfully perhaps, not wanting to understand.

'The leg is nothing but trouble. I can't work, I can't think – I'll be better off without it.'

She felt the colour drain from her face, taking her breath with it. A horrible sick sensation churned in her stomach. 'Oh, Jos, no – you can't!' Her voice emerged as an anguished whisper.

He grinned faintly, a pale shadow of her dear cheerful laughing Jos. '"If thine arm offend thee, cut it off . . ."'

'Don't!' She held his arms as if to steady him, but in some way she knew it was she who had more need of support. 'How can you joke about such things?'

He laid a hand on her hair. 'It's better than weeping, Sally. Besides, it's not the end of the world. You'll see, it'll be for the best. Send word to Darwin to come as soon as he can. And now give me your arm down the stairs – I've kept Swift waiting long enough already.'

Sarah helped him into his coat and stockings and shoes, and they went together down the stairs; but she moved mechanically, while her mind struggled to take in what he had said, with all its implications. He might make jokes about it, but he could have no illusions about what his decision meant; and nor had she. No surgical operation, however small, was without the greatest of risks, from infection and gangrene if not from the surgery itself. But an amputation was perhaps the most dangerous of all, killing more often by shock than by any later complication. It was only ever done when there was no alternative. She searched her memory for the cases she had known and, shivering, could remember none which had not proved fatal. They said the surgeon's speed was all-important; but even then . . .

Perhaps after all Dr Darwin would advise against it. Perhaps she could speak to him before he saw Jos, and ask him if there was any other way, less dangerous. But that hope was short-lived.

'M-much the best course,' Darwin said briskly, when she approached him. 'I've long thought it would c-come to this in the end. It's either that, or resign yourself to having a p-permanent invalid about the p-place – and he's well on the way there already, as you know. N-no life for a man of his kind. I suggest c-calling in Mr Bent – a very able s-surgeon: you can rely on him . . .' He paused and laid one vast hand on Sarah's shoulder, bending solicitously over her. 'It'll be worse for you than him – b-but it is for the b-best, you know.'

Sarah looked up into the ugly kindly face. 'What are his chances?' she asked in a low voice.

'Hm – I never l-like questions like that. Who's to s-say? Every case is different. But if he g-gets through the first f-five days or s-so with no s-sign of any further trouble, he's more than a fair chance of pulling through.'

When the doctor had gone, leaving instructions to prepare for the operation to take place 'all b-being well' on the following Saturday, Sarah stood for a long time at the parlour window staring out at the hazy green and gold of the May afternoon, and shivering. Even here in Burslem the new young leaves quivered shining and fragile in the filtered sunlight, the buds on the rose bushes in the little garden nodded to the breeze, a blackbird sang with liquid fluency from the apple tree in the corner; and a dark abyss opened before her, cutting her off from all the sweetness of the day.

Richard's thin weary crying broke in on the numb horror of her brain. She moved quickly then, running up the stairs to lift him from his cradle, rocking him in her arms, trying vainly to soothe him.

'I canna quiet him, madam,' said Nan, coming herself from some task which had taken her downstairs. 'He inna hungry. I think he's got a pain somewhere – happen the cold's settled on his belly, poor little mite.'

Sarah went on rocking him. Eight months old, less well grown than Susannah or John at that age, he was liable to catch any infection; though when he was well he showed every sign of a sweet sunny nature, all smiles and gurgles and brightness. 'He's a fighter, like Jos,' she thought now. 'He'll come through too.'

She had not seen Jos since he had retired to bed after the doctor's departure, exhausted and in pain. Now, when she realised that Richard was as far as ever from calming down, she allowed Nan to take him – she had a way with babies – and went to the bedroom.

Jos was awake, propped on pillows with *Tristram Shandy* open before him: it was a favourite book, brought to mind

214

again lately when its author Lawrence Sterne had died, but she doubted very much if he was taking in any of what he read. It was odd though: in some way he looked calmer, more relaxed, as if now that his decision was made there was nothing further to worry about.

'I expect Darwin told you he thought it a good plan.' He might, Sarah thought, have been talking of a proposed holiday, so lacking in emotion was his tone.

'Yes,' she said. She wondered if he had considered the possibility that he might not survive the operation; but he could not have done otherwise, surely? He was no fool. Perhaps he simply accepted that it was a risk worth taking and tried not to think about it. She was not used to this sudden reversal of roles, in which he was serene and untroubled and she was the one who looked to the future with fear and a cold crawling horror. She ought to be giving him strength and support, as she had done so often in the past; and instead she felt helpless.

Perhaps he understood, for he held out his hand to her, and she sat on the edge of the bed and laid hers in it.

'My dear good Sally: I know what I'm putting you through. But it'll be all right, you'll see.'

She smiled feebly, trying to look as if she believed him. For a little while he said nothing, his thumb roughly caressing the back of her hand; then he looked up again and said, 'Sally, I'd like Bentley to be here.'

It was then she knew that he was not after all wholly certain that he would recover.

It was Bentley, not Sarah, who stayed at Jos's side during the whole horrible agonising business of the operation.

'Dear God, don't let him die!' The prayer leapt unbidden from Sarah as she sat in the nursery with Richard clasped in her arms, straining her ears – though she did not want to do so – for any sound that might tell her what was happening behind the closed door of the bedroom.

And then she thought, 'No – no, not that prayer.' Memory flooded her, bringing anguished panic. It was the very same prayer that the little girl had spoken into the empty church – the prayer which had been so harshly answered. If it had been answered then in the spirit of its

215

making there would have been no need for her to repeat it today.

She bent her head, tightening her hold about the baby, aching for some release from the tension of knowing that grief stood waiting at the door, and being able to do nothing, absolutely nothing, to keep it out. If only she could have been with Jos now, instead of sitting here trying not to remember the quiet parting just a short time ago: the light kiss, the touch of the hand, and Jos's cheerfully courageous smile as she left him knowing that she might never see him alive again. Bentley, standing by Jos's chair (Jos had insisted on undergoing the operation seated, though it meant he would see everything), had not even glanced at her while she was in the room.

'Why?' she asked herself more than once, 'why Bentley and not me?' But she knew the answer to that, and understood – in spite of the little inescapable hurt – that Jos's choice of companion was no reflection on all the love and care she had lavished on him over the years. She alone knew him and understood him wholly and completely; she alone had been with him in all his moments of weakness, and shared his times of deepest despair and grief. She alone had ever seen him broken, his courage stripped away; no one else, ever, had been allowed so close to him, least of all Bentley whom he admired so much, whose respect he wanted in everything he did. And so, when he knew that his very life might depend upon his courage, when for his own self-esteem he must not weaken, it was the friend who would expect that courage of him who was at his side, and not the wife who would go on loving him however far he should fall below his own high standards. She understood, but that did not make it any easier to bear the waiting.

Richard was quiet now, almost asleep. And then she wished he was not, for the sound she heard next carried clearly across the landing and through the intervening doors: unmistakably, the brisk rasping sound of a saw. It was just such a sound as she had heard often in Tom Lovatt's butcher's shop in Burslem, as he sawed through a bone whilst cutting up a joint of meat . . .

She wished desperately that her hands were free, so that she could cover her ears against the sound. She found she was shivering, and began violently to retch, taking hold of herself only just in time. There was no other sound in there, no murmur or groan of pain: if Jos could be strong, then so could she – but it seemed hours before the sawing came to an abrupt end and there was silence again; and then, a little after, a quiet exchange of voices, though she could not tell if Jos's was among them.

She heard a door open and then close again. She rose to her feet and laid the child in his cradle. 'Don't hurry, keep calm,' she told herself, but her hands were trembling. She walked with careful steadiness out on to the landing, just as Bentley laid his hand on the nursery door.

It was the first time she had really looked at him since his arrival last night: she had been too wrapped up in Jos for any other thought. And now it was with Jos in mind that she scanned his face – pale and drawn, the eyes shadowed as if like her he had not slept for a long time; and smiling, just a little.

'It's all over, Mrs Wedgwood. He . . . he made not a sound from start to finish . . .' He paused, and she saw that his mouth was trembling beneath the smile. 'The surgeon says you may go in now.'

She did not even pause to thank him, only ran past him into the bedroom.

Mr Bent and his assistant were busily clearing away the bloody debris of the afternoon's work, but Sarah did not look their way. She went to the bed where Jos now lay, pale and drowsy with laudanum against the pillows, looking as if he would never again have the strength to move from there. She pulled a stool to the bedside and folded her hands about his where they lay motionless on the counterpane.

'He'll do now, Mrs Wedgwood,' said Mr Bent behind her, pausing in his work. 'I'll call again this evening just to look him over, but he'll need nothing until then. Just let him sleep. No need to worry.' He patted her on the shoulder, and a little later finished his work and left her alone with Jos.

His eyes were on her face, and though he was too weak at present to smile she knew he would have done so if he could. She felt his fingers move against hers, reassuring, and telling her he was glad she was there. Then, after a little while, he drifted gently into sleep.

217

'Five days or so' before they could start to believe he was safe; five days of constant watching and nursing for Sarah and Bentley, taking turns at the bedside, Sarah by day, Bentley by night. There was little sleep for either of them. The works did not come to a standstill because Jos was sick. 'Just as well if I learn a little about what goes on there, if I'm to be his partner,' Bentley told Sarah, reassuring her for not having much time herself to give to anything but sick-nursing. At night, when Bentley sat with Jos, watching at the bedside or dozing in a chair by the bedroom fire, Sarah would be in the nursery watching over Richard. Once she had thought him a little better; but then he had suddenly become very much worse, screaming endlessly with pain and steadily weakened by a diarrhoea neither she nor Nan could do anything to ease. Dr Darwin, calling to see Jos, cast an eye over the baby and prescribed some medicine which, for an hour or two, seemed to help; but that night he was more violently ill than ever, his crying only growing less because he had no strength left.

Next morning as Sarah came to his bedside, Jos said, 'How's the little one?' His voice had more of its usual robust sound today, Sarah thought.

She smiled calmly and sat down, taking his hand in hers and hoping he would not notice how exhausted she was. 'He'll mend, like you,' she said with deliberate cheerfulness, though the words sounded hollow to her. She could not prevent him from hearing the child's crying, but she did not want him to guess how bad things really were. She was thankful at least that Jos was too often in a drugged sleep to know how much the baby cried.

'Five days now,' he said next, with a faint smile. 'By tonight, if there's still no sign of infection, I should be over the worst, so Darwin says.'

'Yes.'

'Let's hope this is the last time you'll have the nursing of me. As soon as the wound's healed I'll have a wooden leg made so I can get about. Then there'll be no stopping me.'

He sounded happy, optimistic, as if he were genuinely looking forward to the prospect, with no trace of regret for the lost limb; but then he had suffered so many years of torment from it that to be without it could only come as a relief. It was not so easy for Sarah to adjust to what had

218

happened, but the need to nurse and dress the wound helped her to grow used to it, so that after the first few times she no longer shrank inwardly as she unwound the bandages from the stump which was all that was left of Jos's leg. It was over, and life would go on . . .

But not for baby Richard. Early in the morning of the sixth day after Jos's operation, the child tensed in one last moment of agony and then quietly died. Sarah sat on for a long time staring down at the motionless little body in her arms; and felt nothing at all.

They buried the baby at dusk the next day. It was not usual for a woman to attend a funeral, but Sarah could not bear it that neither of his parents should be there. She gave Jos his night-time dose of laudanum – enough to make sure he slept for several hours at least – and kissed him gently and left him with a light clasp of the hand. He would read no more into that than the tender goodnight of a loving wife. She closed the door very carefully behind her, so that no sudden sound should trouble him.

She went next, moving with the same quiet unhurried step, to look in on the children. She pushed open the door of their room and stood there, watching them. Both of them, thank goodness, seemed to be already fast asleep, the bed curtains pulled half around the bed, deepening the shadows about their still forms. She stepped softly closer, just to make sure that neither of them was lying wakeful in the dark, afraid or racked with grief. It was almost her undoing. They lay so still: John curled up like a small animal with his thumb in his mouth, his dark lashes resting light as feathers on the curve of his flushed cheek, his hair all soft loose curls about his face; Susannah stretched out on her back, relaxed, one arm flung wide on the pillow near her head, the small fingers curled – she looked so pale, so quiet, but Sarah could see the little lace frill of her nightgown moving gently with her breathing. They were alive, alive and well and sleeping. But there was a terrible wrenching pain at her heart for their infant brother, whose small body had lost all that sweet relaxation long before they laid it today in the little coffin; and for them, with fear at what terrors the future might hold, at the fragility of their young lives, the slenderness of the thread which might suddenly, at any moment, be severed for ever.

With an abrupt gesture she pressed her hand to her mouth,

turned swiftly on her heel and ran from the room. Outside the door she halted, head held rigidly high, eyes closed, letting her arms fall, tensed, to her sides, and drew a long shuddering breath. Deliberately she forced her mind to emptiness and set herself to think only of practical matters.

The burial first. Then the two letters to be written, to William Cox, now at the London warehouse, with the invoice for the goods sent off yesterday, and to Tom Byerley (also in London) to let him know that his uncle would consider his plea to go to Philadelphia when he was well again. That was enough to be going on with. 'Sufficient unto the day . . .' she thought, as she straightened the black silk tippet about her shoulders, pushed a stray thread of hair back under the ugly cap and made her way downstairs.

The curate of Burslem had bent the rules to allow William Willet to conduct the funeral, which as a Dissenting minister he was not by law permitted to do within the precincts of the established church. Willet was waiting quietly in the parlour beside the little coffin. 'So small – so small . . .!' Sarah thought, the reaction breaking through the new emptiness of her mind. But it must not; she pushed it back and came quietly to the minister's side. Kate reached out and pressed her hand but she did not respond, her fingers lying limp in her sister-in-law's sympathetic clasp. She heard the other woman sob and took care not to look at her, concentrating instead on the minister's calm grave face.

Bentley came in, with Peter Swift and the four men from the works who were to carry the torches. One of them, she saw with a little sense of shock, was Sam Hunter – after all that had happened! She bit her lip and tried not to look at him.

Willet began to pray, his voice quiet and level, almost monotonous. She was glad there was no emotion in it.

The little procession set out at last, leaving by the front gate, Bentley and Peter carrying the coffin between them though either could have managed it alone. The torch flames flickered and bent in the little breeze, shedding hesitant red-gold light on the white velvet pall, the black of the bearers' coats – Peter's homespun, Bentley's velvet – and on the single unopened white rosebud laid on the coffin.

'Unopened – it will never open now, cut off too soon . . .'

Panic seized Sarah. Why could she not keep her thoughts safe, clear of the dark chasms which lurked somewhere beyond consciousness waiting to trap her into losing the control which she must not lose – not ever, not while Jos needed her strength so much, not while there was work to be done, and the children, the two left to them . . .

She swallowed hard, and clasped her hands tightly together in front of her, the fingers rigidly looped. It seemed a long way to the churchyard tonight, much further than usual – a long long way, as if she were a child again and all the houses enlarged, the distances extended by her own smallness. Oh to be a child indeed, with hope before her, and all the possibilities and wonders of life lying just around the corner, and not to know that so many of them would be for ever out of reach! She could not at the moment feel that she had ever been happy since then. It was as if a film of ash covered the good times, veiling their brightness, deadening all colour, all joy. 'It will pass,' she told herself, without believing it.

The familiar stench that had haunted her through the years enfolded her, stifling, reminding her that from this place had come Jos's years of pain. Now it was about to swallow up her child, for ever and ever. 'No,' she tried to tell herself, 'he is not here, only his body – the living thing that was Richard is far away, beyond its reach.' The thought gave her no comfort.

As they stood at the graveside the bats squeaked overhead, swooping and darting, bewildered by the torchlight. An owl hooted in the distance, punctuating the insistent monotony of the minister's voice as the coffin was lowered into the dense blackness awaiting it. The pallor of the wood gleamed almost luminously from the depths, and against it the faint grey outline of the rose that would never bloom.

Afterwards Kate held out her arm, offering support.

'No thank you,' said Sarah quietly, and walked alone ahead of them all. It was over now – there was work to be done at home.

She had ordered a light supper to be made ready for their return, but no one ate or drank very much, nor was there a great deal of talk. The Willets left, once she had insisted again that there was nothing more they could do for her – 'You've done so much already – thank you,' and 'Yes, of course I'll

221

send word the moment I need you.' Peter Swift and Bentley retired; the workmen left quietly, not waiting to speak to her, wary of intruding. She sent Nan and Betty to bed, giving Nan a final quick hug to show that she knew the loss had been hers too, and then she extinguished the parlour candles and went upstairs to see if Jos needed anything.

He was sleeping soundly, unmoving and quiet, his face smooth and trouble-free. It would be a long time before he would wake and want her again: that gave her long enough to compose the letters.

She looked in once more on the children, though this time she only stood in the doorway, forcing herself to be reassured by the dimly discernible shapes and the sound of gentle even breathing, choking down the fierce urge to stand over them and remain there, watching, until daylight brought wake-fulness and the certainty – if such there could ever be – of safety.

Instead she left them and went softly downstairs and into the parlour. She closed the door behind her, and then turned and leaned back against it with her eyes closed, swept all at once by a terrible overwhelming sense of exhaustion and despair. 'I cannot go on,' said her brain. 'I can do no more . . .' Tiny incidents flooded her mind, momentary visions of the baby – the first smile, the little hand waving at the newly opened buds of the chestnut tree above the cradle, laughing on Jos's knee while she held out her arms to him across the room . . .

What other joys had she missed when work called her away? Had he wanted her sometimes, when she was not there?

She had no resistance left. Slowly, one by one, the sobs came, hard painful sobs forced out in spite of all she could do, in spite of her iron will and her anger that she could no longer hold them back. She crooked her arm across her face and stumbled forward towards the cold hearth.

Only she did not reach it, for suddenly there were hands at her elbows holding her, strong yet gentle hands; and a deep soothing voice murmuring she knew not what; and then in a moment arms about her, and a velvet coat beneath her cheek, and a sense that at last she was not wholly alone.

Held close there she gave way totally to her grief. She could

222

not have done otherwise now. She was all tears, every part of her, every limb and joint flooded with a desperate sense of loss, with the need for release from the long days and nights of pain. She was scarcely aware of the voice and the arms, except as a help and a supporting strength, there when they were needed most.

It was a long time – or so it seemed – before finally some realisation of what was happening intruded on her grief. As it did so she caught a sob midway and choked it back, and pulled herself half free of the enclosing arms. It was dark in the room and she could not see the face above her, or anything but a greater blackness; but she knew who it was.

'Mr Bentley – I . . . I did not know there was anyone here . . .'

Shame swept her, at her weakness and that he should have seen it, and that she should have allowed him to hold her as only very few men should be allowed to do; only a husband, a father, a brother – not Jos's friend, whom she must not love.

She broke from him and moved away, feeling about for a candle, more than anything else to give herself something to do, though she had a sense too that it was not quite wise for her to be alone in the dark with this man. 'Let us have some light,' she said with brittle brightness.

She heard him move away and then come nearer again. His sleeve brushed hers; she felt his warmth very close, was aware of the smell of him that was like the smell of Jos, but not quite – pipe smoke, clean linen, and that something indefinable which would have told her who he was anywhere in the world if she had no other sense but that of smell to guide her. There was another sensation now driving out the grief of a moment ago and setting her trembling, and it shamed her more than her own sudden outburst had done, for there was even less excuse for it at this time of all times.

She heard the scrape of the tinder box, and a flame shot up, and she saw Bentley's hand – that long elegant hand framed in its snowy ruffle – reach out to light the candle. She bent her head and turned away so that he should not see her face.

She knew he was watching her though; and when he spoke she realised with surprise that he too was tense with emotion. He said abruptly, speaking very fast, 'Josiah – is he still . . .?' and then broke off, as if he dared not complete the sentence.

'Of course!' thought Sarah. He feared that her tears meant bad news. After all, why else should she break down with her husband recovering and the worst over?

'He's sleeping peacefully,' she said quietly, her tone veiling the bitterness at her heart. But then she herself had not meant to break down, and she despised herself for it. She heard him draw in his breath with relief, and added in a crisp tone designed to keep the tremor from her voice, 'Forgive my weakness.'

'Weakness? – Oh, Sarah!' The compassionate indignation of his tone almost set her weeping again. He came to her side and took her hand in his, looking down at her bent head in its concealing cap. 'My dear, if you are weak then we are all of us creatures of straw.'

She felt his touch with every part of her, the impulse running through her from that clasped hand, waking her body to life. 'I did not mean to break down – there is so much to do . . .'

'You have done too much already,' he told her gently. This time she did raise her head to look at him, and she saw that something in her appearance shocked him, as if the toll of suffering was only too clearly imprinted on her features. Yet even now she was far from giving way, the outburst of a moment ago already put behind her, over and done with except for her regret that it had happened at all.

'No,' she said. 'The work doesn't stop because I don't feel inclined to give it my attention. You know that.'

'I know. But it can at least wait until morning. You ought to rest while you can.'

'Rest!' she exclaimed bitterly. 'How can I rest?' She thought of last night, of the long wakeful hours of grief embittered by self reproach, and almost laughed. 'I'm a bad mother,' she said harshly. 'I don't deserve to rest.'

She saw that she had startled him; and yet after a moment, amazingly, he seemed to understand.

'Don't feel guilty. He was always ailing, Sarah – you know that. Nothing you did could have made any difference. You were always the most loving of mothers.'

'When I was there to be loving. When there weren't more important things to be done at the works.'

'You know how Josiah values that. You would neither of

224

you be where you are today without all you have done. The children have a good nursemaid. You see more of them than most fine ladies do of their little ones. And Josiah is always telling me what a good mother you are. You have no cause to reproach yourself. Your baby was sick and suffering for nearly all of his little life – that's over now. Don't wish him back, or regret that he did not live longer: *that* would not be loving of you. Now, I suggest you go to bed and take some of Josiah's laudanum. The surgeon comes again tomorrow, and there's enough to spare.'

She shook her head. 'I can't risk being asleep if I'm needed – I must be able to wake easily.'

'Then let me watch while you sleep.'

'You have a journey tomorrow. You have done more than enough already.'

He laid his hands on her shoulders and swung her round to face him, his voice raised with exasperation. 'Sarah, for God's sake stop trying to be superhuman! You are not, and if you will not admit it then you'll suffer for it later.'

She gazed at him, her lips set in a hard line, and wished – yet did not wish – that he would hold her again as he had just now. 'I must be, if anyone can. Jos must not know . . .' She broke off, suddenly unable to go on. Bentley led her to the sofa and made her sit down beside him, his hands resting on hers.

'That's the worst, isn't it: not to be able to share it with him? But it won't be for much longer. It's been a week now – the worst is past: if he continues to go on as he is doing then we need have no fear for him. This is the blackest time: it can only get better.'

She held herself stiffly, resisting the longing to lean against him. She was so tired now it was hard to keep her self control. 'You . . . you lost a child once – and your wife . . .'

'Yes,' he said quietly. 'Though the child scarcely lived at all. That's different of course. But I know that grief can tear you in pieces, and that almost always it brings some sense of guilt – mine was because I was not there when she died, but you know all that. I do know that to be busy can help, but that you need to give way as well. The mind can only bear so much without breaking, unless you find ease in tears.'

225

'How can I weep, whilst Jos is so ill? He needs a cheerful wife.'

'At his bedside, yes – but not everywhere.' He smiled gently. 'There, you see, that's another service of friendship – to provide a broad shoulder for his wife to weep upon.'

'A service of friendship,' she thought wryly. 'That ought to bring me to my senses. He is Jos's friend. To him, I am Jos's wife, and that is all.' Wearily, she rose and went to the window, pulling aside the curtain to gaze out on the little garden, shadowed in the faint moonlight. She had a sudden longing to escape into the air, to walk out on to the hills and feel the wind in her face, to turn her back, just for a little while, on everything. But Jos might need her, so she must stay. She let the curtain fall back into place, remaining where she was, staring at its heavy crimson folds.

'Don't wait up any more,' she said. 'I'm grateful for your sympathy. But I'm all right now.'

She did not expect him to come to her, but he did, turning her once more to face him, scanning her face closely. 'Are you sure? I can stay if you wish – I'm happy to . . .'

Those dark, dark eyes, she thought; they hold so much, at the moment kindliness, and understanding – a measure of understanding at least. She could not ask for more than that; or rather, she must not. 'Thank you,' she said hoarsely, 'but there is no need.'

The next moment he bent his head and kissed her, lightly, on the cheek. She knew quite well it meant nothing, except that as Jos's wife she had his friendship, and that he admired her courage. But it was too much for her now, worn down as she was, starved for so long of the comfort of touch or caress. She gave a little cry and reached up and clasped her arms about his neck.

For an instant she felt him tense, draw back; heard the sharp shocked intake of breath. Then almost at once his hands slid from her shoulders, ran down her arms to her back, pulling her close, and he bent his head again and found her mouth with his. She clung to him, her limbs melting against him, wishing with a desperate aching intensity that this would not end but go on and on.

It had to end, of course. For both of them their love for Jos was deeper than any need for one another, and the knowledge

226

of what they were doing broke through like a sudden icy wind on a hot day. Sarah felt him tense again, and then his hands fell and he pushed her gently from him. She stood, head bent, dishevelled, and cold to the very core with the knowledge that she had betrayed herself, and Jos.

Without a word or a glance she turned wildly and ran from the room, across the passage, up the stairs, on and up to the tiny attic store room. And there she flung herself on the floor and gave way to a flood of bitter tears.

Some time well after midnight she came down to find Bentley asleep in the chair by Jos's bed; and she did after all take a few drops of the laudanum before curling up beside the children to sleep.

So it was that she was not up when Bentley left, soon after dawn. Nan said that he had insisted that they should not disturb her; but had asked them to convey to her when she woke his thanks for her hospitality, and his best wishes for Josiah's further good recovery.

When she went to Jos, after a breakfast for which she had no appetite, she saw to her dismay that his face, yesterday recovering its colour, had a new pallor. For a moment she stood quite still just inside the door, thinking, 'Does he know? Did someone see?'

Then he said, 'Bentley told me, when he came to say goodbye – about Richard . . .' She saw that there were tears in his eyes.

'He had no business to tell you! I didn't want you to know until you were stronger.'

Jos studied her gravely from where he lay propped against the pillows: he seemed to be reading in her face all the tensions and griefs of the past days. 'I asked him how Richard was – and then I made him tell me. It's right I should know, now he's not here for you to confide in.'

She bent her head in case he should see the guilt in her eyes. She heard him say gently, 'Sally . . .'

Looking up she found that he was holding out his arms to her; and after a momentary hesitation she went to him and allowed him to draw her down beside him on the bed. 'Sally, my own dear girl, you've had more to bear than I ever dreamed of . . .' He held her gently while she hid her face against his shoulder. 'Poor little baby – perhaps it was for the best, though we can't see it now.' Comforted in spite of everything she began to weep, quietly and with relief. 'Things will get better, love, you'll see,' said Jos. 'The worst is over.'

CHAPTER ELEVEN

1769 (I)

'Bentley will come and keep you company while I'm away,' Jos said cheerfully. 'Give you someone to look to if there are any problems; and if the weather turns bad and I can't get back for a few days longer then you'll not be alone. You mustn't be doing too much in your condition.'

'There's Tom,' she pointed out, 'and Peter Swift.'

'I'll need Swift in London – I want him to chase up those outstanding accounts. That quiet trusting manner of his would stir the hardest conscience – and I shan't have time to bother about such things myself. As it is I can't see how I'm going to get everything done in the time.'

'Then take me with you. Bentley can manage here alone.'

He shook his head and reached across the breakfast table to pat her hand. 'You had enough of London last time: you said so yourself. Besides, Bentley's still learning how we run things here, and this is a good opportunity for him to find out more, with you there to provide a guiding hand. If he's going to be in full partnership from the summer then he needs to know what's going on. As for Tom, he has all the work he can handle with the queen's ware orders to meet. No, I need you here. Until I get to London I shan't know exactly what the chief selling items are – Cox isn't always very clear, and I need to be able to send urgent orders that I know will be met quickly and efficiently. You're the only one I can trust to do that, at least as far as the vases are concerned. Though if Cox is right and the demand's as great as he says it is I don't know how we'll ever hope to meet it, at least not before the Etruria works are ready – still, that's another matter. No, it's the best solution for Bentley to come here. You can show him how his house is getting on – he'll like that. He can start planning where to put his furniture.'

Sarah could think of no other argument she could bring forward, except what by its very nature was closed to her –

229

'Don't let him come – I am afraid to be alone with him here . . .' As it was her silence puzzled Jos.

'What's wrong, Sally? You get on well with Bentley – you're good friends aren't you? Is it that you don't feel up to the extra work of a guest in the house? You know he won't expect to be cosseted, and Nan and Betty are good girls – even if Nan has taken leave of her senses lately – and I'll not be here to trouble you.'

A little wanly she returned his smile. 'You know he's always welcome here. It's just that I'd rather be with you.' Which sentiment, she reflected, had the merit of being absolutely true, in its way.

'I'll not be away any longer than I have to,' he promised her. 'I've too much to call me back here for that.'

So on a cold still day in February he went on his way to London; and Sarah had the guest room made ready, and put in several hours of concentrated work going over the entire stock of vases, sorting and grading and listing them; and went back to the house when the bell rang at dusk to wait, with apprehension turning every part of her to water, for Bentley to arrive. She prayed for some kind of miracle that would spare her this ordeal – an urgent problem at the Liverpool warehouse, a slight indisposition of Miss Oates that would make it impossible for him to leave her, anything at all so long as she did not in the next moment or two have to hear the hired chaise from Newcastle rumble to a halt outside the house.

But she did hear it, exactly on time, just as the first fragrant aromas of supper reached her from the kitchen and the children's laughter rippled down from the bedroom where Nan hurried them to wash and dress for the meal.

She stood quite still where she was, just outside the parlour door, as if she had no idea what to do now. She ought to go and open the front door: she was near to it and she could hear the garden gate open and close again (she must grease the hinge tomorrow), and knew that in a moment there would be a clatter of the knocker. But it was as if something close to terror had frozen her into immobility, preventing her from translating will to action and setting herself in motion; or perhaps it was the will that was lacking – she did not know.

Betty came running almost as the first knock sounded, and

in a moment the door stood open and Bentley, smiling, stepped into the hall. Sarah thought she saw just a hint of reserve in his expression, as if he was wary of showing too much warmth for fear it might lead him where he did not want to go.

She stepped forward, not smiling at all, and Bentley gave a little bow and continued to remove hat and coat and gloves and hand them to Betty; he was not smiling either now.

'I hope you had a good journey,' Sarah said stiffly.

'Thank you, yes,' he replied with equal formality. He followed her in silence to the parlour, and went at once to stretch cold hands to the blaze. He looked, she thought, pale and tired, a little strained as if, like her, he had passed the last few nights in wakefulness.

'Wine? Tea?' she asked, with an abruptness far removed from her usual good manners. 'Supper will be ready very soon, but I expect you would like something first.'

'A glass of wine would be very acceptable,' said Bentley, with his back to her.

She poured it and brought it to him, and he turned then, but without looking directly at her. 'How is Josiah?'

'Very well, thank you. Better than he has been for a very long time.'

A silence followed, and seemed to grow and grow. They stood there with an empty expanse of floor between them, and tried not to look at one another, gazing into their glasses, at the fire, the ceiling, towards any imagined sound from beyond the door – anywhere so long as it shielded them from the possibility that their eyes might meet.

It was a relief when they heard Susannah scamper across the hall, brought up short just outside the parlour by a sharp command from Nan. There was a moment or two of stifled giggling, and then a gentle knock, and the door opened to admit the children. Susannah's eyes were bright with suppressed laughter, though outwardly she was a picture of sedate femininity in her best pink satin gown, stiff-bodiced and demure, with its decorative embroidered silk apron. Beside her, solemnly holding her hand, trotted John, not quite three and still in his baby petticoats; and behind them both, her hands fluttering protectively over them, was Nan. 'Betty says supper's ready, madam,' she said.

Sarah thanked her and took Susannah's hand in hers, and led the children forward to greet their guest.

The presence of the children seemed to release Bentley from the awkwardness which had held him. He dropped on one knee before them and held out his hands. 'And how's my little friend Susannah? And John – what a big boy you are now to be sure . . .'

Susannah, laughing freely now, loosed both hands and flung her arms about Bentley's neck, kissing him noisily. 'Bentley! Bentley!' she cried in the precise piping little voice which never failed to delight him. Sarah looked on, envying the unselfconscious demonstrativeness of her daughter; but then Susannah had no cause for restraint, for her love for Bentley, like all her loves – and she was a loving child – was simple, wholehearted and untouched by guilt or doubt or pain.

They went to supper, Sarah and Bentley silent and withdrawn, John solemn and a little sleepy, Susannah skipping along with her hand in Bentley's, chattering away enough for all of them. Bentley, Sarah noted, ate no more than she did – which was hardly anything – and spoke only to the children. If it was a lively meal, that reflected no credit on the adults concerned.

Afterwards Sarah herself saw the children to bed before coming down again to where Bentley sat quietly smoking his pipe by the parlour fire.

He looked up at the sound of her entrance and made a move to put out his pipe, but Sarah intervened quickly, 'No – please – I don't mind at all. It makes me think Jos is not so far away after all.' And then she coloured, and wished that even the simplest and most natural of observations did not always seem to be burdened with hidden meanings. It made conversation so difficult, knowing that there was almost nothing one could say that was completely without danger. Yet, she thought, as she took a seat facing Bentley across the fireside and picked up her sewing, even that seemed heavy with significance, as if all the thoughts they could not voice clamoured for admittance.

After a time, Bentley took his pipe from his mouth, and cleared his throat. 'I gather you've a Methodist in your midst.'

Sarah looked up, startled: it was a moment or two before she realised what he was saying, since it was so far removed from her present reflections. Then she smiled. 'Oh – yes. You've been talking to Nan.'

'A dramatic conversion when the Reverend Mr Wesley came to open the new meeting house last year, so I gathered. He must have quite a following here to warrant a chapel.'

'Oh yes – sometimes it seems as if half the population have gone Methodist – all hysterical meetings and wild preachings. Religion as a substitute for drink, Jos says; but maybe that's no bad thing. However, it was Nan's change of heart which was the most difficult. Jos saw it all as a sign of rooted instability of character, and feared she was unfit to look after the children. Mercifully though she doesn't seem greatly changed, so we hope for the best. After all, the children love her dearly. But there you are – so much for rational religion!' And they were back at Liverpool again, talking of the Octagon Chapel – or in Buxton. She returned with concentrated ill-humour to her sewing.

They neither of them spoke again after that. Now and then, to break the tension, Sarah would pause to throw a fresh log on the fire, trim the wick of a candle or glance at the clock whose hands seemed to have come to a near standstill, and Bentley would upend his pipe over the hearth with a tap and begin the lengthy cleaning process prior to lighting it again, while Sarah tried not to watch how his hands moved, or his eyebrows set at an angle, or his mouth closed about the pipe stem. She tried to think of something harmless and generalised to talk about, something she could say without fear of bringing a tremor to her voice or a heated colour to her face; but there did not seem to be anything at all. It was, she thought, the most uncomfortable evening she had ever spent.

Eventually, after what seemed like twenty-four hours but was in fact nearer one, she glanced yet again at the clock, folded her sewing and laid it aside; and said, 'I think I shall go up now if you don't mind. We shall need to be awake in good time to go to the works. You know where your room is, don't you?'

It was not exactly the most courteous way to treat a guest but Sarah was too uncomfortable to remember her manners. And Bentley seemed only too relieved to say goodnight and watch her leave the room – as relieved as she was herself.

Only, illogically, she found herself wishing as she mounted

the stairs that she had stayed and tried harder to talk, so that they might perhaps have found again some of their old freedom in one another's company.

Next morning was much better, once breakfast was over. It was to be given over entirely to practical matters; and in talking of vases and urns and the popularity of the unglazed black basalt ware recently developed by Jos from the 'Egyptian black' already made locally, somehow the awkwardness between them melted away.

'I gather it's a question of demand outstripping supply at the moment,' Bentley said as they walked together across the yard to the works.

'Yes. Or perhaps more truthfully demand outstripping the necessary improvements. Apart from anything else, we're having to sell poor-quality items touched up and repaired because we haven't enough of the good ones – and as you can imagine that's not something Jos is happy with. He wants to bring in all kinds of new designs, but he just hasn't the time at present, and nor have we the men or the facilities here in Burslem. The sooner the Etruria works are open the better.'

'And how are they progressing?'

'Well enough, though it could always be better. And Jos will keep changing his mind about how the rooms should be arranged – for very good reasons of course. But the men are already set on making the saggars for the new works, and Jos hopes to start making pots there by the summer, if all goes well.'

'And then you'll need new hands.'

'By then it'll be "we",' she reminded him; and instantly regretted the intrusion of a personal note. She went on quickly, 'It's going to be a matter of training boys and girls – the older workmen are not very ready to learn new techniques. We need to take them on young and start from scratch.'

'But who will do the training to begin with?'

'Jos, to a considerable extent I suspect. Though goodness knows how he'll find the time – how he always has, I suppose, by working twenty-five hours in the twenty-four.'

'He's not alone in that,' Bentley commented. 'You're no sluggard yourself.'

She gave him a faint embarrassed smile. 'But we have some

234

good trained hands of course – some of the newer and younger men.'

'Ah, John Voyez perhaps? How's he shaping up? Jos said he'd worked for the Adam brothers, modelling in wood and so forth. Has he settled in well here? It must be quite a change from London.'

'Oh, he's a very skilled man, that I can't deny,' Sarah said, but with such a sharp note in her voice that Bentley looked down at her in surprise.

'You don't share Josiah's view of him then? Or has something turned up that Josiah hasn't mentioned?'

'No, nothing at all. In fact,' she admitted, 'I know of no reason to doubt his ability. What's more, he seems to have a considerable gift for teaching what he knows.'

'He sounds just what is needed then. But I gather you have your doubts.'

'Oh, it's nothing I can point to. He drinks too much sometimes, but that's hardly a rare fault, and at least he keeps his drinking to his spare time. But there's something shifty about him that I don't quite trust. I'd have looked into his background a bit more before taking him on, if I'd been Jos. It all sounded very fine – experience with silver and china as well as wood and marble and any other medium you care to mention – and his skill was spoken of very highly, and with justice too. But everyone was a bit too quiet about his character. However, I could be quite wrong. It's just that Jos never has been a very wise judge of men . . .'

'Present company excepted, I trust,' put in Bentley with a smile. She smiled back, warmly this time and without self-consciousness, almost as if talking of Jos brought him there with them, returning them to the exhilarating friendship of earlier days.

'Of course – but that's just it, he never stops to think. He meets someone, sees something that attracts, and then jumps in with both feet. Only afterwards does he look round to see where he's landed – and then he may find it's not entirely to his taste, by which time it's too late to go back.'

'Yes, that's Josiah all through – I think it's that warm, impulsive quality of his that first attracted me to him. It's very endearing.'

'Ah, but then he was right where you were concerned, as it

happened. But it's a dangerous way to go about hiring workmen. Still, Voyez may yet prove me wrong and go on to be a credit to the works. If he does, then he's just what we need. Would you like to see the work he's doing now, before we go and speak to Tom?'

In a newly partitioned corner of the throwing shed they found the lean wiry little Londoner at work, modelling wreathed handles for an urn. He did not look round as they approached, but continued with swift dextrous fingers to shape flowerheads and trailing leaves of ivy to twine about the handles. At his elbow an apprentice looked on, as impressed as they were by his artistry. Once Bentley caught Sarah's eye, and smiled; but neither said anything until Voyez sat back to study his handiwork.

'That's very fine.'

'Thank you, ma'am.' He spoke coolly, still without looking round. Sarah had a feeling that he was wholly indifferent to her praise, and would have been equally so had she been rebuking him. Perhaps he was so supremely confident of his own ability that he felt no need of comments from others; but Sarah found his manner irritating in the extreme.

'How's young Billy getting on? Is he working well?' Billy was the lad – not very bright, but willing enough – whom Voyez had taken on to fetch and carry for him, bringing clay, tidying away the debris, anything that was needed. It was usual for the more skilled men to take on such help, paid for from their own wages.

Voyez did not answer at once, as if unwilling to take his attention from studying the urn. Then at last he said, 'Billy?' He shrugged. 'Solid from the neck up, but he'll learn.' He stood up suddenly, scraping back his stool on the stone floor, and half-turned to Sarah. 'I'm taking a break now, ma'am, if you don't mind.' Not waiting to learn if she did, he walked out into the yard.

Sarah looked ruefully at Bentley. 'You see. When he *does* work, he works well – but he chooses his own way and his own time. It has an unsettling effect on the other men, just when they were learning good steady ways at last – especially when they know that on thirty-six shillings a week, and piece work on top, he's one of the highest-paid hands we have. But then Jos says all artists are coxcombs and will call no man master.'

'I suppose it's in the nature of the artist to want to put his own insights first. But I can see it might make life difficult in a pottery – especially with an artist in his own right at the head of it.'

Sarah laughed. 'Don't tell Jos you said that!'

They paused next to watch Sam Hunter shaping a vase on the wheel. His own son, nine years old, was shaping balls of clay for him at the bench; he turned to smile at Sarah, and more shyly at Bentley.

'Do you know where Billy is?' Sarah asked him, and was surprised that the boy looked almost frightened. 'It's all right – I only wanted to ask how he was getting on. I suppose he's away on some errand for Mr Voyez.'

'Hidin' from him, more like – the lad's nigh scared out his wits by him.' That was Sam's growling intrusion into the conversation.

'Oh? Why?'

'Poor lad canna do nowt right for yon stuck-up Londoner.'

'That,' Bentley observed as they walked slowly on in search of Tom, 'could simply be natural suspicion of an outsider – a clever one in particular.'

'Perhaps – but in any case it doesn't sound as though he's likely to last long here, poor lad.'

They spent some time talking to Tom Wedgwood – or rather, watching him as he walked about, supervising here, taking a hand there, and looking almost harassed with so many competing demands on his attention and time. Afterwards Sarah took Bentley to see how the kilns worked, since he had not as yet done so at close quarters.

She led the way to the first of the five kilns and pushed open its outer door. They went quickly in, closing it at once behind them, and were instantly enveloped by a fiercely penetrating heat. On four sides of the central oven the arched firemouths opened on to the furious greedy flames fed by coal from the shovel of the great broad sweating figure of the fireman. They walked carefully right round the outside of the oven, while Sarah explained how the temperature depended wholly on the fireman's instinct and judgement, since there was no other really accurate guide as to when to add coal, when to increase the draught, when to damp down; and how a small mistake on his part could ruin a whole ovenful of pots.

'He has to be here for the whole time of the firing – and that can be as much as three days sometimes.'

'A vital workman then,' Bentley commented, picking his way round a pile of empty saggars; and then he stopped, looking down. Sarah came to his side, to see what he had found.

There, staring back at them from a pinched frightened face was a bony boy of about eleven, hunched on the floor behind the saggars.

'Billy!' Sarah exclaimed. Above the roar of the flames the fireman heard her, and came over to them, shovel in hand.

'Lad's all right there, Mrs Wedgwood. I said he can stay.' He rested his hands on the handle of his shovel, holding it upright before him like a crusader's shield and with much of a crusader's defiant aggressiveness in his stance.

Sarah turned to the boy. 'Does Mr Voyez know you're here?' Billy shook his head.

'He looks terrified,' said Bentley softly. He bent down and gently drew the boy on to his feet, and the light from the firemouth fell on two ugly bruises on his temple and cheek.

'What happened there?' Sarah asked. The boy gulped and hesitated, and then said brusquely, 'Nowt, Mrs Wedgwood,' and she had to leave it at that, for she could get no more out of him. In the end he ran from them leaving the outer door swinging on its hinges.

'That Voyez did it, I'd say,' was Harry the fireman's view; but since Billy had said nothing to him either, that did not help very much.

They went back to talk to Tom in a quiet corner of the yard, but he had seen no obvious sign of ill-treatment, beyond young Billy's clear terror, and he thought the bruises had been on him when he came to work that morning. 'Could have got them yesterday, I suppose. Voyez has a temper and not much patience at times, but I can't believe no one would have said anything if he gave the lad more than the odd tap.'

'You know Jos wouldn't allow even the "odd tap".'

'I know – but things do happen sometimes. I tell you what though: Hunter told me something I didn't like the sound of. You know when Voyez came here we paid his expenses and so forth – and Jos told him to charge everything to him through Cox in London?' Sarah nodded: they had also had to endure a week or two with Voyez and his wife and child as guests under their own roof, until a house was found for them. It had not been easy. 'It seems Voyez was boasting in the Bear one night last week that he put one over on Jos by fooling Cox into paying for a few little extras – such as a bottle or two of porter and the like.'

Sarah sighed. 'I'm afraid I can well believe it. I thought his expenses were on the high side at the time. Have you said anything to Jos?'

'I only heard this morning. I wonder if it might be best to let it be for the moment – wait and see like.'

'Maybe. I'll give it some thought. I just wish the man wasn't so good with his hands.'

Later, as they walked back to the house for dinner, Sarah said to Bentley, 'I can't help thinking about that child – it worries me, to see him so frightened.'

'Would you like me to have a word with Voyez?'

She smiled. 'Not at the moment I think. We can hardly accuse him of something without knowing the truth of it. For all we know it's the boy's own father who's to blame.'

At the house a letter from Jos in London demanded the urgent dispatch of all the 'invalids' (as he called them) amongst the rejected black vases, those not quite bad enough to merit total destruction; since he had found someone willing to try and make them fit for sale. 'He wants them by Sunday's wagon,' exclaimed Sarah. 'So much for my plan to take you to Etruria this afternoon – I'll have to see to it at once. Poor Tom will tear out his hair.' She looked at the letter again. 'Oh, and he says "My love to you all, share and divide it as you please" – I imagine that includes you.' Her voice was rough, and it was a moment or two before she found the desired note of controlled coolness to go on. 'Will you come to the works again after dinner?'

The constraint had returned between them. There was a grim line about his mouth. 'I'll go and see William Willet I think. I promised to call next time I was here. I may even stay the night there, if it seems convenient.'

Sarah felt rejected, almost desolate; but that was ridiculous, for she had no right to do so. 'Just as well I've plenty to do,' she told herself that afternoon as, having seen Bentley on his way, she went in search of Tom.

'I'm afraid you'll have to see to it, Sarah,' he told her. 'I've not a spare moment. If Jos wants more vases he'll have to do something about Voyez – the man's not in again this afternoon.'

Sarah selected the 'invalids' and packed them herself, since there was no one free to help her; and then she went to make the arrangements for sending them to London. By the time she reached home it was already growing late, and she was very tired.

And then in the middle of supper (for which Bentley had not returned) Tom Wedgwood came to the house and asked for Sarah, so Betty said, having shown Jos's cousin into the parlour to wait.

'I'm sorry to interrupt your meal, Sarah, but this is serious.' His face would have told her so without words, and the way he was standing planted firmly in the middle of the room. 'Voyez is in gaol.'

Sarah stared at him. 'So that's why he didn't come to work!'

'No, I'm afraid not – he *did* come in, almost at going home time, very drunk. If I'd seen him come I'd have sent him straight out again, but I didn't, and the first I knew was Hunter coming for me, because Voyez lost his temper over some small clumsiness of young Billy's and beat up the lad. By the time anyone could do anything Billy was on the floor knocked out by falling against the bench, with a split lip and several broken ribs. I had him taken home, and sent for Mr Bent to see to him – said we'll pay what's needed – and then we got Voyez into the hands of the law as fast as we could. The next thing his wife storms into the works – God knows how news travels so fast – and she rants at me for being the ruin of them all.' Abruptly he sat down, as if exhaustion had at last overtaken him. 'What a mess!'

Feeling in much the same case, Sarah sank down in a chair facing him. 'What did you say to her?'

'Oh, that there was no place at the Wedgwood works for vicious drunkards, and she was to take herself off and look to her own child – poor mite, with a father like that.'

Sarah smiled ruefully. 'Poor Mrs Voyez too. It won't be easy for her. I'll go and see her – it's not her fault after all, and she may need help. But first I'll go and see Billy. You get

240

yourself home – you look as if you've had enough for one day.'

It was a relief to find that Mr Bent was reassuring about Billy's condition, and that the boy had regained consciousness and seemed likely, in time, to make a full recovery. She found it less consoling that Billy's parents had known for some days that Voyez was ill-treating their son, but were quite unconcerned and regarded this latest development as no more than unfortunate. She wondered if Voyez would now be under arrest if it had been left to them.

It was fully dark by the time she reached Voyez's house and knocked – somewhat apprehensively – at the door, uncomfortably aware of curtains twitched aside in neighbouring windows: as Tom said, news travelled fast.

Mrs Voyez let her in, but with marked reluctance. Her eyes were red-rimmed, as if she had been weeping; but she looked sullen and mistrustful rather than grief-stricken. In the kitchen, smelling of onions and damp washing, she turned arms akimbo to face Sarah. 'Well?'

'I came to see if you needed anything. It must be hard for you at the moment.'

'Oh very kind I'm sure! I'd not be needing anything if it hadn't been for your Mr Wedgwood. What did he have to bring the law into it for?'

'Because a child was seriously injured. Think how you would have felt if someone had used your son so.' She glanced towards the little boy – younger than her John she thought – who lay curled up asleep in a chair by the fire.

'Children need correction – "spare the rod and spoil the child" don't they say? What's wrong with that?'

Sarah felt there was little point in arguing, since it only made her feel less inclined to help. 'Never mind about that now. Is there anything you need? Have the neighbours been helping?'

'I don't want no help from the likes of them. All I want is my man back.' She turned away suddenly to look into the fire. 'What will he get, do you know?' Sarah heard fear there, and an appeal for help.

'I don't know,' she said gently. 'A month or two in prison perhaps. And it's not long to the Assizes.'

'And when he comes out there'll be no job – will there?'

There was a plea in her eyes as she turned round to ask the question, but Sarah ignored it.

'No, no job,' she confirmed. 'But he's a clever man. He'll find something. And meanwhile you must look after yourself and the child.'

Like Tom earlier this evening, Mrs Voyez slumped into a chair. 'I wish I wasn't so far from home.'

Sarah went to the table beyond the fire to draw up a stool for herself; and there came to a sudden standstill.

Amongst the untidy jumble of utensils and kitchenware on its none-too-clean surface lay a pile of papers, with pen and ink nearby; and just visible near the bottom of the pile was a drawing – very careful and detailed – of a vase. The satisfying curve of lip and base and handle seemed familiar somehow, and the simple flowing line of the pattern upon it; and on the lower portion of the paper was written in Voyez's neat hand a list of the ingredients, exact in every proportion, used in the making of the black basalt ware which was their best-selling item.

She stood for a long time staring at it: stoneware clay, manganese, iron oxide – there could be no doubt at all. She felt cold from head to toe. Jos was very strict about secrecy: no one, ever, was allowed to take drawings out of the works – and the only written records of the clay for black basalt were in Jos's personal code, locked away in the Brick House. Inevitably the men who mixed the clay would have some idea what went into it, but they were trusted men sworn to secrecy. And John Voyez had nothing to do with mixing the clay, and no business to know how it was done. What was she to do? There could be no innocent explanation, surely . . .?

In the end Mrs Voyez seemed to realise that something was wrong. She looked round and caught the shocked expression on Sarah's face.

'This paper – what is it doing here? It's a rule at the works that designs aren't brought home.'

'Oh? Is it?' Mrs Voyez did not sound as if she cared very much. 'John was doing those for a friend – to show him what he could do, he said. Someone who might put a bit of work his way – in his spare time of course.'

'Who was the friend, do you know?' Sarah's mouth was

242

dry. Mrs Voyez had said he was doing 'those' – were there other drawings too concealed in the pile; and other notes?

'I don't know. He never said. Someone back home I thought – but it might have been round here. He'll not be doing it now, will he?'

'Then I'd better take the papers back with me, hadn't I?' She held her breath until, unconcerned, Mrs Voyez agreed.

When she reached home it was close to midnight; but she was so seething with anger that she knew there was no point in going to bed, for she would not sleep. She dismissed Betty and Nan and went to the parlour, and there found Bentley smoking his pipe by the fire. For a moment she almost had to remind herself who he was and what he was doing there, so possessed was she by rage. 'Oh! – you've come back.'

He laughed. 'You don't sound very welcoming.'

She relaxed a little and sat down, and then on impulse passed him the papers she was carrying: there had been others, one after another, copies of Jos's best designs. 'What do you make of those?'

He laid down his pipe and quietly looked through the papers. She watched him frown a little, but from puzzlement rather than anger.

'I don't understand: these are Josiah's designs, I presume – but it's not his writing, and besides he doesn't list his materials as openly as this. Where did you get them?'

She told him the whole story, and he listened in a dismayed silence until she had finished; then he said, 'An unpleasant business all round. I wonder how much Voyez has sent off to his "friend" before this?'

'I had the impression these were the first, but I don't know. Jos will be furious.'

'With good reason. The trouble is Voyez is in a good position to go and sell what he knows to the highest bidder, supposing he remembers enough of it without these papers.'

'The only consolation is that Voyez does his best work under close supervision. His craftsmanship is good but he has no real sense of design. Though,' she added with a renewal of pessimism, 'I suppose he has only to remember the designs. We have enough trouble with cheap imitations as it is.'

'Yes – and so far they have none of them been very good imitations. Voyez could be just what these people want.' He picked up his pipe again and began the laborious business of cleaning it. 'Still, he's safely under lock and key for now, and with luck he'll not trouble us for some time to come. When's the next gaol delivery, do you know?'

'The Lent Assizes are due soon, so he could be out then. Still, as you say, that does give us some time. Perhaps there's a solution somewhere.'

By the time, a little later, that they went to bed, Sarah felt calmer, consoled by having a friend with whom to discuss the problem. There had been no dangerous moments in their talk that night.

The next day was bright and sunny, with a mildness unusual so early in the year. In the little garden the snowdrops opened pure and clean above the clay, and the jasmine was bright with yellow stars.

'I'll have to spend some time at the works this morning, after yesterday. But we could go over to Etruria after dinner. It's a lovely day for a walk.'

'You're a real country girl aren't you?' Bentley was wryly amused.

'Why, would you rather ride? We've no second horse at present, but I could hire something for you.'

'Now you know you haven't yet managed to convert me to such energetic means of transport, try as you will: I'm afraid my idea of healthy exercise is a snug coach. But I'll risk the fresh air today, since it's so unseasonably mild. How far is it?'

It was about two miles to the site of the new works which were rapidly taking shape alongside the straight line of the new canal. Down in the valley bottom there was noise and bustle everywhere: men swinging picks with a rhythmic clash against stones, thrusting spades into the heavy clay where the canal was to be; men climbing ladders with bricks lodged on hods on their backs; men laying slates; men pushing barrows; men hammering and banging and digging; everywhere men moving like ants in constant activity, with the busy shouting figures of foremen and builders directing and urging them on.

Sarah and Bentley paused on the hillside and looked down on the scene in fascination.

'They've made some considerable progress since I was last here,' Bentley commented.

'Shall we look at the works first?'

They descended the hill by the path, not looking behind them or to the left, where the two new mansions were taking shape.

'Jos wanted them to put a curve in the canal there, so it would look more natural. But poor Brindley nearly had a fit at the very idea. The lie of the land there calls for a straight stretch of water, and so straight it must be. So Jos now has great plans for the garden – gracious clumps of trees and so on in true Capability Brown style, just to try and counteract the canal. You know Jos met Brown at the Duke of Bridgewater's London house two years or so ago? Brown promised us a visit to Burslem some time – but not in the business line of course; we could never afford his prices.'

'I imagine that between you the two of you could do as well without his help,' Bentley observed. 'Tell me, on the near side of the canal there – is that the wharf for the works? And over there beyond the Newcastle road – that will be the area for the public wharf, I suppose?'

'That's right – and there across the road and beyond the works, that's where the workmen's cottages will be, some day.'

They walked on, coming to the canal side and standing to gaze for a moment at the growing façade of the new works, as elegant and pleasing in its proportions and with almost as many concessions to the prevailing classical taste for porticos and pediments and cupolas as any country mansion.

'Josiah said he had Matthew Boulton's Soho works in mind when he set about the design,' said Bentley. 'I can see what he means. But I think Etruria's gone one better than Birmingham.'

'Just as our pots far outdo Matthew Boulton's metal ornaments for style and quality.'

Bentley looked down at her with a smile. 'Who am I to argue with that? But then Boulton aims at a rather more showy market. What he does make is very good of its kind – but Josiah has no need to fear competition from that quarter.'

'He doesn't very much – but he was a little worried when Boulton started talking of trying his hand at potting. He has considerable respect for the man.'

'They have a good deal in common, even if Boulton's a more

hard-headed character. They both have lively inventive minds, an enthusiasm for new ideas, and a tendency to get carried away by them sometimes. But from what Josiah says I gather that his latest obsession is steam power – that should keep him away from pots.'

Sarah laughed. 'Yes, we spent a day at Birmingham last month so Jos could attend the Lunar Society meeting, and we heard of nothing else but steam power – and some young Scot. What was his name now? James something? Oh, Watt, of course – James Watt. He has apparently been working on some kind of steam engine. Boulton has hopes of luring him to Birmingham.'

'Knowing Boulton he probably will.'

They crossed the canal bed on a makeshift bridge and picked their way through mud to the works. It was here, already clearly visible, that Jos's dream was at last taking shape: a potworks designed and built for the kind of men he hoped to train and foster to create the kind of pots which would one day perhaps make the name of Wedgwood renowned worldwide – or more than it was already, for even now the queen's ware was exported as far as India and America as well as to almost every country in Europe.

Sarah led Bentley beneath the arched entrance into the courtyard behind. 'You can see how it's all laid out so every room is self-contained – outside steps to the upper rooms and so on. That makes sure every process is separate and secret if need be.'

'To prevent a future Voyez, one hopes.'

She gave him a rueful glance. 'If possible, yes. Also the rooms are all arranged in a logical sequence, so everything should be much more efficient. The flint mill there, and the shops for preparing the clay. Throwing room, modelling room, turning room . . . biscuit kilns here and glost ovens there . . . a yard behind there for rubbish, easy for clearing; and one for coal storage, handy for the kilns. Drying rooms, crate shop, and so on . . .

'Come and see the turning room – Jos and I spent hours in the kitchen at home trying to work out the best position for the window. Then of course we had to go and try it out with the actual lathe and a man working it. Jos thought the best light would be from the front, but when we tried it we

246

realised it should be from the side – and then of course it was a question of *which* side. However, we got it right at last, and here it is.' She led him through an opening, still doorless, to the as yet unplastered room, stark and not obviously designed for any purpose; but as she explained it to him, Bentley could see it all take shape before him. It was some little time before she realised that it was her he was watching so intently, and not the room; and what was in his expression set her heart beating fast.

Her flow of words dwindled to stammering silence, and she felt suddenly afraid of the oppressiveness of the emotion in that enclosed space hidden from the bustling scene outside. 'Come and see the kilns,' she said quickly. 'We had even more of a time getting those right.' She felt a sense of relief as they stepped out again into the open amongst all the people, but it stemmed more from a feeling of danger deferred than of danger defeated.

'You can see my house from here, can't you?' Bentley asked, pausing to stare across the canal. Sarah came to his side.

'Yes – there it is.' Bentley's first idea, in a flight of romanticism, had been for a battlemented, faintly gothic edifice, but Jos and Sarah together had dissuaded him. The house that stood there now, a little way up the hillside beside the Newcastle road, was solid, built in pale brick, and austerely classical in style.

'It looks finished from here,' Bentley said.

'It very nearly is, as far as the outside goes anyway. Having the roof on makes such a difference. But there's all the inside work to do still of course. Shall we go and see?'

They walked side by side towards it, uncomfortably conscious of one another, making stiff disjointed conversation. 'Why does it have to be like this?' thought Sarah, 'when I thought we were at ease together again, and could be friends quite naturally – and now in a moment we're back where we were.' She wondered how far his awkwardness was due to his knowledge of what she felt, and how much to his own feelings. Perhaps he did not after all think of her as anything but his friend's wife – though it had not seemed like that once, and there had been other times . . .

It was better when they reached the house where once

247

again there were workmen, and there was something to talk about. Mr Pickford, the architect and builder, was there and came to meet them: he had met Bentley previously to discuss the plans. Sarah left him to show Bentley over the house, and wandered away by herself.

Just behind her, to her right as she stood looking down at the busy scene by the canal, was the old disused stone pit where once she and Jos had sat by the flowering gorse and shared a simple meal, in the days when he was poor and struggling and had only his dreams to offer her. Now, in that very place, sheltered just enough by the brow of the hill, were growing the walls of the mansion that would one day be their home: Etruria Hall.

She did not turn to look at it. She felt curiously reluctant to bring to mind either Jos himself or that shared past. She had an odd detached feeling, as if she were floating in some kind of indeterminate state, adrift from all the values and certainties which bound her to him and patterned her life. Somehow she seemed to be no longer in control of her body, as if her mind had gone to sleep leaving only instinct – an instinct undirected by reason or conscience – to guide her. What was left of her conscious mind stirred uneasily somewhere, brushed by fear; but she let it sleep again. The air was warm, soft with the coming spring, golden with sunlight, and she let it soak into her, giving herself up to whatever it brought.

Bentley came towards her, alone, from the house. She watched him as he walked steadily up the slope, his face glowing with exertion and fresh air, his soft dark eyes unusually bright. She felt the familiar disturbance of her body, the quickened breathing, the tensed nerves, the painful twist of desire. 'Just once,' she thought, 'only once, and then no more . . .'

She brought herself up short, shocked that she could have allowed that wish to take shape even for one tiny interval of time. 'I am Jos's wife,' she told herself, 'and I love him. That is that, and must always be so. And I wouldn't have it otherwise.'

It was true; and yet – how would she be able to bear it when Bentley moved into his fine new house and they into theirs, and they would meet daily, hourly perhaps, and always she would be torn by this forbidden longing? 'It must be conquered,' she told herself firmly. If she had been sure that Bentley felt nothing, it would have been easier. Only she was not sure that she wanted him to feel nothing.

He reached her, smiling, warm.

'Do you approve?' she asked.

'Of what? Oh, the house – yes, indeed. Shall we look at yours now?'

'If you like. We can go back to Burslem that way, through the wood.'

Etruria Hall stood first-floor high, a little desolate in its abandoned state. 'Jos wanted your house finished first,' she explained. 'And there was some difficulty with the design for his laboratory.'

'The most important part of course,' said Bentley with a faint smile.

'Yes,' said Sarah. The thought of Jos calmed her, as if he were in fact walking between them, his presence a tangible barrier, keeping them safe from the danger that she knew was very near. Without thinking very clearly what she was saying she began to talk rapidly about anything she could possibly think of concerning Jos: his current experiments, his dreams and plans. Unfortunately, with a kind of inevitability, these brought her back to Bentley and his eventual move to Etruria. 'Jos has feared all along that you'd change your mind. He knows what a wrench it will be for you to leave Liverpool.'

'I thought I'd set his mind at rest on that score.'

'I doubt if he'll really believe it until you're safely here. After all, you're such a townsman at heart, aren't you?' Without thinking she glanced smiling at him, and then had to look quickly down again as her colour rose, 'You will mind leaving it all, in many ways, won't you?'

He did not say, 'To be near you I would give up everything,' which for a moment she feared he might, though it had not been in her mind when she asked the question. Instead he said, 'Of course there will be things I shall miss. But Liverpool's not so very far away. And when I weighed what I have there in the balance against all that Josiah could offer, then he won. If anyone can understand that, you must.'

Another reminder that she belonged to Jos: was it deliberate?

They reached the house and Sarah led him over the site, explaining everything in a hurried breathless tone. 'Here will be the hall, with the dining room opening from it – this is where the laboratory is to be, but there's a problem about the back door. The doors must be secret you see. Come this way: it's less muddy, and we can see the outbuildings and stable – this is the dairy . . .'

They picked their way carefully over the muddy ground, amongst head-high walls, beneath empty wooden lintels propped upright with nothing to support. 'Quite a mansion,' said Bentley. There was an abstracted note in his voice, as if what he said bore no relation at all to what he was thinking but was simply a defensive observation designed to keep his real thoughts hidden. After a moment he raised his head and gazed across the site to the further hill. 'The sun's setting already.'

Sarah followed his gaze to where a band of rose-gold edged the horizon and spread up to merge gently into the pale green of the winter sky. Beyond the house the path to Burslem passed through a little wood, dense with heavy undergrowth. There, under the trees, it was already shadowed.

'We should be going,' she said, pulling her cloak more closely about her, more in a movement of self-protection than for warmth – it was still very mild for the time of year. 'It'll be dark soon.' She turned, moving quickly, and stumbled on some hidden obstacle. She felt his hand at her elbow, steadying her, and then it was drawn back as sharply as if the touch had scorched him. She walked ahead of him into the trees.

'With every step,' she thought, 'it grows worse.' The darkness closed about them, hiding them from the world, shutting them in together. In the dark, unable to see the other's face, it would be easier to talk of intimate things, things that must not be said. Sarah wished they had gone the other way, skirting the wood and up the hill on to the open moor where the light would linger for perhaps an hour yet. She walked more quickly, trying to put as great a distance as possible between the two of them. But, perhaps from some instinct to protect, Bentley only moved faster too, keeping close behind her. After a moment he touched her arm, very lightly. 'Sarah – wait!'

Here the trees grew most densely of all. Sarah's every instinct told her to ignore him and go on; every instinct but one, which was the one she obeyed. She halted and turned to face him, standing perhaps a yard or two away from him, but able to see no more than the impression of a darker outline, and the grey glimmer of face and hands.

Her heart was thudding painfully, and so loudly that it shut out every other sound but the rustle of some night creature in the leaves and the distant hoot of an owl. She had a desperate, almost unbearable longing to burst out of the rigid fetters which bound her – fetters of her own making, forged by her own free will – to let go and seize this moment when they stood alone together in the dark, unseen and unseeing, to feel his arms close about her, as once for so short a time they had done before. What harm would there be? No one would ever know.

She ought to turn now and run, away from desire and temptation – now, before it was too late. 'How can I want this, loving Jos? How can I love Jos, wanting this?'

Bentley was speaking at last, his voice low, hesitant, a little ragged with emotion. 'Sarah, we must talk – we can't just let things go on like this . . .'

'Run, Sarah, run!' But she did not run, only said, very carefully, 'There is nothing to talk about.'

'You know that's not true.'

'Nothing we ought to allow ourselves to talk about then.'

'Sarah,' he pursued urgently, 'very soon – perhaps this year – I will be coming to live just a few yards away from you. We shall find ourselves always together – like today, and the days before. We will not be able to pretend there is . . . nothing . . . not as we can when we scarcely meet – though God knows even that's hard enough. But this will be worse because we will not be able to count on almost always having Josiah between us.'

'Jos is always between us! You know that. Dear God, he is your friend, your dear best friend – how can there be any question . . .?' The indignation of her cry was not against him, but against herself.

He stepped nearer. With a little shudder she felt his hands clasp her arms.

'I didn't say there was any question, Sarah – only that we must talk . . .'

251

'Don't touch me!' There was such anguish in her voice that he let go instantly.

'I'm sorry.' His breathing sounded harsh and uneven in the stillness, matching hers. 'Sarah,' he began again after a moment, forcing his voice to calmness. 'I have often wondered – if I had stayed in Buxton a little longer, that first time we met . . . if we had met again, might it have been any different?'

It was a question she had often asked herself, always coming back with a kind of bewildered inevitability to the answer she gave him now. 'I have loved Jos from the first moment we met, when we were children. And I knew then, as I know now, that he and I were meant for each other, always.'

There was a little silence, quite different in kind from the last. She knew she had shaken him.

'Then – then did I imagine . . .? Have I been wrong all the time? I thought in Buxton – but that was little enough to go on. There were other times though. Last year most of all, when Josiah was ill . . .'

Wearily, Sarah shook her head. 'Oh, I don't know . . .' She searched for the truth, wanting it for herself as well as for him. 'No,' she admitted, 'you aren't wrong, of course you're not . . .' She looked up at the dim blur that was his face, her voice suddenly sharpened with inquiry. 'Do you think it possible for a man and a woman to love two people in this way – to love them both, wholly and truly and with equal depth?'

'Yes.'

'Then that is it.'

'I see.'

He stirred, and she thought from the sounds that he had leant his back against a tree. She heard him sigh.

'What are we going to do, Sarah?'

He sounded very tired, as tired as she was of being torn this way and that by longing without hope of ease. She bit her lip.

'Nothing,' she said quietly. 'There is nothing we can do. I am Jos's wife, and you are his friend: we both love him. There is no way out of that – except to hope that we may not meet too often, and then not alone, and never again like this.' But she knew with every word that she did not want it to be true; and that something in her tone gave the lie to what she said. With a sense of seizing a last chance she burst out, 'If we don't go home now we'll lose our way in the dark.'

252

She turned from him and began, stumbling, to walk along the path. She heard him follow, and without any consciousness of choice slowed her pace to let him catch up with her. She felt his hand on her arm turning her to face him again. 'Sarah . . .'

She was in his arms; she felt his mouth move from forehead to eyelids to cheek, to her lips, parted now. And she knew she was lost. There was no turning back, not now, not tonight. The path they had taken had brought them here and nowhere else, and they would follow it to the end.

His hands slid beneath her cloak, warm and firm on her waist, pulling her in towards him, and moving on then to caress her back, stirring to life every last sleeping fibre of her body. Beside the path was a bank, thickly layered with leaves, and somehow they were on it, holding each other in a desperate need for nearness, which at last they found.

This then was what she had longed for all these years: the fire and tenderness of his coming, and the sweet fierce moment of completion that ended it. She lay back with arms outflung and cried in joy to the silent wood.

After a time he moved away to lie at her side, one hand resting still on her breast: Jos's friend, as she was Jos's wife. They did not speak but lay still, allowing the realisation of what had happened to seep into the drowsy peace of their relaxed bodies.

At last Bentley withdrew his hand and leaned up on one elbow. 'I want to say, "Come away with me; leave everything and come."'

'You know I would not.'

He flung himself back on the leaves. 'Nor could I – oh, Sarah !' The words came in whispered anguish, and then were carried away on the wind. 'I did not want this to happen; and yet I wanted it – I should not have given way . . .'

'I wanted it too.'

'But I who have always preached reason, and right conduct . . .'

She turned and found his mouth and laid her hand over it. 'Hush – not now! Let it be for tonight.' She sat up. 'We must go back – supper will have been ready long since.'

They walked side by side back to Burslem, saying nothing,

not touching at all; almost, Sarah thought, as if they had never shared that deepest and closest of all physical unions. It was no longer a fear of what might happen that kept them apart, for it had happened. It was more like a kind of grief, a mourning too personal and deep for sharing.

They sat at supper in a tranced state, not really aware of what they ate or what – if anything – was said; and afterwards, somehow, they made their separate ways to bed. If the servants saw anything, it was that the two had somehow quarrelled.

There was a letter from Jos next day, another of his warm delightful letters which seemed to speak to them in his own characteristic tones, full of life and enthusiasm. Sarah, her eyes deep-shadowed from sleeplessness, read it first and then handed it to Bentley, saying nothing; but some deepening of pain in her expression warned him to expect an equal hurt.

The letter ended, lovingly, with greetings to 'my dear friend and my dear wife, for this belongs to both'.

Sarah left her dinner untouched, and turned from the table and went and stood by the window, staring out on a garden drowning in rain. One finger idly traced a pattern on the polished surface of the little table nearby.

She heard Bentley fold the letter, and then there was an interval of silence; and then he said, 'We have eaten of the tree of knowledge, and found only bitterness.'

'Yes.'

'I thought before that we were not happy, that it was hard to live like that – but it was not so bad, looking back.'

Sarah's finger traced on, shaping leaves on a twining stem like the border on queen's ware plate. 'It was a joy, last night – just for a little while – but—'

'But it would have been better if we had never known what it was like.'

'Yes.' She turned round suddenly and faced him: he sat at the table, arms stretched before him either side of the empty plate. 'When Adam and Eve tasted the forbidden fruit they were shut out of Paradise for ever.'

He stared at her, puzzled for a moment; and then he understood. 'It was the natural consequence of what they did,' he said.

254

CHAPTER TWELVE

1769 (II)

They were building a bonfire on the hill just below the newly roofed shell of Etruria Hall. Sarah paused for a moment on what would, eventually, form the garden before the austerely classical front of the house, and watched them running to the wood and back again, laden with sticks for the bonfire, and then once more to the wood for a further load. Most of the bonfire builders were children: the errant Tom Byerley's young sisters; Kate Willet's little girls; Tom Wedgwood's small son Ralph, toddling along under Nan's watchful eye in the company of their own John; and Susannah, of course, bright-eyed and bossy because the bonfire was in honour of her father's works.

Tomorrow, Tuesday 13 June, the Etruria works – still far from complete – would be declared officially open with appropriate ceremonies to mark the occasion. There was to be a luncheon for all the workmen and servants and as many of the closest Wedgwood relations as could be accommodated; and later, at dusk, the bonfire, to mark the close of an important day.

This morning Sarah had brought the children with her while she supervised the carrying of trestle tables from the works to their temporary storage in the house, from which they would be brought tomorrow and set out in the shade of the trees and spread with the food which she and Dolly and Nan, and Kate Willet and her household, and Tom's wife, had all been preparing for some days. Building a bonfire, she thought now, was an ideal activity for the children – all that fresh air and exercise to use up some of the troublesome energy which had begun to bubble over into wild excitement. A pity, she thought ruefully, that Jos was not so easily calmed.

But she tried not to think of Jos, for thinking of him reminded her – as if she could hope to forget! – that Bentley

255

would be at the Brick House by the time she reached home. Jos had gone this morning to meet him at Newcastle, where he had spent last night with the Willets, and bring him back to Burslem for dinner and the expected warm friendliness of her welcome. Her stomach twisted in a knot of panic at the thought. How could she face him again, with Jos there, and the knowledge of that terrible betrayal heavy on her conscience? They had not met since then.

She tried to push the thought out of her mind now and made her way back down the hill and across the canal bed to the works, to see that all was going well there. Today the workmen had been banished, but the activity in the completed rooms was as frantic as ever: only now it was not the bustle of hammering and building, but of crates being unpacked, vases set out on shelves, floors swept, flowers arranged in empty corners and on benches and tables (but not where they might be in the way).

There seemed to be little left for her to do, and it was almost midday and very hot. She went outside the works and looked across at the distant laughing figures of the children. If the bonfire grew any larger it would be in danger of setting the neighbouring trees alight, not to mention the Hall itself. It was time to go home.

All the excitement did not seem to have made a great deal of difference to Susannah, although the younger children were tired and more subdued. She was skipping and laughing as Sarah came up the hill and Nan called them together; and she danced along with her hand in her mother's as they set out for home. 'That way, Mama?'

The blue eyes sparkled, the small hand pointed with un-erring directness towards the shady path through the wood. It looked invitingly cool, and it was the quickest way home; and Sarah, slow and heavy these days, was very tired. But without hesitation she shook her head. 'No, not that way – come along now, and hurry.'

Not once since that February evening had she set foot in the wood, though at times it had been very difficult to explain her unwillingness to do so to Jos or the children. She only knew that if it was possible she did not ever want to go that way again, as long as she lived; though she knew full well also that once they were living here she would have to face it, somehow.

'Oh, madam,' Nan protested, 'that way's much better – you look tired, and it's cool as well as shorter.'

Sarah was about to overrule her, but then she thought, 'Nan's right, and they will only think it strange if I refuse to go that way; and I am tired, and if I reach home exhausted then it will be even harder to face – everything.'

So they went through the wood, and Sarah walked with a painfully fluttering heart and a dread of finding herself at the place where the trees grew most thickly and the bank lay quiet under its carpet of leaves. Then she realised with a little shock that they were already at the far edge of the wood; they had passed the spot, and she had not even known it. The wood looked so different now, all dancing green and dappled shade, leafy and lush and alive. She felt a great sense of relief. She had faced it and found nothing to fear; perhaps the rest would be not quite so unendurable either.

The men were not after all waiting at the Brick House when they reached it. By the time the children were washed and ready, the table set and the dinner prepared, there was still half an hour of painful anxious waiting before Sarah heard the men's voices at the door.

She was trembling, uncontrollably she thought. 'I can't face him – least of all with Jos there. He'll see that something's wrong.' But Jos called cheerfully from the hall and she had to go; and there in the mercifully dim light she came face to face, for the first time since the spring, with Jos's friend, with whom she had betrayed him.

He was bowing and murmuring something she could not quite hear, perhaps because it made no sense; though to her he looked calm and assured, his usual self but for a little scarcely perceptible stiffness which Jos certainly would not see. She tried to match his coolness, and forced some kind of smile and stepped forward, hand outstretched. In a confusion of awkwardness she saw him reach out to take it; and then realised as she prepared to flinch at his touch that he had not done so after all. He was standing quite still gazing at her with a blank pallor, as if in a state of shock.

It jolted her out of her own self-absorption. If he was so disturbed – so uncontrolled – at seeing her again, then she must be the calmer, to cover his confusion as well as her own. She allowed her fingers to touch his for a single trembling

257

moment, and then said (a little too quickly), 'Dinner's ready – do come in.'

'He would keep arguing over some little matter with Willet, though I told him you'd be fuming over the dinner,' said Jos cheerfully.

So he had tried to put off coming here for as long as possible, just as Sarah would have done in his place. Now, shaking off his discomposure – though he still looked pale, Sarah thought – he turned from her to Jos, smiling affectionately. 'That little matter was only the question of the essential creeds of the Christian church,' he pointed out.

Jos waved a careless hand. 'What of them, when Sarah has dinner ready?'

So, laughing, they went to eat; and Jos's good humour carried them somehow through the meal. Afterwards it was easy for Sarah to leave them to sit in the garden over their pipes and talk; and she was free to retreat to the parlour and sink into a chair in the exhaustion of reaction. Only, in the next moment, Tom Wedgwood called to discuss some problem with a kiln at the Brick House works and Jos had to go.

'You go and keep Bentley company,' he said to her. 'Sunshine and quiet and good talk – just the thing for you. You've been doing too much lately.'

And so she found herself seated on the wooden bench beneath the dining room window with the hazy sun on her face and the scent of wallflowers in her nostrils underlying the smell of smoke; and aware of nothing but Bentley at her side, though she kept her eyes on her folded hands and did not look at him.

She knew that he was looking at her. She could feel his gaze with every nerve of her body, and sense too the tension in him. Like the shock on his face as they met in the hall, there was something unexpected in it, an anxiety which seemed greater than the anticipated discomfort at meeting her again in Jos's presence.

'Sarah . . .' he began after a time, in the strained tone of someone trying to find the courage, or the words, to put a difficult question. 'Sarah – the child you are carrying – is it . . .?' He broke off, and she raised her head and looked at him, trying to understand what he was asking; and then she did.

She felt herself go white, as he had done in the hall, almost as if her answer would confirm his worst fears. It had been bad enough – almost beyond bearing – without this. But to imagine – she shivered, cold with horror to think that it might have been possible; only she knew it had never been possible.

Full of compassion for what he must be enduring, what perhaps he had endured ever since their last meeting, she laid a warm consoling hand over his – despite the sun it felt cold. 'No – no, not that. Oh, don't think it for a moment! This child is due in about a month, and that will be full term.' His eyes were on hers, hungrily drawing comfort from them; there was even a little returning colour in his face. She went on more slowly, lowering her voice, 'I think – I know – if I had not been pregnant, it would not have happened. I did not think of it that way then, but I knew I was safe. I suppose it took the last restraint away.'

There was a little silence, during which she saw the colour flood his face and relief soften the strained lines. For a moment he pressed his hands to his eyes. 'I thought – I feared – that would have been the worst betrayal of all . . .' His voice cracked and fell silent. He sat with eyes closed against the sun, clearly trying to bring himself under control; and then at last, more calmly, he said, 'You haven't told him?'

'No! We agreed . . .'

He nodded. 'Yes – and that's right, I'm sure. The hurt would be more than he could bear. It might make us feel easier in our consciences, but the cost is too great.'

Sarah nodded, burdened with a sudden renewed sense of misery. They had no secrets, she and Jos – or had not until this year, and now this was one she could never share with him as long as she lived, for ever and ever. But there was no choice in the matter, not if she loved him as she did.

'The other thing,' she said slowly; 'your not coming here – have you thought further about it?'

'I think I can make a good case to Josiah, but I've said nothing to him yet. After tomorrow perhaps: I don't want to spoil his day.'

It was a triumphant, magical day, even for the two people whose sense of guilt removed them from a free and total enjoyment of it.

First thing in the morning the family guests arrived at the house: Kate and William Willet; Sarah's father, full of pride in his son-in-law's achievement, and her brother John; the uncles from the Big House with their wives (Uncle Thomas too had married at last); Tom from the Brick House works, now in full partnership with Jos; Margaret Byerley (of whose son there had been no news for some time); and a confused hubbub of assorted Wedgwood, Willet and Byerley children.

The house was full of flowers, though with so many people it was not easy to see them; and everyone was dressed in their celebratory best. Susannah was very proud of her young lady's pink silk with hair ribbon to match, and John for the first time wore grown-up breeches and coat and flowered waistcoat. Sarah had remodelled an old gown of blue silk into a loose and surprisingly becoming robe in honour of the occasion; and Jos himself was resplendent in new brown bob wig, fine three-cornered hat, blue coat, black silk breeches and scarlet waistcoat trimmed with gold. Since the amputation he had lost much of the fragile look that had hung about him for so long. He had even filled out a little, regaining some of the appearance of sturdy good health which had struck Sarah on their first meeting; and he had learned to walk with considerable agility on the wooden leg, carefully shaped to be practically indistinguishable from the real one when clothed – as now, in cream silk stockings and buckled shoes.

He came to join the party in the hall with a smile full of pride and love and joy, and drew Sarah's arm through his. 'Well, we're all a credit to the Wedgwood name, are we not?' He caught Bentley's eye and added, 'Not to mention the Bentleys, Byerleys and Willets.'

They went on horseback to Etruria, a happy procession riding through sunlit lanes patterned with dog roses and the last of the May blossom, and at the works found the men crowded on the half-built wharf to cheer their arrival.

Jos made a speech that said little more than that it was not a speech, and invited as many as could do so to follow him to the throwing room. It was freshly plastered, smelling of the new wood of the benches and shelves, and furnished with one of the recently developed mechanical potter's wheels, without a treadle. On the bench, prepared and shaped by Sam Hunter, who stood nearby, lay six balls of black clay.

Jos took off his hat and coat and handed them to Hunter, put on a workman's apron, rolled up his sleeves and sat down before the wheel; Bentley stationed himself beside the rope-driven flywheel at the other end of the bench, watching Jos attentively for the signal to begin. The room was full and faces crowded at the window, but there was not a sound. Jos gave a nod and a little brief smile, and Bentley set the wheel in motion.

Sarah watched Jos's face as he bent over the wheel: absorbed, with the look of secret happiness that was not a smile and yet lit his face. He took a ball of clay, shaping it more exactly in his hands, watching for the moment when the wheel was turning at just the right speed; and threw the clay, centring it unerringly with those swift strong supple hands.

Hollowing, shaping, drawing up and out the hands moved, so quickly that it was scarcely possible to see how it was done – until Jos signalled to Bentley and the wheel ceased moving, and a vase stood there before him, one of those restrained classical shapes that he liked so much. He put it aside on the bench, reached for the second ball of clay, nodded to Bentley and once again set to work.

At the end six vases stood in an orderly row upon the bench, identical, beautiful, perfectly made. Jos looked up with a faintly dazed expression, as if he could not for a moment remember why all those people were there. Then he smiled suddenly and announced, 'When these are finished they will have inscribed upon them: "13 June 1769. One of the first day's productions at Etruria in Staffordshire by Wedgwood and Bentley – Artes Etruriae renascuntur". And one day I pray that Etruria in Staffordshire will be as renowned for its artistry as the Etruria of old. Then all will agree that on this day, as the Latin says,' he shot a grin at Bentley who had coached him in it, 'the Arts of Etruria are reborn!'

There was a restrained clapping from the company in the room, which Sarah, standing there with a lump in her throat, felt was somehow inadequate for the occasion: she was glad that from outside the door came a ragged cheer from some of the men and women waiting there.

261

And then Jos stood up and said briskly, 'Now for the luncheon – you are all heartily welcome'; and as he washed his hands and resumed his coat the gathering became noisily convivial, full of laughter and joking and the giggling chatter of children.

The trestles were set out on the hillside in the shade, spread by Nan and Betty with help from other wives and servants, with cheeses and hams, poultry, loaves of freshly baked bread, ale and fruit, in such abundance that Sarah feared they would be eating the remains for days afterwards.

She was wrong: the workforce were clearly determined to make the most of a feast laid on at their employer's expense, and even the children did more than justice to it – Susannah was already showing signs of an unladylike appetite. Sarah, not very hungry herself, moved among the happy crowd, asking after a difficult child or a sick wife, and deliberately avoiding Bentley as best she could.

As Jos's partner he had as much right as anyone to rejoice and play his part at the opening of the works for which he had given up so much; certainly Jos would think so. But though she did not in any way resent it that Bentley had become so closely linked with the enterprise that meant so much to her, Sarah felt that today must be, first and before everything, Jos's day, for he was at the heart of it. To honour him as she ought she must somehow shut out Bentley, for fear he should once again usurp even a tiny portion of what belonged by right to Jos. Perhaps Bentley himself knew how she felt, even felt something of the same himself, for he did not come near her all day, except when Jos called them together.

After the luncheon, at Jos's insistence, Sarah returned to Burslem leaving the children with Kate, to rest quietly away from the drinking and dancing that filled the afternoon. Only later, at dusk, did she come back for the lighting of the bonfire and the brief breathtaking firework display that followed.

She stood with the children jumping and squealing excitedly around her and watched the flames leap against the dark hill into the luminous blue of the summer night, with her hand in Jos's and a warmth that was not quite contentment at her heart. 'Shall I ever be really happy again?' she thought. 'Or will all my joys now be blighted because of what I have done?'

As they rode home Jos called to Bentley, 'Your house is

ready, you know. We'll have to talk about when you can move in.' And Sarah heard Bentley say, 'We'll discuss it tomorrow,' and flinched at the hurt that was lying in wait for Jos; though not worse than the other hurt from which they were shielding him.

Back at the Brick House it all seemed a little flat. The family guests crowded into the small rooms for supper, the children were hurried to bed, and Sarah felt suddenly overwhelmed with exhaustion. It must have shown on her face, for Jos said, 'You go off to bed, love – we don't want young Jos arriving before his time.'

Sarah smiled faintly. 'Jos is sure this will be another boy,' she explained to Bentley. 'And being born at the same time as Etruria he has to be Josiah, you see.'

She said goodnight to everyone and made her way slowly upstairs. 'If only,' she thought, 'if only it had not happened, today would have been perfect.' But she slept soundly all the same, for the first time in many weeks.

She awoke with a sense of depression and weariness that made her ready enough to acquiesce with Jos's wish that she stay quietly at home and rest today. 'I'm taking Bentley off to Etruria – there's no time to waste,' he said.

She watched them go, knowing that some time that day Bentley would seize the opportunity to break to Jos the decision they had made, though he would put it to him as an irresistible proposal. It *did* make good sense from a business point of view; or so they both believed. But it is easy to make yourself believe that something is the right course when it happens to suit your own interests. It was going to be very much harder to convince Jos that it was so.

Sarah worried about it all day, the more so because she was – as Jos had demanded – lying idly on the parlour sofa, doing nothing more strenuous than reading Richardson's *Pamela*. Its sentimental eulogy of impregnable female virtue was not exactly soothing to her mood nor was it sufficiently absorbing to hold her attention for long. But she was tired, very tired, and she could not have done anything more demanding; nor was there anything for her to do about the house. Kate Willet had taken the children off her hands. 'I'd love to have them for a day or two,' she had assured Sarah; Nan and Betty were dealing efficiently with the clearing up from yesterday; and

263

even if she had been needed at the works she would not have felt well enough. The day seemed interminable.

When Jos came in with Bentley at supper time, one glance at his face told her that Bentley had indeed brought up the subject of a move: Jos's eyes had a bleak look, and there was an angry slant to his dark brows.

'Sally, you must put him right,' he began almost at once. 'I can't make him see sense.'

Sarah smiled (though with some difficulty) and carefully refrained from looking at Bentley. 'What's he done?'

Jos sat himself down on the end of the sofa. 'It's what he proposes to do that is the trouble. He suddenly says he'd be more use in London, keeping an eye on things there. He maintains there's enough supervision here with me and you and Tom, and it's London that needs an extra pair of hands and eyes. I tell him it's nonsense, with his fine new house all ready for him – just two days' ride from Liverpool, too, if he wants to keep in touch with old friends. He'd hate to go and cut himself off in London. Besides, there's no need. You tell him, Sally, for he won't listen to me.'

Sarah looked down at her hands, and the open cover of her book laid face down on her lap. 'I think he's probably right, Jos,' she said quietly. She looked up then, and saw with a pang how her contradiction had dismayed him. 'Think how often you have to go to London at present – you've spent more time there than here in the last two years, I should think. And all the time the business there grows and grows. It does need someone with more experience and knowledge than Cox to keep an eye on things, and take decisions on our behalf. It was all right when John was alive – he was just what was needed. But as things are at present you're constantly trying to be in two places at once, which is no good for you or anyone else. Besides, you're needed here – very often things are held up because you haven't had time to try out a new design, or do the necessary experiments. You've said that yourself.'

'Then Bentley can do the travelling. But at least he'll be here between whiles, and we can plan things together over a pipe . . .'

'Jos, that wouldn't be fair on Bentley – all that travelling. And there should be someone always on the spot in London,

264

I'm sure there should. For one thing, you talk of seeking out the best artists to work on designs for you, but you won't find them in Burslem. You need someone settled in London and able to find his way about artistic society there, not an occasional visitor. And Bentley is very knowledgeable about painting – he's just the man. Maybe you wouldn't have employed Voyez if you'd had someone reliable to advise you, someone who lived nearby and knew all about him . . .'

'Yes, what's become of Voyez?' Bentley broke in, succeeding briefly in diverting Jos.

'He came out of gaol a few weeks ago, after a three-month sentence – that was for injuring the child, of course. We couldn't pursue the matter of the drawings, without concrete proof. But now of course he's found himself a post with Palmer's potworks at Hanley, and I imagine he's doing what he can to turn out Wedgwood imitations – however, that's another matter. He *is* a skilled modeller, whatever his faults. There's no saying it might have been different if you'd lived in London. If you were here I'd still have your advice, and your company too.'

'But you'll still be able to see each other – you just won't actually be neighbours. It's a pity perhaps, but I'm sure it would be for the best.'

He scowled at Sarah, angered that she had not supported him; yet she could see that he was wavering, seeing the sense of what she said. By the morning perhaps he would be ready to admit it. Now it was time to leave the subject. She smiled at him. 'Just think it over, love. Let's have supper now.'

Next day, almost as if it had somehow been planned in advance by Bentley or Sarah, came a letter from Cox, full of frustration and bewilderment. The demand for vases had reached such a point that he felt sometimes he could no longer cope with all the pressures upon him. There were never enough goods to sell; the warehouse was sometimes empty when fashionable visitors called; he had no time to arrange what goods there were in the most pleasing manner, as Mr Wedgwood wished; he had no time either to go chasing up unpaid bills. 'Sometimes,' he wrote, 'I don't know if I'm on my head or my heels. Could you see fit to come to London again and put things in order it might mend matters a little.' Jos looked up from the letter at his wife and his friend, the one seated by the empty hearth, the other standing motionless at the parlour window, looking out.

'Well,' he said, with a hint of bitterness in his tone, 'it seems you were right.' He passed the letter to Bentley. 'You win. Read this – and then let Sally see it. You can move yourself to London as soon as you see fit.' He laid a hand on Bentley's shoulder, shaking it a little. 'So much for my dreams – the evening talks, the meals together, like one family.' His hand fell. 'But there we are. Dreams have to end.'

He left them then, and a little later Sarah heard the front door open and close again. 'I expect he's gone for a ride. He'll have cheered up when he comes back.'

Bentley finished reading the letter and brought it to her, and stood looking down at her as she took it. They did not touch, but there was something almost tangible in the meeting of their eyes. 'I wish,' said Sarah, 'that it was sometimes possible to escape the consequences of one's actions – once at least, just this once.'

He smiled, rather sadly. 'There's no escape from that; and if there could be, then perhaps we'd regret that too. I don't know.' He laid a hand carefully on the back of her chair, just a tiny distance from her head. His voice now was very soft. 'Sarah, you know that I shall always love you. Perhaps I shall never say that to you again, but I wanted you to know that whatever regrets I have – and you too – that does not change. It will be a torment to part from you and live so far away – just as it is as much a torment to be near.'

'I know,' she said quietly, without looking round. 'It is the same for me.'

CHAPTER THIRTEEN

1769–1770

Sarah looked across the dinner table at Jos's bent head. She could see very little of his face, but that he was frowning was clear even from here; and though he had tried at once to stifle it his dismayed exclamation on opening the letter had been audible enough. Sarah said nothing, but simply waited until he should be ready to tell her what was wrong.

He read the letter through twice and then folded it and laid it aside: his hands, performing the action, were clumsy and trembling with suppressed emotion. And then at last his eyes met hers, and she was surprised to see that there was something almost rueful in them. 'Cox,' he said cryptically. 'And don't say "I told you so."'

She did not, of course. Instead she commented quietly, 'Oh dear.' Her eyes travelled to the letter; she had recognised the hurried crowded writing of the address at once, and the delight with which Jos had pounced on it. A letter from Bentley always put him in a jubilant mood; but not, it seemed, today.

'It was worse than we thought,' Jos explained. 'It was bad enough having complaints about bills being sent out twice – no, on reflection, I suppose that's still the worst part of it for it puts our good customers out of humour with us. But I expect it could have been put right quickly enough. Only now it seems Bentley's ordered a full examination of the books and finds everything's in complete confusion. He says it will take him weeks to put it right – not,' he added quickly, 'that there's any question of dishonesty.'

'No.' Sarah's tone was dry. 'Just total incompetence.'

'Yes.' Again there was ruefulness in his expression. 'Bentley wants someone there to help sort things out – now he's so busy setting up the workrooms for the painters and enamellers he just hasn't the time, without neglecting other things. He wondered if you would do it, with your head for figures – he suggests we both go.'

Sarah was swept by a suffocating sense of panic. It did indeed sound like a logical course of action, inescapably, threateningly so. She had the necessary ability to deal with the problem; whilst Jos, supremely indifferent to the intricacies of book-keeping, had not. But for the past months, since that last meeting at the opening of Etruria, she had struggled with her feelings, fought to come to some measure of calmness and acceptance, and she thought she had reached that goal, as nearly perhaps as she could ever hope to do. She could not bear to think that now, suddenly, all her fragile peace was to be destroyed.

Then she remembered baby Josiah, at three months old too young to be left behind, and said in a sober practical tone designed to hide her relief, 'I think it's too late in the year to trail a tiny baby to London. But you go – you must of course – and Bentley will make sure you have all the help you need. Maybe you can take over his duties and leave the books to him; that might be best. As for me, I – oh!'

'What's the matter?'

It was perhaps a smaller blow than the one she had just fended off; but it was enough all the same to shadow her face with desolation. 'The move next week – you'll never be back by then.'

There was disappointment in his expression too, but he said simply, 'It'll have to wait, I'm afraid – I'm sorry, love, but it can't be helped. I think now, what with one thing and another, we'd better wait until spring.'

Just in time Sarah stopped herself from pouring out all her bitter regret at this last and most serious deferment of their move to the new house at Etruria. Time and again it had seemed that it would be only a matter of days before they moved; this time, at least, she had thought that nothing could stop them, and now it had. But what after all would be the use of burdening Jos with her disappointment? He knew how she felt, and doubtless felt it too; and it was not his fault that this had arisen – or not immediately and obviously, she amended, remembering his insistence that Cox be employed as book-keeper. It was hard all the same when she wanted the move so much.

She forced a kind of smile to her face. 'Ah well, it'll give me time to see about setting out the pattern room at Etruria, so that all our wealthy visitors will be able to view our wares in comfort. Then, if we're busy with the new house in the spring when they've company at Trentham and all the other grand houses we'll be ready for them.'

Jos smiled too, both reassured and cheered by her philosophic acceptance of the situation. 'A good idea, love. That should help the time pass usefully until I'm home. Send Jack and Sukey to Kate if you want more time for yourself.'

She saw him on his way at daybreak next morning, and when he was out of sight closed the gate and crossed the little garden – somehow always looking tattered and dirty despite the care Jos lavished upon it – and went into the house, shutting the front door behind her. Then, just inside, she halted, looking about her and liking nothing that she saw of the dark little hallway, from which the small living rooms opened, and the short narrow uneven flight of stairs leading to the cramped rooms above, which were lit like the rest of the house by windows that had constantly to be cleaned yet could rarely be opened because of the gritty smoke outside. For a long time now the house had been far too small for their needs: they had nowhere suitable for the entertainment in appropriate style of the increasing numbers of well-to-do guests who called to look and buy; and there were three children now, and one day Susannah would grow too big to share her brothers' room; and Jos longed to be at work in his own laboratory, secret and planned and built exactly to his needs.

She stared into the depths of the little house to which she had come with so much hope on her wedding day, and hated it. She hated it with an intensity that made her clench her fists at her sides and set her trembling. And she knew that her hatred had nothing whatsoever to do with the good sound practical reasons which had led them to build the house at Etruria. It was emotion and association that fed her hatred, and not reason at all.

Here she remembered almost every day how she had held Richard in her arms as he went into his last convulsive agony and died; how she had waited and waited and waited through the longest slowest most lonely hours of her life as Jos, without her, suffered the amputation of his leg; how she had known the first disappointments of married life, on her wedding night; how, lately, she had lived each day in the constant company of unhappiness and guilt. So much anguish, borne in an atmosphere of dirt and smoke and with the lingering pervasive unmistakable smell from the church-yard permanently there, as if to remind her that all life was pain and must one day end in death for herself and for all she loved. Somehow as the years passed these things had come to drive out the happy memories, of love and good times shared, of the births of children, laughter, talk, joy. One day, she thought, she might be able to retrieve them, to hold them close again; but not for as long as she lived here, caught in the growing shadows.

She made her way with slow deliberate steps to the parlour, and went to the window there and looked out over the garden and the muddy lane to the muddle of houses and potworks beyond, which hid from her the church and the green fields that led over the rise to Etruria Hall.

There, framed in trees, its windows opening on to countryside and clean air, the house waited, offering a new beginning, a new life even: a house without a past and with-out memories on which she and Jos together could make the marks they chose, unhampered by anything that had gone before. She longed, with an intensity so strong that it hurt, to be there, closing the door once and for all on the things she did not want to remember.

'There's nothing you can do about it,' she told herself with some severity. 'You will just have to be patient.' She turned away from the window, her expression resolute. 'Now for the pattern room.'

It was a bright cold breezy day, and she wrapped the children in warm clothes and took them with her, though she left the baby with Nan; the walk would do them good and they could be home by dinner time. Once at Etruria, how-ever, it did not take her long to regret her impulse; Susannah, under the impression that she was helping, carried vases and teapots, rearranged them, gave advice in her bright piping tones, while John showed his usual astonishing ability to disappear the moment his mother's back was turned. Sarah had to retrieve him by turns from the throwing room, a kiln – fortunately not at the moment in use – and the side of the canal. After that last time she gave up any attempt to work and took the children home, trying very hard not to let her frustration and irritation show. Perhaps she should take Jos's advice and send them to Kate at Newcastle: she knew Kate would not mind. But she was their mother and they were her responsibility; it was not quite fair to be always handing them over to someone else for her own convenience. At least after dinner they were tired from the exercise and settled for a sleep, and she was able to return to Etruria for an hour or two and do far more in that time than she had all morning.

Walking home in the dusk she felt her spirits sink as she turned her back on the works and the canal and set her face towards Burslem. It had not been like this at one time; once Burslem had meant everything to her, Jos and the potworks and all that she loved. She felt miserable that it should no longer be so, although the Brick House works were the one part of Burslem where she could still feel happy and at home. She could not help but recognise that much of her longing to be away was her own fault; that it was she herself, by her own actions, who had destroyed her hope of happiness. But perhaps that was not quite fair. After all, they had outgrown what Burslem had to offer. You could not achieve what she and Jos had done and not need to change, to move on to new ground.

Next morning she left the children in Nan's care while she went to Etruria. By evening she knew that one more day would see the pattern room ready; and there were still goodness knows how many days until Jos was likely to return. Feverishly she found work to do, filling the time with a ceaseless activity that she could not allow herself to acknowledge was neither essential nor urgent. She began to go daily to open the wide long windows of the Hall and light fires in every room; she went to the Etruria works, hovering about the men working there, checking stocks and accounts and equipment, making herself something of a nuisance to the ever patient Peter Swift. On the days when even she could not find the shred of an excuse to take her to Etruria she would wander into the Burslem works and plague Tom instead. A letter from Jos, asking for an order to be sent or a new line to be discontinued or increased, would send her running eagerly to see it put into effect.

By early November the bright days had given way to rain.

271

Sarah plodded, drenched, through the downpour to Etruria and back, rising before dawn and going to bed long after dark, and busy for every waking moment. She was tired and tense but would not allow herself to rest. Jos sent word at last that he would be leaving for home next day. She was glad she had that prospect to look forward to; but the day she heard from him was otherwise not a happy one.

At Etruria, two of the key men – needed to instruct the apprentices as well as to keep up the supply of pots – were absent, sick. Sarah trailed back to Burslem through the rain to take broth and other good things to their homes, to offer her sympathy and find out, if she could, how long they were likely to be away from work. And then it was back to Etruria, to make the necessary arrangements at the ornamental works so that the absences did not result in too much disruption; and a last trip to the Hall, to close the windows and see that the fires were safe, and to cast a longing eye over the space everywhere, thinking how good it would be if she had no further to go today, tired as she was; and then back to Burslem again. She arrived for supper cold, shivering and soaked to the skin, to find that Susannah had cut her head running in an excited state around the dining table and that John had subjected them all to a tantrum because Nan would not let him play outside. Some samples of clay from Cornwall that Jos had been wanting, destined for Etruria but arriving too late to be sent there, had been dumped unceremoniously in the hall, where the casks took up most of the space and the path of their coming was marked by a trail of muddy footprints. And finally, Peter Swift called just after supper to say that Will Adams, from whom the Brick House works were leased, was to be married next year and wished to set up as master in his own pottery.

It took Sarah a moment or two to grasp exactly what Peter was trying to tell her.

'Then we all have to be out of here – the useful works as well?'

Swift nodded. 'Aye, ma'am. But not till next year.'

'Not till next year' – as if that gave them all the time that was needed! She knew Jos had thought that one day, if all went well, he might move the useful works too to Etruria, so that the whole Wedgwood enterprise would be within its own

individually planned buildings on a single site. But that had
been something for the distant future. Before that there were
cottages to be built for the workmen, an inn for their recreation, additional kilns and other improvements at the
ornamental works. Business was good, but there was no spare
capital at all.

Sarah thought quickly. It was the vases made at Etruria,
exactly suited to the whims of fashion, which sold best. If
there was to be any speedy increase in profits, then it would
come from there. The essential was – somehow – to increase
output, concentrate time and energy on building up stocks
and not, she realised, to waste those valuable resources on
long walks or rides to and from Burslem. If Bentley had been
resident at Etruria as had been intended, then there would
have been no problem; but he was in London, and there was
no one on hand at the ornamental works.

'Peter, we'll move house tomorrow.' She saw the astonished dismay on his face. 'The day after then – but we'll start
tomorrow. How many wagons can we lay hands on, that
won't be needed for two days or so? And we could do with
help – three or four men who can be spared from here or
Etruria . . .'

Peter gave a wry smile. 'I'll see to it, ma'am.'

'And we'd better send word to Mr Wedgwood on the road
to tell him to come to Etruria on his return.'

'Yes, ma'am. I'll see to it.'

Sarah began that night, packing as much as she could long
after everyone else was in bed, until exhaustion overcame her.
Next day she did despatch the older children to Kate, and
was glad she had done so when she began to realise how huge
was the task she had set herself. How was it possible, she
asked herself more than once, for so few people to acquire so
much in this little house during a mere five years? More than
once she felt a panic-stricken doubt about their ability to
move it all within six weeks, let alone two days.

By nightfall the house had been turned upside down and
had become an obstacle course of crates and boxes, parcels of
books, upended furniture, piles of linen and rolled rugs,
cooking pots threaded together through their handles or
heaped one inside the other. To find what was needed to
make a meal, change a garment, even to reach the cradle

when the baby's crying told her it was time for a feed, were lengthy, uncomfortable and even hazardous processes. Sarah's only sensation, when at last the household had subsided round her into quietness and sleep, was one of depression at the conviction that nothing would go right for them tomorrow and that this chaos would last for ever.

One thing did favour them however: it stopped raining. Next morning as they began to load the first of the wagons, it was neither very bright nor very warm but at least it was dry. Sarah and Betty travelled with the wagon to Etruria, ready to receive and unpack each vehicle as it arrived; Nan and Peter, with the help of the men from the works, were in charge at Burslem.

By what seemed little short of a miracle to Sarah, the last wagon-load had completed its journey when Kate brought the children to Etruria in the middle of the afternoon – and that despite the delays caused when two wagons stuck in the mud on the way. But the real surprise was to see how those possessions, packed and moved with such an effort, seemed so few when set out in the vast rooms of the new house. Just for a moment, pausing to look about her, Sarah was awed by the realisation of what she had come to.

It had all happened so gradually and inevitably, in the natural course of things, but now she realised with sudden force how far they had come from the struggling little potworks by the churchyard; even from the simple yet prospering business of the early days at the Big House. At one time the Brick House Wedgwoods had seemed men of wide vision and startling enterprise; but now, from the head of the grand staircase of Etruria Hall, looking out on the bustle of the new works, with the canal taking shape alongside, and on the whole green expanse of land that was theirs, the Big House seemed somehow as dwarfed and insignificant as did the furniture brought from Burslem. Sarah wondered, with the fleeting ghost of a smile, what her mother would have said to see her today, taking her place in a house as gracious as any of the great houses of her other potential suitors. She would, at the very least, have been astonished that Jos Wedgwood could have achieved so much.

The children, unimpressed by the grandeur, quite unaware of the great step in their fortunes it implied, were simply delighted to find themselves confronted with so much empty space. They ran up and down stairs – 'two staircases, Mama!' – slid across polished floors, rushed shrieking and laughing from one room to another in sheer excitement.

Kate, smiling, shook her head. 'Silly pair – you can see they have no regrets. Now, what can I do to help?'

'I think we should get a meal under way and set up the beds – the rest can be done bit by bit.'

By supper time the children had run off sufficient energy to go to bed afterwards with a good grace and fall quickly asleep. Kate went home – escorted by Peter – and Sarah called a halt to the unpacking, sent the servants to bed and set out on a last tour to check that doors were locked, windows closed and fires safe. She had reached the dining room – empty of all but a few boxes and still uncurtained – when she heard the sound of an approaching carriage. She ran to the side window and looked out on the moonlit drive, and saw the lanterns bobbing on either side of the vehicle coming to a halt there, the horses stamping and foam-flecked from their exertions; and Jos himself haltingly descending on to the gravel. She gave a little cry and ran to the door to meet him.

She stood on the top step dwarfed by the vastness of the house, with the candlelight spilling around her from the hall, and thought, 'Will he mind that I came here while he was away, without him?' For some reason she had not thought of that before.

Then he paused at the foot of the steps, looking up at her with a brightness of expression in which pride and love and tenderness were combined in equal measure, and she knew it was all right. She felt a lurch of her heart, the familiar pang of guilt overlaid by warmth and gratitude. He was home, here at the house which had no past but only a future – a future they shared, in which no one but themselves as yet had any part.

She reached out to him and he came and folded her into his arms. She need not have feared: there was no disapproval, only love and happiness. 'Oh, Sally, my wonder of the world! How ever did you do all this by yourself? I'd never have thought it possible. What a grand homecoming!'

She smiled, allowing her head to rest for a moment on his shoulder, and then she drew back a little and slid her hand into his. 'You'll want something to eat, I expect. We must

have known you would come today, for we left you some.'
She began to lead him into the house. 'I'm sure you won't
mind eating in the kitchen, just for tonight. Everyone else has
gone to bed.' She began to help him out of his travelling
cloak, leaving it with hat and gloves draped over a chair in the
hall. 'How was your journey?'

'Wretched.' He spoke with feeling. 'Everything that could
break down on the coach did so. We had delays everywhere,
and dirty roads – but now my patience is rewarded, so it was
all worth while after all.'

The kitchen fire was easily revived to a comfortable heat,
and Jos ate at the table near it while Sarah sat facing him,
asking him questions, listening to him talk. She did not ask
after Bentley: she had a kind of superstitious feeling that so
long as his name was not spoken aloud in this house then
everything would be well, the past would not intrude, he
could no longer disturb her peace or come in the way of her
happiness with Jos.

But of course she had no hope at all of avoiding his name.
Where Jos was, there Bentley must be, in thought and word if
not in deed. She heard him say, 'Bentley's new house in
Chelsea is pleasant – a good garden, and a hayfield so he can
feed his carriage horses – and it will be comfortable enough in
time. He's not fully moved in yet of course – but then he
hasn't a Sally to put him to rights.' He reached out to lay his
hand caressingly over hers, but she let it rest there only a
moment before she drew away and jumped to her feet, going
to the fire to place on it a wholly unnecessary lump of coal,
just so that he should not see her face.

'Why does he want to move anyway?' she asked irritably. 'I
can't see that he'll be able to supervise the warehouse properly from Chelsea. And Cox will only get things in a muddle
again if he's not supervised.'

'I made sure before I left that there'd be no more problems
of that kind,' explained Jos patiently. 'Cox is to come back
here for good when everything's finally sorted out. He has
been very fair about it all – apologised to the offended
customers and so forth, and taken full responsibility for his
own errors.'

'I should hope so! But maybe if Bentley hadn't been so
busy moving house and looking after his own affairs things

would never have got to that pass, and you'd not have needed to go to London at all.' She wanted to stop talking like this, finding fault, being difficult. It was not really what she felt, if she gave herself time to think about it. Only she did not want to talk of Bentley, to think of him, to feel what even now she felt for him. There was no escape, no more here in the new house than there had been at Burslem. And there was nothing she could do about it.

'Sally, what's the matter with you? Think what he's given up in going to London at all! The lodgings in Newport Street left a great deal to be desired – he must have a comfortable place to live. You'd want the same for us if we were there.' He sounded justifiably bewildered by her attitude.

'I'd want to be as near as possible to my work,' she retorted, conceding nothing.

She did not look round, but she heard Jos get up from the table and come to her, and felt him put his arm about her. 'Come now, love, don't let's get at cross purposes, just when I'm home and everything's put to rights again.'

The coaxing tone stirred her conscience: she turned into his embrace and held him a little desperately. 'I'm sorry, Jos. I'm tired I think.'

'And that's no wonder, my girl, with all you've done today. So let's to bed before we fall asleep where we stand.'

They went upstairs to the room where their marriage bed, which had left little space for anything else in the bedroom at the Brick House, seemed dwarfed by the emptiness around it. But Sarah had seen that the sheets were warmed, and it was comfortable and welcoming and familiar.

What was not familiar, as they lay at last in the dark, was the silence, the deep country silence in which the hoot of every owl or the bark of a fox seemed deafeningly loud. It was a very long time since Sarah had known such quiet, and it soothed her, reminding her that whatever its difficulties this was still a new beginning, offering opportunities such as they had never known until now.

Across the room far beyond the foot of the bed the long uncurtained window looked across the valley to the black outline of the hill against the velvet moonlit blue of the sky. Somewhere on the darkness of the hill a light glowed:

someone was later to bed even than they were – sitting on by a sick bed perhaps, or staying up to finish some urgent task.

Jos felt for her hand and held it, and she rubbed her foot gently against his: his left foot, whole, and strong and supple from the great use it had. 'I'm glad we're here at last,' he said, and she murmured her agreement as they slid into sleep.

She did not tell him until next day that they had received notice to leave the Brick House works. He took it calmly enough, with only the hint of a frown and the comment that, 'We'll just have to get every pot we can make out in the world and sold as soon as possible.' But he set out at once for the works, as if anxious to begin on the process without delay.

His next move, a few days later, was to transfer a number of key workers from Burslem to Etruria. Sarah, calling to see Tom with a new order, found him in a bitter mood.

'I've lost James Bourn now, the only decent engine-turner I had. There'll be no one left soon – as it is, I've had all my best men taken from me. Everything has to give way to Etruria – yet I'm expected to keep on sending out good wares. It seems to me Josiah has no time for his old long-serving partner.'

'It's just that the vases are the best-selling item, and if we're to hope to build new premises for the useful works we need money quickly.'

'Maybe, but there's still a demand for creamware you know.'

'Yes,' agreed Sarah ruefully. 'That's why I'm here now. You know we sent a set of vases to Russia with the ambassador, Lord Cathcart? They've been much admired it seems, and now he wants us to supply a full range of creamware for the use of the Embassy.'

'And I've to meet an important order like that without men? I'm only human you know.'

'Of course. Jos knows that as much as I do. But there are no new men to be hired, with business so good all over the district – at least, no men good enough. There are youngsters in plenty in training, but it'll be some time before they're ready – and there are very few men with the right skills for the work we do. The vases *must* come first – the demand's already far greater than we can meet. It's fashion I know, but there it is. And it's the surest way to be able to afford the new buildings. If you keep the good men you'll be out in the street next year with no works at all, and what good would that do, to you or anyone else?' She smiled coaxingly. 'And you'll manage to meet this new order, won't you?' She handed over the paper with the details of what was wanted. 'I know it's hard, but you've a great deal of experience and so have the men left to you.'

'I'll manage, because I always have,' he agreed glumly; then he softened a little. 'I know it's not easy – not for Jos either, torn between two partners who both want the best for their own side of things. But just so long as it is just a short-term hold up. The queen's ware's not a mere sideline you know.'

'Of course not. It's the bedrock and staple of everything we've ever done or ever will do. I'm not likely to forget that, and nor is Jos.' But she suspected even as she spoke that Jos, bound up as he was in his splendid new works, his partnership with his beloved Bentley, and the vases of whose fashionable appeal he was so proud, did sometimes forget that it was the queen's ware which had set him firmly on the path to prosperity, and which still sold in every corner of the world with a steady reliability which might well endure if and when the fleeting fashion for vases ever came to an end. After all, people needed dinner plates before ever they wanted ornaments for shelf or alcove.

There was little time during the following weeks to reflect on the problems facing the two potworks, or even to enjoy the new house. Sarah had to give some thought to furnishings and curtains for the windows, and see about hiring more servants, but with little money to spare anything that was not absolutely necessary must wait. Much of the rest of the time had to be set aside for the children, the more so as Kate Willet was close to her time with the child she was carrying, and though very well could not be burdened with the care of her brother's children – on the contrary Sarah, in fairness, felt obliged to have the little Willets at Etruria as often as she could. She wished more than once that she shared Kate's wholehearted delight in the company of children, any children. She loved her own, of course; and for short periods of time could enjoy others, so long as they were good-natured and well-behaved, but after a while she would always find herself longing to be at the works, among adults, concerned with other things than dolls and lisping chatter and grazed knees.

Christmas was coming fast, their first at Etruria. There would be space for family feasts, dancing and talk and all the good things they both enjoyed so much: it was the one time of year when even Jos was prepared to shut the door of his works and give himself up to the holiday. Her father and John would come from Spen Green, the Willets and Margaret Byerley from Newcastle, for a day or two at least, the uncles from the Big House, Tom Wedgwood and his wife and children from Burslem, and as many of their other relations and friends as chose to do so. All, unfailingly, would be welcomed with all the warmth that Etruria could offer.

Then, two days before Christmas, a letter came from Spen Green: Sarah's father had been feeling a little out of sorts, and preferred to stay by his own fireside for the time being.

'Now this!' thought Sarah, with an exasperation of which she was immediately ashamed. 'I'll have to go to him,' she said aloud, handing Jos the letter.

He read it, and then looked at her with an expression which showed as clearly as any words that his reaction was just what hers had been: more so, perhaps. 'He doesn't ask for you,' he pointed out.

'Would you have me leave him all alone at Christmas time?' Sarah demanded sharply.

'No – no, of course not.' He was quick to mollify her. 'But perhaps he'd rather be quiet.'

'I must at least go and see – you know how little he says of himself in his letters, and he does sound very low.'

'So you'll leave us alone at Christmas then?'

'Oh, Jos, I'll not be gone long – and you've got any number of people to care for you. He is my father!'

Jos shrugged, pushed back his chair and stood up, as if making ready to go to the works for the day. 'I didn't tell you I might go blind,' he said casually, pausing to push his chair up to the table. He spoke as if he were simply talking of an unimportant decision – whether, say, to ride or to walk down the hill today. Sarah stared at him, not sure if she should take him seriously or not; though certainly his expression was grave enough.

280

'What do you mean?'

'What do you think I mean? I've had trouble with my sight for some weeks now – specks and dots and lines dancing in front of my eyes. I told Bentley when I was in London.'

'Then why on earth did you say nothing of it to me?'

'I suppose I hoped it would get better of its own accord.'

'But it hasn't.'

'No.'

'You should see a doctor about it then.'

'I saw Mr Bent – he said to use them as little as possible and on no account to read or write by candlelight . . .' So that, Sarah thought, explained why he had been so restless lately in the evenings, when once he might have relaxed with a book or written to Bentley. 'He says I may be able to keep the blindness at bay for a little while if I take care.'

For what seemed a long time Sarah said nothing; and then she murmured, 'Oh, Jos!' She wanted to weep, that this should come to him after everything that he had suffered already, and at a time when above all he needed his full strength for his work. She rose to her feet and went to him and led him back to the table. 'Sit down again, love, and let's talk about it.' He sat down, and she stood with her hand on his hair – he had not yet put on his wig – stroking it tenderly. 'Mr Bent is a good surgeon, but he doesn't know everything. Perhaps you should seek another opinion – Dr Darwin's for instance. You were at Lichfield last week: did you say anything to him?'

'I spoke of it in passing, as nothing much.'

'What did he say?'

'He said it was very common and to take no notice.' There was a markedly reluctant note in his voice, as if he did not want to be consoled by Darwin's unconcern. But Sarah was conscious only of a considerable relief: if the doctor she most liked and respected thought there was nothing to worry about, then she was reassured. She smiled gently and sat down, taking both of Jos's hands in hers.

'Then what are you afraid of, love? Have you ever known Dr Darwin to be wrong, even when he disagrees with every doctor for miles around?'

Jos looked at her, from the grey eyes as clear and steady as ever, in outward appearance at least; though she could see

281

that he did not share her relief. 'We only spoke for a moment, in a room full of people. I had no time to describe the symptoms in detail. He was only trying to cheer me, I think. Mr Bent gave me a very careful examination.'

Sarah would not allow any doubts to shake her optimism – or at least none that she would show to Jos. 'For all that I'd guess Dr Darwin's right. You'll see.'

'I hope I shall,' said Jos gloomily; and she hugged him, laughing at the bitter little joke.

'You take Mr Bent's advice for the time being – it can do no harm. And then as soon as you can, have a good long talk with Dr Darwin.'

She stood up again, smoothing her skirts ready for the day's work. 'We'll both go to Spen Green – only little Jos need go with us. Then we can see for ourselves how my father is. We need only stay the one night, unless we find he's worse than we think. It will do you good to get away for a little.' Perhaps, she thought, a change of scene would stop him brooding gloomily on the troubles of his eyesight.

'And how,' Jos protested, 'do you suppose I'm to supervise thirty troublesome hands here at Etruria while I'm jaunting at Spen Green? You know they can scarcely be left for a moment if they're not to make a mess of everything they do.'

'And you know everything's being wound down for Christmas, and they'll be closed altogether in a day or two. There's not much can go wrong in that time, and you can be back to see work start again, even if we have to stay longer than we think at Spen Green.'

To their dismay they found Richard Wedgwood very ill indeed, laid on his bed with a high fever and a look of wasted exhaustion. John, who had taken up residence in the house, was helpless with anxiety and markedly relieved to see his sister. It was clear that Sarah's stay was not to be for the single night of their plans, but for very much longer, an indeterminate time longer.

'Of course you must stay, for as long as ever he needs you,' Jos assured her. 'I'll have to go back to Etruria – as soon as Christmas Day is over at least – but I'll come back here when I can. Nan will manage Jack and Sukey as long as I'm there for her to call on, though you'll have to keep young Jos here with you of course.'

Sarah thought often during the following weeks that it was just as well the infant Josiah was an undemanding baby. That adjective could never have been applied to his grandfather, least of all now when he found himself unwell. He was not accustomed to illness, and once over the worst resented it enormously, trying all the while to relieve weakness and boredom by seeking any diversion his daughter could offer. John thankfully handed over all responsibility to his sister; but then, Sarah supposed, he had endured a good deal before her arrival, and perhaps deserved a rest. She was in any case grateful for one piece of advice he had given them while Jos was there.

'I've heard Dr Elliott's the man to see for your sort of trouble: he's often at Trentham, I believe. They say he knows more about eyes than any man in the country – he is said to have cured the Duke of Bedford and others of very grave disorders.' As a frequent invalid, John's knowledge of medical matters was second to none.

So Jos had left Spen Green eager to consult this expert, and Sarah hoped fervently that he would find reassurance there. She did indeed trust Dr Darwin, but even he was not infallible, and Jos had said there had been no real consultation. She fretted a little that she could not be with her husband at this worrying time, but there was nothing she could do about it except make the best of a trying situation. She was relieved at least to hear from Jos that Kate had been safely delivered of a son, the first after four girls, and that Margaret Byerley had taken Susannah and John into her care, and Nan with them.

Jos came, sometimes, at weekends, to stay at Spen Green. He seemed withdrawn, Sarah noticed anxiously, but obviously glad to snatch a little time with her. He had seen Dr Elliott, he told her during his first visit; the man had looked very grave, but said he thought the case not entirely hopeless, and had prescribed a lotion of elderflower water, camphorated spirit of wine, sugar of lead and other ingredients, which Jos assiduously applied – though not, as yet, with any noticeable effect.

It was during the second visit that William Cox came with messages from the works for Jos. 'I'll have to go back today, love,' he told her. He had intended to stay another night, and she could not hide her disappointment. But it seemed there were difficulties at the useful works, the architect clamouring for an interview and a Mr and Mrs Wilcox, skilled painters, offering their services if Jos chose to take them on. 'I wish you could be there to take some of the load off my shoulders,' Jos said wistfully, and then braced himself again. 'But your father's improving – it shouldn't be long now.'

He went to gather his things together and Sarah stayed talking to Cox, to pass the time while he waited. She had already gained the impression that the man was uneasy about something but could not bring himself to mention it; now, breaking off in the middle of some other trivial matter, he said abruptly, 'Voyez has been gossiping in his cups again – says Mr Wedgwood's broke and fled away owing ten thousand pounds or more.'

Sarah stared at him. Palmer's pottery had already begun, under Voyez's instructions, to produce 'Etruscan vases' which passed, with some, as the genuine article, though Jos had been reassured to find that their quality left a good deal to be desired. Now it seemed that Voyez's malice had not ended there.

'Is he believed, do you think?' She was thinking of the impending move from the Brick House works, which must be general knowledge, and Jos's anxiety about the need for new buildings, not yet begun. To an outsider, unaware of the real situation, it might look as if Voyez was right. 'Has the rumour spread very far?'

'I've heard it from one or two,' Cox admitted, 'and they doubted enough to ask if I knew the rights of it. There's been a man at Etruria asking if his order would be completed, now the works are to close.'

'What's that?' Jos asked sharply, coming in on the end of the conversation.

'I think he should know,' Sarah prompted Cox gently; and so the man repeated his story. Sarah watched Jos colour with anger, biting off an exclamation half spoken. But he held his tongue only until Cox had finished.

'I'll sue him! I'll sue him for every penny he has, for libel and defamation! I'll make him take back every damaging lie, and ruin him as he's tried to ruin me!'

Sarah laid a hand on his arm. 'Jos, he's not worth the trouble. He's a mean-minded little man without the skill or the sense to know where his own interests lie. He's an annoyance, yes – but certainly not worth all the trouble and expense of a court case. Deny the rumours and then forget about it; and before you know where you are it will all have blown over.'

Jos shrugged. 'Maybe you're right – I'll think on it. But if I find he's harmed our business . . .!' He relaxed again. 'But I must be gone or there really will be no business. Let's have a kiss, love.'

It was several weeks before Jos was able to come again, and Sarah had little news of him meanwhile. Her father was making good progress, though slowly enough, and she found it hard to fill the days. She tingled with frustration and boredom, trying to hide from her father and John how much she longed to be back at Etruria; and trying to make herself believe that it was here that she was needed most, when every instinct warned her that her place was with Jos. It was his silence which troubled her most, though she told herself it was only that he was busy, and she would have heard if anything was seriously wrong.

Then at last she did have a letter, but it was not from Etruria or Burslem in Jos's familiar flowing script. Here, instead, was the close upright lettering she had grown used to seeing addressed to Jos; but it was her name that was written there today.

She took the letter up to her room and there stood looking at it, making no move to open it. She could feel her heart beating quickly, chokingly fast; and she knew she was afraid. Why had he written to her, after all this time? He had been so firm – they both had – that all must be over between them, above all that no hint of what had happened must ever reach Jos. Yet how was he to know, writing from London, that Jos would not be with her when she received his letter? And if Jos had been, how could she ever have explained its arrival?

She felt almost angry as, her hands trembling uncontrollably, she broke the seal and unfolded the page.

'My dear Mrs Wedgwood.' She felt a pang of disappointment, sharp and very painful. There was no hint in that opening of love, scarcely even of friendship. In just such terms a man might write a business-like letter to the wife of his best friend.

But why then had he written? Had something else gone wrong? Torn by apprehension both for him and for Jos she read quickly through the rest. 'I think Josiah has not told you . . . he is greatly troubled and low-spirited. He believes – how justly I do not know – that his life as well as his sight is threatened . . . I know he does not wish you to be troubled when already burdened with the care of your father, but I know that you would not wish to be ignorant of anything that concerns your husband . . . believe me at all times your most respectful servant &c, Thomas Bentley.'

Her mouth twisted into a rueful half-smile: so much for her fears that this might be a love letter! If anything, the love that had provoked it was for Jos, wholly and exclusively. It left her with a painful tangle of emotions: fear for Jos, hurt that there was no hint from beginning to end of what they had shared, and – just a little – relief that it should be so. She had not had time to read the letter through again to decide what to do about it when the apothecary came to see her father.

'I think we can safely say the danger's passed,' he pronounced, when his examination had ended. 'He can come downstairs for a little this afternoon. Your careful nursing has been just what was needed.'

That, she supposed, was some comfort; but it would be a few days yet before he would be well enough to be left. It was agonising to know there was nothing she could do but write a cheerful superficial letter to Jos, telling him that she hoped she might soon be home. But almost before she could have hoped to have an answer, Jos himself was at Spen Green, arriving with the first snow of the winter.

'You'll have to stay quietly here for a few days,' Sarah told him with satisfaction. Secretly she was shocked by his appearance. He looked as if he had not slept well for a long time, and very likely not eaten sensibly either. She had not seen him look so ill since the amputation. It seemed that Bentley had been right to be alarmed.

When they had eaten supper and exchanged news of the children and seen Richard Wedgwood to bed, they sat by the parlour fire while the snow rattled on the panes of the shuttered windows, and she showed him Bentley's letter; it seemed the easiest way to reach to the heart of what troubled him.

286

He read it in silence, and then looked up at her, still saying nothing.

'Is he right?' she asked. 'What's all that about fearing for your life? Surely it's not as bad as that?' She had not believed it when she read the letter, taking it to be a gloomy fancy of Jos's; but now, suddenly, seeing the look on his face, she was afraid.

'I've heard of three or four people who had the same trouble with their sight – and afterwards suffered convulsions that carried them off.'

'Who? Which people?'

'Oh, I don't know – but more than one person mentioned it, when I spoke of my eyes.'

'If only I knew,' she thought. 'If only there was some way of being sure there was nothing to fear.' Aloud, she said, 'Have you seen Dr Darwin?'

He shook his head. 'I've had no time, Sally. You don't know what it's like. I've had such troubles with the men – poor work, grumbles about this and that – and we still can't find enough good painters . . .'

'How were the people you were to see – Mr and Mrs Wilcox, wasn't it?'

For a moment his expression lightened. 'Oh, they were just what was needed – Mrs Wilcox in particular has a rare gift. When the weather's fit I'm sending them to London to work in the new rooms there. But two people won't go far – and to be honest Wilcox hasn't his wife's skills. Bentley's been trying to find fan-painters, as having the right delicacy of touch, but they seem hard to come by.'

'Then there's a case for training new hands, as we're doing with the other branches. You said that taking on young William Hackwood was the best thing you ever did, since for all his youth he has such promise. If we can do it with modellers, why not painters? Perhaps Mrs Wilcox would help train young girls for the work.'

'Maybe,' said Jos, his gloom returning. 'But I need someone to do the work now, and none of the youngsters are ready yet. Sometimes I think Voyez was more right than he knew, and we'll end up broke. I can't decide what to do about the buildings for the useful works, and the workmen's housing, and all the rest of it; but something must be done soon – only there are so many difficulties.'

Sarah went to him swiftly and put her arms about him. 'Oh, love, this isn't like you! I'm sure things aren't really so bad. Only you've got so low-spirited you can't see where you're going. It's high time I was home, I can see that.'

'You're right there,' he agreed with feeling. 'That great house seems all dark and cold and full of empty spaces without you. I want you back there more than anything.'

'Then let's get my father on his feet as quickly as we can and I'll come home. But with this snow we'll be stuck for a few days at least, I should think. We can spend some time thinking out what's needed at Etruria, and planning some of the buildings.'

'It's time that's needed most, that's the trouble,' put in Jos.

'Then we'll have to find time somehow,' she said cheerfully, trying not to wonder how that might possibly be achieved.

'If I go blind or die, then we shan't have need of time either,' was Jos's only retort.

But the snow thawed, and the first snowdrops sent up green shoots and Richard Wedgwood grew strong enough to be left; and Jos took Sarah and the baby home to Etruria. She had been five weeks away.

One Saturday night, soon after Sarah's return to Etruria, Jos did not come home from the works at the expected time. It had been dark for about an hour, and the men would by now have long since ended their day's work and be making their way to the alehouses to spend some of their week's wages. Sarah, impatient to tell Jos her good news, began to grow anxious.

From the house the ornamental works appeared to be in darkness, but for the glow of the kilns. Jos might have gone on somewhere else from the works – there were many possibilities – but Sarah could not set her uneasiness at rest. In the past few days he had looked a little less careworn, she thought, but she knew he was not yet his normal self. What if he had been taken ill, alone and unable to call for help?

In the end, prepared to wait no longer, she pulled on her cloak, lit a lantern and made her way down to the works, not really expecting to find him there but hoping to come across some clue as to what had become of him.

288

She found a lamp still burning at one side of the courtyard, and from there she could hear, clearly, the whirr and thump of the wheel in the throwing room; she saw now that the window was brilliant with light. She ran up the flight of steps outside and pushed open the door.

Jos was there, stationed by the flywheel and turning it for the benefit of John Morton, one of his best throwers who was smoothly shaping a vase in black basalt to match a number already completed and set up on the bench. As Sarah came in, Jos was saying, 'Good – when that's done we should have enough.' He turned then and saw her, and smiled briefly.

'I thought you weren't supposed to work by candlelight,' she said softly, coming to his side: it cheered her a little to find him like this, for it suggested that perhaps he was less anxious about his sight.

'I'm not doing much – and besides it had to be done. Bentley wants the vases for painting as soon as possible. If we let them dry tomorrow they can be turned on Monday and fired by the end of the week – but they had to be thrown today.'

She turned to watch the potter's skilful hands, comparing them with Jos's own: he was good, but to her eyes no one was as good as Jos. 'A parcel of books came for you this afternoon.'

'Let's hope it's the rest of Hamilton's *Etruscan Antiquities* at last. It's been very tantalising having only the first volume, though it was kind of Lord Cathcart to give it to me.'

'I'm done now, Mr Wedgwood.'

Jos stopped the wheel and came to look. 'Good – well done. You can be off home. I'll see you're paid for the extra work.'

The man removed his apron, washed and tidied, and made his way out into the night; and Jos sat down thankfully on a stool. He looked very tired, and more than a little anxious. 'What brings you here, Sally? Is anything wrong?'

'Yes,' she said. 'You should be home by now, and you're not.'

His face cleared. 'Oh, is that all? Well, now you can see why I'm not.' He stood up again. 'Now you're here, come and look at the latest batch of bronze vases – I'm rather pleased with them . . .'

She went with him, saying casually as he paused on the top

step to lock the door behind them, 'I saw Will Adams today.'

He turned and looked at her. 'Oh?'

'He says he must be in the Brick House this summer, as soon as he marries. But he'll wait for the works until we have the buildings ready, so long as that is not later than the end of next year. I assured him that gave us ample time.'

He came slowly down the steps to where she waited at their foot, her lantern held high. 'It's time enough,' he said with renewed gloom, 'if my sight lasts that long. But you know I'd make a wretched walker in the dark with a single leg.'

'Oh Jos don't!' There was exasperation as much as pain in her voice. 'Your eyes are no worse are they? They don't hurt you, or do anything but irritate a little because your vision's not clear?'

'But I know what the prospects are. My eyes are no better for all the treatment I've had – so I know they can only get worse.'

'I think,' said Sarah with emphasis, 'that it's high time you saw Dr Darwin.'

So they went to Lichfield and Darwin, after a careful examination of Jos's eyes, was wholly reassuring. 'A m-minor irritation, that's all – n-nothing wrong, to s-speak of. Anyone who s-says otherwise is only after a f-fat fee.'

And somehow after that there was no more talk of failing sight.

Instead, Jos began to realise how much of a burden Sarah had carried during the past weeks, for as winter turned to sping he said one day, 'The moment little Jos is fully weaned we'll go to London, love. How should you like that? I need to go anyway – I'd have gone with Swift last week if it hadn't been for all our colds – and you'd enjoy a little fashionable society, wouldn't you now?'

'And to see Bentley,' she thought, with a painful quickening of the breath. 'To see if the coolness of that letter was a true indication of his feelings towards me now, if it's all over, in fact as well as in deed.' And then she thought, 'But I don't want to see him – better to think it's all over than that, just in case it isn't – or, worse, that it is . . .' Confusion, uncertainty, filled her mind. She sat there trying to understand what she really wanted; and realised that Jos was staring at her in some bewilderment.

'You'd like to go, wouldn't you, Sally? We can see a play or two, hear some good music – and you'll like to visit Bentley's new house. We can see how the painters and enamellers are doing – and maybe find a few good bits and pieces for the house.'

In the end, because she could think of no good reason why they should not go, Sarah yielded to the part of her that ached with a kind of desperation to see Bentley again, however great the heartache; and in two weeks they had left the children with Kate and were on their way south.

Sarah had always felt there was a certain intensity of intimacy between two people travelling together in a chaise, particularly when they travelled alone over a long distance. In the past, the few journeys she and Jos had taken together had seemed to Sarah to bring them both closer than ever, forcing on them the leisure to concentrate on one another.

But this, the first long journey alone since the day, over a year ago now, that she could not bear to remember, was not quite like that, for all the softness of the spring weather, the hedgerows bursting into leaf and the primroses on the high banks. There were too many things she must try not to talk about for that; and those, very often, the things that mattered most to Jos as to herself. In company, Sarah found herself able to talk of Bentley while yet hiding what she really felt; but it is hard to hide such things in a coach, face to face with the person who knows you best in all the world – or ought to do so. Perhaps it was just as well that Jos did not often want to probe beneath the surface of what she said, that he took so much on trust.

She found herself longing for the old days, before last year, when there had been no constraint, no sense of shame, no part of her life from which she shrank and of which she did not speak. In the past she had resented the fact that Bentley seemed to come between them, but now by her own act she had placed him there, a barrier to the old happy innocence and freedom of their love.

At one point, after two days of travelling, as the darkness was slowly filling the coach and they were nearing that night's resting place, she had an overwhelming urge to confess. The words sprang, shaped and ready, to her lips: 'Jos, love, there is something I must tell you . . .'

She had courage enough, the moment was right and might never be so again. She imagined the sense of release there would be, the joy of having no secrets, no dark places, of being once again wholly open with the husband from whom at one time she had kept no secret – no more fears, no more guilt; and reconciliation . . .

But as she opened her mouth she saw suddenly with blinding clarity what would be the cost to him of her own peace of mind – trust destroyed, love betrayed, the terrible hurt of knowing that the two people he loved most in all the world had wronged him irreparably. Would he ever be able to trust again? He might be able to forgive – he was not a man who found it easy to hate, or to bear a grudge, however sharp his initial anger; but what she had done merited more than a grudge. She saw as clearly as if she had already spoken how the knowledge of this thing would shadow his life and destroy his happiness for ever, beyond hope of repair.

No, to tell him might seem, from the outside, right and good and honest, might offer her the hope of healing, the comfort of confession; but for him it would bring only disaster. For that reason she must bite back the words and return her secret to where it belonged, deep within her, unspoken for ever.

She reached for his hand and folded hers about it, and in the dimness saw him turn to look at her and smile; and she wanted to weep.

They went of course to Chelsea, to Bentley's large and comfortable house in Little Cheyne Row. Miss Oates, growing deaf now and more than a little stiff in the joints, welcomed them with tea and cakes and a good fire, and told them Bentley had been unavoidably detained by some difficulty with the painting of the services for Lord Cathcart: that work was being done in the new workshops not far away. 'Nothing serious I gather,' she added reassuringly. 'But I think the gold supplied was not up to standard, or some such thing.'

Bentley came home as they sat by the fireside, hurrying first to embrace Jos with uninhibited warmth, and then to kiss Sarah, lightly, briefly, and without meeting her eyes. She felt herself colour, but not enough – she hoped – to be noticed; and then they all sat down again, and talked of the journey, and Sarah was able to leave all the conversation to the men. Jos was too glad to be with Bentley again to be troubled by her silence. She did not sit watching Bentley, glancing at him only now and then when she could not avoid it; but nevertheless she was wholly aware of him, of every gesture he made, every turn of the head, every movement of his body in the chair. She was ashamed at the strength of the desire that had been aroused in her from the moment he stepped into the room. She had forgotten how powerful was the physical attraction that bound her to him, and how hungry her body still was for the completion that it had known for that one brief moment.

It was an uncomfortable evening, and it told her only too clearly that her own feelings were unchanged, though she could not tell whether or not Bentley still felt for her as once he had. But she survived somehow without disgracing herself, and went to bed with a sense of relief tempered by regret that there had been no ease, no talk, none of the excitement of the mind which as strongly as that of the body had first drawn her to Bentley.

By the end of the next morning she felt sure that as far as he could he was avoiding her; and when they did meet he behaved almost as if she were not there, or at least had no importance to him. It hurt her, the more because she still did not know if it stemmed from too much or too little feeling. Once she would have known; now she felt she had no longer any means of judging. Nor, she knew, ought she to wonder, or even to care.

After dinner, while Jos and Bentley smoked their pipes and talked quietly together, and Miss Oates fell asleep over her sewing, Sarah took herself upstairs to Bentley's library, filled with so many books, the titles and much-handled bindings of which took her back to that long ago day in Liverpool. It was in the library, as if he too remembered it, that Bentley came to find her.

'Josiah proposes a ride – you know how energetic you country people are! Will you come?'

So it was not memory that had brought him. He spoke as he might have done to any guest – friendly, a little teasing, light-hearted. Sarah turned to face him, colouring, even stammering a little because she could not find the words to reply to him in kind. Then she heard him say, 'I hope you did not mind my writing to you. I thought you would want to know.' There was no lightness in his tone, but its gravity might have been as much for Jos as for herself.

'Yes, of course – thank you. I was grateful . . .' she replied hurriedly. She felt she ought to leave the room quickly, to get as far away from him as possible; but as she moved to pass him she heard him say softly, 'There were things I could not write, of course. But I would not have you think them not felt.'

She stood still, and looked at him. 'No. I . . .' she faltered, and struggled to begin again. 'Perhaps it would be better if they were not felt.' Even then she did not think she meant what she said, but it seemed to strike some chord in him.

'Perhaps – you are right, I am sure. I wish you were not.'

She thought for a moment, with an inward flinching, that he was about to reach out and touch her; but at that moment they heard Jos's halting step outside the door, and moved further apart, as if conscious of some danger averted.

'Are you two lazy folks coming or not?' Jos demanded, coming in. 'I'm in need of exercise after all that sitting in a coach, even if you aren't.'

For the next few days Sarah allowed herself to be limited to purely feminine activities, while the men visited the warehouse and the workshops and called on patrons and clients who might be of use to them: it seemed the best way of avoiding Bentley's company, and the temptations it might bring. So she went shopping with Miss Oates, sewed, or played on Bentley's harpsichord, and made numerous social calls.

At supper on the fifth day, Bentley said suddenly. 'Stamford is in London, Elizabeth, and Miss Stamford with him.'

'How delightful!' exclaimed Miss Oates. 'But why did they not let us know they were coming? We have room for them here, have we not? Are they in lodgings?'

'At present, yes – and not very satisfactory ones, I gather. I am sure they would be delighted to come here, if you did not think it would be too much for you.'

'You know it would not, for they know my ways.'

So the Stamfords came to Chelsea, and it was easier still for Sarah to avoid Bentley's company. Mr Stamford, an engineer from Derby, was a friend of Bentley's of many years standing and was also known very slightly to Jos; his daughter Mary, a governess between posts, was young and plain and so self-effacing that Sarah felt that to talk to her was like conversing with a mist, intangible and without substance. But she was good-natured, able to sew or play or sing when absolutely required to do so, and without drawing much either in the way of praise or blame upon herself; and she was rather touchingly pleased to be taken by Sarah and Miss Oates into good London society when they made their morning calls.

It was during one such call that a fellow visitor observed to Sarah in passing, 'I hear your husband is to be honoured by a visit from the Queen this afternoon.'

Sarah turned to gaze at the woman, whose name she could not now remember though they had been introduced (she was beginning to find the constant round of new faces and identical small talk rather trying). Now she tried to keep her voice calm, as if such occurrences were everyday events. 'Really? I had not heard.'

'Ah, but I have a dear friend in the Queen's entourage. It seems Her Majesty has heard of the services that have been made for Lord and Lady Cathcart in Russia, and is most interested in seeing them before they leave the country. Where is it your husband has his rooms? Newport Street?'

It took enormous self-control on Sarah's part to maintain the flow of polite small talk until she could with decency extricate herself from the gathering; but once out of the house she said to Miss Oates, 'We've no time to go anywhere else – or you two may go alone if you wish. But I must get word to Jos. Which is the quietest way to Newport Street from here, do you know?'

Briskly Miss Oates hurried them to the waiting carriage and directed the coachman to take them to the warehouse; but in vain, for it was occupied only by Peter Swift and two assistants – and there were, Sarah noticed with alarm, very few items on display. She drew Swift into the office and explained the situation. 'Do you know where Mr Wedgwood is?' she said.

'He spent an hour or two here first thing, and then some gentlemen came in. I believe they had some antique urns to show him – he went off with them. But where they went I don't know.'

Sarah felt close to despair. Once Jos got talking of Etruscan vases, making drawings, perhaps seeing how they could be copied, he might well be there all day. And the warehouse at present was quite unfit to receive a royal visit. 'Was Mr Bentley with him, do you know?'

'I think Mr Bentley and Mr Stamford had business with a Liverpool gentleman, nothing to do with pottery. They left when Mr Wedgwood did.'

Sarah frowned, trying to think what to do. 'How much of Lord Cathcart's order is finished, do you know?'

'We've a set of plates here. The rest are still at Chelsea with the painters – we were there yesterday to see them. They'll be all but ready, I'd say.'

'Very well – then we must bring as much as we can here this morning. Can you see to sending the cart to Chelsea, and I'll meet you there?'

'But why, ma'am?'

'Because I have heard that the Queen intends to visit us here this afternoon.'

Sarah did not think she had ever been more grateful for Peter Swift's unflappable good sense. For one moment he stared in open-mouthed dismay; and then without another word proceeded to lock up the warehouse and set to work.

Sarah left Miss Oates and Mary Stamford at the house in Chelsea, took just time enough to put on her newest gown – a sacque of sky-blue lustring with a modest train – and a clean white cap under a bergère hat (to re-do her hair would have taken too long), and hurried to the workshops to meet Peter Swift who was already selecting the best of the completed pots and supervising their careful packing on the cart. Sarah made some suggestions as to which further items to bring, and then left them to complete the packing while she set out in the carriage for the warehouse.

There, she cleared the shelves and tables, set a man to sweep and dust, and rearranged those articles in stock which were fit to be shown to the Queen. By the time Peter Swift arrived with the cart she was ready for him; and it was by now almost midday.

'After all this the Queen may well change her mind – or perhaps my informant was wrong anyway.'

'Never mind, ma'am,' said Peter phlegmatically. 'The rooms wanted putting to rights. Mr Wedgwood had it in mind to do it some time soon.'

Even working so hurriedly, within an hour Sarah was pleased with the way the room looked. A dinner service was set out on a table, as if in readiness for a meal; fruit baskets and tea services filled other tables; and a variety of vases was arranged on the shelves so that the colours and shapes appeared to best advantage. In another hour the room would be fit to be seen, even by the Queen of England.

But at that moment there came a hammering at the door. Sarah looked at Peter, and he at her, and then he went to draw back the bolts. A man stood there, resplendent in the royal livery. 'Her Majesty the Queen has expressed a wish to call on Mr Wedgwood's establishment. She will arrive in a few minutes, and does not expect a formal reception.'

'Which is just as well,' so Sarah said, when he had gone. 'It will just have to do as it is.' She did, though, send a man for flowers, accepting that he might well be too late. But by the time the shouts of servants clearing the street outside heralded the arrival of Queen Charlotte's coach, the flowers were in place: violets and primroses bought from a street-seller, looking frail and self-effacing against the splendours of the painted flowers and leaves decorating the plates that surrounded them.

The coach rumbled to a halt outside, the warehouse doors were flung wide, and Sarah stepped forward with Peter Swift and the two other men forming a little party behind her.

Spring sunlight flooded in from the street, throwing the small neat figure of the woman who entered into momentary relief against the bright colours of the group of attendants behind her. Sarah sank into a curtsey, and said with quiet clarity, 'On behalf of my husband may I welcome Your Majesty to these rooms.'

The Queen gestured to her to rise, and came to her, smiling with an unaffected warmth which would have made many a court lady seem false and self-conscious. Long ago at Buckingham House the Queen had been too far away for Sarah to see how she looked – and besides, then Sarah's thoughts had all been for Jos. But now she saw a pale brown-haired young woman in silver-grey silk, whose nose was too large and mouth too wide for beauty, but whose simplicity of manner was immediately appealing.

'You must show me what you have here,' she said, in her lightly accented English, thoroughly learnt since her marriage to King George III nine years ago. 'I am most interested in the services that go to Russia.'

Slowly, Sarah led her about the room, introducing Peter Swift and the other men, displaying the goods as best she could, pointing out a detail of the pattern here, a particularly well-thought-out design here, and glowing with pleasure at the enthusiastic praise that was lavished upon the wares.

'It is a source of wonder to me that Mr Wedgwood can create so very many fine things, and always to so high a standard. I have the greatest admiration for his taste as for his character. It seems to me entirely fitting that our ambassador in Russia should be able to display the very best that England can produce to that strange and barbarous people. They will see that our civilisation extends even to the dressing of our tables.' Later she asked, 'And do you, Mrs Wedgwood, play any part in this great enterprise – other than as a most charming hostess to your Queen?'

Sarah murmured her thanks for the compliment. 'Mr Wedgwood always seeks my advice on the shapes of household wares, Your Majesty. I think it is very important that women should have the greater say in the design of the articles they use: after all, it is they who are inconvenienced if the spout of a teapot pours badly or a handle is difficult to hold, or a flower pot is a troublesome shape.'

'If only,' said the Queen with a smile, 'such practical good sense could be more widely applied.'

She stayed at the warehouse for nearly an hour, and before she left asked that one of the vases should be sent after her to be displayed at Buckingham House. 'I have greatly enjoyed this visit – it is very pleasant to have so sympathetic a fellow member of my own sex for a guide. Thank you, Mrs Wedgwood.'

Sarah and Peter and the other men stood at the door and watched her go, waiting until the coach was out of sight before relaxing, turning to smile at one another in triumphant pleasure.

'Won't Mr Wedgwood be mortified to have missed all this!'

Peter Swift exclaimed with an unaccustomed note of jubilation in his voice. 'To think, I've spoken a word or two to the Queen herself!'

Peter Swift was wrong in one respect: Jos was not in the least mortified that he had missed the Queen. He was, quite simply, delighted that his work had been so honoured, and proud of Sarah for having coped so magnificently.

He had come home late in the afternoon to be met by Miss Oates's account of the Queen's proposed visit; and he was on the point of hurrying anxiously to Newport Street when Sarah made her triumphant return, bringing Peter Swift with her to add his weight to the story.

They were all gathered in the parlour to meet her and hear what had happened: Miss Oates and Mary Stamford, Bentley, Mr Stamford and Jos, all ready to listen with the fullest attention to what she had to say. She took her seat by the fire and told them, and was conscious all the time of Bentley's eyes upon her though she would not look his way.

The moment she finished Jos came and took her hands and pulled her to her feet and into his arms, to an embrace as warm and wholehearted as if they had been alone. 'Oh, my jewel of a girl, where would I be without you?' Only then, like Sarah herself, he could not leave Bentley out, for holding her still in the crook of his arm he turned, smiling, to his friend. 'Isn't that right? We'd be lost without her?'

There was a certain constraint in Bentley's answering smile – it did not quite reach his eyes. 'Certainly,' he said rather stiffly, his gaze moving very briefly to Sarah's face and then on to Jos. Sarah looked down, so as not to risk meeting his eyes, and in that moment caught a brief passing glimpse of Mary Stamford's face. The governess was watching Bentley with unexpected attentiveness; there was something wistful, almost hungry in her expression.

'You too, poor soul,' thought Sarah with compassion; and then wondered if Miss Stamford were not the more to be envied of the two of them. Unreturned love, unsatisfied passion, were painful emotions to carry with one, but she had learned what it meant to arouse in Bentley something more than a civilised affection, and made the discovery than love shared to the full could bring a greater pain than love denied. If she had been like Mary Stamford, single and innocent, then it might have been different; only she did not want to be like Mary Stamford, for then there would have been no Jos either.

The edge had gone from the day's triumph. She felt very tired, looking forward longingly to bed time, although then the man who lay with her was not the one who could bring peace to her body. When he was asleep she wept a little in silence, alone in the dark.

Next day, still full of tender pride, Jos suggested a walk alone together, and they wandered through the fashionable London streets while he talked of future plans and projects with such enthusiasm that after a time Sarah was able to put her unhappiness aside. Passing a jeweller's, Jos came to an abrupt halt and on impulse asked her to say which item on display pleased her most. When, laughing a little at the game, she selected a ruby and diamond ring, to her astonishment he drew her into the shop and promptly bought it for her.

'A good wife is more precious than rubies,' he said tenderly, with a blithe disregard for accuracy; and there in the shop, watched by the jeweller, his assistant, and two rather scandalised customers, he drew her into his arms and kissed her.

CHAPTER FOURTEEN

1772

Sarah had not meant to stay so long sitting on the stool beside Tom's cradle, watching her small son as he sat there in the relaxed collected manner of the very young. Kate had said once, 'I love the way babies sit, when they first learn – legs tucked in to balance, everything just right without thinking about it.' But then Kate adored babies, as she doted on children of every age. Sarah was not like that and never would be, but for all that she loved to watch Tom. He was always so intent, so wholly concentrated on what he was doing – as now, while he gravely poked and pulled and prodded at the little wooden horse young Josiah had given him to play with this morning. But however absorbed, after a time the concentration would suddenly be broken off, and he would look up and give a great crow of delight to find someone there with him; and she would want to pick him up and hug him to her, so much did that smile clutch at her heart. None of her other children had been as beautiful as he was, so delicately perfect of feature, with that soft downy golden hair and those great long-lashed grey eyes, clear and direct and seemingly full of grave baby wisdom.

Yet she had not wanted him. She could remember now, with astonishment rather than with shame, the bitter despair which had gripped her when she realised she was pregnant yet again. Nine more months of sickness and infirmity, she had thought then; and at the end of them another helpless creature dependent on her for life and sustenance, demanding so much of the time she wanted to give to her work – her other work, she had amended, for however unhappy she was she could not deny that the children, too, were part of her work.

Perhaps she would have been happier about it if the moment of Tom's conception had been one she could look back on with pleasure; but on the contrary it had been one of those occasions when she had been wholly disinclined for Jos's attentions, and had endured them with a kind of grim stoicism – below the surface at least, for she had not let Jos see what she felt.

And then, after all that, Tom's birth had been as quick and easy as it was possible to be. Jos had gone to a meeting of his fellow potters, leaving her reading quietly by the library fire, and had come home two hours later just as Tom opened his eyes on the world. And every last trace of resentment had left her at that moment. 'Shall we call him Thomas, for my dear friend?' Jos had suggested; and she had found no cause to quarrel with that.

So, ten months later, as the March wind set the daffodils dancing in the bed below the window and tossed the birds like dead leaves, as if trying to fool the world that it was autumn again; here she sat at nine o'clock in the morning doing nothing more constructive than gazing at her son. What was unusual was not that she should want to do so, but that she should be yielding to that inclination when there was so much else to be done. Her will power seemed somehow to have deserted her this morning, for it had taken a tremendous effort even to get out of bed; and she had not after that been able to force herself to face breakfast and the family and all the other morning duties.

Half an hour later Jos passed the open nursery door on the way to his dressing room, and stopped. 'Sally!' He came in, and she looked round, starting guiltily, but did no more than press her hands down on the chair at her sides, as if about to rise. 'I thought you were going to see young Hackwood this morning.' He sounded more puzzled than angry.

She forced a smile, and tried to make her voice sound matter of fact and light-hearted. 'Yes, of course – I was just spending a little time with our son, that's all.'

Jos crouched down beside the cradle, reaching out to touch the baby's cheek. Tom laughed delightedly, dropping the toy and holding out his arms towards his father, who promptly lifted him up. 'And what better way to spend the time, eh Tom my lad?' Tom tugged at the linen cap on his father's head, pulling it askew to reveal the cropped greying hair. 'Three fine sons now – who would want more? Except the same number of sprightly little lasses – we'll have to even it up, won't we, Sally?'

'Oh no!' she thought in dismay; but if anything showed on

302

her face Jos was too busy talking to his son to see it. She watched him for a while, her mind empty of anything in particular, and then said at last, 'When does Mrs Crewe want William Hackwood to call?'

Jos returned Tom to the cradle, where he resumed his playing and his gurgling – he was an extraordinarily good-natured baby. 'She didn't name a day,' he said. 'As soon as possible, that's all. There's no reason why he shouldn't go today.'

'So long as I let him know in time,' commented Sarah ruefully. She rose to her feet, slowly and with an effort which was not lost on Jos.

'You look tired, love – and a bit peaky. Stay quiet here today if you like: I'll go and see Hackwood.'

Sarah smiled faintly. 'And let Mrs Massey know what to do about dinner as well, I suppose?' Mrs Massey was the new housekeeper at Etruria, a warm motherly woman who had once boarded the young Thomas Bentley in her Derbyshire home when he was a student at Findern, and who remembered him kindly still.

Sarah watched Jos's face, alerted by the slightly blank look it had. 'You hadn't forgotten that the Brindleys are dining with us today?'

'Of course! Make it a good dinner then; you know how Brindley's been overworking, and it'll do him good to enjoy a leisurely meal – nourishing food, and something to talk about that isn't work.'

She thought of saying, 'You know you'll end up talking of canals all the same,' but somehow she did not have the energy to do so. She felt she needed what strength she had simply for things that had to be said and done. At the moment her chief concern was to stay on her feet; she put out a hand to steady herself on a table close by. 'I'll see Mrs Massey now, and then go to the works.'

Jos looked troubled. 'Are you sure you wouldn't rather I saw Hackwood for you?'

She shook her head. 'I don't think you'd be able to talk to him without letting him see your doubts. He must believe we trust him to do the work exactly as required, and then I'm sure we'll find he'll not let us down.'

'I hope not. Mrs Crewe dotes on that son of hers. She'll

want the models to be perfect. But Hackwood's still very young and inexperienced.'

'And gifted. Anyway, we'll see. Did you say you were going to the farm today?'

'I want to see how the ploughing's going, and talk to Evans about turnips.'

John Evans was the man who managed the home farm of the Etruria estate; it had surprised Sarah to discover how delighted Jos was to have land of his own, and how relaxing and enjoyable he found the time spent on it. It would have taken more than a certain weariness to cause her to deprive him of that pleasure today. 'I expect I'll look in on the works later, before I settle down in the laboratory,' Jos added now. He leaned over and kissed her lightly. 'Take care, love. Put your feet up a bit when you've seen Hackwood.'

'I *am* tired,' Sarah thought as, more slowly, she followed him from the room, 'he's quite right.' Tired of deception, tired of emotion, tired of the constant demands of children and servants – yes, even, it must be confessed, tired of the works. Today she would have liked best of all simply to crawl back into bed and sleep. But then she had often been tired lately, and she knew better than to give in to it; that would only mean even more to do later on.

She met the children on the stairs, walking sedately step by step with Jane Hillyard. Last year, suddenly, Nan had married, and was now expecting a child of her own; Sarah still missed her very much. But Jane Hillyard who had replaced her was well recommended and the children loved her; and she had already proved herself willing and efficient and good natured.

Now she paused to let Sarah pass, gathering the children round her – though Josiah escaped, scampering on up the stairs and declaring breathlessly, 'Joss go see Tom.' He spent a great deal of time hanging dotingly, and with a touching protectiveness, over his small brother's cradle.

'Let him go,' Sarah said to the nursemaid who had made a move to follow. 'At least you'll know where to find him.' The words came easily enough, but in the next moment exhaustion swept over her, and a cold dizziness. She tightened her grasp on the banister rail. 'Let the children play outside for a while, Jane. I have to go to the works, but I'll be back about eleven.'

'Yes, madam. It's such a beautiful day after all the rain and cold it'll do them good to be running outside.'

Later, when Sarah set out across the garden on her way to the works, she could not bring herself to agree with the nursemaid's view of the day. It was bright and sunny, certainly, with a brilliantly blue sky swept free of clouds and the spring flowers gold and white and blue in the sheltered corners; but all she felt was the coldness of the wind, chilling her through the thick folds of her cloak and the heavy wool of her gown, setting her shivering. She did not remember ever having been so cold, even in the middle of winter when the Hall exposed on its hill caught every wind that blew.

The formal part of the garden – already taking shape under Jos's enthusiastic guidance – was separated from the parkland which sloped down to the canal by a neat brick wall, just high enough to give a little shelter without obscuring the view from the house. Sarah let herself into the park through the gate that was set in the corner of the wall, and began to follow the path down the hill between the carefully planted groups of trees, which were designed like the wall to improve rather than shut out the view.

She had come only a little way yet already she felt exhausted, her body so tired that it seemed to ache in every part. She paused, half leaning on a tree, trying to gather what strength she had left. She was not likely to inspire William Hackwood with confident creativity if she arrived hardly able to stand upright; and this commission was important, both for him and for the works. The demand for vases was showing some signs of slackening at last, and there was a need to diversify: portrait busts were a promising possibility

She looked down at the works now, blinking to try and clear her vision which seemed for some reason to be spotted, a little blurred. The buildings looked a long way off: the fine classical frontage of the ornamental works, and the newer buildings to the north where the useful works had been housed since the end of last year; and the neat rows of workmen's cottages so ideally constructed that men sought work at Etruria just for the privilege of living in them.

The ache in her limbs was worse than ever now, a pain like

red-hot needles piercing her joints. She moved on again, hoping it would ease, but it only seemed to grow worse. Her head throbbed, too, bringing on nausea and a frightening dizziness.

'Keep to the path,' she told herself; 'that's right, not far now.' She reached the path beside the canal, still waterless since the tunnel through Harecastle Hill three miles to the north was not yet finished, in spite of Brindley's years of ceaseless work (though to the south the canal was open as far as Stoke). The new stone that edged the bank seemed to glitter in the sunlight, dazzling her; for a moment she halted again, closing her eyes.

Turn right now, on to the bridge; just a few yards more and she would be there. A cart rumbled by and someone called to her, but she could not make out what was said and she was concentrating too hard on forcing her legs to do as they were told to look round.

Beyond the bridge the charming round domed building – also echoed at the far end of the façade, and housing the colour-grinding mill – loomed before her. It seemed to be swaying, as if caught like the birds in the strong wind, rocking against the sky. The wind roared in her ears too, very loud, shutting out all other sounds.

She was aware now, very dimly, of the pale gleaming bricks of the elegant façade that faced the canal, and of someone coming towards her: a tiny shrunken figure very far away who was, she knew somehow, Peter Swift. He was gesturing wildly, and his mouth was moving, but she could hear nothing but the noise in her ears, not like a wind any more, but like a drenching cascade of water pouring, pouring over her. Perhaps that was why she was so cold . . .

Then not just the round house but everything – works, canal, trees, sky – seemed to be turning, turning, faster and faster about her like a whirlpool sucking her into its heart deeper and ever deeper. She felt a hand on her arm – or did she imagine it? – but the light from the day was going, and she knew only the pain in her limbs and a horrible sickening sensation of falling.

Somewhere, somehow, the fall must have ended, for she came to rest at last after a long blackness. The world had stopped spinning and she lay supported on softness, wrapped in warmth. Beyond her closed eyes there was light; and slowly, cautiously, she opened them.

She was in her own bed at Etruria Hall, with the sunlight filtering through half-closed curtains and Jos sitting at her side holding her hand in his. She rested her gaze on his face and saw that it did not look as it had done the last time she had seen him. Something had aged him, drained the colour from his skin and set lines of anxiety and fear running from nose to mouth and between his brows. He was watching her with a painful intensity, which, as she looked at him, gave way very slightly to a measure of relief.

'Sally – Sally my love . . .' he murmured, stroking her hand and bending nearer; though to her he seemed still very distant, veiled from her by something invisible and yet almost tangible. He had a look, she thought, of a starving man in dread that his last hope of nourishment might be torn from him. It was a moment or two before she realised that it was for her that he feared.

She wanted to smile, to reassure him somehow; but she felt so desperately weary. She drew together all her last faint reserves of strength, directing them with all the will power at her command, and slowly, after what seemed an age, succeeded in forcing her lips into some kind of smile. Jos smiled too, though as wanly, and reached out to stroke her hair. 'I've sent for Dr Darwin, love – he shouldn't be long. Can I get you anything?'

'No,' she tried to say, but no sound came and only the faint movement of her lips told Jos what she meant. She could not find the strength to add 'thank you'.

Soon afterwards she drifted again into a haunted pain-racked half-conscious state, emerging only now and then to see Darwin's vast bulk bending over her and to hear voices talking, far off and incomprehensible; to see candlelight, and then again the day; and Kate smiling, bringing a damp cloth to wipe face and hands; and always Jos, hovering there with the look of anguish on his dear face that she could do nothing to smooth away, sometimes crouched at the bedside, sometimes bent over a table writing, sometimes standing at the window, a black outline against the light.

Between whiles there was only a chaotic nightmare world

in which the carved devils from Astbury church tormented her, or monsters padded after her that she could not move to run from; and coming nearer they had the face of the man she must not love; or worse, Jos himself would turn from her and become a monster too. It was a world in which the familiar landscape was shadowed with fear, distorted, and in which the only constant, shared with the few lucid intervals, was pain.

At last there came a sleep that was not shot through with nightmares, a deep dreamless sleep that brought her finally to a coherent wakefulness. It was morning, she thought, and fully daylight, but Jos was sleeping still in his customary place at her side. She lay there, not moving, filled with thankfulness that the nightmare was over. It had all been a dream then, an evil, terrible dream; but she was awake now and she knew that none of it was real. Even the pain had gone, like the rest of it.

She turned her head to look fully at Jos, surprised a little to find how much effort that simple movement demanded of her. He was sleeping like a child, but he looked thinner than she remembered, and some of the lines of her nightmare lingered still. Slowly, she began to suspect that it had not all been a bad dream; even that it had been real.

She wanted to turn on her side, and her brain sent the necessary message to muscles and limbs, but nothing happened. She tried again; and then with a growing sense of panic tried to raise her legs, move her arms, or her hands. Only her fingers responded at all; and then only very slowly, awkwardly, as stiffly as a hinge rusted from long disuse. She knew Jos needed to sleep, for otherwise he would be awake by now; but she needed him more, too much to be considerate. She moaned aloud, 'Jos!'

Her voice sounded feeble, rusted like her finger joints, but he heard it. His eyes opened and he smiled and raised himself on one elbow the better to look at her. The look of harrowing anguish had indeed gone from his face, leaving a great weariness overlaid with tenderness.

'The worst's over, Sally my love. Darwin says you'll mend in no time.' He bent to kiss her. 'What would you say to some good strengthening broth?'

She had been hungry; but now her fear was greater than

her hunger. She marshalled all her resources and managed to whisper, 'I can't move.' She was thinking, 'How can the worst be over? What could be worse than this?'

Jos kissed her again. 'Give it time, love. You've lost all your strength, you know. But we'll build you up – have you jumping about the house in no time.'

She studied his face, trying to read the truth there, wondering if his eyes would tell her that the glib reassurance was only bravado, that he was hiding some terrible reality from her. But Jos had never been a good liar, and she saw now only a tender steadfast clarity in his grey eyes.

It was a new Jos who revealed himself to her over the days and weeks of slow halting recovery. Until now it was she who had always been the strength and mainstay of their marriage, supporting and comforting, encouraging and fortifying, but suddenly she found that all turned upside down. It was Jos who brought her tempting food – sometimes, wickedly grinning, against all the doctor's orders, because it was what she most liked; he who urged her with gentle encouragement to force her limbs to move, slowly, gradually, painfully, and would not allow her to be defeated; he who guided her first feeble steps to a chair near the bed, and teased her and laughed to conceal the tears of joy that she knew had sprung to his eyes; he who saw that she was comfortable, read to her, talked to her, listened to her fears and reassured her. And though, sometimes, Kate or Margaret Byerley took a turn at the bedside, it was Jos she wanted there, and he knew it and rarely left her for very long without his comforting presence. 'The lame leading the lame,' he joked once, as held by his arm she stepped haltingly towards the chair; and she was reminded of the time, long years ago, when he had been lame and ill and it was she who had coaxed and bullied and encouraged him back to some kind of normality.

Very slowly, day by day, she did regain her strength, and almost imperceptibly movement returned to her limbs. Darwin came often, each time nodding approvingly at the progress she had made since his last visit. 'Good,' he pronounced. 'B-best of all, though, you n-need a trip to Buxton – just the thing for those s-stiff limbs. Good for you b-both – have a holiday. Get about a bit more, then you c-can go.' She did not tell him that she feared to go to Buxton, because of all the memories it held. Instead she merely smiled and hoped it would be a long while before she had to think of it again.

She learned at last what exactly had happened on the day she had been taken ill: how Peter Swift had called for help when she collapsed, and arranged for her to be carried back to the house; how Kate, sent for at once, had come to look after the children and help in any other way she could; how the Brindleys, invited to dinner, had arrived to find the house in chaos and no dinner prepared, since Jos had completely forgotten they were expected. They had realised all was not well when they met Darwin in the hall, on his way to bring medicines from his chaise.

'He took one look at Brindley and told him he looked as though he needed a doctor's ministrations too,' Jos told Sarah. 'He's since found that Brindley has diabetes – he had some hopes of persuading him to rest and take things more easily, and take care what he eats, but you know what Brindley's like. I'm afraid things will go badly for him.'

Sarah was sorry to hear it, the more so because Jos had, she felt, enough troubles of his own without having to worry about his friends. She grew a little anxious about the works herself, because Jos steadfastly refused to talk about them at all; and that could only mean that they too had their problems. All the more reason then for her to get well as soon as she could.

There came a day at last when, leaning on Jos, she was able to walk as far as an armchair by the window; from where, wrapped in rugs, she could look out on the brilliant green of the April day, feeling the soft air on her face from the window, just opened a very little, and hearing the thrush sing from the beech tree which was bursting into new and dazzling leaf in a corner of the garden.

Once she was settled, Jos hovered about her, a little restlessly, as if afraid she might need something and for some reason forget to ask for it; but she sensed there was rather more than that behind it.

'I'll be very comfortable here, if you want to go and get on with your work, love,' she said at last. The look of relief on his face, short-lived though it was, confirmed her instinct.

'No, Sally – you might get cold, or want something and not be able to call for help . . .'

'There's a bell within reach, and with all these rugs I'm more likely to get too hot. Go on, love – you've not been near that laboratory of yours for weeks, have you? And your trials for the new body were going so well.'

He gazed at her speculatively, as if trying to judge whether or not she might really be left without harm. 'I've got the white to a very satisfactory stage – there'll be time enough to make a trial of the coloured bodies later on, when you're well.'

She remembered the result of the final trial before she had been taken ill: he had shown her the fine hard white rectangle of newly fired clay with great pride. 'Do you really think the same body would work for both the ground and the relief? I know the white polishes beautifully, both for gems and cameos, but surely you want a different texture to set it off?'

'A different texture, yes – but think how the white looked *before* it was polished – hard, not porous at all, smooth certainly, but without a shine. The same body coloured would be perfect – the white detail could be modelled and moulded and then the vase or plaque made in the coloured body, and the white relief applied to it. And then they'd be fired together and there'd be no difficulty about different reactions to the firing . . .' The careworn look was rapidly leaving Jos's face, his eyes had brightened, his hands moved to emphasise the eager words.

'And all this time you've been itching to go and try out what cobalt would do, or zaffre, or those other magical powders, and I've kept you dancing attendance on me! Now go on, love – I'll be better all the more quickly for knowing your work's going well.'

She had convinced him and, after a final delay to tuck one of the rugs more firmly about her, he left her. She sat there enjoying the warmth of the sun on her face, and watching the gardener busy weeding and planting just below and the cattle grazing in the park, and far off beyond the canal the carts moving to and from the works, and the men, tiny like ants, fetching and carrying back and forth, back and forth. Before too long perhaps she would be strong again, well enough to walk down the hill to the works; but for now she was content just to sit and watch.

She was startled when Jos burst suddenly into the room;

311

and a little alarmed, for he had been gone a very short time. Then she saw his face, bright and split by a joyous grin. He was waving a letter, and she knew without asking who it must be from.

'Well, here's a piece of news to cheer you.' He pulled up a chair and sat beside her, and took her hand in his. 'You'll never guess – I can scarcely believe it myself – such news!' He was almost incoherent with excitement, his eyes sparkling, the words tumbling out too fast to make much sense. Sarah smiled, happy for whatever it was that had so delighted him.

'Tell me then.'

'It's Bentley . . .' Her heart turned a somersault, though she had expected his name, having seen the letter. She knew she had coloured deeply, for weak as she was every emotion showed with alarming transparency. But Jos was looking at the letter now, as if even having read it he could still not quite believe what it told him. 'What a surprise, after all this time alone!'

Her heart turned again; and this time she felt the colour ebb from her face, leaving it ashen.

'He's to be wed again at last – and to Miss Stamford of all people! Who would have thought it: that quiet little governess – but a dear good woman, I'm sure, and if she makes him happy . . . There now, how does that make you feel? News to cheer an invalid, is it not? I must write at once and give him our hearty congratulations. Get well as soon as you can, Sally, and then we can go visiting – you and Mrs Bentley will soon be firm friends, I'm sure. Mrs Bentley, eh? What a turn of events . . .' The words flowed on, full of happy enthusiasm, and Sarah forced smiles and made some approving noise at intervals, and all the time her dazed senses tried to take in what he said. It was not surprising perhaps that in her weakened state she should be quiet, hesitant in her reaction; and Jos was voluble and happy enough for two.

Slowly the sense of the words reached her. Bentley to be married again – to quiet meek Mary Stamford. He had chosen her out of all the women in the world, a woman as unlike Sarah Wedgwood as it was possible to be; and she would share his talk, his bed, his life, sing duets with him and play to him, hear of his troubles and his joys first of all, before anyone else. She would be more to him than any other woman alive . . .

There was that roaring again and the room spun round – she clutched wildly for Jos's hand, and felt it hold her last of all before the darkness closed in.

When she came round she was once again in bed, with Jos seated at her side; but this time at least he had no look of deep anxiety on his face.

'You were up too long, Sally,' he told her; and then he grinned. 'Shall I tell Bentley how you took his news?' Sarah felt cold with horror at the thought. She stared at him, wondering if he meant it, and what he meant by it. But he only patted her hand soothingly. 'No, Sally girl, I was only teasing. But it is good news, and I know you'll want to join me in wishing them both well when I write – you go on getting well in your own time, and you'll soon be enjoying it all as much as I do. You're just not quite up to it yet, are you?'

'I was, almost,' she thought; 'if only . . .' She closed her eyes to keep the tears at bay. She must not weep, not before Jos. And what cause had she to weep when all was said and done? Bentley had as much right as anyone to happiness; and she had no right at all to expect a fidelity from him that she could not begin to offer in return. He could never look to find happiness with her, and she of her own free will had made that clear to him, as he to her. Why should she, who loved him, grudge him the loving companionship that she had with Jos . . .?

The tears did come then, flowing fast, marking her shame. How could she feel this sense of loss for a man she had no right to love, when she had Jos? – Jos who loved her so much, who through the past weeks had given up all his precious time to care for her with such devotion and tenderness. There ought to be no room in her heart for anyone but him, not even a tiny little chink to admit his dearest friend. 'What kind of woman am I,' she thought despairingly, 'to feel like this?'

Jos gave a cry of distress at her tears and came and folded her into his arms, smoothing her hair and kissing her. 'Love . . . love . . . don't now. I know how disappointed you must be to find you're not as strong as you thought, but you will get well, you'll see.'

He was right, but it was for Sarah a long weary road; and many times she feared she would never reach the end. Sometimes, too, though she tried not to admit the thought to her conscious mind, she doubted whether she really wanted to be well, or wanted it enough to fight for it.

It was Jos, again, who brought her out of her despondent mood. 'I know Darwin recommended Buxton,' he said one day, 'but I think we should go to Bath.'

'It's a very long way,' Sarah said doubtfully. She saw that Jos looked a little shamefaced and added with a smile, 'Come on now, why do you want to go to Bath?'

His answering grin had a sheepish look to it. 'I did have a fancy to take a look at our showroom there and see what progress it's making. Bentley led me to believe it should be open by now, but he's said nothing – but then he's had other things on his mind.'

So to Bath they went by slow stages. It was hot, and most of the fashionable visitors had gone, and Jos and Sarah spent part of each day driving on to the downs above the town in search of a breeze; and Sarah was quite sure that the water – whether for drinking or bathing – made no difference at all to the persistent stiffness in her limbs. But one thing at least did do her good.

On their first day, Jos left Sarah in the afternoon to rest at their lodgings while he went to Westgate Buildings to inspect the showroom; and he came home half an hour later in an unexpected state of agitation. 'I don't know what's been going on, Sally,' he burst out, once he saw that she was not actually asleep. 'The showroom should have been ready months ago, but nothing's been done, nothing at all – just an empty room, dirty and shabby and full of cobwebs and broken shelves – and no stock at all. I tried to find Ward, but he wasn't at home and his wife hadn't much idea what was going on – said they'd had no instructions and thought nothing was to be done before the next season. So that means we've lost the whole of this season. I'm not happy about the situation either – the street's noisy and full of carts and the like, and too far from the Pump Room. But I suppose it'll do during the season, when the great folks want something to pass the time . . .'

'Jos . . . Jos . . .' Laughing, Sarah broke in on his flow of talk. 'Give over now – let's have some tea and talk about it quietly. It's a good thing we came here, because we can see it all set to rights before we leave.'

Jos looked at her doubtfully. 'We came here so you could get well, Sally – you shouldn't be worried . . .' and then he caught her eye, and broke into a smile. 'On second thoughts, perhaps it's just what you need: something to keep your mind busy. I'll send for that tea, and then we'll get to work.'

After that, Sarah seemed to find all the energy that she thought she had lost for good. Jos wrote at once to Bentley, and to Etruria, ordering vases, teapots, dinner services and all manner of smaller items for the showroom; and next day they went together to Westgate Buildings to see what must be done.

Jos had been right: the showroom was in a deplorable state. Sarah's first instinct was to rush headlong into a frenzy of cleaning; but she had enough common sense to know that she was by no means strong enough yet for such demanding physical activity. Instead they applied to Mr and Mrs Ward, who had been appointed to manage the showroom once it was open, and asked them to send men and women to clean, mend, put up shelves, paper walls and paint.

'We need green baize for shelves and tables – yellow paper for that wall where the black vases are to go – blue there, don't you think, to set off the pebble vases?'

Jos grinned. 'It does my heart good to see you so much your old self again, love. And yes, you're quite right. We may need to send to London – we'll see.'

'Do you think we'll make better sales of vases here than in London? My impression is that most of the fashionable people have all the vases they want now.'

Jos gave her a sharp look. 'Have you been hearing things? Or is it just your usual uncanny instinct for what's going on? I didn't want to worry you, but yes, sales have fallen off. At least this room will do to display some of the stock we've had in so long.'

'Have you thought of lowering prices?'

'Of course – but I'm not sure. The vases cost a good deal in the making, what with the wages we must pay our best throwers and turners.'

315

Sarah frowned a little, thinking; and then after a moment said, 'Jos, have you thought of making them more cheaply – using moulds, for instance?'

He looked startled. 'Indeed I haven't – after all, it's the quality people want. The grand folks who buy a Wedgwood vase don't want some cheap moulded article such as can be tossed out by the dozen by any half-handy apprentice.'

'Of course not – and I'm not suggesting we should ever make poor-quality goods. After all, the items we do make at present using moulds are very carefully made. But don't you think that the time has come to make a slightly cheaper range of vases for the less grand people – those who want fine things in their houses, but can't afford the highest prices, the middle sort of people, who want everyone to see what good taste they have.'

Jos gazed at her for a while, and she watched as the speculative light in his eyes turned slowly to enthusiasm. 'I think that may be just what we need, my clever Sally! We'd have to keep some things just for our grandest customers, of course – special lines, to be kept apart . . .'

'Perhaps some displays to be seen by ticket only,' suggested Sarah. 'When we have a particular order, for instance, like the service made for the King last year. Then people will still associate us with quality wares of the highest order.'

'Shall we begin now, here – set that small room aside for the best things?'

Sarah shook her head. 'We haven't the full range of goods yet – and there isn't really room here. And I think it would be best to begin in London – with a proper showroom perhaps. We can think about it carefully, and plan it all in good time. There is one thing though . . .'

'Yes?'

'Have you noticed how much more showy the displays in the shops are here than in London? Much more colour, more goods – a much more bright and crowded look.'

'Yes – and I don't care for it much.'

'No, of course not – but we'll have to be careful not to let this room look too bare and spartan by comparison, or we'll put people off altogether. Maybe when they're in a holiday mood they like a bit more in the way of lavish display.

316

Perhaps a deep red hanging there, near that window, and a few of the gilded vases in front of it.'

'But gilding's right out of favour – remember what Sir William Hamilton said in his letter.'

'A few items there won't hurt, just to brighten a dark corner. And there'll always be some people who'll like them. We may well manage to get rid of that old stock at long last.'

'Right!' agreed Jos. 'I'll ask Bentley to send them. If you think it's right, then I'm sure it is. I've never known your judgement to be at fault.' He rubbed his hands gleefully together. 'We'll be open in a couple of days at this rate.'

Crates came from London and Etruria, packed with the goods they had ordered; and with them a hasty note from Bentley saying that he was leaving next day for Derby to be married. Sarah forced a brittle smile, listened for as long as she could bear to Jos's jubilant comments, and suggested that they set about unpacking and arranging the goods at once.

'We'll call on them on our way home,' Jos decided as he eased the lid off the first crate. Sarah, reaching in to feel gently for a vase amongst the enclosing straw, stood quite still, not looking at him.

'It's not exactly on our way,' she said, as lightly as she could. 'And I *would* like to see the children again soon.' Her voice sounded more wistful, even complaining, than she had intended; and it made Jos look at her with a concerned intentness.

'Of course, love – and I will keep forgetting how ill you've been, now you're so much better. I'll forget that idea – it would be much too far to drag you all the way to London.'

Sarah closed her ears to the note of regret in his voice, and began vigorously to set out the vases on the shelves.

Hours later they had at last unpacked the final item and placed it to its greatest advantage on a shelf, when a carriage drew up in the street outside and a liveried servant jumped down and hammered peremptorily on the door.

Sarah looked at Jos, wondering; and then he shrugged and went to unbolt the door.

'Sir Harbord Harbord wishes to make arrangements for his mother to view the showroom,' said the servant.

'But we're not open yet . . .' began Jos; and then broke off as Sarah came to his side and tugged at his sleeve.

'However,' she put in, smiling briskly, 'we would be happy to open the room for a private viewing tomorrow morning, if that would be convenient.'

And so the next day they found themselves welcoming the elderly lady and her son to the showroom, and by the end of the visit – full of courtesies on both sides – they had sold two green fluted flower vases, a painted teapot and a creamware dessert service with a simple purple border; and had taken an order for further items to match the service. When the carriage had trundled noisily away along the street, they turned to smile happily at one another. Jos held out his arms and Sarah came to be folded into his embrace.

'My dear girl . . .' He kissed her. 'Bath was best for your health after all – but not the water. All you need is a little work to do.'

She laughed. 'Of course! The best cure there is.'

They walked back to their lodgings arm in arm through the sunny streets, and Sarah felt as if wrapped around with love – warm, and safe, and overwhelmingly grateful.

That night in bed she turned to Jos and gently, tenderly wooed him. 'Are you sure, love?' he whispered as he came to her, and she murmured yes, and he made love to her for the first time since her illness. It was not as it had been with Bentley, but there was such a wealth of tenderness between them that she felt contented afterwards. She had so much, and all of it given to her by Jos; and so she said softly, 'Let's go to London, Jos. I'd like that,' and was glad the darkness hid her lie.

It was much worse than she could have imagined in the warm impulsiveness of that night at Bath. Afterwards, she did not know how she had endured those ten days in London without breaking down altogether.

In the first place she had not realised how weak she still was, and the journey left her exhausted, intensified the lingering pain in hands and knees, and confined her to bed for two days the moment they reached the neat Chelsea house. But it was when she had recovered a little that the ordeal began in earnest.

On the surface it was all exactly as it had been on their last visit, except that Miss Oates, retired to Derbyshire on a

318

comfortable pension, had been replaced by the soft shadowy figure of Mary Stamford. But that change of course was everything.

Sarah first came downstairs in the evening, to the parlour made charming with flowers and some of the finest products of Wedgwood and Bentley. The small dark woman at the fireside rose to her feet in a rustle of modest grey silk and came arms outstretched to welcome her and guide her to a comfortable chair.

'Mrs Bentley,' thought Sarah, with a sense of unreality, almost of disbelief. This quiet, neat little woman whom she scarcely remembered so unremarkable was she; this was Mrs Bentley. 'A nondescript mouse of a woman,' Sarah caught herself thinking; and was at once appalled at the unkindness of the phrase – and its unfairness too, for Mary Stamford – Bentley – was gentle, friendly, kind-hearted, and if Bentley loved her she must also be something more than that, something special, outstanding even. Did he love her? She loved him, certainly, for happiness glowed from her eyes and her face, transforming their plainness to something almost approaching beauty. But Bentley?

She hardly dared to look at him for fear their eyes might meet, but he was coming to ask after her health, and she could not help but smile and give him some courteous reply. She was too confused and uncomfortable though to study his face or try to gauge his mood; and in a moment he had turned away from her to resume his interrupted conversation with Jos.

'You'll have heard something of the case Mr Granville Sharp is bringing on behalf of the slave James Somerset, I suppose? . . . No? . . . Ah, it's crucial for the argument against slavery. Rather like the other cases Sharp brought, but there are greater hopes this time that judgement will be found against the slave owner. Once again a slave – one James Somerset – escaped from his master whilst in England, and then was recaptured and shipped for sale to Jamaica. Certainly by West Indian law he was the property of his master – but Sharp hopes this time for a clear judgement that slavery is contrary to the laws of England, so that any slave landing on our soil is automatically free and cannot lawfully be recaptured.'

'That was the argument with the other cases, wasn't it?'

'Certainly, but the judgement was never very clear – one suspects Lord Mansfield of being afraid to attack the slave owners by stating the law too emphatically. But this case is much more clear cut than the others: I can't help but feel Sharp will win. You must meet him, Josiah – a charming man. And you'd be assured of good music at his house, Mrs Wedgwood. He is an accomplished – one might almost say, passionate – musician.'

Sarah felt that errant uncontrollable colour rise again, and simply forced a polite little smile. Once – always in the past – she would have been excited by his talk, and full of eager questions and lively interest. But she was too weary now for intellectual excitement. She wanted quietness, the solid security of Jos's companionship; best of all not to be here at all, but at home with all that was safe and familiar.

Even so, in spite of everything, she could not help but watch him as he turned away from her again, with a concentrated attention that had nothing casual or superficial about it. She felt, as much as saw, the way his head was set upon his shoulders, the grave sweetness of his expression, the curve of lashes on cheekbone – everything about him just as it had always been; and still able, painfully, to set her stomach churning and quicken her heartbeat. 'It is not fair!' she told him in her thoughts. 'You are free now, free of the torment that binds me! Why you, and not me, when I want it so much?'

For she was sure that he had at last put her behind him. She had little recollection afterwards of those days in London, except of weariness, aching limbs and an apparently permanent blinding headache, lightened only by a theatre visit, an evening at Ranelagh, and the respite of a few tranquil yet busy hours at the warehouse with Jos. But she did know that through all that time Bentley scarcely spoke to her, except when courtesy forced him to do so; that not once did she find him looking her way or trying to steal a moment alone with her; and that his manner towards his wife had all the tenderness of a man in love – and she had every reason to know how Bentley looked when in love. 'I must be glad for him,' she told herself; but despite her determination that it should be so there was no gladness in her heart.

320

When at last the goodbyes had been said and the chaise moved away on the first stage of its northward journey, she was swept by an overwhelming sense of relief, so strong that every part of her felt limp with exhaustion at the release of long-held tension.

'It has all been a bit much for you,' Jos said with compunction, troubled by her pallor.

She forced a smile. 'I'll be well when I'm with the children again.'

She was wrong: coming home again did not somehow work a miraculous cure. Worse still, she realised very soon that she was pregnant again. This time she felt neither despair nor joy, only a kind of dull depressed resignation. She wished it had not happened, but it had a kind of inevitability about it and there was nothing she could do to change things. Jos was pleased, but his concern for her outweighed any gladness of his own.

She said nothing to Jos, but she knew that this pregnancy, so soon after her illness, was not going as it should. Sickness she expected, but not the constant nagging pains in her belly and the perpetual exhaustion worse than any she had known since she came home. Jos insisted that she rest as much as possible, so it was easy enough to hide how ill she was simply by doing as she was told. He seemed to see nothing suspicious in such uncharacteristic meekness.

Not that he had much time to worry over her health. She was improving, she told him: it just took time, that was all. And he accepted her assurance. At the works he put into effect the changes they had agreed on at Bath, setting the men to mould vases in large quantities. She knew from his face and the little he told her that the men were not happy with the changes, that there were mutterings about low wages and the ending of overtime work; but though it troubled her she felt no inclination to go down to the works and try to help him put things right.

At the end of June, in the midst of the Etruria haymaking, a jubilant letter came from Bentley. 'Sharp has won his case. It is now stated for all time that no man can remain a slave on English soil! Now for the greater fight, against slavery everywhere!' Jos, sunburned from the happy hours he had spent

321

each day in the fields with the haymakers, handed the letter to Sarah; and for a little while they shared a time of real and unalloyed rejoicing. Sarah thought of the slave ship all those years ago: were they at last to see an end to that horror, and all it meant?

The summer passed, hay harvest and corn. Susannah came home from her first term at school in Manchester, thinner, taller, full of chatter and odd little refinements of manner; and Tom took his first unsteady steps and began to follow his brother Josiah about the house, to little Joss's delight. James Brindley took to his bed, and it was obvious to all his friends that he would never leave it again.

Brindley's illness stirred Sarah to activity. Almost daily she travelled the four miles to the Brindleys' home at Turnhurst Hall on the other side of Tunstall, on the pretext of taking gifts of tempting food, but in reality to provide the sympathetic companionship that the distraught Mrs Brindley – burdened also with the care of two young children and her elderly parents – so desperately needed. Each visit left Sarah drained, with no resources on her return home for anything but to drag herself to bed. A week of this and she miscarried.

Even in the spring she had not been so ill as she was now. Jos, frightened by the white pain-racked and bleeding spectacle of his wife, sent at once for Dr Darwin.

There was no regret in Sarah for the child that would never be born, only relief. But she did not, even so, make a quick recovery. She seemed to have lost any desire to be well again. She lay day by day not moving or thinking, without will or purpose, wholly disinclined for anything at all. It was as if the long fight had at last become too much for her, and she had given up.

Darwin tried every possible line of attack – medicine, diet, bullying, persuasion – all to no avail. In the end it was Jos, tormented with worry, who gave the doctor the weapon he needed.

'I'm n-not very happy about that m-man of yours,' he said one day as he heaved his great frame into the creaking armchair at Sarah's bedside. 'Have you s-seen how he's losing weight? Walking round like a s-scarecrow with his clothes hanging off him.' He studied Sarah's face intently, noting with satisfaction the flicker of interest, even of alarm, in her eyes as he spoke. 'He's had a l-lot to f-face lately, one way and another. He's n-not tough like you, either – can't c-cope with the s-strain. Needs s-someone to lean on, peace and t-tranquillity at home. I tell him he needs rest, but where's he going to g-get it, I ask myself?'

It was obvious that he knew the answer quite well; and that Sarah did too. She was weak, weary, dizzy, subject to violent shivering fits; but she could if she chose find the strength to force herself to get up and dress and resume some of the duties of the house; and to show Jos a cheerful face.

Darwin was right about Jos: shaken out of her self-absorption, Sarah saw that at once. In the years since the operation on his leg he had begun to fill out a little, but now he was almost as thin as he had been in the days of constant ill health; and, worse, he had the pinched haggard look of a man worn down by cares too great for him. He had been at her side, her loving strength and support, when she needed him; now, never self-sufficient as she was, he needed her. So when, two days later, Brindley died at last, Sarah was there, a quiet understanding presence, providing the consolation Jos needed.

Her renewed strength lasted only until the funeral was over and Hugh Henshall, Mrs Brindley's brother, had replaced his irreplaceable brother-in-law as engineer to the canal scheme. And then the fits of shivering and sickness struck her down again, more violently than ever. She lay in bed, helpless and filled with despair, because Jos needed her and she had failed him. She had nothing to give, because she was empty, except for the ugliness like the hidden place under a stone which no one must ever be allowed to see.

Darwin came again, and stayed two nights, subjecting her to examinations, purges, doses of this and that; and finally banishing Jos from the room and seating himself on the ill-used chair at the bedside with a look of brisk determination. 'Well now, Sarah, this won't do you know. I c-can't find any good cause for all this – n-nothing that good food, gentle exercise and fresh air shouldn't p-put right. But it's not getting p-put right, is it?'

Sarah shook her head, not trusting herself to speak. Darwin laid his great paw over hers. 'Seems t-to me it's not the

323

b-body but the s-spirit that's out of sorts. Don't you think so?'

'I don't know,' she whispered; though she did, only too well.

'We're going to g-get to the bottom of this s-somehow. I think a s-stay in Lichfield is the answer – then I c-can keep an eye on you, eh S-Sarah?'

She felt a sudden tremor of fear; but of what she was not sure. She was in any case too weak, too wrapped in apathetic misery, to do anything but accept what was decided for her. So, with Jos riding beside her in the chaise to see her safely lodged, to Lichfield she went.

The room made ready for her in Darwin's fine house bordering the Cathedral close had, she thought, been chosen with care. High up, its windows looked over angular roof tops to the cathedral itself, and towards the morning sun. From here, the clamour of the streets came only distantly, a faint disturbance, and nothing but the music of the cathedral bells – which she loved to hear – and the sound of the birds in the tall rose-tree in the little garden below intruded on her quiet.

The room was simply furnished, but the good fire in the hearth and the flowers placed on the little table told her of the thought that had been taken for her comfort. 'Rest – that's what you n-need first and foremost – rest, and n-no worries,' decreed Darwin.

And so rest she did, for five days. She lay between smooth sheets, dosed at night with sleeping draughts, tempted by day with delicate morsels of food brought up to her on a tray, and visited from time to time by Darwin himself, who would come soft-footedly to sit by the window and talk idly of this and that: windmills and poetry, politics and the oneness of all living things, the evils of strong drink and salt, and the great benefits conveyed by fresh air and fruit and vegetables. 'T-tell me if I tire you,' he would say to Sarah; but he seemed by instinct to know when she had heard enough of his lively unpredictable conversation. If she wished to join in, he was happy for her to do so; but for the most part she liked to listen, amused by his wit and his flights of fancy.

Besides which, when she did say anything she knew he was watching her intently. She remembered Jos saying once that

324

when Darwin was puzzled as to the nature of an illness, he liked to observe and talk to the patient, seeing what, off-guard, would be revealed of its causes; for he believed that the mind was as crucial as the body to its health. Sarah had a feeling she did not want him to probe too deeply into what lay behind her inability to recover. She wanted to get well, of course she did, but she had an uncomfortable suspicion that Darwin already guessed rather more of what lay hidden even from herself than she wanted him to know.

At the end of five days, the doctor decreed that she was well enough to be helped downstairs to spend some time there in the company of his three sons: Charles, fourteen, charming and dauntingly intelligent; Erasmus, thirteen, grave and sensitive; and Robert, a bright six-year-old. They all had a considerate gentleness about them which Sarah found touching; clearly their father's dislike of the cruelty and roughness of most small boys had affected them, though they were very much in awe of him, only relaxing completely when he was out of the room.

Darwin was, however, rarely out of the room while Sarah was there, unless a patient called him away. She knew how little he was at home as a general rule, and the thought put her more than ever on her guard; most of all when he sat quietly in a corner saying nothing but merely watching her and listening to what she had to say.

At the end of a week she said to him one evening, after the boys had gone to bed, 'I think it's time I was going home.'

'D-do you indeed?' he returned, smiling a little. 'You think you're w-well again then?'

She would not allow herself to be disconcerted. 'I am no worse,' she said steadily, 'and probably better for the rest. And you reminded me once how much Jos needs me there. You surely don't want him ill again?'

'He won't be able to be well until you are f-fully recovered. In any case, he n-needs you, yes – but n-no one can go on carrying all the burdens for ever, without b-breaking at last.'

'Someone has to carry them.'

'Hmph.' He paused a moment, then said, emphasising the words with a prodding finger, 'You know your t-trouble, Sarah? T-too much conscience – relax and forget your consci-ence and you'll feel much better. I've always noticed, it's the people with s-sensitive consciences who have least need of them.'

'How do you know? You can't know everything of someone just from looking at the surface.'

'T-true. But I think I know you – like the m-man in the bible, ask you t-to go one mile and you'd go t-two. Too much g-goodness is bad for the health, you know.'

'If you think me too good, then you don't know me at all!' she burst out. She had feared his perceptiveness, yet it seemed he had not even guessed at the dark places beneath the quiet surface. Thinking of them now she could feel her colour rising.

'Ah, b-but no one alive is without something they look back on with shame. But it's no good l-letting it poison your life. That makes t-two wrongs, n-not just one. Can't you see that?'

She was torn then by two impulses: the one to repel him, wish him goodnight and make her way upstairs to bed; the other to stay and talk, and let herself be taken where she began to suspect he wanted her to go. If she chose the last, the journey might – no, would – be painful, but at the end perhaps would be healing.

She stayed; and after a moment said quietly, 'But if you do something very wrong, and have no means ever of putting it right, how can you help but be poisoned by it?'

'What's done is done. T-turn your back and face the f-future, and make the best you can of that. It's the only way.'

'Sometimes it's not as simple as that.'

'N-nothing's ever simple, of course it's n-not. But most things are p-possible, given the will. And will p-power you have in p-plenty.'

'Not any more,' she said wearily. She was beginning now to feel like weeping, and fought angrily against it.

'Only because you do n-not choose to l-let yourself be healed.'

'How can that be true? I desperately want to be well.'

All Darwin said was, 'S-sickness can be very convenient. Stops you facing up to l-life. Every doctor worth the name knows that.'

'That's nonsense. No one likes being ill.'

'It's easy though, isn't it? N-nothing to do but give way to it. Look at Wedgwood with his eyes – certain he was g-going blind, even going to die, but all that was wrong was that things were a b-bit hard at the works, and you were away. You came home, I t-told him it was all nonsense, and he was well in no t-time.'

'I haven't noticed that I am well because you say there is nothing wrong. And if Jos isn't to be ill again then surely I should go home?'

'You will b-be well when you choose.' He paused, as if suddenly realising that the conversation was simply going round in circles. Sarah watched him, feeling in spite of herself a mild curiosity as to what he would say next; but when he did speak she was caught quite off her guard.

'Fine m-man, Thomas Bentley.'

She knew he had seen how deeply she blushed, and was quite unable to save the situation. She tried to smile a measured agreement, but knew she did not deceive him. She wished with all her heart that he was not watching her so closely.

'Odd thing, I've found n-no one who could resist him: Wedgwood, that s-scapegrace nephew of his in America, your g-good servant, for all that we fell out over his c-canal pamphlet, men, women, all like him – m-my wife thought him irresistible, you know. But you and Wedgwood are c-closest of all, of course – you know what I m-mean. I've often wondered, though . . . he and Wedgwood are so close – Wedgwood tells me they find sometimes that they write the same things t-to each other at the same t-times, the letters crossing in the p-post. That's quite a friendship for a wife t-to contend with. Some might be jealous.'

'So they might,' she said guardedly, wishing her colour would fade.

'But n-not you?'

'No.' Her reply was curt, abrupt.

He waited for a moment, and then said casually, 'That leaves the other p-possibility then. Like my d-dear late wife, you f-find him irresistible. That must be hard for a g-good loving wife, must it n-not?'

Speechless, she nodded, and suddenly without warning burst into tears.

It was as if some long-closed door had been suddenly

opened, releasing an emotion which until now she had never dared to set free. Now she wept uncontrollably, a wild harsh sobbing that seemed to tear her apart, flooding every part of her with grief. In all her life she had never wept like this, with such total abandonment, such an overwhelming sense of relief.

When at long last she came to an end she found Darwin was still sitting there, quiet and thoughtful; and she raised her head and met his eyes with a sense of weary relief. She knew that if he did not yet know everything, he would before long; and she was glad that the time had come.

'I thought it was s-something like that,' he said quietly. 'Poor Sarah. Hard t-to go on, when you're so much t-together. S-strange thing, the human heart – so much capacity t-to love. But for a woman it's harder, if her feelings go astray – more g-guilt, more shame.'

She did tell him then, simply, without excuse or self-pity. He listened, saying nothing, looking only thoughtful with no hint of censure in his expression; and only when she had finished did he make any comment.

'It's over then – as far as anything b-but your f-feelings go. There's no s-sin in love, or friendship, is there? Enjoy the love you have, for b-both of them – and put the rest behind you.'

'How can I, when I did such wrong?'

'You do more wrong by allowing it to p-poison what comes after. That makes it worse, n-not better.'

She could not at the moment feel that it was possible to do as he suggested, and simply put what had happened behind her and move forward, living each day as it came without carrying that burden of guilt with her. Yet, somehow, when she lay at last in bed that night she had a great sense of relief, almost of cleansing, and she slept afterwards more deeply and more peacefully than she had for many months.

Next day she looked forward with embarrassment to her first meeting with Darwin, but when it came, last night might never have happened for all the comment he made. She had talked and he had listened and advised, and that was that: as far as he was concerned, it was over. And for Sarah it was as if a great burden had been lifted from her.

CHAPTER FIFTEEN

1774

'Very prettily done, Mrs Wedgwood. I am gratified that industry and ingenuity should receive their just reward, as they are certain to do. Her Imperial Majesty cannot but be delighted with this very fine example of our English manufactures.'

Mrs Delany, close friend of King George and Queen Charlotte, bestowed on Sarah a last approving smile and moved on to examine the tureens set out on the next table.

After that there was a small pause, during which for once no one caught Sarah's eye or came to compliment her. She relaxed her mouth, by now stiff from smiling so much, and even leaned a little against the wall to rest her feet. But though she was tired her spirits soared.

It was a triumph: there could be no doubt at all of that. Almost the whole of London's fashionable society must have come here today. At the door they jostled one with another to show their tickets of admission, with all the restrained rudeness of those not quite so lacking in politeness as to stoop to crude shoving. Outside, Greek Street had been brought to a standstill by the throng of carriages, and now and then the undignified sound of a fierce and earthy altercation between coachmen drifted in above the decorously modulated exclamations of interest and wonder.

The admiration was sincere and, Sarah thought with pride, wholly merited. Here, in the new showroom in Portland House, Greek Street, Soho, five rooms on two floors were spread with the nine hundred and fifty-two pieces of one single dinner service, the most important special order, Sarah firmly believed, that any English manufacturer had ever received. To mark its importance only ticket holders were admitted to the display, and tickets had only been issued to the titled and the great. Among them, of course, were those whose own great houses or estates were especially honoured by being depicted upon a plate, a tureen, a fruit basket or some other item of the service. Looking round now, she saw Lord Gower stoop to gaze at a view of Trentham; watched Lord Carlisle admire a painting of Castle Howard, and Lord Fortescue one of his house in Wimpole Street. Somewhere among these aristocratic landscapes was a plate showing Etruria Hall, and a larger dish adorned with the Etruria works: for all his wish to flatter his potential patrons, Jos would not resist adding this little concession to his own pride in what they had achieved.

One thousand two hundred and twenty-four views of English scenes and English estates were displayed here today: all painted in a subtle dark purple black with a border of twining flowers and leaves, and each item marked with a frog: a frog for La Grenouillère – the frog palace – country residence of Catherine, Empress of all the Russias. For a few days more the service would be displayed to the aristocracy of England, and then it would be packed with the utmost care and sent on its way to the strange far away country emerging slowly beneath the ruthless hand of its Empress into some kind of civilisation. The very thought of it all could still send a tingle of excitement down Sarah's spine.

They had lived with the project for a year now, ever since the Imperial consul in London had called on Bentley to commission the service. Now that at last the work was done Sarah felt almost sorry, for – despite all the anxieties, the need to put all other schemes to one side, the increasing costs, the problems of negotiating with touchy landowners, the practical difficulties involved in trying to match all the many varied landscapes to the unyielding shapes of tableware, and yet have at the end a service which was both functional and beautiful – despite everything, the past year had been one of the happiest of her life.

It was poor Bentley who had faced the worst problems, scouring booksellers and print shops for views when access to the originals was difficult, searching out artists, supervising the enamelling once the unpainted creamware had reached him from Etruria; above all painstakingly discussing costs with the Russian consul so that, though the firm's profits would not be high, they would at least not make a loss. They all knew that the prestige of the order was such that a profit was of secondary importance.

For Jos and Sarah it had been almost a holiday year, full of

330

jaunts to great houses, taking tea with their owners, impressing on them what a social disaster it would be not to be honoured with a view on a dish or plate. Or there had been the picnic meals eaten on a sunny hillside (and some wet and windy ones) where they had gone to discuss progress with a painter as he worked, or to decide – helped by the camera obscura which was Jos's new toy – on the best angle for a view. Excitement and a sense of shared enterprise had brought them together as nothing else had for a very long time.

Now, today, Sarah was glad that Bentley was not here as she and Jos welcomed the first visitors to the showroom: she wanted this to be their moment alone, savoured to the full, to be carried with them in memory for the rest of their lives. She looked along the room to the door beyond, where she could just glimpse Jos talking animatedly to someone out of her line of vision, his face alight with happiness. She did not think she had ever seen him look so well.

He moved then across the room to speak to someone else, and just for a moment caught her eye and smiled. The little secret glance passed between them, holding them together for a moment as if no one else was there. Just for that time they could almost have been young again, joined by a love rooted in the very heart and centre of what they were; in those far off days before Bentley had come into their lives.

Then Jos turned away and Sarah gave herself a little shake, smoothed the flounced grey satin of her skirts, and began once more to move about the room. If Jos was better in health than he had been for a long time, then so was she, her joints almost free of pain and with a new suppleness this spring. She felt well, full of energy and new life – in more than one sense, she thought a little ruefully, for she was already three months pregnant. With a daughter this time, Jos had decided; and Susannah, tired of being so greatly outnumbered, fervently hoped he was right.

Not once during the afternoon did the crowds in the showroom dwindle; as each group left, another made its entrance. When the time came to close it took over an hour of tactful hinting to clear the last of the visitors from the rooms.

As Peter Swift bolted the doors behind them Jos came to Sarah and folded her into his arms. She nestled close, smiling into his face, and thought, 'We are going back to Chelsea now; but I am safe.'

She had not seen a great deal of Bentley since they came to London a week ago, and when they had been together they had all been far too busy for any personal feelings to intrude. Now that the work was done and they were likely to have a little time for talk and rest, then it might be different; but Sarah did not think so. Or if it were, then she felt able to face whatever might come calmly and without fear. It was as if at last she could see clearly again through eyes which before had been misted by guilt and misery.

The Bentleys had a splendid festive supper ready for Jos and Sarah's return, anticipating what a triumph the day would bring. There were oysters, and cold beef and tongue, fruit tarts and cheese; and a good wine from Bentley's cellar.

'It's early for toasts, I know,' Bentley said as they took their seats at the table, 'but this is one I feel sure you will agree should begin our meal, not end it – the Empress Catherine of Russia!'

They drank her health, and Bentley added a little wish that her people might one day know freedom too –

'Like we do?' Jos put in with a grin; and Bentley said, 'More than we have, of course – as one day, please God, we shall all know. I suppose we must be thankful we are at least not ruled by a tyrant, whatever the faults of our King.'

'A fine sentiment from one of the King's potters!'

Bentley laughed. 'Ah, as his loyal friends we long for his improvement – what else?' He began to carve meat for them. 'I meant to ask if you have news of young Byerley. I wonder what he thinks of the rumblings in Massachussetts.' They had themselves wondered that, when they had heard how the citizens of Boston had thrown the East India company's tea chests into the sea as a protest against the duties imposed by the British government; but Bentley had clearly reached the same conclusion as themselves. 'I expect he has enough troubles of his own without worrying about unjust taxation. Though if it comes to outright war he may find himself involved more than he likes, being an Englishman.'

'I think that has crossed his mind, as a possibility,' said Jos; and Sarah broke in.

'You'll never believe what he's doing now – he's turned schoolmaster!'

Bentley paused, carvers raised above the rosy joint. 'Schoolmaster? Tom Byerley a schoolmaster? I don't believe it!'

Sarah nodded. 'It's true. He wrote asking us to send him a pair of globes for use in the schoolroom. What do you think of that for a reformation of character?'

'I can only say that if Tom Byerley can turn schoolmaster then anything is possible – miracles – the freeing of slaves, of America, ourselves, Russia, the French, anything at all! What happened to the playacting? I know he'd not found much demand for his talents, but I thought it would take more than that to discourage him.'

'I suppose,' said Jos, 'that he found he did not after all want to go on for ever without a roof over his head or a settled place or the certainty of bread to eat – the more so when his gipsy life landed him in gaol. So he's to try what schoolmastering can do for him.'

'Let's hope the New Englanders realise what a rarity they have in him!' Bentley resumed his carving. 'Did he give an opinion then on these latest troubles? After all, such a pillar of the community as the village schoolmaster has surely a view worth knowing.'

'He says there is great ill feeling against the Governor of Massachussetts, and of course the King and Lord North whom the Governor represents. But I think young Tom is not a very political animal – and talking of such, is Benjamin Franklin still in London?'

'Indeed yes. He had little joy with his petition against the Governor of Massachussetts, as you can guess – and he has been dismissed from his post as Deputy Paymaster General for the colonies – but it is a delight to have him amongst us again. You must meet him this time – he has the most inventive of minds, as I've often told you.'

'Another Darwin!'

'Rather more practical, I suspect,' observed Bentley drily. 'His inventions work, for the most part.'

'Be fair – Darwin's windmill at Etruria is working very well grinding flints for us.'

'True – but that reminds me, what became of Darwin's carriage? It was only after I'd seen your order for a carriage last winter that I remembered you'd talked of having one made to Darwin's design. What happened to it?'

Jos and Sarah exchanged a laughing glance; and Sarah said,

'That was a vehicle worth seeing – so well sprung it was like sailing on the clouds. But sadly the body and wheels weren't quite up to supporting all that superfluity of springs. It overturned more than once – mercifully without injuring anyone – and finally fell to pieces altogether. Poor Darwin was so disappointed – for an hour or two at least – and then he was back at his desk working feverishly on a new design. But this time I don't think we shall be in a hurry to try it out.'

It was in every sense a festive meal. Bentley himself was at his best tonight, witty, charming, full of lively anecdotes about London life; and later, after supper, ready with a store of newly composed satirical songs for their entertainment, which Jos declared would have lost them all their wealthy patrons at once had anyone been listening at the door. Not that there was any malice in his humour, for Bentley shared with Jos the capacity to be intensely critical of a man's actions while yet retaining an affection, even a respect, for the perpetrator.

Sarah realised very early that the attraction was there still, as strong as ever, but tonight somehow she was able to relax and allow it to set her face glowing and give an edge of excitement and vivacity to her talk, without feeling troubled or torn apart. It was a very long time since she had enjoyed an evening in Bentley's company so wholeheartedly. Later, as she and Jos went up to bed, she thought, 'This is how it should always be, how it should have been right from the start – a happy loving friendship, like there is between Bentley and Jos.'

Next morning Jos insisted that she stay at home. 'Maybe you're not tired, but we don't want to risk your becoming so,' he told her. She made a token protest, and then gave in; and secretly she was glad to leave the showroom to the others today. Yesterday had been so special, so very good, that nothing else in the following days could hope to have quite that magic – it might even be that today would be, just a little, an anticlimax. So she was content to stay quietly in Chelsea in the restful company of Mary Bentley, talking, reading, playing music, perhaps going for a sedate walk.

When Jos had left, Sarah came downstairs to seek out her hostess, but instead, looking into the parlour, found it occupied by Bentley himself. He was standing at the window, studying some papers he was holding – drawings of some kind, she thought. For a moment, caught by the old panic, she hesitated and almost fled; and then he turned and saw her, and she drew in a deep breath and calmed herself and smiled.

'I thought you'd gone with Jos,' she said casually. 'I was looking for your wife.'

He smiled. 'I'm going on to Greek Street later. I'm afraid the queen's ware catalogue keeps me here this morning.'

She moved a step nearer and saw that the drawings he held were of the shapes of tureens and teapots, done in simple clear lines. Last year a catalogue had been produced in English and French for the ornamental works and it had already led to increased orders, as much from overseas as from England itself. Very soon it was hoped the new catalogue would be doing the same for the queen's ware.

'Are those the drawings for the printers? They're very fine.'

'Yes, I'm pleased with them. I shall take them to the printers this morning, on my way to Greek Street.' He gathered up a second pile of papers from a nearby table, shuffling them together between his hands. 'Mary is giving her day's instructions to Nanny in the kitchen. She'll be here soon, if you'd like to make yourself comfortable.'

Sarah sat down on a little gilded sofa, expecting Bentley to leave her, and he did begin to move towards the door. But there he came to a halt again, and turned back to her, like a man suddenly finding the excuse he wanted to stay longer.

'You're looking very well, Sarah – and Josiah too. The past year was a better one, I think.'

She looked round, smiling. 'Yes – we've had our troubles, but on the whole it was a good year.'

He came some way back towards her. 'What became of the widow who was giving such trouble – what was she, the second wife of Josiah's brother Thomas?'

Sarah nodded. 'That's right. Tom's affairs were left in such a terrible tangle when he died – and it didn't help to have his widow so very difficult and uncooperative. But it seems to be sorting itself out. Jos has been endlessly patient with her. He took the Churchyard works off her hands, you know – it was

335

such a millstone and she needed something to live on. Now he is looking for a suitable tenant.' Her smile had a wry twist to it. 'Strange to think he might have been there all along himself, if Tom had taken him into partnership . . . But perhaps not – it would never have been in Jos's nature to stay in a safe rut.'

'Nor would you have let him, would you?'

She shook her head. 'It's not a case of one of us allowing or not allowing the other to do something. We work together in everything, even if sometimes the first impulse comes from one and not the other.'

He stood looking down at her with a gravely thoughtful expression. 'Yes.' She guessed that his thoughts were not of a kind to make him comfortable; perhaps that was why the next moment he appeared to change the subject. 'The children – how are they? Is Susannah well? Is she still happy at school?'

'Happy enough, yes. But we have some doubts. We think she could learn more than she has done – they don't ask enough of her, I think, and she can be such a scatterbrain sometimes. But she hasn't been well lately. Jos thinks it's lack of exercise. Whenever she's at home he takes her out for vigorous rides, or sets her gardening.'

'I envy him the closeness he has with her. But then I envy you all of your little ones.'

There was a brief silence, and Sarah was struck by the sombreness of his face. 'It's still not too late for children you know,' she said gently. 'We have another on the way, and I am forty this year.'

His smile was faint and a little rueful. 'No, but I think perhaps that is one joy we must accept that we shall never know.'

'You have each other. That can be enough.'

Abruptly, he sat down facing her, and for an instant she glimpsed in his eyes a bleakness that frightened her. 'Yes – yes, of course,' he said, but she knew he was trying to convince himself as much as her.

For the first time in years she did not feel consumed by a need to spare herself pain, to avoid what might hurt or disturb; instead, unselfconsciously, she recognised that he wanted to talk, but could not quite bring himself to do so, and she set herself to draw him out.

336

'You are happy, though?'

He sighed, and then said slowly and softly, not looking at her, 'Who knows? Who can say what happiness is? Ecstasy, perhaps, or joy or exhilaration? Perhaps those are something no rational man should wish to have – and if they are happiness, then no, I am not happy. That kind of deep intense emotion I knew once, long ago . . .' Very briefly he glanced at her, though if she had not been watching him so intently she would not have seen it. He cleared his throat then, and went on, 'I am comfortable, cosseted even – a well-cared-for married man with an agreeable wife who loves me, and everything I could wish for in the way of material comfort. I have good books, fine pictures and good friends, theatres and music within reach, the best opportunities possible for good talk and good company. What more could a man want? That surely is happiness.'

It was at that moment that she knew with certainty that all he had ever felt for her was still there, unchanged, that his marriage had in fact made no difference, except to underline his acceptance that only the emotions remained of what once they had shared; the rest must be over for ever.

'And you? Are you happy?'

What could she say? She could answer much as he had done, acknowledging the satisfactions of success and wealth, the secure devotion of a loving husband. She could accept as true for her too his quiet wistful acknowledgement that he had as much of happiness as anyone ought to hope for; and she could imply beneath that admission that at the heart of it all was an emptiness, as of a house where the fire had burnt out, leaving in the hearth only the cold ashes of the blaze that once had been there.

Only she knew all at once that to take her cue from him would be dishonest. What was true for him was not after all true for her. At the heart of her world there was a richness he had never known, even in that fleeting forgetful moment long ago. If there was little in her life of passion and ecstasy, she had children, work that she loved, and a man who had been part of her, bone of her bone, almost since infancy. To ask for anything more – to ask perhaps for one further moment of consuming passion – would have been unpardonably greedy, demanding more from life than any human being ought to expect or hope for, too much, beyond any deserving.

'I think,' she said carefully at last, 'I am as happy as I can hope to be. One thing only is missing – I must be thankful that it is only one.'

He met her gaze then, holding it steadily without smiling, and then he reached out and took her hands in his. He sat quite still for a little while, looking down on the long fingers, the ring glowing against the pallor of the skin. 'You have beautiful hands, Sarah. I have always thought so.'

There was such a tender softness in his voice that in spite of everything Sarah felt her heartbeat quicken suffocatingly. Her first instinct was to pull her hands free, but she did not want there to be any room for fear or awkwardness between them now. So she let her hands remain, still and unmoving in his grasp. After a time, still holding them, he said, 'Some things we can never have, Sarah – but there are others we shall always have, for ever.'

She was able then to smile at him as he looked at her; and she knew that something had changed irrevocably between them, and she was glad of it.

CHAPTER SIXTEEN

1775

'"And he that sat was to look upon like a jasper and a sardine stone." Kate says she's always wondered what a jasper was, and William doesn't seem to know – so here's our answer. I don't think it's being presumptuous, do you? Look at that one there.'

'That one' was a cameo, the modelled face a little roughly done and not quite in proportion with the background rectangle, for it was only a trial piece. But it did not need perfection in the modelling to show her what Jos meant. The pure shining white of the face stood out beautifully against the blue ground – a subtle blue, at once warm and yet delicate, with a hint almost of grey, the texture smooth without a sheen, like the surface of a fine pebble.

'That's the mix with cobalt added, of course – here's the green . . . They were fired together.'

Sarah took up the second cameo, soft grey-green behind that clear white. 'It's lovely – it couldn't be better. Which mixture did you use in the end?'

He pulled open one of the shallow cabinet drawers near his table and showed her the coloured rectangles that exactly matched the blue and green of the cameos. 'There – numbers 3726 and 3741 . . .'

Sarah leaned over to look: below the numbers incised on the rectangles of clay were the coded letters TTBO. 'The hottest part of the biscuit oven,' she translated. 'You fired them the same way, I suppose?'

'Oh yes – though making sure the temperature is the same each time isn't easy of course. What I must get right one day is some means of measuring oven temperatures really accurately – all these years racking my brains and I've still not come up with anything foolproof.' He smiled up at her. 'But never mind. It looks as if we might be making jasperware very soon now, and I had begun to fear it would never come right. The next stage is to make it in large enough quantities for the men to use. All along I've found the tiniest variations in the mix can throw it all wrong. The 3681 basic mixture is the only one that's worked, out of all those I tried.'

Over three thousand trials, Sarah thought, gazing down at the two pieces in her hand; and about five years of careful painstaking experimentation, when time and the demands of factory and family permitted; and even now there was still a great deal of work to be done before this beautiful new ware could make its appearance in the showrooms. But the turning point had been reached. Sarah bent and kissed Jos tenderly on the forehead, and then laid the trial cameos on the table before him. 'My darling hard-working clever Jos.'

He grinned up at her and then turned on his stool to face her. 'What do you think, Sally? Should I take out a patent on it?'

'Now you know what I think about patents. They're very hard to enforce, and it seems to me they only end in lawsuits. Keep as much of it quiet as you can – but you'll always be one jump ahead of your rivals, you know you will. Otherwise Voyez and his like would have made their fortune by now, instead of desperately scraping round for something else to imitate.' For a time Voyez had disappeared from the scene, only to turn up recently in the West Country selling poor-quality cameos stamped with 'Wedgwood and Bentley': a threat of legal action against him had eventually proved effective.

Jos nodded. 'My wise Sally – I expect you're right. And now, I don't doubt you came to tell me it's dinner time.'

'*Nearly* dinner time. I know better than to leave telling you until the last minute, or we'd never begin on time. But there was something else – the two crates have come from Naples.'

'From Sir William Hamilton?' He laughed softly, with excitement. 'What perfect timing!' The ambassador to the kingdom of Naples had written some time ago to say he was sending a large number of casts he had taken from Greek and Roman bas-reliefs, which he had found in his ceaseless collecting of antiquities. He had a great admiration for Jos's skill in adapting ancient designs for his own purposes. 'Now I'll have some new ideas to try out in the jasper.' He stood up and began to put the trial cameos away in an empty drawer of his cabinet. 'I'll tidy up and come as quickly as I can.'

Sarah turned to go; and then paused. 'Jos, talking of William Willet: don't you think he's aged a great deal lately?'

Jos looked round. 'Yes, I suppose he has. But he *is* an old man, Sally. Maybe we forget that because his mind's so active.'

'He's always been very active too. But he looks tired and ill – or so I thought at church yesterday. I suppose I'd never considered that a day might come when he would no longer be minister there.'

'Please God that won't be for a long time yet.'

'I'll say Amen to that – and talking of old men I'd better go and let my father know it's dinner time or he'll be late too.'

For nearly a year now Richard Wedgwood had been living at Etruria Hall, ever since John Wedgwood, ill for so much of his life, had died at last. The old man had been left lonely and desolate, and the suggestion that he should live at Etruria had come from Jos – Sarah never failed to be both astonished and moved by Jos's patience with his father-in-law. It was much greater than her own; though on the whole, she had ruefully to concede, it was on her that most of the burden of caring for the old man fell.

She was glad that, at present, her joints were going through one of their better phases: making one's way to and from Jos's laboratories and workrooms with aching joints was not to be undertaken lightly. Whichever way one went there was no direct or easy route back to the main part of the house. One could take the door from the passage outside the room where he was working at present, which led outside and, by means of a narrow high-walled twisting passage, came eventually to the stable yard behind the house; or – as she did now – one could go along the passage in the opposite direction, up a narrow flight of stairs, through a trap door – always kept closed – and into Jos's study above. It was forbidden territory to anyone but herself, and sometimes Tom Byerley, who had this summer returned from an America now wholly at war with its mother country.

Her father, she knew, would be in the library at this time, and so it was there that she went. He sat in the most comfortable chair close to a blazing fire, leafing his way with a faintly disapproving expression through what she supposed must be one of Jos's many scientific books. He looked round as she came in, as if he had been longing to have someone to hear his opinion on the work. He closed the book over the fingers of one hand and waved it up and down.

'What does he want things like this for in his library? Can't you tell him it shouldn't be lying around for anyone to pick up?'

She came nearer and saw that the book was the *Émile* of Jean Jacques Rousseau, that enlightened treatise on education which Bentley had so enthusiastically recommended to Jos all those years ago, when Sarah had feared that Jos no longer had any need for her. Now she smiled soothingly, looking down at her father. 'It's a very highly regarded book, Papa – but not the kind of thing you'd enjoy, I'm sure. We have Berkeley's sermons somewhere, you know – and a great many novels . . . There's *Tristram Shandy* for instance – Jos has been trying to persuade you to read that for years.'

'Hmph!' Resolutely undiverted, her father opened the book where his fingers marked the place and tapped the page in an irritated manner. 'Listen to this rubbish: "At twelve years old, Émile will scarce know what a book is . . . when reading is useful to him . . . he must learn to read." What kind of educational principle is that, to teach nothing at all? Where would you have been if we'd not seen you were well taught from your earliest years?'

'I think if you read a little further on you'll see that Monsieur Rousseau isn't quite saying there should be no teaching at all, just that the impulse should come from the child.'

'And what child is going to ask for lessons when it can be out at play? What nonsense! But I suppose that's why you don't spend your mornings teaching your little boys to read, as your mother would have done?'

'They'll learn soon enough, when they go to school. John reads very well now, you must admit that – and he couldn't read at all when he left home.'

'If this is what you believe in . . .' he waved the book again with a kind of emphatic disgust, 'then I wonder you sent them to school at all. And I suppose that's why young Susannah's kicking her heels at home these days.'

Sarah restrained any impulse to answer him angrily and said

with all the mild reasonableness she could muster, 'Now, Papa, you know she's at home because she's not been well, and also because we felt she wasn't really learning as much as she should. Even you wouldn't want her to go through life able to do nothing but draw and play the harpsichord, however well she does that. No – Rousseau's work is interesting, and one can learn a great deal from it, but we've no intention of following it to the letter.'

That seemed to reassure him – in part at least – for he laid the book aside; but he had not finished with her altogether, for he went on, 'I don't know what your mother would say about your way of going on, Sarah. Maybe you don't believe in teaching your children to read, but you could at least spend more time with them. You're never here in the daytime – always gallivanting somewhere.'

This time there was no keeping the sharpness from her tone. 'This morning I was showing a party of visitors from Trentham around the works, at the end of which we sold three classical statuettes, a bust of Shakespeare, a pair of candelabras, a vase, and two queen's ware tea services. That is the kind of work which takes me from home. I hardly call it gallivanting.'

'A mother's place is with her children.'

'I am rarely very far away, Papa. And they have an excellent nurse.' She returned the despised Rousseau to his shelf and went on briskly, 'Now, dinner's ready. It's your favourite roast sirloin – so come on now, and forget my delinquencies for a while. After all, every child's a disappointment to its parents at some time or another.'

Richard Wedgwood eased himself slowly out of his chair. 'Oh, you're not a disappointment, Sarah. Only sometimes I can't understand why you should behave as you do.'

'If you see my children suffering, then you can complain. But I don't really think you need worry.'

Jos came to dinner with a glow of satisfaction about him that was almost tangible; and a letter from Bentley, brought to him as they left the table, simply crowned his happy mood. He waited to open it until he had reached his study, but almost at once came in search of Sarah, who was by now – doubtless to her father's satisfaction had he not fallen asleep by the library fire – putting the infant Catherine into her baby carriage, so that Jane Hillyard, the nurse, could wheel her about the garden. Jos paused only briefly to talk the baby into a chuckle and a smile, before he said, 'Well, Sally, we have Bentley's opinion of the schools at last.'

Mrs Massey the housekeeper had told them of two girls' schools in Derby, but knew little about them, and so Jos had written to Bentley to see if he could advise on their possible suitability for Susannah. 'He confirms that Mrs Latifier, though sound as far as learning goes, is very High Church, so that won't do. But he has no very encouraging report of Mrs Denby either. However,' he went on before Sarah could speak, 'he does thoroughly recommend Blacklands' school in Chelsea, as an excellent establishment for young ladies.'

'Chelsea! But that's London!'

'And thus very near to where the Bentleys live.' There was a mixture of pleasure and – just a little – regret in his expression. 'He suggests that Sukey comes to live with them and, as soon as she seems strong enough, attends the school in Chelsea as a day pupil. Until then, he and Mrs Bentley would undertake to teach her themselves.'

For a little while Sarah said nothing. They had not thought of sending their daughter so far away, much more than the day's journey to Manchester or Derby; but to Bentley, dear friend of them both, cultivated, deeply interested in education, his wife a governess – that was different somehow. 'Yes,' she said slowly, 'perhaps that is the answer, if it wouldn't place too much of a burden on him.' But she had a sudden vivid picture in her mind of Bentley during a recent visit here, walking in the garden with Susannah skipping and dancing at his side; and of the light in his face as he did so. He and his wife were childless, yet longed for children – yes, what could be more right, for all concerned?

'Then let's take that as settled.' Any regret had gone from Jos's face, though Sarah suspected it would linger still beneath the surface: he had always been closer to Susannah than to any of the other children. 'Where's Sukey?'

'In the garden, in the play house with the others.'

They left Catherine to Jane's care and walked out to the garden, where the magnificent play house, a gift from Bentley to the children, was set up on the lawn in the sunshine. Tom and Josiah were marching towards it, carrying books and a cushion between them. 'For Sukey,' they said.

'Bossy lass that she is!' Sarah remarked. She lifted the curtain covering the play house doorway, and bent down to see Susannah seated cross-legged upon a rug like some oriental potentate. 'She *is* getting better at last,' Sarah thought in passing; there was colour in Susannah's face now, from the fresh air and sunshine of the past weeks, and her blue eyes had a new brightness. But she was still far too thin, with a frail look that sometimes frightened her parents.

There was, however, nothing disturbing about the impudent grin with which she greeted her mother.

'Come now, Susannah, let your brothers play in peace for a while – your Papa and I want a word with you.'

The girl uncurled herself and emerged into the sun, shaking out her flowered chintz skirts with a startlingly mature gesture. Sarah sometimes forgot that at ten Susannah was coming very near to young womanhood, already older now than her mother had been when she first met cousin Jos. She was going to be pretty too, once she had filled out a little, with those fair curls framing the sweet oval face and the gentle blue eyes liable so often to sparkle with fun and laughter.

Behind her now the boys had tumbled into the play house and their squeals and giggles floated out through the little doorway. Susannah cast a half regretful glance over her shoulder, but Jos took her arm and steered her gently back to the house. 'We think we've solved the problem of your schooling, Sukey.'

It was settled then. Susannah, who loved Bentley and was excited at the prospect of living in London, was entirely happy with the arrangement. It was decided – as had already been proposed – that the Bentleys would come to stay for a few days at Etruria in October, and then they, together with Sarah and Jos and Susannah, would enjoy a short holiday in Derbyshire to better acquaint Susannah with her new guardians before she accompanied them back to Chelsea.

It was Mary Bentley's first visit to Etruria, and as she stepped from the carriage and paused to look at the house, her start of astonishment was clearly visible to Sarah, coming down the steps to welcome her. The size and grandeur of it all clearly overawed her for quite some time, and she said nothing at all until the first greetings were over and they were

345

walking together to the drawing room. When she did recover her poise sufficiently, she was full of shy praise for the graceful proportions of the rooms, and the growing loveliness of the garden. Sarah remembered her mother's fulsome raptures over the house at High Newbold all those years ago, and was very thankful that Mary Bentley's modest good manners allowed her to be appreciative without irritation. Sarah exerted herself more than usual to make their guest feel at home.

Tom Byerley dined with them that day. There was – to Sarah's secret regret – little left in him now of the wild young man who had run away to America. He had become diligent, hard-working, even rather dull; and a new stoutness had given him a generally middle-aged appearance though he was still only twenty-seven. It was all a little sad, though the new Tom Byerley was of considerably more use to Jos and Etruria than the dreamy young man of the old days.

Just now and then, however, when enthusiasm kindled it, a distinct vivacity of manner would bring to mind the youth he had been; and today, with his hero Bentley present, was just such a moment. Bentley even delighted Tom by giving a lively account of all the latest news of the London theatres.

It was later, as they sat over tea in the drawing room, that the talk became more serious, moving inevitably to the war with America which was daily growing more bitter.

'I always said it would come to this if Lord North persisted in taxing the Americans against their will,' observed Jos, not, Sarah knew, for the first time – but since her father had come to Etruria, such observations were fraught with danger for domestic peace. She tensed and glanced at Richard Wedgwood, who, inevitably, had coloured angrily.

'And why should they not pay taxes like the rest of us? They expect us to defend them at our expense.'

Bentley turned to the old man. 'But their objection, sir, is that they play no part in electing the government that taxes them. It is essentially a question of liberty.'

'Liberty – hmph!' grunted Richard Wedgwood; and Sarah moved quickly to divert the conversation into less controversial channels. She was sorry about it; she knew how Jos had looked forward to the long lively political and philosophical discussions he so enjoyed – as did she. He had been the more eager this time as there was a great deal he had not written about to Bentley, or Bentley to him, during the past months, because it was only too common for letters to be opened in the post, and the consequences of expressing treasonable matters in writing during a war might be uncomfortable, to say the least; the more so as it was a very popular war, nationally speaking. It was Richard Wedgwood who expressed the general, patriotic view, as most people would see it.

But unfortunately, though her father was quick to express his own strong opinions, however much he knew they differed from those about him, he hated any kind of contradiction: it only upset him and made him bad tempered. And so now Sarah soothed him – helped by Jos, who realised quickly enough what she was doing – and resigned herself to spending an evening in the company of her father and Mary Bentley, so as to leave Jos and Bentley free to retire to the study with their pipes to talk in peace.

'Never mind,' she consoled herself. 'We'll be away from here in a day or two, and free to talk of what we please.' She felt a little guilty that she should so look forward to leaving her father behind for a time – Kate had promised to look in often, to cheer him – but the past months had not been easy. It was a big house with many rooms, yet even so her father seemed always present, depriving herself and Jos of most of the private shared moments of intimacy they had once enjoyed, outside the few they spent in bed.

It was a relief that next morning Richard Wedgwood was not with them as they walked down the hill to the works to show Mrs Bentley round the provincial portion of her husband's enterprise.

'I've been having a good long think about the creamware lately,' Jos told Bentley as they walked two by two, the women a few paces behind – a little to Sarah's irritation, for she did not want to be shut out of what would certainly be the more interesting conversation. But courtesy directed that she should put Mrs Bentley at her ease; and so she did her best, while making sure there were enough breaks in the talk for her to be certain of missing nothing. 'I think,' Jos was saying, 'that it's sure to go out of favour before long – it's had a good run after all. And I wonder if, now I've broken the back of the work on the jasper, I should try my hand at porcelain.'

Bentley glanced behind him. 'And what does Sarah say?'

Jos smiled ruefully. 'She thinks the creamware will always sell well, as a good useful decorative range, and all that might possibly be needed is to work at whitening the body a little.'

'I think Sarah's right: don't you? Developing porcelain would take a vast amount of time and expense, I imagine, and others are already well advanced with it. I think we should concentrate on the jasper, which is something completely new.'

'That's what Sarah said. But I'm still not sure.'

'In any case,' put in Sarah, 'you have a fair amount of work still to do on the jasper, if it isn't to be limited to small cameos and bas-reliefs. Time enough to consider porcelain when you've achieved those jasper vases you've set your heart on.'

The tour of the works was not, Sarah thought, a total success, at least as far as Mary Bentley was concerned. That quiet young woman was disturbed by the dust and noise of the flint mill, troubled by the heat of the kilns, and clearly – for all her valiant efforts to hide it – bored by the numerous fascinating processes which each successive room opened up to her. Only the pattern room interested her at all, since there on the shelves were displayed the most beautiful products of the two works; but since she had lived surrounded by those products since the day of her marriage they could offer little to excite her.

'What does he see in her?' Sarah asked herself as they set out for home again; but she knew the answer well enough, without having to think very hard about it. Mary Bentley was accomplished and reasonably intelligent, and an able hostess in her quiet way, and demanded little from her husband in return for the honour he had done her in asking her to become his wife. It must be restful for Bentley, after the torment he had suffered in loving the wife of his best friend, to find peace with a woman who could never, whatever she did or said, put him in mind of Sarah. In marrying Mary he had turned his back on passion.

They returned to the Hall for dinner to find that Richard Wedgwood had not apparently forgotten the short-lived disagreement of yesterday. He was in the library, where they joined him until the meal should be ready, and reading a pamphlet of which a further number of copies lay in a pile at his elbow. 'These were sent over this morning, by some gentleman who hoped you'd distribute them – I don't doubt Mrs Massey will tell you who he was.' He tapped the pamphlet with his finger. 'Very instructive – you should read them.'

Jos took one from the pile and looked at it with a puzzlement turning swiftly to distaste. '"*A Calm Address to our American Colonies* – John Wesley" . . . What's this?' He turned a page or two, read a little, and then with an exclamation passed it to Bentley. 'So they've got him working for them now, have they? Can't they see that this kind of tyrannical behaviour can only lose us the colony for good? I'm surprised at Wesley.'

'Are you?' queried Bentley. 'I thought you always doubted that he was a real friend to liberty.'

'His *Thoughts upon Slavery* last year raised my hopes that I'd misjudged him – but it looks as if I was wrong.'

Sarah went herself to examine a pamphlet, seeing that it was clearly designed to win the colonists over to the point of view of the British government and King. 'Do you think this will help our fight at the meeting house or not?'

'Probably not,' said Jos. 'I fear it'll be only too popular with some elements.' He turned to Bentley. 'We have a good number of would-be Methodists in our flock at Newcastle,' he explained, 'and, now it begins to look as though we must think of a successor for Willet, the Methodist faction are flexing their muscles for a fight.'

'Then Willet's no better?'

Sarah shook her head. 'He grows worse every day. More than once he's not been fit to preach, and you know how hard that would go with him. I think Kate fears his mind may be going. But even he seems to know his days as minister must be numbered – and he *is* nearly eighty.'

'So if you hear of a good minister firmly of the Unitarian persuasion let us know, and we'll try to entice him here, before the Methodists or anyone else bring in one of their protégés.'

'At least the Methodists are sound on doctrine,' Richard Wedgwood broke in. 'And it would seem that one at least of them has a grain of patriotism left.'

'I think dinner will be ready,' said Sarah quickly. 'And

afterwards I think we musicians should have our way and enjoy a little singing and playing – don't you, Mary?'

'Ever a lover of harmony, Sarah,' murmured Bentley with a grin. The intimacy of the interjection set her heart lurching; but it did not trouble her, only sent her happy in to dinner.

The journey to Derbyshire was meant to be a holiday, but as Sarah knew very well Jos could never wholly leave his work behind. They began their journey by following the route over the high moors through Leek to Ashbourne, so that they could view the course of a proposed new portion of canal designed to ease the transport of raw materials from the quarries and lead mines of Derbyshire to Etruria and the pottery towns.

After that it was, decreed Jos, 'Matlock first, for the ladies.' Sarah would have objected to being considered so dismissively, as if her only thought was for frivolity, had she not known that it was for Mary Bentley's benefit that such arrangements had been made. Besides, she knew that Matlock was ideally placed for a number of other attractions which Jos had mentioned in passing: lead mines, rock and fossil hunting, and the new cotton mill at Cromford built by Richard Arkwright and fitted out with a revolutionary new design of spinning machine.

The little village nestling beneath the rocky tree-clad hillside, with its resemblance to some Alpine scene exactly suiting the new taste for scenic wildness and grandeur, was fast coming to rival Buxton in popularity. It had spa waters of its own, a sparkling river, dances and assemblies, boat trips with music provided for the entertainment of guests; and if one did not wander too far afield it was possible to miss seeing the huts of the lead miners on the fringes of the more fashionable areas.

For the first time in her life Susannah found herself treated as a young lady, dressed for the evenings in modest but pretty silk gowns and allowed to stay up for the dancing or the torchlit river journeys. Sarah had never seen her so glowing with happiness. 'I fear our Susannah has all the makings of a fine lady,' she observed a little ruefully to Jos.

'Don't worry, Bentley will make sure she grows up with something more serious in her mind as well,' Jos reassured her.

Sarah made another more startling discovery during those days at Matlock. Mary Bentley, shy, quiet and unassuming as she was, suddenly blossomed in Susannah's company, and the two quickly became firm and devoted friends though neither seemed to forget that one was older and in some sense in a position of authority. At first Sarah ascribed her success to Mary's skill with children, acquired in her years as a governess. Not until later did it occur to her that Bentley's wife was wholly at ease only in the company of those much younger than herself; and further, that she was more than a little in awe of the forceful, independent Sarah Wedgwood.

By day there were walks up the rocky hillside to admire views and collect samples of fossils and minerals to send to young John, at school at Bolton. Jos sent long explanatory letters to his son and to the other pupils there, to whom he had become a kind of unofficial visiting lecturer on mineralogy and related subjects.

Sometimes they hired horses or mules and went further afield, once to visit the grandeurs of Chatsworth House, another day to explore Dove Dale – 'your own native waters,' Jos said to Bentley, whose home village had been on the more level reaches of the river. They rode, too, towards Middleton, to see the lead mines in which Mary Bentley's father had shares and which supplied Etruria with cawk, the hard white stone which was an essential ingredient of the new jasper; and on the way home enjoyed a picnic in a sun-drenched hollow commanding a splendid view of the deep course of the River Derwent as it wound its way through Matlock and on towards Derby.

Finally, near the end of their stay, Jos ordered the carriage for the trip to Cromford.

It was not, after all, the delightful day Jos had anticipated. It started well enough, with an invigorating drive along the steep-sided valley beside the river in the bright October sunlight. And they reached Cromford without difficulty, recognising at once the insignificant scattering of cottages, dominated by the great five-storey bulk of Arkwright's mill striding the Bonsal Brook as it cut its way between high crags to run towards the Derwent.

'I gather he works night and day,' Jos observed, 'that being the only way he can make full use of the machines, since he depends on the water to power them. I wonder what his men think of working such hours.'

'I expect that depends on how much he pays them,' Sarah suggested drily.

But if Jos had hoped to talk to the mill workers and find out for himself what they thought of their working conditions, he was soon disappointed. The single arched doorway into the mill was firmly closed, and when they knocked the man who came refused to admit them.

'Then we wish to speak to Mr Arkwright,' Jos insisted. The man closed the door again and they heard him turn a key on the inside, and it was some time before it opened again just wide enough to allow through a pot-bellied figure in a brown coat and wig, whose look of ill-tempered suspicion was not encouraging.

Patiently, as smiling and courteous as the other man was the opposite, Jos explained how he and his partner and their wives had heard of Arkwright's remarkable water-powered spinning machines, and the growing success of his Cromford mill; and being in the area were most anxious to enjoy a tour of the mill.

The man confronting them glowered. Sarah, watching the various manifestations of bad temper succeed one another across the podgy face with its disfiguring wart and small sharp eyes, decided she did not like Richard Arkwright; and that, further, he had no intention at all of allowing them the kind of gracious welcome that she and Jos insisted on offering to all visitors to the Etruria works.

'I let no spies into my mill,' he said unpleasantly.

Sarah would at that point have made a sharp retort and left, but Jos was very anxious indeed to see the new machines, so he only said, mildly, 'Come now, Mr Arkwright, what would a potter want with spinning machines? Our interest is purely scientific – an acknowledgement of your ingenuity and skill.'

For a moment the Lancashireman looked them all up and down, first Jos and Bentley, then the two wives, and finally Susannah, who was staring with ill-concealed hostility at the unattractive figure before them. Eventually he said, 'My wife will make you some tea, if you like to call at the house up there.' He gestured vaguely towards the hillside above the lane that skirted the mill. His tone was very slightly more welcoming, but only grudgingly so.

'That,' Jos returned mildly, 'would be very disappointing, when we have come so far. It would have been pleasant to have shared a pipe and a talk with you, as businessmen together.'

Sarah, watching Jos's face, could see no sign that he was

otherwise than in earnest, though 'pleasant' was not the word she would have used to describe such a prospect.

After a moment or two more, Arkwright said, 'Give me a few minutes then, and I'll take tea with you – but I'm a busy man, and if I'd wasted my time gossiping with every caller then I'd not be where I am today.'

The coach took them to the solid house on the hill overlooking the mill, where Arkwright was to meet them. Sarah resisted the temptation to give her opinion of their unwilling host, since Susannah was present, but once she caught Bentley's eye and exchanged a smile and eloquently raised eyebrow which showed that he shared her opinion. Jos on the other hand simply said, 'He's right, you know – visitors can be a great interruption. I've often felt it myself.'

'But you always treat them with courtesy,' Sarah pointed out.

'Ah, but then I live in hopes that they will buy my wares. Arkwright only needs to get his spun cotton to the weavers – he has no direct customers to please.'

It was true but did not, Sarah thought, excuse him. However, she knew that Jos still hoped to persuade their host to give them the guided tour which he had so looked forward to, so she resolved to put on her most charming and sociable manner. Of the others of the party she had no fear, for neither Bentley nor his wife could ever have been less than courteous; but she prayed that Susannah would behave as she should.

There was nothing civilised or relaxed about the gathering in Arkwright's parlour that day, but Sarah guessed that it was as close as one was ever likely to come to such qualities in this house. She looked about her, noting the absence of books which at home littered every available surface, and the signs that it was Arkwright's personality above all which dominated here: there were none of the softer, feminine touches of flowers or ornaments or musical instruments. It was the house of a man with an overwhelming personality, but without education or taste. She was struck suddenly by the extraordinary contrast with Jos. On the surface the two men were much alike, for both had risen from humble origins by their own efforts to a growing wealth and success. Neither had received much in the way of schooling, both were gifted with an ability to use and develop new techniques and new

353

ideas. And yet Arkwright was crude, boorish, overbearing, insensitive; and Jos – her Jos . . .

She studied him with new eyes, seeing not simply the sturdy figure of a man of forty-five who looked young for his age, tanned, his expression bright, alert, full of intelligence and curiosity and all the warm impulsiveness of his nature, but also the spirit beneath, rooted in the earth and its practicalities yet reaching out always to some place visible only to some inward eye.

It had never occurred to her before that all the things that gave him most joy came from the ground on which he trod with that halting and yet vigorous step: the clay from which the pots were made, and the flint and stones and lead; the seeds, sown by him in that same soil, which grew into flowers and fruit in his beloved garden; the fossils and minerals that so absorbed his interest. All these humble earthly things were yet turned at his hands into something fine and rich and good – a delight for the mind, a pleasure to the eye, a joy to the spirit, as if he had some rare power to transform the ordinary to loveliness.

He must have realised at last that she was watching him, for he turned his head to smile at her; she felt a new warmth run through her, which had in it desire and a love all at once renewed and enriched. It was some time after that before Arkwright's talk impinged again on her thoughts.

The mill owner had become almost affable and had thawed sufficiently to talk of the mill, however adamantly he still refused to admit them to it.

'Do you find any difficulties in getting your men to work at night?' Jos asked him.

'Why should I? Night workers are paid well for it. But most of my people are women and children, not men. I make sure and keep them happy – rewards for good work in cash or kind and the like. That way I've never had no trouble. You ask any of my people – call at any cottage you please – and you'll find a happy worker. It'll stay that way too. I've houses a-building for them and when I've the money there'll be an inn and a chapel. They'd be there the sooner if Meg there,' here he glanced venomously at his silent unhappy-looking wife, 'would sell the property she has to help me. But still, there it is. I've set up a festival too – it takes place each year

354

to celebrate the founding of the mill. Dancing, food and drink in plenty – gives them something to look forward to. No, you'll not find any discontent amongst my people, I can tell you.'

By the time they were forced to accept that tea with the great man was the nearest they were likely to come to Cromford mill, and had at last taken their leave, Arkwright had worked himself into a mood of self-satisfied complacency, carping at the ways of all the world but himself. Sarah thought she preferred him ill-tempered, but was for the most part simply relieved that they had managed to extricate themselves before Susannah had made any unfortunately candid remark; though perhaps at ten she could be trusted now to show a little womanly tact.

As the coach travelled back to Matlock, Jos said thoughtfully, 'Why do you think a man of such a temperament seems able to manage his workers so well? It's true that they are contented – I have heard others say it. It seems he has none of the difficulties I have in that line.'

'I imagine the fact that most of his workforce are women and children has a good deal to do with it,' suggested Bentley. 'I've always found the women amongst the enamellers in Greek Street to be the most eager and flexible of workers. But on the whole there are few women and children at Etruria.'

'I should think even more to the point,' Sarah put in, 'is that Arkwright's mill is using a wholly new process and new machines, and he doesn't need a very skilled workforce. But our men come having had years of apprenticeship in a skilled trade, and they are proud of their skill, independent, used to the old ways. Some of their skills are needed, but they have to be adapted, and for men used to having a say in what they do it comes hard to be forced to follow another man's very different ways. After all, it's the youngsters trained at Etruria from the start – lads like William Hackwood for example – who are proving the best workers, and who have a great pride in being part of the Wedgwood works.'

'Yes.' Jos nodded thoughtfully. 'I think that must be it. One thing I can be glad of though – I get on better with my partners than it's said Arkwright does. Still, he's achieved a great deal – I'm very glad we've met him.'

Sarah realised with some astonishment that Jos meant what

he said; he had even formed quite a favourable impression of Arkwright. She reflected on the contradictory nature of Jos's character, so quick-tempered and intolerant of anything that threatened the perfection of his products, and yet so extraordinarily patient where the failings and foibles of men who did not work for him were concerned – or was it just that he did not see those failings?

That night was their last in Matlock, and by a lucky chance there was dancing at their lodgings, simple informal dancing with a spirited harpsichord accompaniment and a few selected fellow visitors to the spa for company. It was Susannah who was the star of the evening, dancing away as if nothing could ever tire her, as if she could continue all night and never flag. Jos did not dance, of course, but the Bentleys danced together; and then Bentley danced with Susannah; and then once, at last, with Sarah.

She had never danced with him before and for a moment, as he took her hand to lead her on to the floor for the country dance, she was no longer a sober married woman of forty-one but a young girl again, asked to dance by the most handsome man in the room and filled simultaneously with wonder, ecstasy and a paralysing shyness.

He danced well, and so did she, better indeed than quiet Mary Bentley who did not much care to dance. Back and forth, round and round, bobbing and swaying they progressed about the room, flushed and laughing, their eyes meeting brightly as the pattern of the dance carried them away from one another. Later, close to, as their hands joined, he said softly, 'This has been a happy time – and tomorrow we take something of you with us.'

She glanced across at Susannah, temporarily occupying her own seat between Jos and Mary Bentley and chattering animatedly to the former governess, her face alive with enthusiasm and happiness. She looked up at Bentley again. 'I'm glad. She will be happy with you – and best of all that is something I can give you without pain or regret.'

He moved away from her again and she from him, behind the next couple, around and then back again. 'This is how it should be,' he murmured as they met. 'Never Paradise again, but the best that fallen man can hope to have.'

She smiled. Once she had asked him, 'Do you think it

possible to love two people?' and he had said, 'Yes'; and for them then that realisation had been blighted by pain. Now it was still true, but the pain had gone, and the guilt, and they were left simply with the happiness of being together and the joy of sharing all that they could rightly share.

Next day they were reminded that even sharing can be painful. They found Bentley's coach waiting for them at Derby, just as planned, and they all stood in a little group beside it to say goodbye.

Mary, modest and tactful, kissed Jos and Sarah and slipped into the coach. Then from Bentley there was a hug for Jos, a kiss for Sarah, scarcely noticed this time – for now it was Susannah's turn.

Susannah said little, but she clung to them both with a fierce wordless intensity that told them all they needed to know. Sarah prised her hold a little apart and bent to cup that flushed bright-eyed little face in her hands. 'Be good, love – take care now – and love your Mama and Papa Bentley just as you love us.'

'I will, Mama,' Susannah whispered, too proud to weep though Sarah knew it was tears and not laughter that gave such a shine to her eyes.

From Jos there was the same tenderness, and an equally dignified response; and then with his arm about her Bentley led Susannah to the coach.

Sarah felt Jos draw her close and they stood together, watching, silent, until the coach with its little white waving handkerchief had disappeared from sight.

'We've given him some of ourselves,' said Jos at last, huskily. 'That's a comfort.'

So she had thought last night, but Sarah could not yet trust herself to speak. Instead she squeezed Jos's hand and went with him to their own coach, which seemed to have become all at once much too large for the two of them.

CHAPTER SEVENTEEN

1779–80

'I can't bear to think of all those fine marble antiquities going out of the country – Russia buying up all our great works of art. What I would have given to take some copies of them!'

'Yes, very sad, very sad.' Mr Sparrow's lawyer's tones were more moderate than Jos's, less sharp with indignation. 'But how often one sees this kind of thing – the worthless spendthrift heir of a great man. A good thing Sir Robert Walpole is not alive to see how his nephew cares for his inheritance.'

'It seems to me just one more sign of our decline as a nation. Once we were held up to the world as a shining example of liberty and civilisation – and however far we fell short of those ideals even then, there was some truth in it. Now we can't even hold up our heads in a more material sense. We have no influence left for good: we can no longer keep our works of art; France and Spain attack our shipping and unite against us overseas; our armies fighting on our behalf are made up of German mercenaries – we are the laughing stock of the world. And I can't remember a time when there was so much unrest amongst our people as there is now.'

'Your husband's at his unpatriotic talk again,' murmured Richard Wedgwood disapprovingly, but Sarah simply smiled. Her father had heard it all so often before there seemed little point in his commenting on it yet again. She looked across the room, wondering what Susannah was talking about so intently with Mrs Sparrow – they had ceased playing duets on the harpsichord some time ago.

'Did you hear what Henshall was saying this morning about the troubles in Lancashire?' Mr Sparrow went on. 'He says there's a good deal of muttering amongst out-of-work weavers against the new mills that can spin and weave with fewer men.'

'Trade's bad in the cotton business, with the Irish shutting out imports and foreign markets cut off by war. Taken together with the new system of working, that might make it hard for the less adaptable to find work, I suppose. But until now there's been such a growth of trade that there has certainly been an increase in employment on the whole.'

'Perhaps; but it looks as if that might be at an end. Henshall thought things looked ugly – gangs of idle men hanging about looking for trouble.'

The boys were at school in Lancashire, at Bolton, surrounded by the new mills which men like Arkwright had established there. Sarah felt a twinge of alarm, but would not give way to it: the workless weavers of Lancashire had no quarrel with schoolboys or their masters, and the boys were not encouraged to wander the countryside unsupervised. They would be safe enough.

'Mama!' Susannah had come softly to her side. Her face was bright and happy, her thoughts very far indeed from England's decline or the troubles of the unemployed. 'Look, Mrs Sparrow has given me this music to try for myself at home – isn't that kind of her?'

Sarah turned to smile her thanks to Mrs Sparrow, glad to be distracted from the gloomy conversation of the men. 'It will make a pleasant change from the "Harmonious Blacksmith",' she commented teasingly, and Susannah grinned.

'But you like that, Mama – you said so!'

'So I do; but one can have too much even of a good thing.'

She watched Susannah as they talked, touched and warmed – as so often – by the beauty of this eldest child of theirs, her slender poised gracefulness, the fair curling hair framing a face that needed neither powder nor paint to give it the pink-and-white delicacy of a porcelain figure. It was good to have Susannah at home again, recovered from the serious illness that had laid her low for so long in London, much of her awkwardness polished away by her three years' schooling there. Sarah had thought often lately what a joy children were once they had passed the infant stage and grew daily more companionable – separate individuals with personalities and opinions of their own. Susannah at fourteen could be moody, serious, frivolous by turns, always unpredictable, sometimes

359

exasperating; but often when they talked woman to woman, shared pleasure in a book or a piece of music, laughed over some silly private joke, she was simply a delight.

It was Susannah who kept them all entertained next day as the coach carried them home from the Sparrows' comfortable house, where they had passed the last two pleasant days as guests of the family lawyer. The excuse had been Jos's navigation committee, meeting at Stone, but they had all enjoyed the break from routine – even Richard Wedgwood, for all that several times on the homeward journey he re-marked pointedly how much he preferred his own fireside to any other in the world.

It was to that fireside – in the library – that Sarah's father hurried almost as soon as they reached Etruria Hall. By that time Susannah, changed and fresh and smiling, was already seated at the newly acquired harpsichord, tripping her way with more enthusiasm than accuracy through the sonata by John Burton which Mrs Sparrow had given her. Jos had been greeted in the hall by a letter – 'Bentley again,' Sarah thought, and she set off alone up the stairs to see that all was well with the little girls. There were three infants – the 'infantry' as Jos laughingly called them – left in the nursery now: Catherine, not quite five; Sarah, a chubby noisy three-year-old; and Mary Ann, still a baby and not thriving as she should.

'Sally!' Sarah halted halfway up the stairs and turned. Jos was standing below with the opened letter in his hand and his face was strained with shock. She went down to him and saw at once that the letter was not from Bentley.

'Mr Holland has written – Josiah is very ill . . .'

She gave a little murmur of dismay.

'He says they thought it was simple indigestion and tried home remedies, but he grew no better. They sent for the doctor then – and he thinks we should come.'

She reached out and grasped his hand, and for a moment held it, though whether to give or gain comfort she did not know. Then she said, 'There's no moon – we can't start tonight. I'll get everything packed and we'll leave at dawn.'

There was no joy or excitement in the departure in the chill misty dawn of that October day; only a sense of urgency, dark and laden with apprehension. There was no pleasure either in seeing the sun break through to light the trees already tinted with autumn, only relief that it was fine and the roads dry, so that nothing could hinder them.

They halted only once, about the middle of the day, to change the horses and snatch a hurried meal, and then they were on their way again. At the turnpikes they had the money ready, so as to waste as little time as possible.

They were almost there, sitting silently side by side with linked hands, when the coach came to rest unexpectedly without warning.

'There's no turnpike here,' commented Jos, and pulled down the window to look. A noise reached them; an angry rumble of voices, the tramp of clogged feet on hard ground, an argument between their coachman and someone unseen.

Jos drew in his head. 'The road's packed with men, hundreds of them I'd say. I can't see what they're doing.' He looked out again, and Sarah did the same on the other side.

She thought then of Mr Sparrow's words 'gangs of idle men hanging about ready for trouble'. But this was no gang, and there was no sense of idleness. They were purposeful, grim, determined; roughly dressed men cramming the narrow lane from hedge to hedge and armed with the domestic weapons that lay to hand – cudgels and staves, spades, brooms, mallets, anything that would smash or shatter. They were not looking for trouble: they had found it.

Sarah sat back on the seat. 'They're going our way – if they don't let us through we'll be hours getting by.'

Jos nodded. 'Then they must stand aside – I'll go and talk to them.'

She reached out to hold him. 'No, Jos – you don't know what they'll do . . .' But he had gone, out of sight. Quickly Sarah followed him.

He had reached the man arguing with the coachman, a great giant of a man at the rear of the gathering. 'He says they've been smashing looms at a mill nearby,' Jos explained to her.

'Aye, and that's just the first,' the man put in, ready to expand his theme if Jos had not spoken again.

'Can't you see, that leads nowhere? You'll only find your-selves in trouble. You can't halt progress.'

Sarah saw the look on the man's face if Jos did not; she laid her hand on his arm. 'Enough of that, love . . .' Then she turned imploringly to the man. 'Please, we're going to see our son who is ill – let us by, if you have any pity. We've no time to spare.'

For a moment the man studied her, considering; almost as if it took him a long time to admit the possibility of other troubles beside his own, other concerns apart from the iniquities of mill owners. Then he shrugged and turned, and spoke to a man near him, and word rippled through the column. Slowly, shuffling and more than a little grudging, the men moved back, leaving a path just wide enough for the coach to pass.

Sarah urged Jos inside again, closed the door, and the vehicle moved forward between the ranks of grimly staring faces, not exactly hostile but without friendliness or sympathy. She was glad when they were past.

They found ten-year-old Josiah flushed and thin and restless in his bed in a stuffy little room at the Reverend Philip Holland's school at Bolton. Sarah remembered now how the smell of the place had struck her before, a smell compounded of unappetising food, stale air, inadequately washed young bodies. At the time the excellence of the education provided by the Unitarian minister had weighed heavier than those more mundane considerations; now, she felt only greatly alarmed. She went straight to the window and thrust it open, letting in some freshness to the overheated atmosphere. And then she set about plumping up her son's pillows, smoothing the sheets, bathing his hot skin, while Jos held his hand and talked softly to him; and Josiah lay watching them, transparently glad to have them there at his side.

'Dr Taylor will be here to see him again in the morning,' Mr Holland had said as he showed them into the room. 'He'll be able to tell you what he thinks. I'll leave you with him now, so you can settle him. There'll be supper for you in the parlour as soon as you feel able to come down.'

It was some time before Josiah fell into an uneasy sleep, and even then Sarah was reluctant to leave him.

'You can come back when we've eaten,' Jos pointed out. 'We'll take it in turns to sit with him through the night, if he seems likely to be wakeful.'

Downstairs they found John and Tom waiting in the

362

parlour to share their supper. John looked reassuringly healthy, but Tom, Sarah saw with anxiety, had a wan and fragile look. It was, he told her dismissively, 'just a headache, Mama,' but he was unusually silent and ate very little.

Later, when they talked of it, Jos said, 'He often has headaches – I expect he's just anxious about Josiah. You know how close they are.'

'That's taking sympathy a bit far.' She knew that Jos had been simply attempting to reassure her, and that he too was anxious.

The doctor, next day, was encouraging, despite their account of Josiah's restless night. 'He's poorly, certainly, but not I believe in any real danger – he's a tough lad at bottom you know. But in my opinion what he needs now is fresh country air, gentle exercise, and a good long spell without a book in sight. I'll do what I can to get him fit to travel as soon as possible, and then you can take him home for a holiday.'

'We shall take Tom with us too,' Jos told Mr Holland some time later. 'He looks as if he'll be the next one taken sick if we don't do something.'

'I wouldn't recommend travelling tomorrow,' Mr Holland advised them. 'Dr Taylor has an alarming account of troubles yesterday – it seems your little obstacle on the road coming here was by no means the worst of it. A far larger party attacked the mill at Chorley, and in the ensuing scuffle three men died. There was no damage done to the mill but the mob left swearing revenge, so it's said. There's talk of them getting firearms together for another attack tomorrow – and making for every mill in the district, which means Bolton itself is under threat. The powers that be have sent to Liverpool for troops, but I can't see them getting here for a day or two. I think you'd be wiser not to travel until it all calms down again.'

'Arkwright has a share in the mill at Chorley, hasn't he?' Jos commented thoughtfully. 'I wonder if he's had trouble at Cromford too?'

'Cromford's very out of the way,' Mr Holland pointed out. 'There was no weaving or spinning there before, so I imagine it won't have been seen as a threat. Though now, who knows? It is astonishing how men of good sense got together in a mob seem to abandon all principles and all reason and behave like madmen.'

'Poor deluded souls – why can't they see you can't turn back the tide of progress? If it wasn't for men like Arkwright there'd be no improvements in trade at all, and even more men without work.'

'I suppose,' Sarah pondered later, as they walked – a little warily – on to the hills in the evening sun, allowing the wind to blow away the fumes of the sickroom, 'if men are hungry and out of work it's hard to convince them that this is indeed progress. All they see is that once they could earn a living at their own firesides, and now the new mills have all the trade and they are left with nothing. You can understand their feelings.'

Jos turned to gaze at her in astonishment. 'You surely don't condone machine-wrecking and law-breaking, Sarah!'

When Jos called her 'Sarah' matters were grave indeed. She smiled wryly. 'Of course not, love. That solves nothing after all. The changes will come for all their anger. But I do understand why they are angry, and even what makes them vent their anger as they do. I imagine they feel they have no other way to express their grievances. If you have no power even over your own life, let alone over who governs and controls it, then what else is there to do but stamp and shout and smash things?'

'Oh, Sally, that's nonsense! Whatever our troubles as a nation we've surely not declined so far that the only way to right wrongs is by violence. That only makes for greater loss of liberty in the end.'

'I don't suppose those poor men have thought much further than their own troubles. In any case, to understand is not to condone – but if you don't even try to understand you become hard and unfeeling.'

'Hard!' Jos stared at her. 'Do you call me hard? I've brought in new ways and fought for them, just as Arkwright has – and look at the difference. What did our men have before? A poor living scraped together by selling second-rate pots at country fairs. Now they have good housing, clean orderly conditions of work, markets for their goods in every corner of the globe, excellent wages. I don't call it hard, to give them that kind of better life.'

'But you didn't do it for them – or not first and foremost – did you? It was only that you could do nothing without them.

You need the best potters and painters and modellers, and so you attract them with good wages and so forth. But that's only on condition they follow your wishes to the letter. And – admit it – if you found machines to do the work you'd sack them all tomorrow.'

'Oh Sally, I didn't know you thought so badly of me!' His eyes were full of reproach, but he admitted grudgingly, 'I don't know – it's true that machines don't make unreasonable demands, or get drunk, or take days off for no good reason. Properly designed and maintained they don't make mistakes either. But there's no machine in the world can throw a pot or paint a design so finely as can a good man or woman, and I doubt if there ever will be. Besides, if I can do something in my line of work to give the people under my charge a better way of life, and knowledge and dignity and self-respect, then it's my duty to do so. It's that way that changes for the better will come, not by angry mobs smashing machines.'

Sarah turned Jos to face her and solemnly took both his hands in hers, turning them palms upwards. 'And would you not grieve and rage, Jos my love, if these hands were never allowed again to shape a pot just because some man had made a machine to do the job better? That's how the cotton weavers feel, you know.'

'That's different,' objected Jos, though his eyes fell at her gaze. 'And besides, even I couldn't argue with progress.'

Sarah laughed and linked her arm through his, and they walked on again. 'There's no talking you round, is there, my love? Sometimes you're amazingly stubborn.'

'Of course,' he agreed good-humouredly. 'And so are you. That's how we came where we are today.'

They descended the long hill back towards the school, talking little and then not with any seriousness, as if wary at this time of touching again on any sensitive place. It was a Sunday, and for the most part the little town was quiet, and yet not peacefully so. Children played in the streets, but even their noise seemed restrained, and here and there was an odd unaccountable bustle of activity – women converging on an inn in a poor street, carrying dishes and beakers (always the old pewter utensils that generally still served as the daily tableware of the poor), men talking intently on street corners or hurrying along in groups with a kind of furtive haste.

'Holland's right it seems,' said Jos. 'Something's up hereabouts.'

'And there are more than just weavers tied up in it, I would say.'

They quickened their pace, eager to return to the security of the school. 'Jos, what were those women doing, do you think? Providing food for the men, ready for whatever they're planning? But no, that can't be it – they only carried empty plates and so forth, and I can't see why the men would want to lumber themselves with such things on a march. Another strange thing – did you notice how all the things they carried were made of pewter? Why on earth should that be?'

Jos shook his head. 'I don't know . . .' and then he gave an exclamation. 'Yes I do, of course . . .! Do you remember back in '45, when the Pretender was marching south with all his wild Highlandmen at his back?'

Startled, Sarah laughed. 'Yes, I remember, just about. We couldn't come to Burslem because Papa wouldn't risk a journey – and all the grown-ups had anxious looks and talked in low voices of terrible unspeakable things the Highlanders would do to us if they came our way. And then nothing happened at all and all the invaders turned round and went back home. But I *was* only nine. Anyway, what has all this to do with anything?'

'*I* remember something more. I remember your uncles melting down pewter for all the neighbours, to make ammunition for the firearms in case they were needed. It must have done wonders for the sale of pot plates, for a little time.' The lightness left his face. 'But that's what it is, I imagine. Mr Holland said they wanted arms – and the women are doing their bit to help.'

Sarah shivered. 'I know they have no quarrel with us, but I wish we were safe home and the boys with us.'

Jos put an arm about her shoulders and gave them a squeeze. 'That's not like you, Sally.'

She smiled ruefully. 'No, it's not, is it? I think if only Josiah were well I'd have courage enough.'

There at least there was some comfort, for by Monday morning Josiah was already greatly improved. 'If he keeps it up we'll set out tomorrow,' Jos decided.

'I don't think that's wise,' said Mr Holland doubtfully.

'Nothing's happened yet today, but there's an ugly mood in the streets.'

By dawn next day, when in spite of all warnings Jos and Sarah had the carriage at the door and were settling Josiah, well wrapped in blankets, into it, they knew that it was more than a mood or a threat. They heard from a frightened passer-by that well over a thousand men – their numbers swelled by the Duke of Bridgewater's colliers – had marched on Chorley during the night and burnt the mill to the ground, watched helplessly by a tiny troop of invalided veteran soldiers. Triumphant now, the rioters were marching back to Bolton, their goal to destroy every mill on their route and to end at last at Cromford, the source of all their troubles.

'Are you sure you won't stay until it's over?' Mr Holland pressed them.

'We can't risk being from home any longer – if we go now we can be away before the mob gets here, while the roads are quiet.'

'Should we take John too, Jos love?'

'No, I think we were right to think there's no need. These men have no quarrel with schoolboys, as you said. We know he'll be kept safe indoors until it's died down. But Tom and Joss need quiet and country air as soon as possible.'

Sarah went to say goodbye to John, whose disappointment at being left behind was swamped by excitement at the possibility of being able to watch an angry mob at work. 'I don't expect you'll see or hear a thing,' Sarah said cheerfully. But as she went downstairs with her arm about Tom she heard, far off, a strange deep rhythmic thudding.

'Drums,' said Jos as she joined him. 'They said the men marched to drums.'

Mr Holland bustled them into the coach. 'Get on your way quickly – they can't be far off. Whatever you do you mustn't meet them on the road.'

They passed here and there hurrying knots of roughly armed men making their way to join the main force and, sometimes, a mill guarded by a small and apprehensive band of workmen and townsfolk. When they paused at the first turnpike they could still hear the drums.

'Even if they send troops from Liverpool,' grumbled the turnpike keeper, 'they'll be too late to be of any use.'

And then all at once they were in the peaceful untroubled countryside where no sign of unrest or disorder intruded and their only thought was to find somewhere comfortable to spend the night, for Josiah was too ill to bear the journey home in one stage. 'Well, love,' was Jos's only further comment on the troubles. 'We'll have to wait until Jack writes to find out what happened.'

The letter from John was already there when they reached home, full of all the delighted sense of importance of a thirteen-year-old boy witnessing great events, only letting it be known in passing that he had not in fact witnessed anything at first hand. The rioters, he told them, had attacked three mills in Bolton; but then, warned in advance of an approaching militia force, had dispersed to their homes, and the trouble was over. The bitterness and resentment would not so easily be overcome, Sarah knew, and one additional piece of news roused even Jos's indignation.

'Do you know,' he told Sarah, coming home one day from the works, 'one of the bargemen tells me the soldiers in Lancashire were ordered not to fire over the heads of the rioters, but right into them, shooting to kill. To end it all quickly, so they said.'

'You don't think they'd be justified, faced with such lawlessness?' Sarah asked curiously.

'I can't see any justification whatsoever for giving soldiers a taste for shooting their own countrymen,' said Jos with emphasis. 'Where might that end?'

Sarah smiled. 'Then we're not so far apart after all, love. And let's be thankful at least that the whole thing ended without bloodshed.'

Josiah and Tom had endured the journey to Etruria without undue strain, and once home began steadily to grow well again. But both Jos and Sarah knew that their return to health would only confront their parents with a new and different problem. They talked of it first one evening after Sarah's father had gone to bed and left them alone together in the dim quietness of the library.

For some time they sat, relaxed, silent, enjoying the peace and the unaccustomed luxury of being alone with only one another for company. Then Jos said abruptly, 'We're going to have to decide what to do.'

368

She was too much in tune with him tonight to need to ask what he meant, so she said, 'School doesn't agree with them. It may be good for their education but it's been little short of disastrous for their health. Perhaps there are children who thrive on poor food and too little air and exercise, but ours aren't among them.'

'It's not just the boys either . . . Sukey's had one illness after another – even in London, though we know Bentley gave her the best possible care and she was happy.'

'And it won't be long before we have to make some decision about the younger girls. I know we want the best for them all – but we must look after their physical as well as their mental well-being.'

Jos smiled. 'And so, like me, you begin to think we must consider educating them at home, where we have some control over how it's done.'

She nodded. 'It wouldn't be a problem if the schools valued health as highly as book learning, but there we are. Still, it's not something we should rush into. For the present John seems well enough, and it won't hurt the others to have a complete rest from work until after Christmas. That gives us time to think over how they are to be taught, and what they should learn – and, of course, who is to teach them.'

'Then we need to consult the best opinions on the matter – Bentley of course . . .'

'And Dr Darwin . . .'

The opportunity to consult the doctor came rather sooner than they might have wished. This time it was not Josiah or Tom – both fully recovered – who required his services but Richard Wedgwood, down with a chill which at his age was no slight matter; and the very day that they sent for Darwin little Mary Ann was seized with terrifying convulsions, which wrenched her small body for hour after hour in merciless succession. Reminded agonisingly of Richard, Sarah held the child in her arms helpless to do anything, praying in wordless despair for Darwin to come soon, before it was too late.

By the time the doctor arrived the convulsions had subsided to an occasional spasm, but Mary Ann lay limp and exhausted, with one side of her body unable to move at all.

Darwin examined her very thoroughly and prescribed electric shocks for the paralysis and opiates for the convulsions,

369

treatments which distressed Mary Ann's parents almost as much as her illness had done, although after what seemed like hours they did see some signs of improvement. 'That's the trouble with having children,' Darwin said gruffly to Sarah when there was leisure to talk. 'You can't t-tear yourself free of them. As long as they l-live, when they s-suffer s-so do you – worse than they d-do perhaps.'

She studied his face, which was as impassive as usual, but she knew he spoke from the heart. Last year his eldest son, the brilliant Charles, well through his medical training at Edinburgh University, had died suddenly of an infection caught while dissecting – he had been only nineteen. It had been a terrible blow to his father, but only his closest friends had been allowed to glimpse something of what he felt. To the world in general he showed an uncaring face, and simply immersed himself more than ever in his work.

But his son's loss made him the more sensitive to the question of how best to educate the Wedgwood youngsters. When he had attended to Sarah's father – 'N-nothing to worry about' – he sat down with them in the library to give the matter his attention.

'What does it matter what they learn, so long as they live and grow happy?' Sarah burst out without thinking, and then wondered if she had distressed Darwin. But he only nodded his agreement, unsmiling but calm.

'True, my dear S-Sarah. But they won't b-be happy if they aren't well t-taught.' He glanced at Jos, on his other side before the fire. 'You think of s-subjecting them to a t-tutor, do you – like gentlemen's sons?'

'Not necessarily, but it is a possibility. Do you think it wrong? After all, your own boys were largely taught at home.'

'I don't think it wrong at all – much b-better for their health, as you say. But I imagine you'll w-want to ensure they have a more useful education than most gentlemen's s-sons.'

Jos smiled. 'Ah – we thought you'd have views on that. We're seeking the best advice of course. And as Bentley is still considering his reply you can have the first word.'

'I've always understood it was the l-last word that counted for most – but perhaps if I p-put my views very s-strongly they'll t-tip the scales.' He settled himself deeper into his chair, as if preparing for a lengthy dissertation. 'Well now, let's s-see . . . First, don't s- stuff them full of all that classical n-nonsense – Latin, Greek, and s-such like – dead languages, no use to anyone. If they want to read classical writers, the only ones worth reading are already t-translated. But French now, yes – very useful if they mean to s-sell your wares overseas. In fact, I think I know the very French t-teacher for you. Young, very young – b-but educated – French, of course. Went as a s-surgeon on a French ship, and t-taken prisoner – no knowledge of s-surgery at all, but likeable, and s-speaks French like a n-native, as you might say. He's staying at Lichfield, and my boys have learnt more from him in t-two weeks than in years of study before. S-send your boys over for a while, s-see what you make of him. Now then, what else? Book-keeping, accounting, all that k- kind of thing – and, of course, m-mathematics, drawing, all the experimenting you c-can give them. Fit them to be broad-minded well-read l-little manufacturers – a good s-sound *practical* education, that's what you want. No gentleman's s-son ends up fit for anything but t-turning an elegantly abusive Latin phrase in p-parliament – and that's if he ever re-members his L-Latin afterwards. That's n-not for your boys.'

Sarah looked slowly about the room, taking in with fresh eyes the spaciousness of it, the walls lined from floor to ceiling with books, the fine carpets and furnishings, the paintings and ornaments, the long windows looking on to a graceful parkland where once had been only a barren windswept hillside. In her mind she contrasted all this com-fort – luxury almost – with Burslem, with the dust and dirt and cramped rooms of the Brick House, the cottage simplicity of the Ivy House, the muddle and stink and occasional squalor of the Churchyard works where Jos had begun forty-nine long years ago.

Their sons could remember none of that old life, not even John who had been only three when they left Burslem be-hind. It was from here, from the splendour of a mansion as grand as any gentleman's seat, that the new generation of Wedgwoods would set out. Already, they were acquiring a polish of manner and bearing which Jos for all his wide reading and intellectual curiosity could never match; and Susannah, their sister, was in every way the pattern young lady, far more so than her mother had been at her age despite

371

all the hopes centred on her. Would any of these children of theirs be content with the education Jos would have liked, which would have fitted him best for his chosen trade? They were born to riches, to wider possibilities perhaps than the potworks offered, even to leisure; it was certain, she thought, that they would want something quite different from life than Jos asked, and need for it quite another kind of learning.

'Do you not think,' she broke in hesitantly, 'that our children need what is best not only of a useful and practical education, but also of a gentlemanly and classical one? I think you have failed to consider that in many ways, whether you like it or not, they will be growing up as gentlemen. And they will need to hold their own in the company of other gentlemen, not feeling at a disadvantage because that education failed them.'

'They are to be manufacturers, Sally, not idlers frittering away their time on trifles.' That was Jos at his most dismissive, and Sarah was too weary to argue. She could only hope that Bentley would come to her aid.

He did. 'It is to me self-evident,' he wrote, 'that their education must be practical and scientific; and I have always believed that they must be taught that no luxury can be taken for granted, but must always be striven for. But I know I do not need to preach the value of hard work to you.

'However, their schooling must also be designed to broaden their minds, to stretch the capacity to reason to its fullest extent, to develop the imagination and all the highest instincts to which man may aspire. Then, and only then, will your sons and daughters be able to move freely in any society, whether high or low, with the dignity and grace you would wish for them. To this end, I disagree with Darwin: I believe some elements at least of a classical education to be essential. Latin has value as a discipline, and forms the basis of much of our language: it is universal almost amongst educated men, and the key to much of the greatest literature and thought. You follow the best models of classical art in your pottery, believing them to be unsurpassed; does it not follow that in other spheres too the classical world has an ideal of perfection to offer? You will say that you have achieved so much in a lifetime without any taint of classical education – and so you have; but, my dear friend, there are few indeed like you. Your children, I think, are made of more earthbound material, and like most of us need all the help that education can give to repair the deficiencies of nature.'

And so, of course, Latin became part of the curriculum of what Jos called, laughingly, their Etruscan Academy. The weeks before Christmas were busy, absorbing, exhilarating. The invalids recovered, but Darwin continued to call regularly to give his views and help as he could, and, later, to take the boys to Lichfield to see what wonders young Monsieur Potet could work on their rudimentary French. As Darwin had foretold, the results were impressive, and so the shy gentle nineteen-year-old came to Etruria, lodging with a kindly widow nearby and walking daily to the house to teach the children.

By the spring the days had taken on a new routine. At six or seven each day, Jos, full of enjoyment of his new role as headmaster, would ring the school bell on the landing to wake the sleeping scholars. Half an hour later the boys were expected to be washed and dressed and on their way to the works to join Tom Wedgwood's boys for a lesson in writing from Peter Swift. Meanwhile, the little girls (even tiny Mary Ann) would be installed in the newly furnished schoolroom near the nursery to read and write with Jane Hillyard; and Susannah would sit at her harpsichord, vigorously practising her music. After an hour of hard work the children came noisy and hungry to breakfast, and towards the end of the meal Sarah knew Monsieur Potet would be found waiting anxiously in the hall, ready to embark on the French lesson. After that, he took them for drawing (being skilled in that line also); and then until dinner time there would be two hours of riding, or gardening, or chemical experiments, depending on the weather and the inclinations or abilities of the pupils. Dinner gave way to Latin with Tom Byerley, and French conversation followed before tea, often – when it was fine – out of doors as the children walked with their tutor about the garden or in the fields. For the older children the day ended with a lesson in accounting from their mother, before supper at eight and bed at nine.

The twelve months which followed that troubled autumn were rich and happy ones. The country might be in turmoil, with mobs of malcontents ready to follow any demagogue for any cause, the more destructive the better, but at Etruria the noise and activity were all of a fruitful and healthy kind.

Jos planted an orchard and an abundance of vegetables, and discussed gardening at length in his letters to Bentley, whose interest in the subject was less than wholehearted. The children thrived on the new regime, delighting Sarah with rosy cheeks and huge appetites, and an eager thirst for knowledge that set them at mealtimes worrying at ideas like young puppies over a bone in a way that earned her father's deep disapproval. Only Mary Ann's continuing mental and physical backwardness clouded their clear sky that year.

Trade might be difficult throughout most of the country, but even that problem scarcely touched them. Jos had still not solved the considerable difficulties involved in making hollow-wares (vases, bowls, teapots and so on) in his new jasper – the firing temperatures were the chief difficulty – but the bas-reliefs, cameos and portrait medallions had proved popular beyond their wildest expectations. He spent long hours in his laboratory, or trying out one technique or another at the works, and remained optimistic of eventual success. 'Everything yields to experiment,' he would say.

At long last the years of hard work in planning the factory and training the men at Etruria had borne fruit. Often these days when Sarah stepped through the archway into the central courtyard she was struck by the busy, bustling, contented atmosphere. There would always be difficult characters amongst the three-hundred-strong workforce and grumbles about this and that, but Jos's ways had been accepted at last. The young men and women, trained at Etruria, were proud of their skills, and proud to be associated with the name of Wedgwood; and those who had been longer with the pottery realised too that they were an essential part of a great and highly regarded enterprise.

It was Sarah who first suggested a new departure for them: to send out a man with samples of the smaller items produced by Etruria, to travel from town to town visiting shops and other potential clients and encouraging them to place orders for goods. Jos took up the idea eagerly, called in the new minister of the Newcastle meeting house, Mr Lomas, to take over the Latin lessons at the Hall, and despatched Tom Byerley on his travels. Jos's nephew seemed to brighten into new life at the prospect before him.

They had plans for the house too, for large as it was their growing family and a constant stream of visitors seemed to fill every corner. Work began on two new wings and a larger kitchen, and the young artist John Flaxman, who had already done some impressive designs for the pottery, was commissioned to plan the decoration of the extended mansion.

'It's high time we had a few family portraits, don't you think, Sally?' Jos said one day. Bentley recommended his friend Joseph Wright from Derby, but Wright was indisposed. And meanwhile the celebrated George Stubbs had contacted Jos with a view to trying his hand at modelling in jasper and painting on earthenware. So he came to stay at Etruria, and Jos struggled with the problems of producing a smooth flat earthenware surface for painting that did not warp or twist in the drying or firing; and Stubbs was invited to paint the family portraits.

'I think we should have two portraits of the children, one of the boys and one of the girls,' said Sarah. 'You and I can be done separately, and my father too.'

'Yes.' Jos nodded. 'Something that shows them in some kind of characteristic pose. Let's think now – Sukey at the harpsichord while Catherine sings, little Sally and Mary Ann playing on the carpet close by. And for the boys, Jack working on some experiment or other, Tom jumping up and clapping his hands to see the reaction, Joss thoughtfully studying the chemical dictionary. How does that sound?'

'Perfect,' said Sarah.

But George Stubbs had his own ideas, and in the end there were only two portraits, one of Richard Wedgwood, the other a single outdoor study of the family with the older children on horseback.

'He complains that everyone thinks he paints nothing but horses,' commented Sarah ruefully, 'and then he won't paint a scene without a horse in it.'

At the end of harvest time their best-loved guest came to Etruria at last: Bentley, arriving alone for a few summer days snatched from the pressing business that kept him tied so much to London.

As she came to welcome him into the drawing room, Sarah had an odd sense that now, at last, the family was complete: all those she loved were about her and she could ask for nothing more. She held out her hands to him and he took them in his, just for a moment standing still, his eyes holding hers with the warm gravity that never failed even now to reach some deep place within her.

'You've been away too long,' she said at last, and smiled just a little.

'I shall do my best to make amends for that while I'm here.' He went then to greet Jos, who steered him towards a chair.

'Let's have the tea and cakes Sarah's ordered for us, and then I've a scheme to fill the hour or two till supper time, if you're not too tired.'

Bentley glanced questioningly at Sarah, who smiled. 'It's the newest entertainment for all our visitors to Etruria,' she explained; and Jos added eagerly, 'We'll take a pleasure barge through the Harecastle tunnel. I'd have liked to travel the whole length of the canal with you, but you give us so little of your time – so this will have to do. What do you think?'

Since the barge was waiting at the Etruria wharf, it was inevitable, Sarah thought, that they should first have 'just a quick peep' at the latest jasper medallions ready for sale.

'See how Flaxman's head of Medusa's turned out,' Jos said. Bentley had come across John Flaxman in London and had been immensely taken with the young artist and sculptor, who though deformed in body was clearly immensely gifted: it was through Bentley's influence that Flaxman had agreed to model for the firm, and his work was perfectly suited to the new jasperware. Now Bentley took the medallion in his hand, admiring the clarity of the modelling, beautifully defined against the dark blue ground.

'Very fine,' he said approvingly. 'What of his *Apotheosis of Homer*? Have you heard what Sir William Hamilton thought of the copy we sent to him?'

'Yes – did I not tell you? I'll show you the letter at home. He said it astonished all the artists in Naples, being – now what was the word? – "more pure and in a truer antique taste than anything they could do".'

'Far be it from me to interrupt your little bit of honest pride, love,' Sarah broke in, 'but if we're going to get to the tunnel and back before supper we ought to be going. Besides, the children are in a silly mood today – I don't think we should leave them to poor Peter Swift for much longer.'

376

The children – apart from the little girls who had stayed at home – had been left in Swift's care in the courtyard while the adults went to the pattern room; and he was looking more than a little harrassed by the time they returned. John had wandered away by himself towards the canal where he stood patting the horse waiting to tow their barge; Susannah was standing at the window of the modelling room, watching the men working on the jasperware; and Tom had led the reluctant Josiah right inside the forbidden territory of the dipping room, to watch the glazes being mixed. When Sarah came up to them he was arguing fiercely with an agitated Peter Swift, while Josiah, only too conscious of wrongdoing, shifted uneasily from one foot to the other.

'What are you boys doing here? You know it's dangerous.' Sarah's severe gaze was on the whole more effective as a disciplinary measure than Jos's anger; but not to Tom, who simply smiled sweetly in return, in that way which never failed to melt all her disapproval.

'You know we wouldn't break any of Papa's rules, Mama – we won't touch anything. We just wanted to see . . .' There was an inarticulate protest from Josiah, and Tom glanced at him and amended. '*I* wanted to see if they were making the jasper dip.'

Jos came and ruffled his son's fair hair. 'That's not made in there, my lad – now come on. The barge has been waiting this past hour.'

Tom gave a little skip of delighted anticipation, and called Josiah to race him to the canal. Sarah and Jos, joined now by Susannah, watched them disappear through the archway. Bentley shook his head. 'It seems to me young Tom needs a firm hand.' There was a note in his voice which hinted at disapproval, but then, thought Sarah, he did not know how very hard it was to be firm with Tom.

The gentle three-mile voyage along the canal to the tunnel would have been tranquil, had it not been for the children's noisy singing of rounds, interspersed with a great deal of giggling. 'Some visitors hire a band to play for them at the tunnel,' Jos said with a wry grin. 'I thought we'd have a little peace.'

As the canal wound its way about the contours of the land the valley narrowed and deepened, until the green slopes and

377

sheltering trees ran right down to the water's edge, closing them in – and there at last was the tunnel mouth. The children fell silent, as if awed by the darkness of the brick-framed archway in the hill, somehow looking far too small to admit anything so wide as a barge. The towpath came to an abrupt end.

'He has to leg us through,' explained Jos, as the boatman unhitched the horse and jumped on to the barge, reaching out with his arms to guide the boat through the archway and into the tunnel. Once inside, he stretched out flat on his back at the head of the barge and raised his legs so that his feet rested on the brick vault above; and then, slowly, laboriously, he began to 'walk' them through the tunnel, step by slow step.

'He's walking upside down!' Tom exclaimed with a nervous little giggle, but none of the other children said anything. Sarah could see a mixture of fascination and fear on the four young faces.

She felt Jos's hand close about hers where it lay on the cushioned seat between them, and knew he was neither afraid nor offering comfort but simply sharing something of his excitement with her; she could see the same excitement on Bentley's face.

At first it was quiet, but for the slap of water between barge and brickwork, and dim, though illuminated still by the bright daylight from the tunnel mouth. And then, slowly, steadily the light dwindled, no longer able to reach so far into the dark, and they lit the candles they had brought with them, sending a flickering furtive light flowing out to the seven wondering faces, throwing the tunnel around them into a greater darkness still. Far away, if they looked back, they could see the tiny glimmer of the tunnel mouth: 'Like a star,' said Tom suddenly, in a voice just a little rough and tremulous.

Now and then as the barge slid deeper into the hill strange echoing noises reached them, banging and hammering, calling; faint at first and then coming nearer; loud and clamorous and fading again – like voices heard in fever, Sarah thought.

'That's the miners at work, at Goldenhill colliery,' Jos explained, his voice reassuringly cheerful. 'The tunnels run down to join the canal.' It had been one reason for taking the

378

canal through the hill, to provide a link with the mine and so allow coal to be brought out easily and cheaply. Sometimes, Jos explained, there were disputes when coal barges clashed with other users of the canal, since there was no room for two vessels to pass. None of them wanted to imagine what that might be like, though Jos seemed unconcerned.

'There's no light at all, only the candles.' That was Susannah, her voice soft and wondering; and looking round they saw that she was right.

'What a subject for Wright to paint!' Bentley commented. 'Perhaps I'll suggest it to him.'

After what seemed a long time the tunnel exit came into sight, a tiny pinpoint of brightness in the distance. Sarah thought, with a twinge of compassion, that the boatman's legs must be aching unendurably by now. She hoped that the generous payment Jos planned at the end would be compensation enough. It was not a job she would have liked.

The daylight when they reached it was dazzling beyond words, making them blink and shade their eyes; but the warmth was wonderful after the chill dampness of the tunnel, and the ordinary everyday look of everything after the weird nightmare darkness.

'And now,' said Jos as the barge came to rest against the canal bank and the boatman jumped out to tie the mooring rope, and to lie for a time with obvious relief on the bank by the towpath, 'when our friend there is ready for us we shall go back again, if the tunnel's clear. One and three-quarter miles each way – and much of it cut through solid rock, liable to flood and full of evil gases – just think what a feat it was to build it all! The more so when you think nothing on this scale was ever done before.'

'What a pity Brindley never saw it finished,' commented Bentley. 'He would have been so proud of his achievement.

'What better memorial though than this canal? It has opened up the countryside to trade as nothing else could. The way things are going we'll soon be able to send goods by barge not only to Liverpool or Bristol or Hull, but anywhere in the country, including London. When I think how cut off we were from everywhere when I was a boy – with not even a road for wheeled vehicles this side of Newcastle – then I can hardly believe how much has changed.'

'A revolution,' agreed Bentley. 'A quiet one, and bloodless, but a revolution all the same.'

By the time they were once more at the southernmost end of the tunnel they had seen enough of darkness and brickwork gleaming with damp, and were content to relax in the sunlight as the plodding horse drew them the last leisurely miles to Etruria; even the children were quiet now.

There were two barges waiting for the tunnel: one held a party of sightseers, laughing and talking and entertained meanwhile by an inexpert band of musicians; and the other, empty now, was on its way to bring another load of coal to the hungry kilns of the pottery towns, as if to emphasise Jos's words about the benefits of the canal.

When they reached home there was still time before supper for Jos and Sarah to take Bentley to see the family portrait, set up on its easel by the long library windows. George Stubbs himself was still working on it: a big balding man in a brown painter's smock, who was very ready to put palette and brushes aside and point out to Bentley what he saw as the finer aspects of his painting. It showed – to the right – Jos and Sarah seated beneath a tree, with a black basalt vase at Jos's elbow and a kiln smoking gently in the distance; and a little behind, the four older children on horseback against a background of trees, with Mary Ann on the left in her baby carriage, pulled by Catherine and attended by young Sarah. Bentley studied the painting with care, made suitably courteous comments, and then they went to supper.

Later, once the children and their grandfather had gone to bed, Sarah and Jos and Bentley took chairs on to the sun-warmed flagstones in front of the house and sat there, with the men's pipesmoke scenting the quiet air and the blue darkness of the evening closing gently about them.

'Now, let's hear your honest unvarnished opinion,' said Jos at last. 'What do you think of our portrait?'

Bentley thought for a moment, and then said slowly, 'Well, of course, it's not quite finished, as you pointed out. However, taking that into account, it's a fine piece, of course. The horses are magnificent, full of life and character . . .'

Sarah gurgled with laughter and he grinned at her. 'As for the riders, I think the little girls quite well caught, and the

380

boys. But I see none of Susannah's bright spirit in her figure . . . and you two look lamentably wooden – you, Sarah, in particular.'

'I wonder if we mightn't have done better with Wright after all. His painting of you was very fine.'

'I love the way he uses light,' Sarah put in. 'We intend to commission something from him one day anyway, though I can't help wishing we'd waited until he was available to come here. But still, perhaps Mr Stubbs will put right the deficiencies before he's done.'

'If he doesn't, it will still be a fine picture. I'm only so particular because I know and love you all so well. I suppose too I regret that you will have no painted record of your Etruscan school at work. Such a notable experiment should not go unrecorded. The children certainly look as though they thrive on it. I'm only sorry that coming in holiday time I'll not see it in action.'

'Try talking French to them – even to little Kitty – and you'll need no other recommendation.' Jos's voice was full of pride.

'Young Monsieur Potet was a good idea then? But did you not mention some problem at one stage?'

Jos nodded, and Sarah explained, 'Being so very little older than the children he'd no idea of discipline. He'd fool around with them, and then find they were quite out of control – we discovered he was trying to assert his authority by striking them. Of course, we'd have none of that.'

'Indeed no. Neither Sarah nor I nor any of our servants has ever struck any of our children, and we don't allow anyone else to do so either. However, we both had a talk to him, gave him a hint how to go on, and he's managed better ever since, I'm glad to say. But dear me, he's a shy young man – hardly says a word to anyone but the children.'

'Though he did come to confide in me during the late anti-Catholic riots. He was terrified that he'd be attacked in the street.'

'Did the trouble reach you here then? I thought it was a peculiarity of the London authorities to let a mob loot and burn for ten days without lifting a finger.'

'Unfortunately, that was long enough for us to be infected,' said Jos. 'The colliers and potters got together and talked of

381

marching on the Grange – they're Roman Catholics there of course, with a chapel the mob had designs on.'

'And our poor Monsieur Potet was close to tears one day. On his way here he'd heard someone say, "There goes the Frenchman – we'll kill him first." He was all for hurrying back to France at once. But then mercifully the mob in London was quelled, and things settled down again here too. Which is just as well – I shouldn't like to think of the poor lad going home with tales of how the English are a lawless people who beat up foreigners and papists and anyone they don't much care for.'

'No.' Bentley drew thoughtfully on his pipe for a little while, and then said, 'It's a sad reversal, isn't it? Once the French were so tyrannically ruled that they held up the peace and liberty and prosperity of England as an example of what ought to be – and now Monsieur Neckar and his master King Louis are working such wonders in the way of reform across the channel there's no telling where it will end. It has a long way to go, of course, before they have even as little freedom as we have – but it's a considerable step in the right direction.'

'Perhaps it will be the signal for great things here too – perhaps your society for constitutional reform will have its way and persuade our rulers to bring in universal suffrage and annual parliaments.'

Bentley's expression matched the scepticism in Jos's tone. 'I fear that will be a long time coming, my friend. At present we seem to be tumbling headlong back into the Dark Ages. War has a dangerous effect on governments, I think – they become terrified even of the breath of liberty. I fear that our poor anti-slavery campaign is doomed for the time being. Losing America only makes our ministers more anxious to hang on to the West Indies, with all their dubious privileges. And over here any kind of freedom is seen as a threat and not a glory.'

There was a moment of rather gloomy silence, which Jos broke by saying cheerfully, 'Let's forget all our troubles and enjoy our Etruscan peace as if the rest of the world had nothing to do with us. All we need to worry about is whether it will rain before the last of the hay is in.'

'Ah, then I am in time to play the farmer,' said Bentley. 'I thought I might be too late after all the fine weather we've had.'

'There are two fields still with hay to be gathered in. So if that's your wish, we'll have a day in the fields tomorrow.'

In the two highest meadows of the Etruria estate the last of the hay was cocked over wooden tripods to dry in the sun, dun-coloured and aromatic against an intensely blue sky. They all trooped up the hill towards these conical silhouettes, dotting the heights where on another summer day almost exactly twenty-nine years ago Jos and Sarah and Kate had ridden to the fair. It had been open moorland then, where now Jos's new-laid hedges sheltered the meadows; and Jos had been workless, frail, full of doubts, and Sarah burning with indignation on his behalf; and Kate, dear loving Kate, had been filled with thoughts of the man she would meet at the journey's end – that same man who, loved and respected to the end of a long life, had died and left her to a bitter grief, which after two years seemed to have lessened only a little.

It was hard now to imagine what the hillside had been like then, when the valley was a quiet green emptiness and there were no works, no canal busy with barges, no rows of cottages, no bustle glimpsed far off through the young trees. And no Bentley, that essential partner to their lives and their love.

Today it seemed as if they were young again, carefree and happy as perhaps they had never been then. Bentley, unused to country life, did his best to help with the stacking and loading of the hay to be carried to the barns, but so ineptly that they laughed and teased him. He took it in good part, hobbling comically along as if it had all been too much for his back, grumbling with a contradictory grin that Jos and Sarah were unreasonable task masters.

At midday work ceased, and ale and bread and great hams were brought from the home farm – that very Ridge House that they had passed long ago, when Sarah had imagined herself its mistress, never dreaming that she would one day be mistress of a far greater house. They sat with the labourers in the shade of three tall sycamores in the corner of the field, to eat and drink; and Bentley made up a silly song about the haymaking Wedgwoods, going through each member of the family verse by verse right down to Mary Ann (the only absent member, left at home with Jane), and adding a rollicking chorus that they all joined in with increasingly hysterical laughter.

Afterwards, as the heat grew more intense, the adults

stretched out to doze while the children ran off to chase each other, squealing and laughing and tossing the remnants of hay – even Susannah, who was in general far too much the lady for such frivolity.

When dusk came the last of the hay was safely in. Bentley swung the sleepy children on to the cart and took the reins in his hands and drove them home, with Jos perched on one side of him and Sarah on the other. The children slept as the cart rattled and rocked its way down the hill beneath an arching sky pricked with stars where the blue was deepest, and edged at the rim with palest green. The air was cool now, yet soft with the lingering glow of the day, scented with hay and the warmer closer smells of horse and harness and work-weary humans.

They none of them spoke, though Bentley sang a little song under his breath, the happy formless notes keeping time with the clop of the horse's hoofs, the rattle of the wheels on hard earth and the jingle of harness. Sarah sat with his warmth against her, her hand linked in Jos's behind his back, so that they formed a perfect trio, united and complete. Tonight her senses were wide awake, aware of every smell, every sound, every touch, and loving them all. She thought she had never felt so alive, so perfectly and completely happy. Any more, and she would have burst for joy.

Two days later Bentley, his pale townsman's skin just a little tanned by the sun, took his leave of them again.

'One day you must come for a real stay,' Jos told him firmly, as they embraced. 'After all, remember you should really have been our neighbour.'

'I'm that in my heart and always will be,' he said, his glance taking in both of them; and then he came to kiss Sarah. 'Thank you both for giving me so much happiness in these few days as will last me for all the next six months at least – and certainly until we meet again.' The kiss, she thought, was softer, just a little more lingering than usual.

'If that's how you feel, we should have made you less happy, so you'd have had to come back the sooner,' Jos teased him.

And then their friend was in the coach, waving as it moved away. Jos pulled Sarah's arm through his. 'Sometimes I think too much of life is spent in parting.'

'But logically then the same amount of time is given to meeting, so that's not so bad, is it?'

'Except,' said Jos with sudden gloom, 'that the parting has the last word in the end.'

Sarah squeezed his arm. 'Come on, Jos, don't spoil a happy time. It's not so very long to Christmas – the Bentleys will be here then, if it's humanly possible.'

The November wind set the rain lashing against the windows, rattling the casements, whining through every nook and cranny. Even with curtains pulled close to shut out the wild night, the noise of the storm still reached them, and the chill thin threads of cold air curled about ankles and ears, penetrating and relentless. Richard Wedgwood huddled over the smoking library fire, wrapped in a rug and coughing rather more than necessary to emphasise his discomfort and call on his daughter's sympathy. Sarah knew quite well that it was company and attention he wanted, to take his mind off the raging of the elements and reassure him that everything was still safe and normal and orderly. In the end, because she was busy and because Susannah seemed as uneasy as Richard Wedgwood, she sent her daughter to read to him, thus calming and occupying them both.

She wished it was as easy to calm her own restlessness. There was no excuse for it, as she had countless duties awaiting her attention, but somehow she could settle to none of them. She hated the storm. It had been blowing now for two whole days, toppling trees, loosening slates, flattening the last of Jos's flowers in the garden, and she wished it would end. She wished too, even more, that Jos was not still out in it, riding home from his latest navigation committee meeting at Stafford.

'You're being silly, Sarah,' she told herself severely. It was not like her to worry just because Jos was out in bad weather; travelling as much as he did, that was inevitable and not in the least unusual. But her unease persisted, a dread of something hanging over them, some terrible accident perhaps.

She ordered supper early, settled the little ones to bed with a soothing story, gathered the older members of the family into the drawing room for cards and music. She had hoped for one of the light-hearted laughing evenings that often developed when they were together, but some spark seemed to be lacking tonight – perhaps because Jos was absent.

Her father and the children went to bed at last, and peace settled over the house – no, she amended, not peace, but a kind of quiet within the storm, and a quiet that only seemed to jar her nerves the more. She wandered about from room to room, checking a window fastening here, straightening a cushion or a curtain there. She made up the fire in their bedroom, tidying the covers on the already tidy bed where she and Jos would sleep later, when he came home – if he came home.

Trying to drive out such thoughts she went downstairs again, to the morning room where the letter which had come for Jos today stood propped above the jasperware panel set into the chimneypiece. She gazed at the panel, distracted for a moment by its beauty. Jos was right to be proud of this new ware, the crisp definition of Flaxman's white dancing figures clean and pure against the hard unpolished surface of the coloured body beneath. This one was made in the blue he liked best, a soft restrained colour whose blueness was not that of sky or sea, distant hills or spring flowers, and yet seemed to hold in itself the essence of them all.

Tonight, though, even the thought of the work that had captivated her all her life could not really distract her. She sat down for a while, but could not settle to reading a book; she played briefly on the harpsichord; she threw logs on the fire, examined every ornament, looked out of the window at every sound that might be Jos coming home. But it was always just the wind.

And then at long last after what seemed hours she heard that familiar uneven step in the hall. She jumped up and ran to him and flung her arms about him with a desperation that nearly threw him off balance, and set him laughing.

'What's all this then? I've only been gone two days, love!' He held her a little away from him to look in her face. 'What's wrong?'

She shook her head, so swept by relief that she was shaking. 'I just had this feeling you'd met with an accident – I don't know why – it was silly.'

He looked so fine tonight, she thought, gazing at him as if

386

for the first time – fifty years old, yet upright, square-shouldered, muscular, vigorous, his tanned skin scarcely lined except at the corners of the clear eyes, and there only because smiling and laughter were so much a part of him.

He laughed now, and hugged her to him again. 'Well, I'm home and hale and hearty and in need of supper. So I hope you've left me some.'

'I'll ring at once.' She spoke demurely, but felt ridiculously light-hearted as she went to the bell.

They sat together by the fire in the morning room while he ate, and she watched him all the time, as if she could not look at him enough now she knew she had him safe. Only halfway through his meal did she remember the letter and pass it to him. For an instant his face lit in the familiar way, and then clouded again.

'Not Bentley.' But then that was not really to be expected, since they had heard only two days ago. He opened the letter without haste and spread it before him, reading with half an eye as he lifted a slice of ham to his mouth; and then, abruptly, he froze into utter immobility.

The glow had drained from his face, leaving it a dreadful clay-white.

'Jos . . .?'

He looked up with a kind of bewilderment, as if he had forgotten where he was; and then he pushed the letter towards her.

It was from Ralph Griffiths, near neighbour of Bentley in London. 'When I called this morning I found Mr Bentley very poorly indeed,' she read. 'The doctor seemed greatly alarmed – his life is feared for.' For a moment she herself could not breathe, as if something had tightened harshly about her chest. Then she said quietly, 'You'll go to him.'

Jos nodded, pushing his plate aside and rising a little unsteadily to his feet. 'Now, at once,' he said.

'Not tonight, love – it's too wild a night. Rest now and be ready to leave as soon as it's light.'

He shook his head. 'The rain's easing: there'll be enough moonlight I think. I must go.'

She knew she could not make him change his mind; nor, if she were honest, did she wish to do so. She hurried to pack a bag for him, and ordered food to be made ready; and within an hour the four horses were harnessed to the coach in the stable yard.

He held her to him as if he could hardly bear to leave her. 'Pray for the best – I'll let you know.'

'As soon as he's fit, bring him here for a good long holiday,' she said with a brisk cheerfulness that was utterly hollow. It did not reach Jos either, for he said no more, only kissed her again and climbed into the coach.

She stood there in the wind until long after he had gone, staring into the lantern-lit dark with her cloak pulled tight about her and her mind concentrated into a single wordless prayer.

It was six days before she heard, and then there was just a hurried scrawl, not from Jos, but from Griffiths again. 'Mr Bentley died on Sunday. Mr Wedgwood remains for the funeral on Saturday next.' Sarah stood for a long time with the letter in her hand, staring across the shaft of thin winter sunlight without seeing it or anything on which it rested in their elegant dining room.

'Dead,' she thought. 'Bentley is dead.' Somewhere she supposed the sense of it went home, for she felt a sharp pain dart through the surrounding numbness, almost physical in its intensity. With it came an odd conviction that out there, beyond the boundaries of Etruria Hall, there was nothing but a void. The universe had shrunk to this little space, enclosing all she had left.

Except Jos – her thoughts flew to him. In her mind she went back with him through the past few days: through that stormy Saturday night, the calmer Sunday which followed, the next night; and the day after, which was the soonest he could have been there. She felt the tension stretching his nerves through the long hours of the journey, when he could do nothing but wait and fear; and then, at the last, he had come too late.

He had been left no time in which to hold his friend's hand or exchange a last few whispered words; but had been met instead by the blind windows that told him everything, the hushed voices, the still figure on the shrouded bed. So short a time ago that figure had been his friend, and was now an empty shrunken husk from which all that had given it life had gone for ever, beyond his reach; like one of the fireworks blazing up into the night sky to celebrate the opening of Etruria, spending itself in a brief breathtaking brilliance and then extinguished, leaving only a darkness the deeper for its going.

It was Jos's pain she shared now in her own – the terrible tearing wordless anguish of new grief. They talked of mourning when someone died: it was a sorrowful word, sad, heavy, languid with loss. But it had nothing to do with this first shocking moment of unbearable pain that was like being torn in pieces, a torment without limit or hope or light or ease. She wanted to scream or shout, drum her fists on the wall, rage at the darkness until some answer came, some response. But there was only a cold howling emptiness, and Jos was far away in the same desperate solitude, and her searching spirit could not hope to reach him over the miles.

This storm was all inside, for when the girl came to clear the breakfast things she saw only her mistress standing very still near the window with a letter in her hand; and she murmured an apology for the interruption and turned to go.

Sarah stirred as if waking from a nightmare – though from this nightmare there was no waking – and said quietly, 'It's all right, Jenny. You can clear in here now.' Her voice was as calm and unemotional as always, controlled and full of quiet authority. It astonished her that it could be so, when she felt as if nothing of the old Sarah was left.

But it was the old Sarah who took her through the next few days, keeping the news from the children until Jos should be home, directing the household so that there was no interruption to the usual routine. Underneath, she was scarcely aware of what she was doing. It was as if she were adrift in some dark underworld, while the shell of her body went through the motions of daily life like an automaton.

Then at last, the funeral over, Jos came home. Sarah was there at the door when the coach drew to a halt, watching as the footman opened the door; and the bent shrunken grey old man stepped down, slowly, stumbling a little, so that the footman had to reach out and support him.

An old man. Her Jos, who had gone through life with his head held high, whatever the pain and hardship and endless grinding hard work; Jos who could even limp with a spring in his step. Just for an instant she did not know him.

Then with a cry she ran to him and threw her arms about him. She felt his body shake convulsively; and then at last her own tears came and they clung together, weeping for what they had lost.

CHAPTER EIGHTEEN

1781

The wind had risen by the time Sarah made her way home from the works, blowing from the north-west to drag at her cloak and her skirts, and tear the last of the leaves from the trees in the park. She bent her head and pushed against it, plodding steadily on up the hill.

There were wild leaden clouds rushing across with the wind, promising a stormy night. November, and storms – just as there had been almost a full year ago, when the news came. It was only a year, but it seemed half a lifetime since she had last known a day free of this heavy dreary weight on her spirit.

The works offered some solace to her because she was needed and busy there, now Jos took so little interest. When he went to the works it was to shut himself in his new and splendidly equipped laboratory, assisted by Alexander Chisholm, the Scottish chemist who had come in the spring to act as his secretary. Chisholm's coming had shut Sarah out from Jos's experiments, but knowing that the Scot could give help of enormous value, and that only in the laboratory did Jos seem able to forget for a little time his grief for his friend, Sarah could not resent it.

Jos would be at home by now, for Chisholm had undertaken as usual to spend an hour or two this afternoon working on some simple experiments with the boys. She knew where she would find her husband – in the old laboratory below all his study, only she would not disturb him there if she could help it. He did not seem to want her company much these days.

At the moment of Bentley's death it had seemed as if the shared grief would unite them as never before. But those first moments of closeness had been the last. Jos had wept only once to her knowledge, for those few minutes on his return from London. Then, for a little while, he had been quite

391

seriously ill. She had nursed him tenderly, trying to encourage him to talk of his dead friend because she knew that would help them both; but Jos seemed totally unable to share his grief. Even when he was well again, but for frequent blinding headaches, he would not let her help.

Steadily, relentlessly, he had shut her out, shut everyone out as far as his feelings were concerned. He shut them out literally and physically too, outside the locked door of laboratory or study, as if afraid to risk any demands on his emotions. Worst of all, he had taken to sleeping in a separate room, excluding Sarah from his bed as from everything else. The excuse was that he slept badly and kept Sarah wakeful too, but though it was true that did not lessen the hurt. When she mentioned her anxiety – in a general way – to Dr Darwin, he said only that Jos still needed her and that she must not break.

She had not broken, and nor would she, but it had been a terrible year, and the end was not yet in sight. She could only go doggedly on as if nothing was wrong, ready for the moment when Jos should turn to her again. The works were her solace, as the laboratory was Jos's, but it was hard to come home at the end of the day and feel that horrible sense of oppression as soon as she stepped through the door of her own house.

She let herself in by the side door from the orchard, since the main hall was chaotic with builders (the work on the new wings was taking a long time), and slipped into the little cloakroom to remove her outdoor clothes. As usual the boys, coming in earlier from a ride, had left their coats in an untidy heap on the floor. She would have to speak to them about it again – sometimes she thought having servants to tidy up after them was bad for the children. She gathered the garments together and hung them on the appropriate pegs, and then she paused, studying the row of coats and cloaks.

There was an unfamiliar greatcoat at the far end, and with it an unpretentious black beaver hat, rather worn, and a pair of old but well-polished top boots. She stared at them for a moment or two, and then realised they were not after all unfamiliar – they belonged to Monsieur Potet. But it was by now four o'clock, and he should have left the house two hours ago when Chisholm came to give his chemistry lessons. 'Unless

I've forgotten something,' she conceded to herself; but the new arrangement had stood for some weeks now, and she could think of no reason why today should be different, unless perhaps Potet had felt a sudden urge to study a little chemistry himself.

On her way to the schoolroom to investigate, Sarah looked into the library in case her father was there. He was not, and the room was in near darkness, the fire almost out. She went in to revive it, and to draw the curtains; and halfway across the room was startled by a sudden movement from the most shadowy corner.

She looked sharply round, peering into the darkness. 'Who's that?'

No one replied, but she could hear rapid breathing, like that of someone frightened – or perhaps . . .

By now she had made out two figures, close together but standing just apart, one a man, the other wearing pale muslin that gleamed faintly in the dark.

'Susannah! What are you doing?' And then she did not need to ask. The fire, flaring suddenly into life, lit two flushed guilty faces: her daughter's, and that of Monsieur Potet.

For an instant longer she stared at them, and they at her; and then the young Frenchman made a stiff little bow. 'I must make my apologies, Madame.' She ignored him, and turned instead to her daughter. 'Go to your room, Susannah.'

She thought Susannah was about to protest – perhaps Susannah did too, for she looked her mother defiantly in the eye and opened her mouth. But no sound came, and she closed it again and quietly, head bent, left the room with none of her usual tripping lightness of step.

Sarah checked that the door was firmly closed and came back to Potet, who had emerged from the shadows to face her before the fire. He was not flushed now but pale, his wide, rather full mouth pressed into an unusually hard line, as if to force himself to be brave. If John or Josiah or Tom had looked like that, Sarah would have relented at once, whatever their misdemeanour; but she was too shaken by what she had seen – or rather, by wondering what she had not seen and into what undesirable paths the tutor had led her young daughter – to feel anything but anger towards him.

'Monsieur Potet, you are in a position of trust within this household . . .'

Again he made a stiff little bow, and said with a clipped gravity somewhat belied by the gentle sadness of his brown eyes, 'I understand, Madame – I am dismissed.'

Sarah did not like the feeling that he had taken the initiative; but she simply said quickly, 'Don't be hasty, Monsieur. If it comes to that, it will only be after due discussion with Mr Wedgwood, who must, of course, be told.' What would Jos say? He was so unpredictable these days. He was as likely to treat the subject with complete indifference as to burst into a terrible rage. She wished it were possible – or right – for her to deal with the matter without telling him.

She returned her attention to the young Frenchman, with a slight softening of her tone. 'Perhaps you had better tell me exactly what was going on just now – and what led up to it. I realise I may have jumped to an unwarranted conclusion – but under no circumstances is it right for you to be alone in the dark with my daughter. I am astonished that you should have permitted such a ᛿hing to happen.'

He coloured fierily under the penetrating severity of her gaze. 'I have been at fault, Madame – but I meant no insult to Miss Susannah. It was from the heart . . .'

The simplicity of that declaration did touch her, but she would not let him see it. Instead, she pursued relentlessly, 'That is no excuse, and you know it. Nor does it answer my question.'

She had not thought his fair skin could absorb any more colour, but it did. His eyes fell, and he gave all the appearance of painful embarrassment. 'There has been nothing, Madame – one kiss only, now. I forget myself, to my great shame.'

Sarah sighed. His distress was evident enough, and she believed him. But what of Susannah? 'One kiss only' was no trivial matter, if you were sixteen and had never been kissed like that before.

'Go home, Monsieur Potet, and I will send for you as soon as a decision is made. Until then you had better remain in your lodgings.'

He bowed again, and with a murmured, 'Good day,

Madame,' left the room, youthful unhappiness in every awkward step.

'Poor lad,' thought Sarah, in spite of herself. Perhaps it was natural that Susannah should have warmed to him. There was a mere four years between them, and he was gentle and friendless and a long way from home; and not unattractive, in a youthful and rather ineffectual manner. Susannah would have felt able to befriend him without suspecting any risk to herself. But it had been at the least a grave misdemeanour on the tutor's part to have taken advantage of that simplicity, if, of course, that was how it had happened.

She found Susannah sitting on the window seat in her bedroom, very still and gazing out on the uncurtained darkness beyond the window. She must have heard the door open, but she did not look round; and for a little while Sarah said nothing but simply looked at her daughter, trying to see in that demure and maidenly figure some clue to this evening's incident.

She found it without trying very hard. It seemed extraordinary now that she had not realised it was almost inevitable, in the circumstances. But then a mother in daily contact with her children is often the last person to realise that they are growing up. She had known, of course, that there was much of the young lady in Susannah: the veneer of poise and social grace on her high-spirited youthfulness was what gave her such charm. But physically too she was fast becoming a woman. She was slender still, a slight girlish figure whose breasts were small and hips narrow – but they were there for all that, giving a softness and shape to the simple girlish white muslin. She had a glow about her also, in the warm tint of the creamy skin and the eager light in her blue eyes, which hinted at a bubbling vitality beneath the surface polish that her schooling had given her.

Put a girl like this – warm-hearted and impulsive as she was – for hours at a time under the same roof as the lonely young foreigner she had confronted downstairs, and such an outcome as this was not only unsurprising but utterly predictable. And Sarah suspected now that all the blame had not after all been on the tutor's side. If Susannah was physically no longer an awkward angular child, then emotionally too she had very likely left the uncomplicated simplicity of childhood behind – that simplicity which once her mother had envied, seeing her little girl in Bentley's arms. But she did not want to think of that now . . .

'Susannah!'

The girl did look round then, as her mother approached. She coloured a little, but managed still to retain a look of untouched tranquillity as if all this had nothing to do with her. Sarah felt a tremor of doubt. How innocent had Susannah been? Was Potet the kind of man to take advantage of a girl wholly guiltless of leading him on? She doubted it, and watching her daughter just now she had been sure that the responsibility had been shared. Yet . . .

She sat down near Susannah on the window seat, gravely examining the serene young face. 'Well, what have you to say for yourself?'

The volatile colour spread from the white lawn ruff at her neck to the roots of her fair hair, and made her seem a child again. 'Should I have anything to say, Mama?' The note of defiance was muted, just a little unsure of itself, but it was enough to stir a momentary irritation to life in Sarah. She controlled it, however, and said as calmly as she could, 'It is not generally regarded as proper behaviour to be found kissing your tutor.'

A tiny dimple appeared in Susannah's cheek, echoed by a tentative sparkle in her eyes. 'Would it be acceptable if I'd not been found, Mama?' she asked, very softly but with a sly sideways tilt of the head.

'Don't be impertinent!' Sarah spoke more mildly than she felt. 'You know what I mean.'

The next moment all trace of lightness had gone from Susannah. She sprang to her feet and stood facing her mother, red-faced and deadly serious. 'Why should I not kiss him, Mama? What's wrong with a kiss?'

'Do you really think a young girl's kisses are to be given so lightly, without thought? What do you suppose Monsieur Potet felt about it?'

'I *know* what he felt about it. And it was not given lightly. You don't really think I'm that kind of girl, surely?' She bent her head, so that Sarah could scarcely hear her last whispered words. 'You see, I love him – and he loves me . . .'

Sarah sighed. 'Oh Susannah! What can you possibly know of love?'

And then she fell silent, struck by an astonishing realisation: 'I knew. I knew when I was half Susannah's age that I loved Jos, with an unquestioning certainty that all the pains and griefs and betrayals of a lifetime have not been able to shake. What right have I so lightly to reject the possibility that Susannah too knows what it is to love, however undesirable that love may be?'

It was too late to withdraw her dismissive exclamation, and it had already hurt her daughter. 'I am not a child, Mama,' she said with dignity, looking reproachfully at her mother. 'I have given my heart, and that is that.'

There was some reassurance in the flowery phrase, which sounded as if it had been chosen as much for its poetic flavour as its content – it might have come from a novel. Sarah thought that she could never have spoken like that about her feelings for Jos. What had she said, faced with an angry father all those years ago? As far as she could remember there had been no dramatic declaration of love, no impassioned plea, but only a simple assertion that one day she would marry Jos. It was all she had felt was necessary, for the rest was so much grounded in reality that it did not need to be explained or questioned. It had not been a matter of romance; romance, even in its deepest sense of an overwhelming passion, had been unknown to her before that autumn afternoon in Buxton.

But it would be wrong to assume that, because Susannah sounded more like a lovesick schoolgirl than a young woman deeply in love, that was all there was to it. And if it was only that, it was real and painful enough to her at present. Sarah would not make the mistake her own parents had done, and drive Susannah into rebellion.

She was silent for quite a long time and when she spoke at last it was very gently, choosing her words with the utmost care. 'Susannah my dear, if you let Monsieur Potet believe that anything more than an agreeable friendship is possible between you, then you are being unfair to him. You are very young still. You will grow older and change . . .'

'Never!' Susannah burst out fiercely. 'Not in that, never! I shall always love him – and I have told him so!' Her eyes were defiant, daring her mother to rage at her for such unconventional behaviour. But Sarah did not rage.

'It is possible that you may go on loving him,' she acknowledged, a little to Susannah's disappointment, she suspected wryly. 'Certainly a love that endures through time and difficulty is not to be taken lightly. If your love is real . . .'

'It is! It is!'

'Then no amount of separation will destroy it, and in that case one day we shall have to give the whole matter serious consideration. But it would be very wrong of me to allow you at your age to tie yourself for ever to a penniless tutor, however agreeable he may be. It would also be wrong of you to give Monsieur Potet the impression that this is a possibility. Whatever has begun between you must be ended.'

Susannah gazed at her with stricken eyes. 'But I can't, Mama – I can't just shut out what I feel!'

'No one's asking you to, my dear. Only that you should take care never to be alone with Monsieur Potet, never to place yourself in a position where what happened today might happen again. It may sound hard, but you can do it, I know.'

Susannah bit her lip. 'But François . . .?'

It took Sarah a moment or two to realise who François was – she did not think she had ever heard Monsieur Potet's Christian name before. That more than anything else told her how far matters had gone between the two young people.

'Susannah,' she said gravely, 'in very many households a tutor found as he was today would have been instantly dismissed, in disgrace and without a reference. If I did not believe that no harm was intended, and that you were as much to blame as he, then I would have had no hesitation in doing exactly that. As it is, I think it might be better if he were to move without scandal to another post. However, we shall see. But any more misbehaviour of this kind will make his dismissal certain. Do you understand?'

Susannah nodded miserably. 'Yes, Mama.'

Sarah rose and drew the girl to her side, hugging her briefly. 'That's my good lass,' she said, and then left her, sorry for the heartache – however short-lived it might prove to be – that her daughter must suffer.

She went at once to speak to Jos, though whether he would listen to her she did not know. She could be certain of nothing with Jos these days, except that he existed for the

398

most part in some far gloomy place where she could not reach him. Perhaps this news of his most dearly loved child would shake him out of himself, bring him back to the world she inhabited; but she did not really allow herself to hope so.

He was not, after all, locked in his laboratory, or she hoped not, for it was the study door that was locked, and she had no means of making him hear if he was below the trap door. She knocked briskly.

There was no reply, so she bent her head close to the door, listening: no sound at all, of any kind. She knocked again, more sharply this time.

She heard the scrape of a chair on the carpeted floor, and then Jos's slow halting step coming near. The key turned and the door opened, and Jos stood staring at her with the blank unfocussed look of a man disturbed but not yet brought fully out of whatever reverie had absorbed him. Behind him the room was in darkness, though the curtains had not been drawn.

'Jos, something rather awkward has happened . . .'

His eyes settled on her face, their gaze sharpening a little; and then he shrugged and drew back, holding the door wide for her to pass.

She went to the table and lit the candle there, and then pulled the curtains across the window. The fire, she saw, was all but out. He must have been sitting here for hours, unaware of cold or dark or anything but his thoughts. There was a letter spread open on the table facing the chair, as if he had been reading it; but it must have been a long time since he had been able to see what was written.

She looked at him, standing facing her just inside the closed door, and watching her with his old man's eyes in his old man's face, tired, hopeless, without life. She could not grow used to it, even after a year. She still felt her heart give a painful, pitiful twist.

'Mary Bentley,' he said at last, so suddenly that she was startled. She realised that he was looking now at the letter, answering her unspoken question. 'Or rather Griffiths, on her behalf. She needs help. See for yourself.'

Sarah took up the letter and read it through, and was left with a vivid poignant picture of the widow, broken and close to despair. Her physical needs were few, Griffiths said, but the money left to her at Bentley's death was dwindling fast, and the rest of a considerable fortune was tied up in the beautiful vases and bas-reliefs and other unsold products of the Wedgwood and Bentley partnership. He did not want anxiety or hardship to be added to her other troubles.

'Poor woman,' said Sarah, finding it hard to imagine how anyone, however burdened by grief, could be so helpless in practical things as to have to find others to act on her behalf. Yet that was unfair: her own grief was as deep and as real, and she knew only too well the temptation to abandon oneself to despair. If it had not been for the house and the works and the family perhaps she might have done so. And she had only to look at Jos's grey face to see there the mirror of Mary Bentley's sorrow.

'What do you think?' she asked, knowing that he would shrink from facing the question. 'The thing is, she's not able to keep up any involvement in the business, nor does she wish to – and without that there'll be no income. It seems to me the best course would be to sell the share of the assets that is not yours – Bentley's share, I mean.' Why could she still not say his name without pain? 'That should give her a reasonable competence to live on. She'll still have the income from his canal shares too.'

'Yes,' said Jos slowly, his tone as colourless as ever. 'I expect you're right.'

She came to his side and laid a hand on his shoulder, trying, as so often before, to reach him with a measure of comfort; and knowing, as always, that she had failed. 'We shall have to go to London,' she told him. 'I think it's something we must supervise ourselves.'

He did not seem to want to listen to her. 'I'm well on with the work on my pyrometer,' was all he said. 'I hope to have a paper to present to the Royal Society next spring.'

'I'm glad.' Why was there no note of triumph in his voice, no hope, no joy? 'But you'll make even better progress once this business is over. Don't you think this is the right moment for Tom Byerley to come to London too? If he settles himself in well at Greek Street then he'll be able to marry soon.'

Only yesterday Byerley had pleaded with her to make Jos take some action in the matter. During his travels as salesman for the firm he had met a congenial Derbyshire girl and had

400

suddenly lost the urge to wander. Jos had spoken – prompted by Sarah – of making him responsible for the Greek Street enterprise, and he was eager to establish himself there and create a home fit for the bride of his choice. But Jos could not bear to think of anyone taking what had been Bentley's place, and he had consistently refused to give the necessary thought to the matter. Now he said, 'Yes, I suppose so.'

Set against the enormity of the task that faced them, the problem of Susannah seemed suddenly of little importance. Sarah decided in the end to settle the matter alone. There was no time to do more than warn Monsieur Potet to behave himself – leaving the question of his future to a later date – and despatch Susannah to stay with the Darwins during their absence. It would be Susannah's first visit since Dr Darwin had married a wealthy widow and settled in Derby, and so there would be sufficient interest in it to divert the girl's attention from the misery of parting from her François. Sarah did, once, try to explain to Jos the reasons for her action. 'But I might as well have saved my breath,' she thought afterwards, with some bitterness. He had heard her in silence, his expression opaque, and then walked away to find Alexander Chisholm and give him some directions concerning the laboratory.

Once before when she had come to Bentley's house, Sarah had thought it looked both the same as always and yet utterly, irrevocably changed. She thought so again this time – and looked back on the selfish misery of that earlier visit with shame and almost with regret. Now, that earlier change after his marriage seemed an entirely happy one in retrospect, a change for the good, set against this.

There were still the well-proportioned rooms, the air of comfort and simplicity; the same curtains and carpets and furnishings, the rows of books, the ornaments; even the same polished cleanliness, the vases of flowers, the tea at the fireside when they arrived.

And there was nothing tangible of which Sarah could say, '*that* is what is wrong'; merely an absence that took all life from the house.

Perhaps though that absence was not after all complete. Every now and then, hearing approaching steps, she would

401

look up expecting to see Bentley come into the room where she sat, to set her heart fluttering and to delight her with his talk. Once, doing so, her eyes met Jos's and she realised with a little shock that he too had been ready to turn with a smile to greet his friend. She saw the anguish that followed and knew it echoed her own. She reached out then and took his hand and held it, and they sat in silence, not quite weeping, and closer than they had been for a very long time.

They found Mary Bentley broken, defeated, a pale wraith in black bombazine haunting that shell of a house. She welcomed them, soft-voiced, and poured tea, and did all that was proper; but often she would melt into tears and always she hung close to Sarah, as if comforted by her strength and calmness. Where Jos – but for that one occasion – withdrew into himself, Mary Bentley talked incessantly. In any other circumstances Sarah would have found it too much for her over-strung nerves to cope with; but during the last long silent year the need to talk to someone close to her of the man she had loved had been at times almost unbearable, and to be able to share Mary's grief and her memories was a great comfort. But she saw to her pain that always when the subject came up, Jos would leave them, going out to wander in the streets or shut himself in their room upstairs. They shared a bed here in Bentley's house, but it only served to emphasise the separation between them. Perhaps, Sarah thought bitterly, it was better after all to sleep apart than in this apparent closeness which turned their isolation of spirit into a greater torment than ever. But she could not help hoping that she might by some touch or caress be able to come a little nearer to him again.

Tom Byerley, clearly relieved to be settled at last, handled the arrangements for the sale at Christie's fashionable Pall Mall auction room with quiet efficiency, though Jos also went to help him sort out the goods to be sold. It was Jos who decided that all the joint Wedgwood and Bentley stock – and not simply half of it – should be cleared. Mary Bentley was touched, and wept again when he told her of the decision.

'He would have done the same,' said Jos abruptly, and then turned away and rapidly leafed through the pages of a book pulled at random from the shelves. It was the first time Sarah had heard him speak of Bentley for many months.

It was Jos too who placed the advertisement which appeared some days later in the London papers. 'Mr WEDGWOOD having had the misfortune to lose his much lamented friend, and partner, Mr BENTLEY, has found it necessary (in concurrence with the wishes of Mrs Bentley, the widow) to dispose of their joint stock by Public Auction by Christie and Ansell at their Great Room (late the Royal Academy) on Monday December 12, 1781, and on the eleven following week days, in 2,200 lots. The Nature and Quality of the Ornaments made by Wedgwood and Bentley are generally known throughout Europe, as well as in the these kingdoms . . .' Sarah, reading it, smiled a little sadly at the burst of justifiable pride which Jos, even in his grief, had not quite been able to resist. It showed, she thought, that the man she had known and loved was still there somewhere beneath the irritable and taciturn figure who sometimes seemed to have taken him over entirely.

It was decided that on the day of the sale's opening Sarah should stay with Mary Bentley, since the widow so clearly needed her company; and she accepted the arrangement with the best grace she could. 'For Bentley's sake,' she thought.

Jos rose before her on that dark December morning, and she lay in bed watching him dress. She saw how his hands trembled as he wound his stock about his neck, fumbling awkwardly with the fine linen, and when he began to struggle with the black cloth coat, pulling it half on and then reaching unavailingly for the armhole, she slid from the bed and came to help him. She fussed over the task a little, pulling the collar straight, smoothing the cloth, anything as a pretext to touch him with a consoling hand.

As she stood before him to neaten the frills of his shirt, he closed his hand about her wrist. 'I wish you were coming,' he said suddenly. His voice was rough, quiet yet without warmth, but it made her catch her breath. She ached to put her arms about him, but dared not for fear of rejection.

'There's Mary – but perhaps . . .'

He turned from her. 'No, I know. She needs you.' His tone did not say 'but so do I'; only she knew he did.

He left the room without saying anything more, or looking at her again; and she dressed rapidly and hurried, not downstairs after him, but along the landing to Mary Bentley's room, knocking gently on the door.

It was agreed very quickly that the widow should spend the day with Mrs Griffiths – a servant was sent at once to make the arrangements – and Sarah told Jos she would join him at Christie's as soon as she had seen Mary safely deposited in the care of her friend. Jos merely nodded, but the relief in his eyes set her weeping a little after he had gone.

It was like the old days. The London season was at its height, and the auction room was thronged with what Sarah thought must be half the city's fashionable society. The hubbub before the sale's opening was deafening: laughter, greetings, loud-voiced gossip; and animated discussion of the wealth of beautiful items ranged, numbered, about the room. Today only the inferior items were to be sold, with the quality and quantity of the lots increasing each day until the finest wares would be reached on the eleventh day. But there must, Sarah thought, be an example here of every lovely thing made by the firm of Wedgwood and Bentley since that bright summer day of its beginning: vases and ewers, statuettes and busts, medallions, cameos, plaques and candlesticks and flowerpots in every kind of body from the marbled agate ware to the clear beauty of jasper; and among them copies of the great Russian service.

It was strange, Sarah thought, to be there in the bustling expectant crowd and feel not triumph but an ache at the heart and a great sadness.

She pushed her way across the room to where Jos and Tom Byerley were talking over the final points with Mr James Christie, the auctioneer; or rather Byerley was talking, for Jos simply stood in silence wrapped in some gloomy thoughts of his own. Sarah slipped into place beside him, smiling briefly as she took his hand unobtrusively in hers. Christie bowed and excused himself, saying that he must make a start, and Tom Byerley cast a relieved look in her direction, as if he was finding Jos's mood more than a little difficult.

'A splendid crowd,' he commented. From here on the edge of the platform near the auctioneer's rostrum the view was even more impressive, the mass of heads bobbing and swaying, the men's bewigged and powdered, the women's with ringleted hair piled high and adorned – as Sarah's was – with elaborate confections of lace and ribbon, or – as Sarah's most emphatically was not – with spangles, pearls, artificial

404

fruit or ostrich feathers. Fans and catalogues waved, mingled perfumes (not all pleasant) wafted towards them, high-bred voices chattered on.

'Trust the best people to smell out a bargain a mile away,' Byerley went on rather unkindly in an undertone.

But he was wrong. There were no bargains in Christie's auction room that day: from the very first moment that was patently obvious.

A hush, tense with excited anticipation, fell over the crowd as the auctioneer banged his gavel and called to his assistant to bring forward lot number one; and the sale began. Sarah only remembered then how Bentley had told them once that Christie's manner of selling was a drama in itself, drawing crowds even when there was little interest in the sale; now she realised exactly what he meant. Each item was introduced with a flow of superlatives that almost took the breath away, toppling over, often, into excess, but always hugely entertaining. In any other circumstances she would have enjoyed it all as much as did the buyers, listening rapt and open-mouthed as the adjectives piled one on top of another, the convoluted phrases coaxed, cajoled, teased them to bid; and even today she could not help but smile, just a little, from time to time.

There was a black basalt vase wreathed with leaves whose shape, Sarah remembered, had dissatisfied Jos when it was made. 'Permit me, ladies and gentlemen,' the auctioneeer implored the crowd with fine dramatic emphasis, 'to place this inestimable piece of elegant antiquity under your protection. Only observe the sublime symmetry of the form, the exquisite delicacy of the decoration – how can you be less than moved to harmonise your own inexhaustible munificence with the perfection of this unsurpassable work of art?' At which point, suitably allured, the bidding began And it was like all the other bidding, beyond anything they would have thought possible.

Sarah had not imagined such a feverish reckless disregard for expense could exist, and on such a scale. A few items – the elaborately gilded vases which were now so unfashionable, for example – fetched little more than their market price. But almost everything else was held up to a dizzying spiralling bidding that ended often in a gasp of astonishment from some quarter of the saleroom. Even the auctioneer allowed himself a glimmer of a smile and an increasing sparkle of the eyes as the sale progressed. And for the first time in a long while Jos had an alert and interested look.

At the end of the first day the total raised amounted to one hundred and sixty-nine pounds. 'Do you realise,' Jos murmured to Sarah when Christie, his voice hoarse, told them the figure, 'that when I was a lad many a pot bank scarcely made that in a whole year?'

Sarah smiled and risked sliding her arm about his waist, where to her relief he let it stay. 'Bentley would have been proud, and happy.' This time he did not recoil or turn away, but simply nodded, and for a moment put his arm about her shoulder, pressing her to him.

'Thank you,' he said, and she knew what he meant.

Even with her support, the day had taken its toll of him. By the time they reached the house again he was weighed down by a crushing headache and, refusing all offers of supper, went straight to bed. Sarah was concerned, but she was at the same time so relieved that he had, just a little, admitted her once more into his life, that she could not help but feel her spirits lighten.

By the end of the eleven days of the sale Mrs Bentley knew she would be able to live in comfort to the end of her life; and Jos, astonished and impressed by this demonstration of the continuing demand for the products of Etruria, showed heartening signs of renewed interest in the enterprise.

Mary Bentley, helped by her late husband's many friends, made arrangements to move to a smaller, more convenient house nearer the centre of London, where she could live with her unmarried sister. Tom Byerley married and settled in Greek Street, happily absorbed in supervising the showrooms and workrooms (all now under one roof in Soho), and glad to be no longer on his travels. And Jos and Sarah went home.

Despite Sarah's hopes, there was no sudden change in Jos on their return. With visible relief he set to work once more on his pyrometer, for measuring the heat of a kiln; and on designing the ideal scientific pestle and mortar for Joseph Priestley, who was now ministering to a congregation in Birmingham. From Sarah he was as withdrawn as ever, as if the trip to London had never taken place.

Going to bring Susannah home from Derby, and allowing herself a few days' holiday with the Darwins as a break from the strains of Etruria, she asked Dr Darwin's opinion of Jos. 'It's more than a year now since Bentley died, yet he seems as far as ever from getting over it.'

Darwin nodded. 'S-some things one n-never g-gets over.' And then, in case that sounded too discouraging, he added quickly, 'Let him k-keep busy, find n-new interests – d-don't let him brood. And – be p-patient.'

She supposed there was no other answer he could have given, but it did not help. What she did not tell him was that a conviction had been steadily growing in her since Bentley's death that all of this was somehow inevitable, to be expected, even right, in a bleak and horrible way.

Once, months ago during the long despairing night when Jos had first slept apart from her, she had lain staring into the darkness trying to think of some way out of this morass of unhappiness; and she had seemed suddenly to hear a voice speaking to her, close by in her head and yet with a distinct and separate reality, as if it came from somewhere outside herself. 'You see,' it crowed, 'you thought you had got away with it! You thought you could be happy, in spite of what you did. And I let you think that, for a while. But you were wrong; and now you know how wrong. Every sin requires its payment in full – and this is your payment, to lose them both, and be left with nothing, for ever and ever . . .'

The words had tormented her until the dawn came; and somehow in the daylight it had all seemed rather silly, a superstitious night-time fear. Yet she had never quite been able to drive it out, even then; and instead of diminishing in its effect on her, it had grown until she had come to believe that it was true, and that Bentley's death and Jos's separation from her were all part of the natural order of things, the result of that one act of betrayal long years ago.

She had found it comforting once before to talk to Darwin, but she knew she could not tell him what troubled her now. He was too rational, too practical a man to listen to her with patience or sympathy. He would have dismissed her conviction out of hand as superstitious rubbish; and she knew that she could not be helped by someone who did not begin to understand what tormented her.

On the surface she went on as before, and a part of her still hoped that Jos would turn to her again, in spite of everything. Darwin was right in one thing: she had no choice but to be patient.

To her great relief Susannah seemed to have thrown off her undying love for François Potet with amazing rapidity. She did not mention him at all when greeting her mother, but was instead full of the excitements of her stay. Sarah felt that the child in her daughter had come happily back to the surface. There had been rides and card parties, music (she had tried, with a hilarious lack of success, to teach the totally unmusical Dr Darwin to play the harpsichord), and dancing, a theatre trip, and a constant round of visits, including one to the painter Joseph Wright to see how he was progressing with his painting of *The Maid of Corinth* which he was working on for Jos and Sarah.

And, of course, there had been the companionship of the Darwin boys – or rather of Robert, for Erasmus was too reserved and shy a character for ready friendship. Young Robert, though two years her junior, seemed to have taken her in hand. His older brother's death had left him the focus of all his father's ambitions, and he was already beginning reluctantly on the medical studies which were to turn him into the doctor Charles might have been. He tried to impress Susannah with his newly acquired knowledge, but better still he was ready also to join her in any youthful silliness. She had not, Sarah noted thankfully, crushed his pretensions with the grown-up young-lady act she put on sometimes when she thought her brothers were getting above themselves; perhaps, because he was so much larger than either herself or her brothers, she forgot she was the elder. She was even visibly regretful at leaving him.

There was still, of course, the problem of Monsieur Potet. In the end, to Sarah's astonishment, it was Jos who solved it.

'Chisholm suggests Jack and Joss would benefit from a spell at Warrington, with a view to going on later to study at Edinburgh – he has connections there, of course. Tom's not strong enough to cope with the change yet – and besides, he's too young. He'll enjoy a bit of undivided attention from Chisholm. As for Potet, the lads are all as fluent in French as any teacher could make them – it's not fair to keep him here, wasting his talents. There'll be any number of families glad of his services – we'll recommend him.'

'And what about the younger girls?' Sarah asked, rendered almost speechless by this lengthy and decisive utterance.

'They'll do best with a governess, I expect.'

So it was settled; and for a little while Sarah again had hopes that the turning point had come, that Jos had returned to her again.

But he had not. He could, at times, be practical, reasonable, capable of making decisions and putting them into effect. In public he might be more serious than before, inclined to be irritable and no longer given to laughter and high spirits, but it was only Sarah who knew how deep was the change in him. Sometimes she thought that the aching sense of loss at her heart was not for Bentley at all, but for the dear friend who had died with him on that wild November night.

CHAPTER NINETEEN

1783

'Now, I just want to look in on Nan – John Bates went down with a chill last week, so they'll not have anything coming in, I imagine. Then a word with Mr Webber on our way home.'

Susannah laughed. 'That's the third time this morning you've said, "now we'll just"! And I don't think I'd call the works "on our way home".'

Sarah smiled at her daughter. 'It just happens there's a great deal to be done, that's all – the more so with your father away.' She would never have let Susannah know it, but Jos's absence – as always of late – left her with an unmistakable feeling of relief, together with a sense of guilt that it should be so. It had not grown any easier to live beneath the same roof as a man separated from her by some kind of impenetrable barrier, even if she did in some sense believe it was what she deserved. The children did not feel it, of course: with them, if sometimes stern, he was always tender and patient, willing to listen and advise. In the two years since Bentley's death he had become a little less withdrawn, progressively more interested in other matters than his laboratory, more approachable on the whole. His headaches were more frequent than ever, he was often irritable, but she could have borne that had she been able, sometimes, to feel again the closeness of spirit and unity of purpose that had held them together from their first meeting – or, even more, if she had felt sure in any real and permanent sense that he needed her.

The carriage came to a halt in the market place, and Sarah and Susannah, well wrapped in thick cloaks against the chill March rain, made their way round the solid pillared bulk of Burslem town hall – built where once the maypole had stood – along a steep muddy lane between the rows of new cottages, to the little house with the words 'John Bates, cobbler' painted above the door on a wooden board.

Nan welcomed them warmly enough into her scrubbed

firelit kitchen, hurrying – a little flustered with pleasure – to make tea, and asking, in a flow of talk too fluent to allow any reply, if they were well, and how was Mr Wedgwood, and exclaiming at how Miss Susannah was quite the young lady now. At eighteen, Miss Susannah felt she was a little too old for such remarks, but she smiled politely, fond as she was of the woman who had been her loving nurse in infancy. Poor Nan had herself borne no living children; and it was hard now, Sarah thought, faced with the lined harassed woman beneath the temporary mask of cheerfulness, to remember that this had once been the willing carefree parish orphan who had come to work at the Brick House.

'How is John?' Sarah asked at last, when there was a brief interval in the talk. She was sorry the question seemed to suck the life out of Nan, leaving her looking tired and troubled.

'On the mend today, Mrs Wedgwood.' And then, almost as an afterthought, 'Thanks be to God.' The pious phrase sounded automatic, a gesture to the faith that had once fired her young spirit. Sarah remembered vividly the flushed ecstatic face of the girl who had first talked to her of Wesley's preaching, all those years ago, but it was perhaps hardly to be expected that the early fervour would last. If it could still bring her some comfort in difficult times, that was as much as could be hoped for. 'It's a bad time to be poorly,' Nan went on. She sat slumped on her stool, her hands hanging with a pathetic helplessness over her knees. 'You see, madam, times being hard like, he canna afford to lose business – what there is, leastways. Happen you'll not know, but bread costs more by the day – and not just bread neither. John says "Trust in the Lord, He will provide", but I do doubt sometimes, just a bit.' The last words were spoken in an undertone, as if she was ashamed of giving voice to them.

Sarah reached for the basket that Susannah had carried from the coach. 'You know the debt I owe you, Nan. I don't think I can ever repay it. I've some bread here, as it happens – and if there's anything else you need . . .' She saw the tears spring to Nan's eyes and broke in quickly on the stammered thanks and protests. 'What are friends for, after all? At times like these it's only right that those of us who've been blessed with plenty should share what we have.'

411

'I shoulda trusted – John were right.' She smiled tremulously, and then added, 'But there's not many think like you – I've heard talk of grain hoarded to keep prices high.'

'I don't think that's true.'

'No more do I, but there's them that believe it – and some say the poor have the right to take food if it inna given – though John says that's wicked talk.'

'It shouldn't have to come to that,' commented Sarah sadly. 'But you know to send anyone in need to Etruria Hall, don't you? No one's ever turned away from there empty-handed.'

'I know – and God bless you for it. You know,' she confided, 'some of our preachers talk against the folk at Newcastle meeting house, calling them unbelievers and atheists. But I know good Christian folk when I see them, and so does John, and we wunna hear a word against you.'

Sarah, embarrassed and uncomfortable at such lavish praise, steered the conversation deftly to less emotional ground.

When they were ready to go Nan came with them to the door. 'It's no weather to be out in, this!' she exclaimed, a little scandalised, as they pulled their cloaks about them, bent their heads, and stepped outside.

They ran through the rain to the carriage, and Sarah ordered the coachman to take them to the ornamental works at Etruria. There she left Susannah in the carriage by the canal while she went in search of Henry Webber. A skilled modeller in his own right, recommended to them by no less a person than Sir Joshua Reynolds, he had been appointed last summer to manage the ornamental side of the business. That had been Sarah's idea, though she had known it would make much of her involvement with the works unnecessary. But now that Jos was so wrapped up in his other interests, she found that she could not hope wholly to take his place, for there were too many other demands on her time; and besides Etruria needed skills she did not have. The increasing infirmity of her father had been the final blow. He had at last become wholly bedridden, a difficult demanding old man who insisted on her almost constant attendance. She had given it, as much as she could; and felt more relief than anything when at last just before Christmas he had died.

412

Today, though, she had every excuse – once her calls had been made, on the needy and on Tom Wedgwood of the useful works, who was ill – to walk beneath the archway into the courtyard and go in search of Henry Webber, who was to be found in the modelling room as she had expected. There she showed him the sketches that had come today with a covering note from Jos in London.

'John Flaxman has completed the design for the chessmen,' she explained. 'Mr Wedgwood would like your opinion.'

Webber peeled back the covering papers and revealed the drawings, beautifully done, almost three-dimensional, so that one could see instantly how the finished figures would look.

'I believe,' said Sarah, 'that he modelled the queens on Mrs Siddons and the kings on Mr Kemble.' She wondered if Byerley, seeing these idols of the stage in the sketched figures, had felt a twinge of regret for the ambitions of his youth. 'As you see, they're very much in the Gothic style which is so popular these days.'

Webber nodded. 'Very fine – very fine indeed,' he commented with pleasure. 'I wouldn't know about fashion, but I like the look of them. You could almost imagine them springing to life to fight a real battle. But the modelling won't be easy, I imagine. Any idea when he could have them ready for moulding?'

'Not for some considerable time, I should think. But you like them then? You don't need time to think it over?'

'Not at all. I can't imagine better. They're to be done in the jasper, of course – I'll give some thought to the colours. Tell Mr Wedgwood I'll have some suggestions for him when he gets back. And you ask Mr Flaxman to start work at once.'

He came with her to the door, talking of the progress of two or three new lines in the jasperware – Jos had at last solved the problems of firing hollow-wares in the new body. Sarah would have loved to stay and look around, but Susannah was waiting and it was dinner time.

'Did Mr Wedgwood have news of his meeting?' Webber was asking now. 'Was he giving a paper this time?'

'The meeting's not until tomorrow.'

'Ah, I see . . .' He paused, and cleared his throat. 'We're very proud of him, you know, Mrs Wedgwood. A fellow of the Royal Society – quite something, that is.'

Sarah doubted if most of the workforce knew what the Royal Society was, much less cared, but she was touched by the sincerity of Webber's praise. There was a very real affection for Jos here at the works; and certainly those who did understand its significance were proud that he had been elected a Fellow of the Royal Society, to which he had already presented three papers. Jos himself was even more proud of the fact that his election had coincided with that of Joseph Priestley. 'Just think,' he had said wonderingly to Sarah, 'here am I, a mere potter, taking my place with the best scientific minds alongside a man like Joseph Priestley'; and Sarah, warmed by his brief confiding moment, had kissed him and told him the honour was richly deserved.

'He is not presenting a paper this time,' she told Webber. 'I can't remember what subject was to be discussed.' She gazed across the gravelled path to the canal and the hill beyond, all drowned in the same relentless wetness, from the still leafless trees to the barge moored at the far wharf.

'Grain,' said Webber in a low voice, 'bound for Manchester. But I heard one of the men say this morning it was for our own people – he believed it, I think. I just hope no one sees it go this afternoon – feelings are high just now, what with shortages and high prices. I heard a mob broke into a grain warehouse in Newcastle last night. We don't want that kind of trouble here. They sent in the militia, I'm told.'

'I don't think there are any troublemakers at Etruria,' said Sarah soothingly.

'They don't have to be at Etruria – if word gets to Newcastle, or Hanley, or Burslem, there are enough malcontents there . . .'

'Let's hope they realise the people of Manchester have as much right to grain as they have.'

'I doubt if men like that go in for such unselfish feelings,' commented Webber drily.

'Perhaps I would not, if I were hungry, and my children too.'

Dinner was ready when the two women reached home. The savoury smells drifted towards them from the kitchens as they hurried upstairs to change out of their wet clothes. 'Mm,' murmured Susannah appreciatively, 'roast mutton and caper sauce, I should say. What do you think?'

414

'I think you're a greedy young woman!' retorted Sarah with a smile.

But when they sat down to eat, the food seemed somehow to have lost its appeal. The mutton was well roasted, the sauce hot and fragrant; there was a veal pie, and one of Betty's finest soups to begin the meal (she ruled supreme in the kitchen now, a cook that many a great house might envy). And Sarah was suddenly transported back to the almost-forgotten evening at the house of George Lathom, when she had sat at that splendid table scarcely able to eat for thinking of Jos in his hunger and poverty.

'Now,' she thought, 'it is we who have so much, and beyond our walls day after day men and women and children wake to empty bellies and scarce inadequate food. I said to Nan, it is right to give to those who have nothing, but I felt uncomfortable with her gratitude, and her praise of me. How can it be right that the few should eat well, while the many – even those who have work – should be faced with hunger because times are hard and prices high? Bentley wanted the workless to have land, so they could feed themselves, but perhaps that is not an answer for more than a few. And what of those who have work, but still cannot afford bread?' She knew what Jos would say: 'we help them with gifts of food until prices fall again'. But somehow that seemed a haphazard, unreliable system. 'And I don't think I should like it, if I were poor and hungry.'

It was too wet that afternoon for there to be any temptation to any of them to go out. 'We can't even experiment properly with Mr Chisholm away,' Tom complained; but he was never at a loss for long, and he took himself to the library to work on some figures derived from his most recent experiments, while Josiah wrote a letter to his father, and John browsed amongst Jos's various books on plants. Susannah settled down for a long and pleasurable session at the harpsichord, and Catherine and Sarah went to their afternoon lessons with Miss Mulhall, their governess.

Mary Ann, Sarah knew only too well, was unlikely ever to be able to join her sisters. With an unflagging patience which was a wonder to the child's mother, Jane encouraged the little girl to try to walk, to repeat simple words, to develop whatever abilities she had; but they were very few, and very limited, and whenever she seemed to be making any progress there would be another bout of illness and she would be back where she started. This afternoon Sarah spent a little time talking to Jane, and watching how Mary Ann could take three uncertain steps holding tight to the nurse's hand; and then, feeling a little burdened with the sadness of things, she went to her own sitting room upstairs to enjoy the unaccustomed luxury of some uninterrupted reading.

It stopped raining at last. The sudden brightness cast by a shaft of sunlight reaching into the room made her look up: far off there was a furtive, joyous gleam of blue sky. She went to the window, opened it, and leaned out, sniffing the sweetness of the air, feeling the drying wind on her face. It was, after all, good to be alive: she was blessed – they all were . . .

She stilled, her wandering gaze caught and held by some activity on the canal, and the towpath alongside it – a great dark surging mass of people was coming into sight from the Longport direction, more and more of them, a seemingly endless throng; and with them, dragged by a rope from the towpath, a barge moved along the water.

Even here, so far above them, she could hear the noise: shouting, snatches of song, and underneath the spasmodic sounds the regular beating rhythm of an angry triumphant chant. They were moving quickly – men and women, and even little children hurrying with them – steadily on towards the works.

She drew in her head, slammed down the window, ran downstairs. The boys had left the library and she found them instead in the drawing room with Susannah, gathered at the window. 'I'm going down to the works,' she told them.

'No, Mama!' Susannah came and laid a hand on her arm. 'Please don't do that – there's no telling what they're going to do.'

'What they mustn't do is any damage to the works,' Sarah told her, shaking herself free.

'But you might be hurt!' John put in anxiously.

'Nonsense – I don't doubt I know a good few of them.' She had not liked that ugly chanting, reminding her as it did of the beating drums of the rioting weavers in Lancashire three and a half years ago; and of what she had heard of the riots in London a year after that. Angry men gathered together,

416

however rational apart, became unpredictable, dangerous, frightening. But she had no intention of letting the children see that she was afraid.

'Then I'm coming with you,' John announced decisively. She looked at him in astonishment: not quite seventeen, tall but slender and unbearded, his voice not long settled into the deeper tones of manhood – her diffident son, suddenly become protective, the man of the house. She did not smile, because it would have hurt his pride; and in the end she did not need to reply, because Susannah called from the window, 'Someone's coming!'

Sarah went to look, and saw the man running up the hill towards the house. 'I'll go and meet him.'

It was Sam Hunter, coming as fast as he could. By the time she reached him, John a few paces behind, she could see that the crowd was already at the works and had come to a halt there, spreading out either side and up to the very walls of the building, like a dark menacing growth.

Sam tripped, almost falling, and Sarah reached out to hold him. He looked up into her face, his breath coming in long rasping gulps scattered with incoherent words: ' . . . barge – man drowned, nearly . . . crate shop . . .'

'Steady now,' she said gently, though she was trembling with impatience to know what was happening. 'Get your breath first.' She sensed rather than saw John at her elbow, as tense as she was. They waited in silence, watching the man as he struggled to control his breathing. As soon as he could, he told them with a greater measure of calmness, 'There was a barge with grain for Manchester . . .'

'I know – go on.'

'Some thought it was for us, or some such. How they heard I dunna know – happen they'd word from the works – but they came, from all around, and set on the barge at Longport. They took a knife to the boatman – said they'd throw him in the water. Then they took him prisoner along with them. They talk of storin' the grain in the crate shop . . .'

'In the crate shop! What does Mr Webber say to that?'

'He sent me to tell you – but he says he canna say no to a mob that size, without puttin' the whole works at risk. He's sent the men home, all but one or two who stopped to keep a look out, so to speak. They've locked up as best they can.'

John touched Sarah's arm. 'Don't you think we ought to send to Newcastle for help, Mama – the militia . . .'

She turned shocked eyes upon him. 'There are women and children there, John! And if there were not, would you turn guns on hungry men?'

It was John's turn to look shocked. 'Not to shoot, Mama – only to send them home.'

'He's right, Mrs Wedgwood,' Sam broke in. 'It's the only way to stop things getting out of hand.'

Sarah shook her head fiercely. 'No! I'll not have soldiers at Etruria!' The very thought chilled her. To dispel it, she turned her attention to Sam himself, looking close to exhaustion after his run. 'Come into the house and rest – have some supper. Then we'll see what's to be done.' As they went, she asked, 'Was there much in the crate shop?'

'No, it's empty. There was a load sent off this mornin'.'

'Thank goodness for that.'

Now and then one or other of them watched from the window, but there was little more to see: an isolated swirl of movement in the crowd, a drift away of two or three together, tired of the excitement or the waiting and going home. As it grew dark little bursts of flame sprang up and steadied into glowing dots – torches, they supposed – and here and there the throng parted to encircle a fire: it was a cold night. 'I wonder where they found dry wood?' John murmured, but Sarah preferred not to dwell on that quesion.

Sam Hunter came to thank Sarah for his food and rest, and take his leave of her. 'I'll go back down, Mrs Wedgwood. I can let you know what's going on, if I find out.'

She thanked him and watched him walk away into the darkness, and then she pulled the curtains and ordered supper. It was early, but she wanted to be ready if she should be needed, later.

When the strained silent meal was over, Sarah went upstairs to say goodnight to the little girls – rather giggly and difficult in the tense atmosphere – and thought she heard, from some far part of the house, the sound of raised angry voices. Downstairs again she found Tom and Josiah in the hall, standing together rather hesitantly at the foot of the stairs as if wondering whether to come and find her, and visibly relieved that she was there.

'Mrs Massey said there were men at the kitchen door,' Tom explained. 'She said they had sticks. John went, but he's not come back – it's been a long time.'

She reassured them, but it was unbearably hard not to run to the kitchen but to walk steadily, with all the appearance of calmness.

A cold gust of air met her as she opened the kitchen door, telling her how long the back door had stood open as it was now, with a great burly giant of a man, stave in hand, propping it wide. Behind him in the yard she could make out three other figures, faces grotesquely highlighted by the torches they held. And confronting them, a slim dark shadow against their aggressive presence, stood her eldest son, legs planted wide, arms folded, the picture of immovable rectitude. Just for an instant she felt a spark of pride at his courage, but it was driven out by exasperation that he could be so foolhardy.

She passed the huddle of frightened kitchen maids, and Betty standing poker in hand beside Mrs Massey as if she would take action to fight off any threat to her domain, and took her place at John's side. She stared at the men, none of them known to her, seeing them transfer their attention to her, recognising in her grey silk-clad figure the lady of the house.

'We want food,' said the man in the doorway. 'We've the grain store to guard – we canna sit up all night wi' nowt in our bellies.' His eyes travelled round the kitchen: the new ovens, the polished copper cooking pots, the dresser stacked with three fine dinner services, the remains of the meal on the scrubbed table. 'You've enough and to spare.'

Fear gave way to an exploding anger. 'So you come and demand it with staves in your hands from a house full of women and children? How very courageous!'

The man's eyes ran sceptically over John's tall gangling frame, as if to say, 'This is no child.' And Sarah, struck again by her son's demeanour, thought that indeed in this half light there was little of the child about him.

'Give us food and drink and we'll go.' One of the other men had intervened, in what was meant, she thought, to be a tone of calm reasonableness.

'I told you!' John burst out furiously, though Sarah could

hear the tremor beneath the anger. 'My father would give you not one thing – and I speak for him!'

'No one's ever turned away from Etruria empty-handed,' she had told Nan this morning; but then she had not known that anything like this would happen. She said, her quiet clear voice contrasting with John's rage, 'He will always give generously to anyone in need who turns to him for help. But not like this – not when you have forcibly appropriated his property for your own ends with neither his knowledge nor his permission. There is no question whatsoever of your receiving food from this house. And if you do not leave quietly and at once I shall have you removed.'

She saw the man's hand tighten about the stave, and she knew he itched to use it. He watched her, assessing her strength, her stubbornness, her willingness to carry through what she threatened. It seemed a long time, that interval during which they faced one another in a battle of wills: the four men, and the woman and the boy, the flickering light the only moving thing on their tense faces.

Then the first man shrugged. 'You'll be sorry,' he said, and he turned and led the others away into the night. It seemed very dark and cold when they had gone.

It was a moment more before Sarah closed the door and turned to put her arm briefly about John, in relief and thankfulness; but he did not move.

'Mama, you *must* send for help now! We can't let men like that loose on the works and do nothing about it. It'll only get worse.'

She remembered how Bentley had talked of the Gordon riots in London, when the authorities had stood by and done nothing whilst the mob looted and burned for days on end. Swift action at the outset would have put an end to it almost before it began, so he had believed; and he would not have wanted bloodshed. Was this any different?

'Yes it is,' she told herself. 'There are women and children – and they are hungry. Hunger would drive me to desperate measures.' But she knew she could not sustain that argument for ever. 'It may come to that,' she said aloud. 'But not yet. I'm going to talk to them.'

She heard a cry from Mrs Massey, and John's horrified exclamation. 'You can't! Mama, there are hundreds of them! No!'

'No one will touch me. I don't doubt I know most of them

already. It may be that they will listen to reason. I must try – I can't send for troops if I have not tried.'

'Then I'll go!'

She smiled at that. 'You'd only get angry, John, and then there might be danger. I'm a woman, and no youngster at that: who better to go? I'll take William Baddeley with me in case there's trouble; but I'm certain there'll be none.' William Baddeley was the groom, a big strong lad, good-natured yet fearless. John's face brightened just a little.

'You'll ride then?'

She shook her head. 'No. I think that might look a little threatening. Better to go on foot.'

John seemed, briefly, amused at the thought that his mother even on horseback could ever look threatening. Then he began to plead urgently for her to change her mind, to send for the militia, to send some strong man down to the works; anything but go herself.

'John, I'm going – if nothing else I shall be able to see for myself what the situation is and judge what ought to be done. And I must get ready first, so don't hold me up please.'

She dressed with immense care, choosing a jacket, waistcoat and petticoat of stone-coloured cloth, a simple and rather severe ensemble that would show up well in the dark; a neat hat with modest plume set on hair that was dressed tidily rather than extravagantly; boots and gloves. She wished to look authoritative, well dressed, but not rich or lavish in appearance.

William Baddeley was waiting in the kitchen with a lantern and a good stout stick. 'I'll lean on it like a walking stick, but it's there if I need it,' he explained. She did not argue, though she hoped fervently that it was an unnecessary precaution.

They set off down the hill; it seemed a long way in the dark, the familiar path full of unexpected obstacles.

Once, William stopped. 'You're never going in amongst that lot,' he said, staring down at the dark mass at the far side of the canal, stretching away in all directions from the rosy circles of fire.

'No,' Sarah told him. 'I shan't cross the canal. I'll speak to them from this side.'

'You'll never make yourself heard, ma'am!'

But he had not taken account of simple human curiosity:

421

that, if nothing else, sent silence settling over the crowd as Sarah's pale lantern-lit figure took shape on the far bank, standing very still and very upright.

She saw eyes turned on her, hundreds of pairs of eyes gleaming in the light of fire and torch. It was their anger she felt as an almost tangible thing: anger, suspicion, even hatred, reaching her from the watching eyes, the motionless waiting figures.

Then, just opposite her, there was a shiver of movement. The crowd parted, and two people she did not know elbowed their way forward: a wiry man, with eyes set in deep shadows in his bony face, and a woman, tall and thin and very pale. They were unarmed, less obviously threatening than the burly man who had come to the kitchen tonight, but the hatred that reached out to her from them was so strong that Sarah shivered.

'My friends!' There was a jeer from somewhere, but the man on the canal bank raised a hand for silence. 'I have come to offer what help I can – and to beg you to go home!'

For a little while her voice had carried high and clear over the water, but now in an instant it was drowned by a ragged mocking chorus; and as quickly the man with the hidden eyes silenced it again. 'Give her a hearing!' he commanded, but with nothing in his voice that gave her any hope of being heard sympathetically.

'You are hungry, I know. You will not help yourselves by taking the law into your own hands. Go home, let me know at the Hall what your needs are – we will help all we can, that I promise.' She paused, almost expecting more shouting, but there was none. Only the pale woman spoke, her voice ringing fiercely into the night.

'We don't want charity – we want justice! We have as much right to food in our bellies as you – why should we beg for what ought to be ours?'

'I wish I knew,' Sarah thought, stirred to sympathy in spite of everything. But she called out, 'You have a right to eat, but if you take the grain from the barge you steal from someone else – from other hungry people. Can't you see that?'

'Oh yes?' The cry was harsh with derision. 'Don't tell us it would have been given away – or sold cheap. We steal from the profiteers – the hoarders, the cheating shop keepers, the

422

fat merchants with full bellies. That's justice, not wrong-doing. The only laws we break are rich men's laws. To-morrow we will sell the grain for a fair price, so no one need go hungry. The boatman will get his due, for we don't cheat. Go back to your fine house and full larder, and let us be!'

She could not have answered then, for wild cheering broke out and echoed round and round from the walls of the works and the hills, filling the night air with noise and the smoke of the waving leaping torches. Sarah felt Will's hand on her arm, warming and protective, but she did not move. In the end she raised her hands, begging to be heard; and after what seemed a very long time the two ringleaders gave her what she wanted.

'I have been urged to send to Newcastle for soldiers' – the murmur erupted again, and then stilled – 'I do not want to. But if you don't go home, then someone will send – if not me, someone else. You know then what kind of justice you will have. It is not my kind, any more than yours. Go home, before it's too late.'

After that there was no more quiet, only a long derisive defiant shouting that seemed to go on and on for ever. Sarah knew she had lost.

She heard someone coming through the darkness, along the canal bank from the bridge: Sam Hunter slipped into the lantern light. 'I'll go to Newcastle for you, Mrs Wedgwood.'

She gazed at him, filled with sadness. 'How can I . . .? They will only sell the grain, and then go home – if that's all, there's no great harm done.'

'It's not all – there are gangs of them roaming round, smashin' up property and stealin' anything they can lay hands on. It can only get worse, believe me, Mrs Wedgwood . . .'

She stood there for a long time, looking at the noisy crowd that was losing interest in her now, intent on its own pur-poses: and then along the canal to where the lights shone from the workers' cottages, and a flame spurted suddenly into the dark, illuminating roof tops, lighting black running figures making their way along the row. 'House on fire,' said Sam.

She had no choice now, and she knew it. With an aching sense of betrayal she reached into her pocket and drew out a note, written before she left the house in the hope that she

423

would not need it. She gave it to Sam. 'Take that to Major Sneyd. He will do the rest.' And then, all at once utterly weary, she took Will Baddeley's arm and they turned for home. She had pleaded in the note that there should be no shooting, no bloodshed, only the threat of force to frighten the people home; but she knew that did not lessen her responsibility. She did not think she would ever forgive herself that it should have come to this.

She did not sleep much that night, rising often to look out of the window and see what was happening below. Some time just before dawn she saw what she had feared: the crate shop burning. And she heard harsh commanding voices, saw the crowd turned to face a new torchlit mass by the bridge, and knew the soldiers had come.

Two hours after dawn the canal bank was empty but for a scattered debris of charred and broken glass. The crate shop roof was damaged, but that was all. No shots were fired, no blood shed. But Sarah could feel neither relief nor triumph.

By the time Jos came home two men had been arrested, neither of them, so it was said, in any way responsible for the trouble. She told Jos quietly all that had happened and what she had done; and he listened in silence and then said only, 'I would have done the same,' and left it at that.

The arrested men were found guilty and condemned to death; and though one was later reprieved none of the arguments of Jos and Sarah and their friends could save the other. The authorities wanted an example, and a warning; it did not matter very much to them where the real guilt lay. 'Rich men's laws,' the woman had called them derisively; but it was those laws that had won in the end, and Sarah felt she was as much to blame as anyone.

She tried to tell Jos what she felt, but he did not seem to understand. Eventually, as a last resort, she went to see Kate, in the little house Jos had built for her at Etruria, where she had lived with her children since William's death.

Once it would have been the most natural thing for Sarah in a mood of despondency to go and talk to Kate. But Kate, like Jos, had aged greatly in the past years, and she suffered also from increasingly poor health. The months of nursing a husband rapidly dwindling into senile decay had taken their toll, even before his death had left her swept by a bitter loneliness tempered only a little by relief; and the death, from consumption, of her eldest daughter soon afterwards had been the final blow from which she had never fully recovered.

Looking now at the other woman's thin face with its gentle questioning eyes, Sarah thought, 'How can I trouble her with my anxieties?' and she began to talk brightly about the weather. After that, as there was no response from Kate, she fell silent, trying to think of something else to say.

In the end it was Kate who spoke. 'Is it Jos?'

Sarah had a desperate longing to pour out her grief in tears, tell Kate everything, and perhaps find all the consolation she needed. But that would be to ask too much of her friend. Instead, calmly and a little drily, she said how she worried about Jos, how still after all this time she could not reach him; and at the end, Kate said, 'I think it happens sometimes when you lose someone you love a part of you dies too – not always, not inevitably, but sometimes. It may come back, but it may be gone for ever. I think that's what's happened to Jos.'

She knew Kate was right, it was the wellspring of all joyousness in her husband that had drained dry at Bentley's death, the source of laughter and enthusiasm and all the delight that she had loved so much.

She made her way home, calmer, but with the same burden still oppressing her spirits. It was growing dark as she let herself in by the garden door. She hurried along the passage and into the hall. Just at the foot of the stairs stood Jos, with the troubled look of a man who did not quite know why he was there or what to do about it. He turned as she came in, and the relief on his face astonished her. She almost expected him to come running to fold her in his arms.

He did not. Instead, he said, 'You're back. I didn't know where you were. No one saw you go.'

'I went to see Kate,' she said. 'Is anything wrong?'

He shook his head. 'I just didn't know where you were.' He looked her over, almost, Sarah thought, as if he wanted to reassure himself that she was Sarah, and unchanged. And then he murmured something about a book he wanted and made his way to the library.

It was then she understood. However he might have changed, in one thing he had not, however much she might have thought otherwise: he needed her as desperately as ever.

And, having lost so many of those he loved, he had a terrible fear that he might lose her too. It was, she thought, just what she needed, to know that he depended on her still. It gave her something to cling to in the darkness.

CHAPTER TWENTY

1786

There was an atmosphere of fierce concentration in the library. At a large carved table below Stubbs's portrait of her grandfather Susannah was at work, fluently translating three letters to her father's customers in France. She was twenty-one now, fully a woman, happy, outgoing, independent-minded, forthright in her views – in many ways, Sarah thought, pausing to look at the bent fair head, very like Jos had been at her age.

At the little writing desk Sarah was also composing a letter: this one, for Peter Swift to copy later, was worded with extreme care, designed to stir the conscience of one of their aristocratic customers who, like so many of his kind, seemed to regard the payment of bills as beneath his consideration – he had owed a considerable sum to the firm for three years now. Sarah had a gift for striking exactly the right note – part way between deference and contempt – to produce the desired result.

The letter completed, she went to warm cramped fingers at the brisk fire. 'I'm going to Mary Ann in the garden, Susannah. If I were you, I'd not sit there too long – it's a lovely day and a pity to be indoors.'

Susannah turned her head and smiled. 'Don't worry, Mama – I've promised to reward myself with a ride when I've finished this.'

For more than a year now Sarah had been afraid to venture very far from the house, for fear her little daughter might need her – the convulsions had become so frequent and so often nearly fatal. They had tried cold baths and hot baths, electric shocks, even a trip to Buxton which had exhausted the child rather than helped her; but despite all the temporary improvements Mary Ann simply grew steadily more disabled. The only comfort was that her brothers and sisters – particularly the two younger girls – cared for her devotedly, and so gave her a great deal of pleasure.

Perhaps, thought Sarah as she crossed the landing, today would be one of the good times. She hoped so, for she ought not to spend too long with Mary Ann – there was a great deal to do. Lord Scarsdale was coming with a party of friends on his way to Trentham, and after he had visited the works he must be entertained here with tea and polite conversation; and then the Priestleys would arrive in time for supper to stay for two nights before going on to London, taking Jos with them – Jos, who was so visibly excited at the prospect. The thought cheered her: it was so very long since Jos had been excited about anything.

Mary Ann was not after all in the garden. As Sarah descended the stairs she heard the singing first, the clear fresh youthful voice rising up the stairs from the drawing room; and then Mary Ann's delighted laughter in response. Jane Hillyard had pushed the child's wheeled chair as far as the drawing room door and there come to a halt, turning the vehicle so that Mary Ann could look up at the singer high on the scaffolding which filled the room – a sturdy snub-nosed young man with flaming red hair who was painting the ceiling to one of John Flaxman's austerely classical designs. Sarah was still not quite sure what she thought of young William Blake; he was touchy and opinionated and more than a little strange, and Jos found him irritating in the extreme, for all Flaxman's warm recommendation of him. But Mary Ann adored him, for he sang to her and told her stories and set her laughing as few even of her closest family could do. For that, Sarah thought, he could be forgiven a great deal.

'Mary Ann, my chick, say goodbye to Mr Blake for now,' she said to the child as she reached the hall. 'We're going into the garden.'

The young man bent his bright head precariously over the edge of the scaffolding and waved the child on her way. As they emerged into the April sunlight they heard him resume his singing, joyous as a bird.

Mary Ann enjoyed the garden, shouting with laughter as a robin hopped unafraid along the orchard wall, and pointing eagerly with a happy gurgle at the last of the daffodils. Jos came to find them when he returned for dinner, going straight to the child and talking tenderly to her as if she could understand every word he said. The little girl loved her father: only at her

428

very worst did her face fail to light up for him, and today she greeted him with a bright smile and a shout.

'She's much better than she was yesterday,' Jos commented. 'This spring sunshine is just the thing for her.' He came to Sarah's side and waited as Jane pushed the wheeled chair on ahead of them. Sarah studied his face: he looked less tired than usual, and she knew that lately he had been sleeping better. If only this projected trip to London might be the turning point!

'What do you think, Sally?' he asked after a moment. 'Do you think she will ever really be well, like the others?'

'I don't know, love. I just take each day as it comes. We can't do anything else.'

'No.' He paused, then added on an optimistic note, 'Perhaps they'll find some cure for her – perhaps one day Darwin will try something new, and it will work.'

'Perhaps: but until then the most important thing is that she should be as happy as we can make her.'

The rest of the day went well. Lord Scarsdale's party visited the pattern room and a selected portion of the works (only a very few close friends were ever permitted to see where – and how – the jasperware was made), and then were entertained to tea in the library, in an atmosphere of refined politeness.

'I've always admired the jasper plaque we had set in the chimney piece in the tapestry corridor,' Lady Scarsdale told them, as she sipped tea from a queen's ware cup, 'but I had not realised how many other exquisite things were made here. Do all your designs come from antique patterns?'

'I think it's more true to say that I try to capture the spirit of the antique – I have never wished to be simply a slavish copyist.'

Lord Scarsdale nodded approvingly. 'Yes, I think in that lies your success: your wares, and the jasper in particular, recreate in our age the beauty of the ancient world.' From a man who was an enthusiast for anything classical – and had, through the skill of Robert Adam, built his house at Kedleston near Derby on those principles – this was praise indeed. 'I am surprised not to find you in London,' he went on. 'Does the sale of the Portland vase not interest you?'

Jos caught Sarah's eyes and smiled. 'Certainly – I am leaving for London in a few days, with that very object in mind.'

'Ah! So you hope to buy it? May we then expect your interpretation of its beauties in jasperware some time soon?'

'That, my lord, depends on many things, I'm afraid – above all, of course, whether or not I may somehow be able to make a close study of it. I understand that the Duke of Portland is anxious to buy it for himself from his mother's estate. But I have had the pleasure of his acquaintance for some time – I am hopeful that some arrangement may be made.'

'You must let Sir William Hamilton know, if you do decide to work on it. After all, he was the one who brought it to England.'

By contrast, the guests at supper that evening brought unalloyed pleasure, without constraint or formality. The two older Wedgwood boys were away – John in France with Matthew Boulton and James Watt, Josiah dutifully pursuing his studies at Edinburgh University – but, in a way, that only made Priestley's arrival the more welcome, because Tom wholeheartedly shared the enthusiasm of both his father and their guest for scientific enquiry, as his brothers did not. Hearing the eager lively talk about the table, Sarah thought, 'It's almost like having Bentley again.' But it was not, of course, and never could be. For her, as for Jos, there would always, for ever, be something missing.

But these last few days, increasingly, she had begun to feel that Jos was her old dear love again, and not just the empty shell he had become since Bentley's death. He was still inclined to be irritable, and he was more grave in his demeanour than he used to be, dignified rather than ebullient, less given to overwhelming enthusiasms for some new project – except now, when the possibility had arisen of studying the Portland vase. She prayed that nothing would go wrong with the coming trip to London, that it would send him back to her happy, looking to the future, and able at last to admit her again to that innermost part of himself from which she had been for so long excluded. Then she could finally and for ever banish the sense of guilt and responsibility which had haunted her, as the piece of superstitious nonsense her reason told her it was.

The next day the fine weather held, and the younger girls were sent to work in their garden plots while Jane once more pushed Mary Ann along the well-kept paths. Sarah could spend little time with her youngest child today, for she had Mary Priestley to entertain. They walked and read and called on Kate and talked of their children, and generally passed the time in the kind of aimless feminine activity in which Sarah rarely and reluctantly indulged, though she liked her guest and found her good company. Jos and Tom and Priestley spent the morning with Alexander Chisholm in the laboratory at the works, and returned at dinner time with an air of happy satisfaction about them.

They had planned a trip on the canal for the afternoon, but as they were about to leave Jane came to say that Mary Ann seemed a little feverish, and so Sarah stayed behind. The child was fretful and restless; Sarah hoped it was only a chill but she dared not leave her.

When he looked in at supper time, Jos found her sitting at the bedside. 'How is she?'

'Not very well, poor lass,' Sarah told him anxiously. 'The fever seems to be growing worse.'

Jos sat down on the edge of the bed and after a while was able to draw a weary smile from his daughter. 'Shall I send for Mr Bent?'

'It might be wise – I wish Dr Darwin were nearer at hand.'

Mr Bent could only advise bathing and a medicine which might or might not prove effective. The fever increased, bringing a frightening delirium which set the little girl staring and shouting at unseen horrors in the candlelit room, beyond any soothing. Sarah sponged the dry hot skin with cold water and murmured gentle words, and prayed. She knew, with a growing anguish, that she was waiting for the convulsions to begin, as inevitably, inexorably they would, whatever she tried to do.

They came at last some time after midnight, throwing the helpless little body into the terrible tormenting spasms that Sarah knew only too well. Soon after they began, as mother and nurse knelt either side of the bed longing for them to cease, Jos came in, softly, and sat down beside Sarah, putting his arm about her.

'Go back to bed, love,' she whispered, though her body ached for him to stay. 'There's nothing you can do. You have a journey tomorrow.'

'I shan't go to London if she's not better,' Jos told her softly. 'Priestley will have to go on without me.'

Sarah knew what that would cost him, but she did not argue. They sent Jane to bed and sat on together, watching and

431

waiting. Sometime not long before dawn the convulsions ceased at last, and Mary Ann lay very still, eyes closed. She looked white and exhausted, without life. Sarah bent and touched her cheek, and the blue eyes opened, their expression blank and unfocussed. Jos held her limp hands in his, stroking them and murmuring, 'My little girl . . . my Mary Ann . . .' in an endless soft rhythm. After a time the unseeing eyes closed again.

'She always sleeps for a while, when the fits have gone,' said Sarah.

But when the sun rose they knew that Mary Ann would never wake again.

For a long time afterwards Jos held Sarah in his arms, and they stood there together as motionless almost as the little figure on the bed, dry-eyed and saying nothing. Joseph Priestley found them like that when, brought the news by Tom, he came in search of them.

'The journey can wait,' he said when Jos at last reminded him that by now they should have been on their way to London. 'We can think of that later.'

They would have liked Priestley to conduct the funeral, but the rector of Stoke, in whose parish they now were, though not unsympathetic to Dissenters, had read Priestley's recent notorious articles denying the truth of the virgin birth and would not allow such a heretic on consecrated ground. Instead, Priestley conducted a brief service at the house before Mary Ann's little coffin was carried from it for burial, and then stayed to talk consolingly to Sarah and the girls while Tom and his father went to the funeral.

He talked of sufferings ended, and a happier world, but Sarah, calm, unweeping, felt nothing, not even the harshly suppressed pain that she had known when Richard died. She was tired and somehow set apart from everyone, beyond their reach. Perhaps, she thought, trying to understand the strangeness of the sensation, it was because she was exhausted after all her watching, and relieved that at last the burden had been lifted, from Mary Ann as from herself.

That evening, as they sat together in her little sitting room, Jos said to her, 'I've told Priestley to go on to London without me. They'll start tomorrow.'

'Oh no – no, you mustn't do that!' Her voice was sharp with

432

urgency. 'You must go to London – it's so important. Please, love, don't put it off!'

'How can I go and leave you at this time? My place is here, with all of you.'

'I shall be all right, we all shall. You must go – there's nothing more to be done here. Please, love!'

'Then you come with me.'

But she knew that was not what she wanted, though she could not have said exactly why. She argued more vehemently than ever: she would be better for staying quietly here – she had Susannah and Tom, and Kate near at hand. He would be busy in London, and her presence would only hamper him.

In the end he said, 'We'll see tomorrow,' and came to kiss her. She knew with certainty that he wanted her to say 'Come and sleep in my room tonight, so we can comfort each other'; she knew he was reaching out to her as she had always told herself she wanted him to do. But she only said, 'Goodnight, love', and then watched him go, stooping a little with sadness, to his own room, away from her.

He did go to London, because she convinced him that it was right for him to do so. She felt a kind of relief afterwards, and it puzzled her. In the past his absence had been a relief only because he had so adamantly shut her out; and yet now when she sensed that at last the turning point had come, that a very little more would bring them closer perhaps than they had ever been, she could not, would not, open herself to him, and wanted only to be alone. She could not understand it, for it made no sense at all. She felt angry that she could be so contrary, so difficult. Or was it rather that the years of estrangement from Jos had at last dried up all her power to feel, even to love?

That day, when Jos had gone, she ordered the carriage and went, alone, to the churchyard at Stoke, to stand looking down at Mary Ann's grave. She did not know why she had wanted to come here, unless it was in the hope of finding that she could still feel something, if only pain. But there was nothing. She was not even aware of grief. She stared down at the grave and saw only a small red-brown mound in the grass on which lay the flowers, still fresh, that Jos and Tom had brought here yesterday. This, she thought with dull conviction, had nothing to do with her, or with Mary Ann.

She made her way back across the churchyard to the waiting carriage; and returned home.

That night she lay awake for what seemed hours before sleep crept over her; and then she began to dream, a dreadful appalling dream. She thought she was in the churchyard at Burslem, and evil things were crawling over the gaping graves and a sky red as blood stained the grass and the earth and the stones with its light; and she ran from the place in cold terror, on and on through a wood where the branches dragged at her clothes and thorns caught at her flesh until at last she stumbled and fell, down and down in the dark, and came to rest in the arms of the man she had loved long ago; only it was no idyll that followed, but an ugly desperate panting struggle in the dark, all tangled limbs and sweat and a fruitless striving for a completion that was never within reach. Then from somewhere far off a voice cried, 'You have sinned and this is your punishment,' and she was alone in some high place, looking down on Astbury church; and she saw the carved devils swarming like black ants down the columns and across the nave to where Mary Ann lay quiet and still; and they climbed all over her helpless innocent body, pulling and pinching and tormenting until it writhed and quivered in convulsions . . .

With a cry of anguish she flung out her arms and somehow forced herself awake. She was in her own room alone in bed, and it was dark and quiet but for an owl hooting somewhere in the night.

She was trembling, bathed in sweat, sick with horror. The nightmare clung about her, impossible to throw off, though she climbed out of bed, crossed the room and pushed open the window to lean out, breathing in great gulps of the soft spring air. 'It was my punishment – it was my punishment for what I did . . .' the words hammered endlessly, cruelly, in her brain.

She went back to the bed and, fumbling, found a candle and lit it; but the grotesque shadows only seemed to make matters worse, as if the nightmare was taking actual shape about her. In the end she extinguished it, climbed back into bed and lay shivering with her head under the covers not daring to go to sleep again. It seemed an interminably long time before dawn came, and she could get up and dress and tell herself it was nothing, that it was over now.

But it was not over, though she told herself firmly it was all nonsense and she must put it out of her mind. 'Work is the b-best cure for grief,' Darwin would say. 'Keep busy.' Which she did of course, as always, although she was not sure if this empty horror had anything to do with grief at all. Susannah was anxious about her, and Tom when he came home, briefly and late for dinner; but she dismissed their anxieties and went to spend an afternoon checking through the household accounts.

By supper time she had still failed somehow to throw off the taint of the nightmare. 'I wish Jos were here,' she found herself thinking. 'I could tell him about it, and he would tell me it was all nonsense, just a dream.'

It would have been easier if she had not known that it was more than just a dream, had not felt that there was an inescapable logic about it all. It was as if some cruel and relentless power was playing with her like a cat with a mouse: 'Have your happiness for a little while, because you must pay for it twice over . . .' So she had lost Bentley and Jos at once, together, in a single cruel blow. Only she had not after all lost Jos for ever; he had begun, little by little, to return to her, to regain something of his old warmth and tenderness – or so she had thought. And then this had happened, just when it seemed as if happiness might again be possible – their poor suffering child had died in agony while they looked on and could do nothing to help her. 'You see!' that mocking providence seemed to say, 'you were not safe after all – there is no escape. And you alone are to blame.'

That night she did not go to bed, but sat reading – or trying to read – in her room until, now and then, she dozed a little, only to wake with a jolt, fearful of imminent dreams. When she knew it was past midnight and everyone would be in bed she took the candle and went downstairs, wandering through the empty silent rooms without purpose, pausing now and then to read a page of a book, gaze at a picture, shuffle aimlessly through a pile of papers, but settling to nothing. After a few hours of this she was chilled and desperately tired, longing for bed but afraid of what it might hold for her.

Very soon the servants would be about, but she did not want to face them. As quietly as she could she took a thick cloak from the cloakroom and let herself out of the side door into the

435

garden, in darkness still but touched by a faint lessening of the shadows. She made her way by instinct more than sight to a sheltered corner near the orchard where there was a seat, and sank down on it, knowing that when day came she would be hidden from the house by shrubs and trees, safe from intrusion.

Even here there was no escape. Guilt and fear and pain turned together in her mind endlessly, without respite. She began to think she must be going mad; the possibility only increased her terror. 'Help me!' she cried in silence to that terrible emptiness from which no answer came.

Slowly, imperceptibly, the darkness faded to grey, the cold ash grey of the dawn when the world is drained of colour and life and warmth, its deadness matching the bleakness of Sarah's spirit. Small things rustled in the undergrowth, a bird began its hesitant song, but all was lifeless still.

She heard a door close somewhere, the crunch of a step on gravel, and shrank back further into the shelter of the shrubs. The gardeners would not be here yet – perhaps it was Tom going down to the works. If so, he would not be likely to see her.

The steps came nearer, soft-footed but perfectly audible. She waited for their sound to turn away, along the path that crossed the garden to the gate; but they did not, only came on. When she realised that they were almost on her she stood up, too late to do more than turn in a kind of unreasoning panic to face the intruder.

It was not Tom. It was young Mr Blake with a wide-brimmed hat crammed on top of the flaming curls that lit up the greyness, and he seemed as startled as she was.

'Oh – Mrs Wedgwood!'

She looked about her as if in some vain search for a means of escape, and then sat down again, looking mutely up at him. He took off his hat and bowed his bright head, just a little.

'"Night's candles are burnt out, and jocund day
  Stands tiptoe on the misty mountain tops . . ."'

She stared at him, full of bitterness. How could he stand there quoting Shakespeare in praise of the morning – and not even aptly, she thought, for the garden faced south-west and there was no sunlight above the hills? He must know that Mary Ann had died and that he might be intruding on her grief.

'You are grieving for the little girl,' he said after a moment, a flat rather unemotional statement.

'What do you suppose?' she longed to retort; or even to shout, 'I want to grieve but I cannot – I am a monster who loved where she ought not to love and now I cannot love at all.' She wondered if it would shock him if she did; but she had no means of finding out, for she did not say it.

He frowned, and then abruptly sat down beside her. She could not quite bring herself to tell him to go away, though she wanted to. Or did she? She was aware, dimly, of a certain niggling curiosity about him. Suddenly she heard herself say, 'Do you believe it was all a punishment for sin?' She immediately wished it unsaid, but it was too late.

'Sin?' he asked sharply. 'What sin? She was a little child.'

Since she had begun, she could only go on. 'No, not *her* sin,' she corrected him. 'Mine.' And then she was afraid. 'What have I done?' she thought. 'He is almost a stranger.'

He did not question her, as she had feared he might; but he frowned sharply, as if the very thought appalled him. 'What kind of tyrant is your God? Not the Jesus I know, who said, "Woman, thy sins are forgiven thee." Don't you remember?' He might, she thought, have been speaking of a mutual friend met only yesterday. 'As for the child, you wept for her suffering – can you think He does any less than share your tears, and her pain? But He shall wipe away all tears from your eyes, and there shall be no more sorrow nor crying nor pain, only joy.'

'Joy! I can see no cause for joy at all.'

'Not when Mary Ann is running through the fields of heaven with Jesus and His angels, laughing for joy?'

She stared at him, at the bright hair springing up from the broad pale forehead, and the eager dark eyes; for a moment, hesitant and faint, she glimpsed the vision he had conjured up, longing for it to be real. 'I can't see it.'

He threw down his hat and took her hands in his. 'You must, for it's true.'

Sarah freed her hands, turning her face away from him. 'She never did learn to run, not once. She scarcely walked, even for a little while.'

'Then rejoice that she is healed and made whole.'

'But how do I know that?'

'I know. I saw the angels come to take her home.'

The quiet words shocked her more than anything else he had said, but it was a strange kind of shock, not of horror or fear or dismay, only bringing with it a complete stillness that seemed to go right through to the very heart of her. She thought of the consolation she had found in other griefs: from Bentley when Richard died, a consolation that had turned to a poison still lingering in her blood; from Darwin, who had given her the release of confession but somehow, it seemed, had left some place untouched; and now this young man she hardly knew, with his strangeness and his awkward manners and his total certainty, had presumed to lecture her – only it was not quite like that. 'Woman thy sins are forgiven thee' – yes, there is an escape after all, she thought. What was it next? 'Go thou and sin no more' – an end, a door closed, and then a new beginning . . .

Suddenly, she smiled and opened her eyes, though there were tears blurring her vision. 'You're a strange young man, Mr Blake,' she said shakily, 'but thank you . . .' And then she began to weep, gently and for a long time, because it was what she needed. Her companion touched her hand once and then stood up and quietly left her alone.

When the chaise drew up before the front door Sarah looked first at Jos's face, even before she stepped forward to embrace him. She hoped, almost without daring to hope, to find in it the same eager light she had seen so often in the early years, the sure sign that all was going well and that he was about to immerse himself in some new and difficult and rewarding project. She did not find it. He looked calm, thoughtful, perhaps even a little troubled – and, as he stepped down to her waiting arms, transparently glad to see her. He clung to her for a moment almost with a kind of desperation, and then turned to give orders for unpacking the chaise. 'Take particular care with the crate inside,' he instructed.

Sarah stared at him. 'Jos – is that . . .? Have you . . .?' She was not sure. If she was right surely there should have been triumph there, or delight?

He nodded and smiled, though with restraint. 'Yes – the Duke of Portland has loaned it to me. I shall begin work as soon as I can.'

438

'Aren't you going to show it to me?' she asked.

'All in good time. First I want to hear how you are. There wasn't a moment in London when I didn't think of you and worry that you were all right.'

She smiled and came closer and put her arms about him. 'There was no need, love. All is well.' She studied his face with great tenderness. 'I think I should have been worrying about you. What is it, love? Mary Ann, I suppose . . .'

He sighed and bent his head. 'I did come to ask myself if we did wrong – if there was something we could have done differently, something that would have made her life happier perhaps.' It was not the nightmare which had tormented Sarah, only the natural self-questioning of a rational man; but Sarah knew it was real enough for all that, and it was clouding the happiness he might have had; and she knew it was in her power to bring him ease.

'Perhaps there was, love – I don't know. Perhaps we shall never know. We did what we could as we saw it; we could have done nothing more. It's over now, as far as a grief can ever be over.'

His eyes on her face were thoughtful and troubled. 'Sometimes I find it hard to accept – to understand why, make any sense of it at all. Yet it ought to be possible.'

Sarah kissed him. 'Enough to know that all's well with her now,' she said softly. 'That should give us something, almost, to be glad about.' She added the 'almost' because she thought the words would have sounded callous without it. She could not begin to explain that morning in the garden to Jos: she would not have known where to find the words.

What she could do, finding exactly the right words of understanding tenderness, was to help him to find an answer to the questions that were haunting him; and by the time they had talked a little more she knew that for him too the torment had ended.

'Tea first,' she said at last from the comfort of his embrace; 'or are you going to show me the vase? I don't think I can wait much longer.'

So he opened the case and pulled out handfuls of straw, and at last reached in and with great gentleness lifted out the vase and set it on the table; and she saw then that the old light was in his eyes. 'There, Sally – there it is!'

He put his arm about her and they stood side by side gazing at it.

Sarah did not quite know what she had expected. She had seen drawings of it before, but they had somehow looked nothing like this. The body of the vase was of a deep blue-black and had a hard sheen to it, and such an intensity of colour that where the white figures upon it had been cut most finely the body showed through, giving depth to the foliage of the graceful trees and layered rocks, shadowing the folds of garments or the cupids' wings, or the waving hair of the strange bearded heads that decorated the handles. Sarah reached out and ran her fingers over the smooth surface and the delicate outline of the relief work.

'It's beautiful . . .'

'They say it was made to hold the ashes of the Roman Emperor Alexander Severus; but then they say many things.'

'And the figures on it? What do they represent?'

He grinned. 'There are even more theories about that. I've heard it on good authority that it shows the judgement of Paris, Adam and Eve in the Garden, Leda and the Swan, the birth of Augustus, and – oh, I don't know what else. I talked it over with Darwin when I called there on my way home. We decided we thought it represented death and the entrance of the soul into Elysium. But I expect there'll be other theories before I'm done.'

'You are going to copy it then?'

'I am going to try. But look at the shape of it – throwing that on a wheel is going to be very difficult.'

'I suppose it must have been thrown originally . . .' She caught his eye. 'Wasn't it?'

'Look at it again. What do you think it's made of?'

'I know some authorities said it was made of stone, but you doubted that.' She touched the vase again, tapping gently with a finger nail, running her hand around the rim. It was made of some cold substance, very hard, smooth, almost transparent – 'It's glass! It is, isn't it?'

He nodded excitedly. 'Yes, it's glass – I'd never thought of that until I saw it. But my jasper is harder than glass. Just imagine how it might look, if I can get over the difficulties. See how the figures are cut so the body shows through to give them depth. It was a true artist who made this.'

Sarah put her arm about him. 'And a true artist who'll create it again,' she said tenderly.

They called the children to see the vase, and Blake, too, who redeemed himself a little in Jos's eyes by admiring it with a passionate enthusiasm.

Jos and Sarah were very late to bed that night, for they sat together by the library fire long after everyone else was asleep, talking with a freedom and openness which they had not known for many years. They climbed the stairs at last hand in hand and, with no need for words, went together to her room, to the wide curtained bed, and slid beneath the covers into one another's arms.

They found there laughter, and tenderness, and love; and passion fed by the years of separation to a new intensity. And tonight for the first time in her life Sarah passed through that closed door with Jos to the ecstatic contentment beyond, a completion the more wonderful because it was wholly shared and wholly tender and untouched by remorse or regret. Jos himself must have known that somehow it had been different for her, for afterwards he laughed softly and murmured, 'Not bad for two such old folks, Sally my girl,' and she nestled against him and fell asleep, smiling, there in his arms.

CHAPTER TWENTY-ONE

1791

It had been winter still when Jos and Sarah left Etruria for London, the hard earth swept by an icy wind and only a few hesitant snowdrops and crocuses struggling into flower.

Now, little more than a month later, they came home to spring. Primroses covered the banks, wood anemones starred the grass beneath the trees, pear and plum were snowy with blossom, and new leaves, frail and brilliantly green, were opening on the once bare branches of woodland and hedgerow. The soft warm air was loud with the sounds of birdsong and running water.

On the hill above Etruria they were busy with the last of the spring ploughing in the Wedgwood fields, the tiny figures of plodding horses and men moving slowly back and forth on the red earth, with a cloud of gulls following after. John must have been there too and seen Jos and Sarah coming, for as they turned into the drive to the Hall he came cantering on horseback to meet them, his long face flushed and smiling. He was twenty-five now, easy-going and unambitious, happy to drift along as life took him. Jos called to the coachman to halt, and they waited until John drew rein alongside.

'There now, and I hoped we'd have the ploughing finished before you were home! We've been getting the top field ready for turnips. Still, it's nearly done.' They moved on again slowly, John continuing to talk as he rode alongside. 'The grass is growing well – this warm spell was just what was needed. The girls have done a good deal in the garden – they were busy there when I went out this morning . . .' He talked on, about farm and house and garden, but never once about the works. In the end, Sarah broke in to ask him, 'Have there been many visitors to the works? How's business, do you know?'

John shrugged. 'I expect Josiah will have told you most of it.'

'He talked about business as little as possible,' put in Jos bitterly, but Sarah laid her hand over his to quieten him, and John did not hear.

'Tom's seen to that side of things,' he went on. 'He's there now, I think – oh no, he went to see about something to do with his educational institute, or whatever it is he calls it. I don't know: he never seems to be around much when I'm at home. Robert Darwin's been over two or three times, you know – just for the ride. We had a picnic one day in Bradwell Wood.' Robert Darwin was a fully qualified physician by now, in practice on his own account at Shrewsbury, and already prospering.

'We have a scheme for the summer. Joss and Sukey and I think we'll go and stay at Shrewsbury, and then go on to Wales – Pembrokeshire, maybe. Sukey wants to visit the Allens at Cresselly – you know, she met the daughters somewhere or other, and they've been very pressing for her to come.'

'That should please Josiah,' Sarah thought a little grimly, 'I seem to remember they were a very aristocratic family, with ancestors going back to the Cecils.'

They reached the house, where Jones the butler welcomed them smoothly. Mrs Massey had retired now to a small house on the estate to live on a comfortable pension, and a new housekeeper had taken her place; but it was Jones – soft-footed, efficient George Jones – who now ruled the indoor staff.

Jos hurried upstairs, calling greetings to his three daughters as they crossed the landing to meet him. Daughters, he had often told Sarah with feeling, were much less trouble than sons; but then they had never been burdened with his ambitions for them.

None of the remaining Wedgwood girls was a child any longer, in the strictest sense. Sarah, plain, sensible and serious-minded, was fourteen, old for her years and much given to heavy reading. Catherine, slender and fair and lovely, was seventeen and more worldly than her sister, but with a haughtiness of manner that invariably distanced her from many people, particularly, her mother realised in the light of Josiah's recent behaviour, those she regarded as her social inferiors. Susannah, at twenty-six, was the loveliest of them all; and, just at the moment, she glowed with a sparkling warmth of eye and cheek that almost made her seem younger

443

than her sisters. Sarah kissed them and then left Jos to hear their news while she went in search of Tom, in his laboratory in one of the attic rooms. Josiah had said he was over the worst, but she wanted to see for herself.

Her younger son, disturbed at his work, always had the look of someone woken suddenly from a pleasant dream: a little vague, as if not quite sure where he was, but with something of the happiness of the experience hanging about him still. He had it now, as he unfolded his long slender person from his chair and came to hug his mother.

She held his hands to keep him standing where she could study him. She thought he looked no better, even perhaps a little thinner, but his expression was cheerful enough with none of the rather daunting severity it took on when he was in pain. And then he smiled, with the melting sweetness that could overcome anxiety or anger with equal force. 'Come now, Mama, don't look like that. I've had three days without headaches, and the other pain's nearly gone.' He kissed her lightly on the forehead, neatly diverting her attention from his health. 'I was sorry to hear about the vote in parliament – it ought to have gone the right way, when Mr Wilberforce spoke so eloquently – did Father hear the debate? You didn't say in your letter.'

'Yes, he was there. The abolition motion had the support of the Prime Minister and the opposition, but it still wasn't enough – 163 votes to 88 is quite a sizeable defeat.'

'After all our hopes too: it's such a blow. What plans are there now? You must tell me what I can do.'

'You can be sure we shall – we've a great deal to talk over with all of you. I don't doubt you've made some progress here that you will want to show us too – and what about the works? Josiah said you'd hopes of another order for the Portland vase.'

'It came to nothing, I'm afraid. But we've had trouble with the last two made – the ovens overheated, I think. It's difficult to get it right when the wind's high. We've begun again though. Oh, and I've finished the paper on heat at long last.' Jos, Sarah knew, thought the paper might well be good enough to be presented to the Royal Society.

She smiled at her son's enthusiasm, which reminded her so often of Jos himself as a young man. 'He'll be glad to hear it – but now it's dinner time, so you'll have to tear yourself away from your books.'

'Sometimes,' said Tom with a hint of impatience, 'I think I ought to set up house on my own, where I don't get led astray by the lures of family life.'

'Like meals!' Sarah laughed. 'Don't be silly, my dear. It's good for you to relax sometimes. Now hurry up.'

He caught her arm to detain her. 'Mama!' She saw the gravity of his expression, and turned back from the door. 'Josiah wrote – he said he had offended you both . . .' She was not surprised that his elder brother had already written, though he had been only a day in London before they had left him: whenever they were apart, Josiah wrote to Tom with unfailing regularity, for, at twenty-one and nineteen respectively, they were as close as ever. But it did surprise her a little that he had mentioned the disagreement: she wondered how much he had told his brother. 'He said it was the letter he wrote, offering to come and relieve you – I didn't see it, so I don't know exactly what the trouble was . . .'

Perhaps it was in Josiah's favour that he had not shown the letter to his brother; perhaps he had after all been a little ashamed of its tone. But he had sent it all the same, and it had plunged Jos into a depression deeper than any he had suffered for some time. Reserved, correct, with a strong sense of duty, Josiah had suggested that he come temporarily to London to take the place of Tom Byerley, suddenly fallen ill, since Jos and Sarah were anxious to return home and no one else could be spared from Etruria; and then he had hastily qualified his offer. 'I would live in the house,' he had explained, 'and take care of the correspondence and do what other business I could – except attending on the rooms any farther than waiting upon some particular people, for I have been too long in the habit of looking upon myself as the equal of everybody to bear the haughty manners of those who come into a shop.' Sarah had almost been able to see the expression on Josiah's face as he wrote that last word, full of gentlemanly disdain for trade and for the humiliating obsequiousness of those who were forced to live by it.

For Jos the conclusion had been plain, and deeply hurtful. 'I can see how it is – he despises us, his own parents. He thinks he's too good for us, too good for the kind of work we do, all we stand for – a fine finicky gentleman too proud to dirty his hands in the market place.'

445

Sarah had tried to comfort him, but at heart she had known he was right, for all that Josiah later denied it. Their second son would do his duty, but without enthusiasm. It was to Tom they must look to find again Jos's creative and enquiring spirit, his independence of mind; Tom who, now, had sprung warmly to his brother's defence: '. . . .you know, Josiah's real trouble is that he's more at home with books than people. Put it down to shyness if you like.'

She smiled, and brushed his cheek with her hand. 'Shyness it will be then – so long as you're at the dinner table in two minutes.'

He gave a cry of mock dismay and ran to his room to change.

There were no guests at the table today, only the seven Wedgwoods; though as always these days there were one or two additional places set, in case of unexpected callers. It had happened so often that a last-minute arrival had necessitated a hasty rearrangement of the table settings that Jos had decreed they must be permanently prepared. 'It's like sitting down in the showroom,' John had complained once, not very seriously; though Sarah, looking at the great oval table set with the best of Wedgwood queen's ware – one of the four or five services used in rotation – saw what he meant. The atmosphere, however, was always very far from that of the showroom, with so many lively young people at the table. She sometimes thought there must be more good talk and laughter in their dining room than anywhere else in the land.

Today, of course, the atmosphere was a little more serious than usual. Jos and Sarah had gone to London for what they had hoped would be the passing of the bill to abolish the slave trade, that cause which had been so dear to Bentley's heart. As if with a sense that it was a legacy left to him by his friend, Jos had joined the anti-slavery committee which for some years now had worked to bring pressure to bear on parliament and to gather information in support of its aims. Under the leadership of William Wilberforce, the wealthy and devout MP for Yorkshire, it had seemed that success was within reach at last. And then had come the bitter disappointment of the parliamentary defeat.

'What did your committee decide to do then?' Tom asked. 'I suppose there can't be another vote for a long time.'

'I'm afraid not. I think Wilberforce felt it more than most,

446

because he's always been opposed to anything that smacks of extreme measures, and of course now we have little choice but to take them.'

'Revolution at last!' said Tom with a laugh.

'This is not France, Tom,' Sarah reminded him lightly; and then, more seriously, she went on, 'I think that's just the trouble, that since the revolution in France anyone who wants to change anything is seen as a terrible threat to peace and stability – it's foolish, of course, but there it is.'

'Especially anyone who actually had the effrontery to support the French revolution, of course,' Jos added ruefully. 'I think sometimes Wilberforce wishes he had less radical companions in his fight. He doesn't mind fervour in religion, but in politics – that's another matter.'

'Come on then – what are these extreme measures we're to take? Was it decided? Do we give away one of our cameos free with every dinner service?' Tom's voice was teasing, but there was a sparkle of excitement in his eyes.

Sarah looked down at the little jasperware cameo mounted in cut steel which she wore pinned to the collar of her sprigged muslin gown. It was one of Wedgwood's most successful designs, modelled by William Hackwood on lines suggested by Sarah, and showing a kneeling manacled slave set about with the words, 'Am I not a man and a brother?' The cameos had been set in snuff boxes, rings, buttons and all manner of small items, and had proved immensely popular, setting quite a fashion. 'We almost do that already,' she pointed out. 'No, the main thing is that we are to urge everyone to refuse to buy anything from the West Indies – sugar, rum, whatever – '

'Anything that's produced with slave labour,' said Tom thoughtfully. 'Yes, I can see that – if everyone did it, the slave owners would go bankrupt. They'd be forced to give up slavery to survive. It's an imaginative idea.'

'But isn't that an unjust interference with legitimate trade? Won't it merely make for resentment? Besides, I thought you were asking for the abolition of the slave *trade*, not slavery as a whole.'

Sarah looked shocked. 'Oh, John, only because it's a first stage, that's all – we want it all to go, and the sooner the better.'

'Well, yes, of course, I know that: quite right too – but Father always said it has to be done bit by bit. If you hit the slave owners as well as the slave traders, won't there be so much resentment that they'll close ranks, and you'll get nothing at all? They're very powerful, the West Indian landowners.'

'That was more or less Wilberforce's argument,' said Jos. 'But he was overruled by the rest of us. After all, his gentlemanly ways have been tried. It is time for something new, something to make people think again about the whole evil business of slavery.'

'Besides, it can't be right to enjoy food which depends for its existence on slavery,' said Sarah eagerly; and John, never one to assert himself, lapsed into silence.

'So from now on it's no more sugar or rum at Etruria.'

'We shall have to drink lemonade punches instead,' suggested Catherine pertly.

'Since when have you been accustomed to rum punches, miss?' demanded Jos, and she laughed.

The only member of the family who seemed to take little interest in the discussion was Susannah, and that puzzled Sarah. She had thought that of all their children it was Susannah who cared most about the anti-slavery campaign, for she had lived with the Bentleys and learned from her 'Papa Bentley' many of the ideas and principles he held dear. But today she was almost silent and more than a little abstracted, as if some private thoughts of her own absorbed her. It was only when, later, Catherine began to tell her parents about the day of their picnic in Bradwell Wood, to which Robert Darwin had come, that Susannah seemed to come to life again, her face lighting up as if with some inner illumination.

Something connected in Sarah's brain. Robert Darwin – it was a long ride from Shrewsbury, scarcely an easy day's excursion – yet he came with increasing frequency, and had been doing so for some time. It was of course entirely natural that Susannah should form one of the party when the young people rode out together. Her manner towards him was always easy, open, light-hearted, even sisterly, Sarah had thought once – but looking back she began to wonder.

Since Robert Darwin continued to come often to Etruria, Sarah had ample opportunity to observe them together; and any doubts she might have had as to the nature of their relationship soon disappeared. The bond that united them was

448

so strong as to be almost tangible, like an electric charge linking eye to eye.

In spite of everything, Jos was on the whole a happy man that summer. Since cousin Tom Wedgwood's death three years ago, Byerley and the Wedgwood sons had been taken into partnership and Jos had officially retired. But it had, Sarah noted with tender exasperation, made little difference to his life. In fact the four years of work on the Portland vase had kept him tied more than ever to laboratory and kiln, years of unceasing experimentation before he had at last completed a copy of the vase which satisfied him; and even that had not quite come up to his own high standards. In the end there had been other more perfect copies, but each one took several weeks in the making and might at the last moment, for the most trivial of reasons, be ruined in the firing. The best copy had been exhibited in London for a time – to be viewed by ticket only, of course – and then Josiah had taken it to Europe. In all, twenty-four celebrated or aristocratic subscribers had ordered copies of the vase. Jos had been a little disappointed that there had not been more, but it was perhaps just as well, for it would have been difficult to meet any large demand. In any case, nothing could lessen his pride in the work.

It was soon greater than ever, for Sir William Hamilton, temporarily returned from Naples and about to be married to the beautiful but notorious Emma Hart, came to Etruria that summer expressly to see Jos's copy. Sir William had been responsible for bringing the original vase to England, and he was fervent in his admiration of Jos's work. From so notable a connoisseur that was high praise indeed.

Even when Jos resisted the temptation to wander down to the works as if he were still as much in control as ever, he could not be idle. He involved himself in a round of meetings and visits, or long sessions of letter writing, all concerned with the abolition campaign. Sarah knew that his influence was considerable, the more so because it was rarely given so openly on behalf of any political cause. At election times the local candidates would turn in vain for the celebrated Josiah Wedgwood to give them his support. 'Until we have a reformed parliament and a vote for everyone there's no point in supporting one party or another,' he declared, for he despised

449

the corruption of the electoral process. But when, as now, some cause fired his imagination, he gave his time and money and energy unstintingly. Even so, he could occasionally be persuaded to abandon more serious matters and join the family for a picnic, a ride, or a day in the hayfield. Otherwise the garden – as always – provided his chief recreation.

Byerley recovered and returned to his duties in Greek Street, and Josiah came home, bringing a certain amount of tension with him. Since John had as little as possible to do with the works, it was Josiah for the most part who managed the business side of the enterprise; and until now there had been few difficulties with Jos, who had been happy to discuss any problems with his son. Now Josiah found that his father would greet any request for help with some bitter little remark which showed how much the unfortunate letter still rankled. Josiah gave up talking to Jos about business matters, and turned to Sarah, instead, the more hurt that his father continued to take a lively interest in Tom's experiments and innovations.

And then autumn came, and Robert Darwin called one morning with an unusually purposeful expression on his face. Sarah, returning from the works where she had been helping Josiah to reorganise the display in the pattern room, heard the young doctor ask for Mr Wedgwood and, coming in to greet him, drew her own conclusions.

'I think you'll find him in the greenhouse with James Downes,' she said. 'I'll take you there.'

She led the way, along the passage and out of the side door to the bright windswept garden, chaotic with the blown leaves against which James Downes, head gardener, was at present fighting an almost ceaseless war; from which he had temporarily broken off to join Jos in the greenhouse for a discussion over the precious new vine. Sarah pushed open the door, signalling to Robert to pass her, but he hung back, and instead Jos excused himself and came out to them.

'Robert would like a word with you, love.'

'With both of you,' said the young man hastily, in a voice so upset by nervousness that it ended in a squeak.

Many people found Robert Darwin intimidating. Like his father he was a huge man, tall and broad, dominating any room he entered. But this morning, out here in the garden towering over the small figure of Jos, solidly at home with his broad

450

dark-browed face and his earthy hands, it was the younger man who looked shrunken, ill at ease and out of place. For quite some time the two men looked at one another, Jos – entirely unsuspicious still – waiting with friendly interest, Robert swallowing hard, opening and shutting his mouth, fidgeting with his hands and saying nothing at all. Once, he cleared his throat, thrust his hands deep in his pockets and flung up his head; but still he was silent. Sarah could bear it no longer. 'Let's walk along to the orchard,' she suggested gently. 'It's more sheltered there.'

They set out, in silence. Jos was happy to enjoy the day: the sunlight brilliant on swaying boughs, the late roses dancing in the wind, the last apples ripe on the trees. But Sarah was trying desperately to think of some way to bring Robert quickly to the point, before he crumpled completely. It would have been funny, if she had not known how painful it must be for him.

In the end it was Jos who in all innocence forced him to speak. 'Have you come from Derby? How is your father?'

Robert jolted, as if taken by surprise, and then burst out in jerky phrases, 'I don't know – well, I think – no, I haven't come from – I may go on – ' And then he stood still and said abruptly and a little too loudly, 'Mr Wedgwood – sir – I wish to marry Susannah.'

Jos too halted and very slowly turned to face the young man; and at that moment any inclination to laugh was swept from Sarah. She did not know how she had expected Jos to react – with pleasure, at least, if no more. What she had not anticipated for one moment was the look of appalled dismay on her husband's face, mingled with disbelief.

It quelled Robert, destroying all his momentary courage, and he simply gazed back at Jos with a look of mute appeal, as if to say, 'I know I presume too much, but I beg you to be kind.' Sarah longed to intervene, but dared not, afraid of making mattters worse by saying quite the wrong thing – for surely this unexpected reaction of Jos's must give way in a moment to acceptance?

It did not. After a painful interval he suddenly said, 'Marry Susannah? Why should you want to marry her?'

Robert and Sarah alike stared at him, astonished at the stupidity of the question, which should surely have been unnecessary from so doting a father. Eventually, realising that some kind of answer did appear to be required, Robert, red-faced, began a stumbling reply. 'Well – she's – there's no one else, never has been . . . I love her, have done all my life . . . now she – er – loves me, she says . . .'

Sarah smiled encouragement at him, but he did not look round to see it. Jos merely glowered up at the large young man. 'Sukey's not ready to tie herself down yet!' he snapped.

At that Robert's self-confidence surfaced briefly. 'She's twenty-six, sir! Many women have been mothers several times over by her age. Many women,' he added darkly, 'would think themselves past hope of marriage.'

'Oh Robert!' thought Sarah despairingly; but it was too late. Jos glared at him, hostility in every pore, every gesture, every phrase.

'Are you suggesting you're my daughter's last hope? Let me tell you she could pick and choose from a dozen suitors. But what's so special about marriage? What have you to offer her that she hasn't got already? A comfortable, happy home? Love and care? Wealth? Country air, her own carriage, horses, garden, music, books, intelligent conversation? She has them all in abundance – what more could you offer her, pray?'

'A loving husband and, I hope and trust, fine healthy children to grow up under her care.'

'She can live a full happy life without those, can't she?'

'Perhaps you should ask her, sir.' Robert spoke quietly, but Sarah could see that it was only with a considerable effort that he was able to keep his temper.

'Hmph! I know my own daughter at least as well as you do, if not better, much better. I've watched her grow and blossom, and I've loved and cherished her with every year that passes. I don't want to see her tied down to some country doctor who works every hour God gives and has little time to spend at her side.'

Robert opened his mouth as if to say something; but then caught Sarah's eye and let her speak, in a voice sprightly with amusement. 'I suppose a master potter would make a better husband, with all those idle hours on his hands?'

She saw the answering tremor of laughter in Jos's eyes, but he had no intention of allowing it to soften him. 'You know that's different. We've always been a partnership, you and I. My work has never shut you out. But Sukey can't play the

452

doctor. She'd lose all her privacy and comfort, and see her husband at the beck and call of every Tom, Dick or Harry – no, Robert Darwin, that's not the life I want for my daughter. Nor, if she really considered the matter, would she, I'm quite sure.'

Robert's huge frame seemed to sag and droop, as if all the life had been drained out of him. Sarah longed to say something comforting or encouraging; but before she could think of anything he said with a note of hopelessness, 'Will you at least think it over, sir?'

'There's nothing to think over!' Jos snapped back; but this time Sarah did intervene.

'It is perhaps rather too important a matter to be decided quite so quickly. In any case, Robert, you are our good friend, and always welcome here. Nothing changes that – does it, Jos?'

'No – no, of course not,' agreed Jos grudgingly.

Sarah invited Robert to stay for dinner, and sent him in search of Susannah, so that by the time they sat down to eat he was looking calmer and just a little less miserable.

Meanwhile, as soon as they were alone, she turned on Jos.

'Oh, love, how could you? I can't think of a better husband for Susannah than Robert Darwin – he's kind, considerate, educated, reasonably wealthy, and the son of one of our dearest friends. And she loves him. What more could one ask?'

'Why should she want to marry at all?'

'Because she loves him and wants to share her life with him. There's nothing new or strange in that. It happens to most of us, and without it the world would very quickly come to an end. You at least should know that.'

'That doesn't mean Sukey has to throw herself away on a country sawbones.'

'Oh, Jos, what utter nonsense! Admit it – you just can't bear to let her go. I know you love her dearly – we both do – and I know you can't believe any other man is good enough to be trusted with her. Only Bentley was ever allowed that privilege. Every father since the world began has resented his daughter's suitors – my father was just the same, you may remember. But the more you try and hold her the more surely you'll lose her, because she'll turn against you.'

Jos looked at her then, and it was no longer anger that was in his eyes, but fear, and misery. 'I don't want to lose her – I don't want to lose anyone ever again. There have been too many, even Joss now . . .' He broke off, and she went to him and put her arms about him.

'Oh my love, you'll not lose her that way, not in any real sense – and I'm here still and always will be.' She felt him cling to her, and sensed the insecurity that was still there deep down in him. After a while she said gently, 'Think again, love.'

He drew back, shaking his head. 'Not yet – one day perhaps. It's too soon . . .' And with that hint of a possible future concession she had to be content: it was the only comfort she could offer the two young people – that, and the cheerless advice to be patient. It was, she thought, a measure of Susannah's love for her father that she seemed to understand.

CHAPTER TWENTY-TWO

1794

Jos was a little better today. In the afternoon he came down to the drawing room and sat by the window in the pale winter sunshine, well wrapped in rugs against the draughts.

From here he could look out on his beloved garden, with its well-tended lawns framed in pleasing arrangements of shrubs and trees and flowerbeds, which somehow even in winter managed to avoid the bleak dead look of most gardens. There were bright berries on the holly, gleaming against the deep green of the leaves, a scattering of evergreens amongst the bare branches, and in one sunny corner the winter jasmine was already beginning to flower. A few fragile Christmas roses had opened beneath the cherished and cosseted rhododendron, one of Jos's exotic new shrubs – Sarah thought it unexciting for most of the year, but the spectacular display of lavish pink blooms in the spring certainly justified its place in their garden.

Sarah, standing beside Jos with her hand resting on the back of his chair, was not looking at the garden. Instead she was gazing with a certain guilty hunger across it and down the hill to the works, watching the distant bustle of people and carts and barges. It must be three weeks since she had walked down there – almost as long since she had left the house at all – and she felt a wistful desire to pass again through those busy rooms with their familiar beloved sounds and smells: the purposeful rhythmic whirr of the potter's wheel, and the distinctive, unmistakable smells of wet clay and newly fired pots.

She consoled herself with the thought that she would not have been happy going so far from Jos at this time. After all, she was no longer needed at the works. Josiah and Tom Byerley between them managed the business here and in London, with efficiency if not with enthusiasm, and every branch now had its trusted manager to supervise the day-to-day running of the works. If Sarah were to go down there now,

455

it would be a piece of pure self-indulgence, because through all the changes and chances of her life her love for the potworks had been the one constant.

No, she thought with a faint smile; not the only one, nor yet the most important. There had been Jos too of course. She came round from behind his chair and sat down on the cushioned window seat, well to one side so that she could see him without obscuring his view of the garden, though he was not looking at the garden at present. His eyes were closed, and he appeared to have fallen asleep, breathing gently and evenly. She was relieved to see that the hectic flush had gone from his face: the fever had certainly lessened today. But it had left him pale and thin, apart from the swelling about his throat and jaw, and he looked very old.

'I suppose he is old,' she thought with some surprise. After sixty-four years of a life filled with incident enough for three long lives it was hardly astonishing that he should look old. Yet on the other hand both William Willet and her own father had lived until well over eighty, and neither of them had ever seemed old, not until the very last years of their lives. 'It's just that Jos is ill,' she told herself; 'once he's on his feet again he'll look younger.' Once before he had aged suddenly, when Bentley died, and then too he had regained some of his old vitality in the end. Not all of it, of course: something had died for ever with Bentley. But illness had never had the power to crush him as that grief had done: he was a fighter, unwilling to accept the limitations of an ailing body.

She did not, at the moment, examine the realisation that had been steadily growing within her during the last days: that somehow this illness was different. This time Jos was not making any attempt to fight. Instead he seemed to be accepting what came with a quiet serenity, as if he knew that there could be no outcome but one, and over that he no longer had any control.

Her thoughts slid over that dark place in her mind and came to rest on less troubling, more practical matters. Next week it would be Christmas – a pity John could not come, but with Louisa so near her time they could not be expected to travel all the way from London. In his last letter he had sounded a little happier; perhaps after all he would come to like being a banker. But she could not rid herself of the suspicion that John

456

would only really be happy as a country gentleman, living in what Jos would regard as idleness – and none of his sons must be idle. If John wouldn't be a potter, then he must follow some other calling.

Tom was the only one allowed to be idle, because necessity forced it on him; though he was as incapable as his father of actually doing nothing. But pain and sickness, growing more intense and more frequent as time went by, had forced him at last to acknowledge that a demanding career was not for him, and he – like John – had last year relinquished all share in the business. He was, at the moment, staying at Little Etruria, the comfortable house built for Thomas Bentley which was now the home of Josiah and his wife Bessie – and their daughter Sarah, just a year old this month.

So apart from John the whole family would be here this Christmas: Josiah and Bessie and little Sarah; Tom; and Susannah and the two younger girls. Christmas had always been such a time for festivities and rejoicing in the Wedgwood family – a time for welcoming friends and relations, for lavish hospitality and laughter and joy. They would be quieter this year, because of Jos's illness – though he would be better by then of course, and the rejoicing would be the greater for that . . .

But somehow she did not want to dwell on it. Instead she thought of all the Christmases she and Jos had spent together over the years, through good times and bad: that grim dark Christmas after Bentley's death, when the only rejoicing had been forced from them for the sake of the children – Jos had been ill then too; the noisy chaotic happy Christmas when they had decided to set up their 'Etruscan Academy', and all the children were at home and well and happy; the strained, troubled Christmas at Spen Green, when her father had been ill and Jos had feared himself nearly blind, and she had been so tense and miserable with guilt; the second Christmas of their marriage, when Susannah had been just old enough to crawl around amongst the guests, and laugh, and clap her dimpled little hands with delight; above all, that strange, joyous Christmas when she had thought Jos no longer cared for her – and then, suddenly, they were to be married at last. How many years ago was that now? She had been twenty-nine then, and she was sixty now – at the end of January they would have been married for thirty-one years . . .

Her mind sheered away from the thought. It was not

consoling, because it involved looking to the future, and she did not want to look to the future: it was too dark and uncertain, taking her near the hidden place that she must avoid at all costs.

No, she would not even think about Christmas, because that was next week: she would think about today, this very moment, and no further.

Jos had not stirred. His slight body slumped limp against the supporting cushions, somehow looking very small, almost shrunken in the swathing folds of the blankets from which his hands emerged, framed in the cuffs of the blue damask gown and the little frill of the nightshirt: those dear hands, broad and strong and supple, roughened with hard work, a little gnarled – and somehow now too motionless, as if they had no strength left in them; all that wonderful skill faded to nothing, wasting away . . .

Her eyes flew to his face, the features very still beneath the blue linen cap, the broad strong features she knew so well, but with a look of unreality about them, as if they were a copy carved in wax – or a death mask . . .

She moved then, leaned forward to lay a hand over one of his, and found with relief that though cool it was not icy. Then he opened his eyes, clear and grey and direct beneath the dark brows, and smiled. She felt her heartbeat quicken with relief and thankfulness. 'Did I disturb you, love? I'm sorry.'

'A pity to waste time in sleep.'

She did not pause to wonder what he meant, if anything. She said, with a sense of covering an awkwardness, 'I was looking down at the works just now. It all looks very busy. You wouldn't think that so many potters had failed, with the war causing such difficulties.'

He smiled again. 'We've come through worse times.' He spoke slowly, for his throat was still inflamed and his voice had no power in it – if she had not been close to him she would not have heard him – but for all that the words flowed quite easily. 'Bentley was right,' he said after a moment. 'War makes governments afraid of freedom.' He paused again, his thoughts following some reflective path of their own. 'I suppose it's a bad sign for our abolition campaign that the French have abolished slavery. After all, they are the enemy.'

'Yes, that will hardly make our government look on the

458

policy with favour. But there we are: it will come.' It was good that Jos was talking about politics, taking an interest again in something outside the family.

'What would Bentley have said, to see the frivolous French first in the field?'

'He would have been glad that anyone should have taken the step.'

'Yes: he was the most generous of men. We owe him so much.' Jos's fingers turned to move gently, in a caressing gesture, against hers. 'You know, Sally, he told me once that if you had been free, and unknown to me, he would have wanted you for his wife. I've wondered sometimes if that would have made you happier.'

She felt herself go rigid, stilled by shock. It took her some time to draw breath again, feeling the colour return flooding to her face from which for a moment it had drained. What had made Bentley say that, she wondered. Was it the nearest he had come to the comfort of confession? And what of Jos: had he guessed something of her feelings for Bentley?

Then she dismissed the idea. He had spoken casually, as if making a passing observation of no great significance; and he was not a devious man. Carefully, trying to control her uneven breathing, she said, 'No other man could ever have given me what you have done, whether of happiness or anything else. If I had never met you I think I should always have lacked a part of myself.'

He smiled at her, saying nothing, but with a look of great contentment, as if she had laid to rest a last small anxiety and there was nothing further, now, to trouble him. She caressed his hand, drawing comfort from him, sharing that peace of mind.

'Dr Darwin's coming over some day before Christmas, if the weather holds,' she said eventually. Darwin was too far away now, at Derby, to be called to Etruria in times of illness, and Mr Bent the Newcastle surgeon was still their usual medical adviser; but Sarah would be glad of his opinion this time. Though perhaps by the time he came Jos would be fully recovered.

Jos smiled, but said nothing; after all, they had been married too long for words to be always necessary. Very often they understood one another well enough without.

'Josiah said he'd look in this afternoon, on his way back from the works.'

Again Jos smiled. His eyes rested steadily on her face, as if he found tranquillity there, as indeed he had always done.

They were sitting there like that, silent yet comfortable, looking at one another and not moving at all, when the door quietly opened and Susannah came in. She was dressed in the new fashionable gown that Jos liked so much, a yellow sprigged muslin with the waist set high under the breasts and the long skirts falling in straight narrow folds to the floor, the sleeves close fitting but softened at the shoulders with puffed epaulettes, the high bodice ending in a little ruff. 'Ah, my spring-time girl,' he said approvingly.

But Sarah thought that there was little of the springtime about her, apart from her gown: her face beneath the short cropped curls was pale and drawn, marked only too clearly by the strain and watching of the past days. She was smiling, however – cheered perhaps by her father's improved appearance – and came to kiss the invalid and ask tenderly after him.

'Have you slept at all?' Sarah asked.

'A little.' She brushed the question aside, and said to Jos, 'Would you like me to play for you?'

'Yes, lass – play that gentle little thing by the man you heard in London – the German. Not Handel, of course – '

'Mr Haydn: he's an Austrian actually, but I expect he would forgive you. Is this the one you mean?'

She sat down at the piano and began to play; and under cover of the sweet expressive notes, Jos said in a low voice to Sarah, 'High time she was wed, Sally – Robert Darwin's a good lad. He'll make her a fine husband.'

Sarah stared at him in amazement. 'Jos!'

He grinned at her, a little sheepishly, looking for all the world like the boy she had once known long ago. 'Late marriages wear better, I always think.'

'You know full well we could have wed at fifteen and still made a good marriage of it. It was only circumstances that kept us apart.'

'At fifteen Sukey would have wed that Frenchman,' Jos pointed out, and then conceded, 'but I've got to make some excuse for myself, haven't I? Only I don't want to blight her happiness. Life's too short for that, and too uncertain.'

Susannah, unaware of her father's decision, was still playing when Josiah arrived. Tom was with him, and – to Jos's delight – so were Bessie and the baby.

Elizabeth Wedgwood was a firm favourite with Jos, whom she adored, the more so perhaps because most men frightened her – even, to Sarah's surprise, her own husband, though she loved him too. But then her father had been a great believer in the discipline of the rod, using it freely on his large family of daughters, and on his eldest, Elizabeth, in particular. So much, Sarah had thought when she heard of it, for aristocratic birth! Jos, who had never laid a finger in anger on any of his children or allowed anyone else to do so, must have seemed an extraordinary being to Josiah's lovely young wife.

It had been the holiday in Pembrokeshire three years ago which had first brought the two of them together. Susannah had taken her brothers with her to visit her dear friends the Allen girls; and now Elizabeth Allen was Josiah's wife, and her sister Louisa had married John. Louisa was the beauty of the family, spoiled and somewhat wayward, but she and John seemed to have settled down well together. Bessie was beautiful too, and with such a sweetness and charm about her that they all loved her, and Josiah – for all her awe of him – worshipped the ground she walked on. His transparent happiness in his marriage had done much to break down the barrier between him and his father.

Bessie – who was like her sister heavily pregnant – came at once to Jos carrying the little girl. Sarah watched the light on Jos's face as Bessie held the child near, so that she could smile and gurgle at her grandfather, and he could talk nonsense to her as once he had done to his own babies. 'Whatever difficulties there may have been,' thought Sarah, 'the children couldn't have had a better or more loving father.' If only Jos could be spared for many years to enjoy the carefree delights of grandfatherhood . . .

Susannah had ceased her playing when her brothers came, and she slipped from the room to order tea and summon her younger sisters to the drawing room; and so by the time the tea tray was set by the fire all the family but John were gathered there.

Sarah poured the tea, glad to see Jos so happy. He was talking very little, but Bessie sat by him murmuring gently

461

from time to time and holding the child on her knee, and he looked as if for the moment he could wish for no more from life than this. Sarah had her two sons on either side of her, Josiah reporting on progress at the works, Tom full of enthusiasm over some experiment just completed. Susannah seemed to be relieved that for the moment no demands were being made on her: she looked half asleep, leaving her sisters to pass cups and hand round cakes. It was a tranquil happy afternoon.

Later, when the others had gone, Susannah helped to get her father to bed, and then Sarah sent her to sleep in her turn. 'I'll manage tonight,' she said.

Jos was a little feverish again, but perhaps that was to be expected after the exertions of the day. Sarah lay down on the bed beside him, dressed in case he should need anything, but resting while she could. He was tired and lying very still, and she thought he was asleep; but she felt his hand reach out and close about hers, and she turned her head to look at him. He was not smiling, but there was a warmth in his expression which gave him a look of great contentment.

'Just the two of us,' he said softly. 'In the end, that's all we need.'

She thought: is that right? Is it true for me, or even for him? There was Bentley, who gave us both so much: light and fire and colour, ideas and a deeper understanding. Without him life would have been the poorer, and might well have been very different. In a way they all three had been necessary to what they had achieved: Bentley's culture and breadth of vision; her practical common sense and emotional strength; and Jos – no, without Jos none of it would have been possible. All Bentley's gifts, all hers would have been nothing without him. It was that wonderful skill to mould the clay which had so impressed her all those years ago which lay at the heart of what they had achieved together; that, and the fierce striving for perfection which had driven him on against every difficulty. Without that, there could have been no world-famed pottery; and without him, she would have been nothing, just an accomplished well-brought-up woman, aimless and a little bored. If she had been more than that, it was because Jos was the core and centre of her being.

She kissed him, very softly. 'It's always been enough,' she agreed, and knew it was true.

EPILOGUE

Sarah did sleep a little that night, after all. She was wakened by a gentle knock on the door, and turned her head drowsily to see Robert come in, smiling at her and bearing a tray.

'Your breakfast, Mama. I've deputed myself your serving man this morning. Have you rested well?'

He set the tray on her bedside table and helped her to sit up against the high piled pillows: she was always at her most stiff and uncomfortable first thing in the morning. 'Now, have a good breakfast, and then I'll come and take you to see your new grandson. I'm just going to make sure they'll be ready to receive you.'

She smiled at him, but waited until he had left the room before making a start on the hot chocolate and bread and butter he had brought her. She was not always very skilful with her rheumaticky hands, and preferred to take her meals without an audience.

She was hungry this morning, and ate with more enjoyment than usual: happiness gave one a good appetite. She smiled up at Jos's portrait – the fine one painted by Sir Joshua Reynolds in 1782. 'Good morning, love,' she murmured to him. What a silly old woman they would think her, if they heard, but the thought did not trouble her.

She was glad that Jos had been spared the infirmities of old age. He would have found it hard to be forced into the kind of inactivity she had to endure. She would have loved to have his company still, of course; but then she had never felt he had gone very far from her. He was such a part of her that even death had not been able to destroy that closeness. In many ways Bentley's death had been much harder to bear.

It had been worse for Susannah. She had grieved bitterly for her father during that bleak winter and spring of 1795, and for a time had been very ill indeed. It was Robert Darwin who had helped her through those difficult months;

463

and by the end of the year they had been married, secure in the knowledge that it was with Jos's blessing.

It was consoling to remember how Jos's death had been followed almost at once by the births of two more grandchildren, a kind of tangible reminder that life would go on. There had been John's little Eliza, and the third Josiah Wedgwood who was fourteen now, the second of the eight children at Maer in Staffordshire, where Josiah and Bessie had their grand house out in the country a safe distance from Etruria. Duty had compelled Josiah to become a potter, because his father had wished it and left the whole enterprise to him in his will; and Josiah was nothing if not dutiful. He was in effect the head of the family now, on whom all the others depended, and he took his responsibilities very seriously. But that did not alter the fact that he regretted deeply the humble origin of all his wealth, and though he ran the business with reluctant efficiency he refused to live in a house whose windows overlooked the works. Sarah had to admit however that Bessie made their home a wonderfully happy place, where any member of the family was always welcomed with unstinting warmth and hospitality.

Poor John was not even sustained by a sense of duty done. He hated the bank and had no financial sense at all, so that his personal affairs were in a constant muddle; but he had a loving wife and seven children on his country estate, and an enduring love of growing things, and when she had last heard of him he was trying to gather together like-minded friends with a view to forming a Horticultural Society.

Catherine and Sarah had never married, though more from choice than a want of suitors. Her mother suspected that Catherine thought herself infinitely superior to most of the young men who had aspired to her hand; and Sarah was far too busy with her many good works and her large library to consider giving time to cherishing a husband. Besides, they each had a substantial fortune and every material comfort: why abandon the freedom that gave them, for a less certain prospect? They lived for the most part at the little village of Barlaston a few miles from Etruria, in the modest but comfortable house which their mother shared with them. Increasingly these days her infirmity kept them dancing attendance on her: she knew it was trying for them at times, just as it was for her, and all three of them had been glad of the break that this present visit to Shrewsbury had given them.

Then there was Tom . . .

To think of him still hurt her as nothing else could, because of the sense of waste: all those extraordinary qualities of mind and spirit, the charm and perception and boundless curiosity, gone for nothing. She still had, somewhere, the faint fading pictures that he had made by the action of light on specially treated leather. 'We need to find some way to fix it there,' he had told her with something of his father's restless dissatisfaction with the less than perfect; but death had prevented him from finding an answer, to that as to so many other questions. She believed firmly that it was not all at an end, that somewhere he was leading a fuller life without pain in the company of those others she had loved, Jos and Bentley and Richard and Mary Ann. But how could it be right for him to die so young, when he might have given so much to his fellow men – as much perhaps as his father had done?

In her portable writing desk, carefully tied together and labelled, were the many letters she had received after Tom's death: from the celebrated natural philosopher Humphrey Davy; from the members of that eccentric group of poets and thinkers who had been amongst his friends – Samuel Taylor Coleridge and William Wordsworth. She had read the letters so often she almost knew them by heart. Wordsworth's had struck her most – what was it he had written? 'Your son produced in me an impression of sublimity beyond what I ever experienced from the appearance of any other human being.' Bessie, Josiah's wife, had put it more simply, coming with tears in her eyes to comfort Sarah, 'He was too good for this world.' She had found no comfort in the thought then, or since.

Yet now, pondering the four-year-old letters, she thought with a sense of surprise and discovery, 'Was it after all such a waste, if everyone who knew him felt they were transformed because of it? It's as much as any of us can ask, to have left the world in some way a better place for our passing through it.' They had said that of Jos when he died: Joseph Priestley, writing from America, where he had settled; Matthew Boulton and James Watt; Sir William Hamilton; Benjamin Franklin; William Wilberforce (how delighted Jos would have been that a year ago the slave trade had at last been abolished); and so many more – and Sarah had found it easy to believe, and greatly consoling. Tom's life had been briefer, its effect on others less obvious, but that was no reason for it not to have been as purposeful and important in its way as his father's.

She lay back on her pillows and pondered the matter; and knew that the lingering desolate sense of loss was melting away within her. She was at peace with the past: it was over, and there was no longer any bitterness left, any regret. Today was for the future.

She wanted to take some little gift to this new grandson, since she was privileged to see him so soon after his birth. Her old hands were too stiff to make anything. She looked about her for something she could bear to part with, and yet which would cost her something, for a gift was no good if it was not costly. Yet it must be appropriate for a little boy.

Then she knew. In the chest of drawers – the bottom drawer if she remembered rightly – there was a wooden box in which after Jos's death she had packed the precious collection of fossils, begun long ago in Burslem and still carefully ordered and labelled. They were no use to her; she could even believe she had saved them for just this kind of occasion, making it possible to link this new grandson with the child Josiah Wedgwood, setting out on the voyage of discovery that had been his life. For this new child too she hoped that life would be just such a voyage, an adventure for ever opening up new wonders to the view.

Her maid came, to help her dress in her best dove-grey silk, with a pretty ribbon-trimmed cap on her grey hair and a long lacy shawl wrapped about her; and then she was ready for Robert. When he came she said, 'I want you to do something for me.'

He found the box and brought it to where she sat in her chair by the bedside. 'What *have* you got in here, Mama? The crown jewels?'

She smiled back at him. 'A gift for your son,' was all she would say.

The box was heavy, but she would not let him carry it. He put one arm about her, supporting her, and they set out slowly along the passage, across the wide landing and along another passage to Susannah's room, where he held the door for her to pass.

'Mama! Come and see our new baby!' Susannah looked pale

and a little tired, but that was only to be expected: she did not give birth with the same ease as had her mother. But she was sitting up in bed and smiling happily, and Sarah was reassured.

She went to the bedside and laid the box on the table there, and bent to kiss her daughter; and then sat down thankfully on the chair Robert had brought, to wait while he went to bring the infant from his cradle.

She tapped the box with one bent finger. 'For little Charles Darwin – your father's fossils. I hope he'll like them when he's older.'

Susannah laughed gently. 'I'm sure he will, Mama – and thank you. We'll take care of them for him until he's old enough.'

Robert towered over her, the baby a tiny scrap in his great arms. 'Can you hold him, do you think? Would you like to?'

She held out her arms and he laid the child in them; and she held him close, studying the small well-wrapped creature. He was awake, but quite silent, staring up at her with the solemn direct dark-blue gaze of early infancy, his arms bent so that the long fingers splayed out beneath his chin. She had forgotten the perfection of infant hands, so small, with tiny pink nails, yet large in proportion to the little body. He had a soft brown down on his head, neither dark nor fair, and faintly pencilled brows. She smiled at him and murmured something meaningless and tender.

Perhaps after a time he grew tired of staring at the same doting face; perhaps he simply wanted his mother. Whatever it was he began to wriggle, and then to whimper. Sarah looked up at Robert, and he took the child and gave him to Susannah.

'I'll leave you now. But don't wear each other out with talking will you?'

'Now would we do that?' Susannah asked, laughing, as he left the room.

Indeed for some time neither of them said anything. Susannah lay watching the child crooked in her arm, and Sarah studied them both, remembering Kate Wedgwood, dead for five years now, and her devotion to her babies. Susannah was a bit like Kate in that; but then the first moments after a birth are always very special to the mother, however many times she has been through it before.

'Which is he then?' Sarah asked at last. 'Wedgwood or Darwin?'

Susannah looked up. 'Who's to say? Perhaps he's too small-boned for a true Darwin, but it's a little early to tell.'

'He's just himself – but with some of both sides in him. That was one thing I was glad about, that Jos and I were both Wedgwoods, so no one could say you children were anything but Wedgwoods too. And I didn't have to lose my family name. But then, the Darwins were always almost family.'

'And are truly so now.' Susannah paused, and then went on reflectively, 'It's strange to think of all the things that go to make us what we are – so many different things. Some are a part of us, and we can control them – some are not. I have your blood in me, and dear Papa's, and some of what I am must have come to me through you both – your gifts and qualities, your guidance when I was a child – though not always the things you might have wanted. Sometimes I think that although he wasn't any sort of blood relation my Papa Bentley had as much of a hand in the making of me as either of you. He meant a great deal to me, more I think than you ever knew. Perhaps he has a part in this baby too, in a way, because he helped to make me what I am.'

It was a shock to hear Bentley's name, so unexpectedly. It must be years since anyone had spoken of him to Sarah, though he was often in her thoughts. She stared at her daughter, saying nothing, but glad that in old age one did not blush easily any more.

But perhaps even so Susannah sensed something, for she gave her mother an intent glance and went on, 'I've often wondered – he was so close to Papa – closer than anyone but you, I think – I wondered if you were ever jealous. But then he had such charm, such a way with him . . .' Again that intent look. 'I used to think you disapproved of him – you were a little stiff with him sometimes, not warm and friendly as you were with Papa's other friends. When I grew older and thought about it, I wondered – I hope you won't mind my saying this – I thought it might be something else: a shield against attraction perhaps.'

Now Sarah did blush, thoroughly and painfully. She bent her head, not knowing what to say. How dreadful, to be caught in guilty awareness by her own daughter!

Susannah sounded a little breathless, as if she knew she was treading on delicate ground, but was nevertheless determined to go on. 'It would hardly be surprising if you felt his attraction – everyone else did. And he and Papa were so different, for all their closeness – you might have found things in him that Papa never had. There was one time I've always remembered . . .' She hesitated, and then gathered her courage to finish. 'We were in London staying with the Bentleys – it would be the time before I went to live with them, I think. I came downstairs late one night, when I should have been in bed – I can't remember why now. There was a light in the hall, but a door open somewhere and a light beyond – and I saw you and Mr Bentley, in the darkness, just standing there, close but not touching. Just before I came he had been saying something – I didn't hear what – and then you just stood looking at one another. I don't know why, but I felt an intruder, and went back upstairs again. Funny how it should stay in the mind – I don't suppose it was of any significance at all. You were probably discussing pots.'

She grinned; but there was no answering smile from Sarah, who said very carefully, choosing her words, 'He was a man of great charm and culture, as you say. But your father was always first.'

Susannah laughed at the obviousness of the remark. 'I *know* that! No one could ever have doubted it.' She raised the baby a little in her arms, and rocked him. 'Well, little Charles, that's one thing you can be sure of – you were born of love, and it was all around you even before you were dreamed of. You'll have it there to wrap you safe always.' She looked across at Sarah again. 'What would you wish for him, Mama, if you were his fairy godmother?'

'Oh, that's a hard one. Love and laughter, of course – but a good mind too, lively and inquiring and full of boundless curiosity, like your father's, with his ability to pursue an investigation through to its end. Health and strength of body and mind. Integrity, and the courage to go on seeking the truth through everything. Oh, all the best qualities of the Darwins and the Wedgwoods, and all the compassion and creativity and idealism that Bentley would have wanted for him too. Will that do?'

Susannah laughed. 'For a start, Mama! What a great man

469

he'd be with all those qualities, even with half of them! I can't wait to see it.'

Sarah shook her head. 'You may, but I never shall.' She spoke matter of factly, without sadness. 'A pity, but there we are. Still, maybe I'll know all the same what's going on, even if I'm not here to have a part in it.'

Susannah's smile was full of tenderness. 'I'm sure you will, Mama.'

There was a commotion, scarcely suppressed, in the passage outside; and then Robert opened the door just wide enough to admit his head. 'Prepare yourself, Mama; and you, my darling. The children have come to see their new brother.'

After that there was no more quietness for a long time.